Hall, Jim, 1947-
Buzz cut.

$22.95   AUG 0 5 1996

BUZZ CUT

JAMESWHALL

BUZZ CUT

Delacorte ▤ **Press**

Published by
Delacorte Press
Bantam Doubleday Dell Publishing Group, Inc.
1540 Broadway
New York, New York 10036

Library of Congress Cataloging in Publication Data
Hall, Jim, 1947–
Buzz cut : a novel / by James W. Hall.
p.   cm.
ISBN 0-385-31234-2
1. Thorn (Fictitious character)—Fiction.   I. Title.
PS3558.A369B89   1996
813'.54—dc20   96-50425
CIP

Manufactured in the United States of America
Published simultaneously in Canada

July 1996

10   9   8   7   6   5   4   3   2
BVG

For Joe Wisdom, who showed me how to get out there and what to do when I arrived.

And thanks to John and Lisa Timinski and to Mark Goossens for invaluable technical assistance. And to John Boisonault for indescribable help, and as always to Evelyn, without whom none of this would be possible or nearly as much fun.

The race is not to the swift, nor the battle to the strong, neither yet bread to the wise, nor yet riches to men of understanding, nor yet favour to men of skill; but time and chance happeneth to them all.

—ECCLESIASTES 9:11

BUZZ CUT

CHAPTER

1

In his official Fiesta Cruise Lines shirt, Emilio Sanchez stood before the bathroom mirror squinting at his new tummy bulge. The blue rugby shirt was hugging him tight at the belly, showing off the extra couple of inches of flab.

What it was, was too much cruise line food for the last six months. First time in his life he'd had a chance to eat three meals a day. Here he was, only twenty-four years old, way too young to get a gut. He didn't watch out, soon he'd be looking like all those American passengers. Worse than that, with a big gringo belly he wasn't as likely to score with the ladies.

Emilio was sucking in his stomach, staring at his profile when the door to his cabin opened. Tindu, his Filipino roommate, probably ducking in from the first dinner seating for a quick smoke.

Emilio smoothed his hand over his stomach, flattened it briefly, and decided tomorrow he would begin a diet. Eliminate breakfast. That would be easiest. Eat two meals a day instead of three. Drop ten pounds by the time of the anniversary cruise. No problem. An easy decision. Sex was a hell of a lot more important to Emilio Sanchez than breakfast.

He ran a quick comb through his thick black hair and turned from the mirror and the first thing he saw was the glitter of the blade. It was not a large knife. He'd seen bigger. Four times in his life he'd faced knives. Taking cuts on both arms and one deep wound to his left shoulder. But in those Juarez street fights, he had always possessed his own knife.

The man in his doorway held the knife in a comfortable underhand grip, left hand. Nothing fancy. Clearly familiar with its use.

"The shirt," the man said.

"What?"

The man stepped closer. "I want that shirt."

"You want my shirt?" Emilio plucked some fabric at his breast. "This shirt?"

"I want it. Give it to me."

He did something with the knife, a little Zorro waggle of his hand. Then he held up his right hand and Emilio blinked. Couldn't believe what he was seeing here in his own room. A guy with electricity coming out his fingers. Knife in one hand, sparks coming out the fingertips of the other.

"Hey, man, it's okay. You want the shirt, you got the shirt. You can put the goddamn knife away. I give you the shirt, it's yours, man. I never liked the fucking shirt in the first place."

Emilio stepped back, pulled the shirttail out of his pants, crossed his hands over his stomach ready to drag it off over his head, watching the man. "You want it, what, like for a souvenir or something?"

"I need the shirt." Saying it very calm. "Like right now."

The man wore a black Fiesta Cruise Lines T-shirt and a pair of new blue jeans. The T-shirt said he'd been a Jackpot winner. The man looked like a movie star, not the super handsome type, but one of those you've seen all your life, in this and in that, the star's brother or best friend. You've seen him a hundred times, but you never know his name. One of those.

Blond hair hanging loose down to his shoulders. A face that looked like the guy might've been playing with his girlfriend's makeup. Lips a little too red, skin a pasty, powdery white. Like you could take a fingernail and scrape some of it off, get down to the real flesh. But still handsome, and despite the knife, still somebody it looked like you could reason with.

"I got more shirts if you want them. In my drawer over there.

I got three or four, man. Brand new practically. You go and take them all. Start your own collection. I don't give a shit. I never liked these fucking shirts."

Still gripping his shirttails, arms crossed, ready to strip off the shirt, but trying to talk his way past this, find some way to keep from ducking his head into that blue material, lose sight of the guy in his doorway for even a half second. That knife not moving, just hanging there in front of the guy's belly. The blond man very still, not blinking, nothing.

"Go on, take off the shirt." Voice getting quiet now.

Emilio shifted his feet, brought his right one back a half step, gonna kick the man in the groin if he came forward at all. Punt him up to the Promenade Deck if he tried anything.

Emilio tugged on the shirt, made a little feint to see if the guy moved. He didn't. So Emilio went ahead, stripped out of it. Losing sight of the guy for a half second was all it was, a half second, couldn't have been any longer than that.

The shirt came over his head and Emilio felt a cold jiggle in his belly, and something hot spilling out, running wet down his pants, and he heard the noise coming from his throat, like he was gargling, or puking, like he was out in the alley behind the Kentucky Club back in Juarez, too much cheap tequila, drinking in that bar he remembered now, a place where men stood and guzzled beer and opened their flies right there, a beer in their hand, and pissed into the ceramic trough that ran under the lip of the bar and through a pipe out into the street, a river of urine running down the gutters of Juarez. Thinking of that bar, of that border town, how much he'd wanted to escape that river of piss, go away, see the world, wear nice clothes, meet the blond women, only so he could wind up like this, in a tiny, pathetic fucking room on a ship, a man killing him for his shirt, for his stupid goddamn shirt.

And Emilio felt himself falling backward against the sink. Seeing the man in his doorway, holding the blue cruise lines shirt in one hand and the bloody knife in the other. No smile on his face, nothing at all. Same look Emilio felt on his own face at that exact moment. Nothing there at all. Never would be again either. Never. Just like the blond guy, a dead face.

* * *

Butler Jack strolled through the cruise ship casino listening to the clang of coins, the bells and gongs, the incantations of luck at the craps table, shrieks of joy and groans of defeat.

Butler was tall and rawboned and carried himself fluidly. He wore gray slacks and the blue long-sleeved rugby shirt with a Fiesta Cruise Lines insignia above the breast pocket, the uniform for the casino staff. Emilio Sanchez's contribution to the cause. Butler's hair was tucked under a wig. Thick black waves slicked back into ducktails.

In a corner of the room Butler halted for a moment, leaned against a slot machine, and stared up at the TV mounted overhead. Lovely Lola Sampson in a slinky black dress was standing on the Sun Deck of the M.S. *Eclipse* belting out the catchy theme song for Fiesta Cruise Lines, while her husband Morton stood below on the Promenade Deck beaming up at her. The most beautiful sixty-year-old in America. Didn't look a day over forty-five. Body firm, voice lush, face as smooth as a ten-year-old's.

No wonder Morton Sampson snapped her up, made her his wife and a TV star. Two years ago she was an ordinary working woman worrying how she'd survive on her social security. Now look at her, on a first-name basis with America. People in every corner of the televisioned world knew her name. Had her own morning talk show, *Lola Live*. Got buddy-buddy with her new husband's Hollywood friends. Lovely Lola. Singing and dancing, while her low-cut dress displayed her considerable assets. Voice deep and swollen with happiness as she shamelessly pitched her husband's cut-rate Caribbean cruises.

The TV was turned down low, so Lola's song was lost in the hubbub of the casino. But it didn't matter. Ask anyone on the ship to hum the tune, they'd be able.

Butler watched slender Lola as she swayed and sang, her blond hair swishing. Her new shoulder-length cut. Two years ago, the only singing she'd done was to solo in the church choir. Now look. Like she'd been at this all her life.

When she finished her song, she flashed her best smile at the camera and spoke. Though her words were inaudible, Butler knew her speech by heart. Lola Sampson was inviting one and all to join her and Morton on the twenty-fifth anniversary cruise. A week in the Caribbean, rub shoulders with Lola and Morton and a couple of network news anchors, rock stars, a host of Hollywood types. A week of *Lola Live* broadcast from on board the *Eclipse*. Only three weeks away, rooms going fast, so make your reservations now.

Oh yes, Butler Jack had made his already. Wouldn't miss this voyage for the world.

Butler ambled across the smoky room, passing behind a row of blackjack dealers, over to the far corner of the casino where he stood for a moment before the stage where the visiting band was playing their last set of the evening.

Shaggy hair to their shoulders, wearing tight yellow suits with bell bottom trousers, the four members of the Baby Boomers looked like they'd been beamed down from a sixties' hootenanny. Skinny guitars, emaciated bodies. They juked and jived across the stage, trying very hard to make their music fill the big room. But the passengers showed no sign they noticed as they pulled the slot machine levers, slid their stacks of chips across the felt tables, and glanced around with the glazed expressions of men too long on the assembly line.

Butler turned away from the band and, for the second time that evening, he visited a blackjack table, this one nearest the cock-tail lounge. He waited until the dealer had finished a round and some of the players abandoned their places, then he moved to the dealer's shoulder and the man looked up at him. Butler nodded at his rack of chips.

"Getting a little low?"

The young man stared at Butler.

"Name's Jack." Butler pinched a corner of his counterfeit ID and leaned closer. "I'm subbing for Emilio. His father died and he had to fly off to Pittsburgh for the funeral."

"Too bad," the man said as he opened a new deck of cards.

"You need another rack or not?" Butler asked him.

"Well, since you're here," the dealer said.

He tore a sheet off his pad, signed the chit, handed it to Butler who turned and worked his way through the din, down several rows of dollar slots, passing the roulette tables, four poker games and over to the pitboss station where he filled out his own request form, countersigned the dealer's signature, and stapled the two together. Then he headed to the banker's cage.

Butler passed his chits through, waited while the young black woman with round glasses tore off the receipt and passed the rack through the window to him. The tray of chips was sealed tight inside a stiff plastic wrap. Butler reached for the tray, but this time the young woman held on to it.

"Wait just a minute," she said. "Do I know you?"

He gave her the Emilio story, dead father, Pittsburgh. She leaned forward, squinted at his ID.

"Hey, this is my second trip tonight."

"I don't remember seeing you before."

"I'm Jack. You've seen me. From engineering."

"Jack, from engineering?"

"I'm usually covered with grease. That's why you don't recognize me. They got me filling in tonight."

"Your I.D.," she said. "It's not right."

"What?"

"I got to call somebody, verify you. Just take a second."

"What's wrong with it?"

Butler unclipped the plastic card and studied it for flaws.

"They're not issuing those anymore. Five months out of date. I'm sorry, but we got orders. Some special deal going on."

She had her phone pressed to her ear, tapping numbers.

"I told you," Butler said. "I'm from engineering. I'm just filling in till Emilio gets back. A last-minute thing."

"Just the same I got to report. Sorry. They're tightening security. Something's been happening, got everybody spooked."

She gave him an apologetic shrug and he watched her as her face changed, focusing now on the voice in her ear.

Butler glanced around. No one in line behind him, a small crowd gathered around one of the nearby blackjack tables groaning in unison as the last card was flipped.

"Mr. Sugarman? It's Annette in the casino."

Butler stared at her. Annette turned her back to him and cupped a hand around the mouthpiece.

Butler took one more quick look around, then swung back to

Annette and snaked his right hand through the bars of her cage and touched the voltage to the nape of her neck. A puff of dark smoke. Her legs sagged, the phone spilled from her hand, and the young woman sank to the floor.

Carrying his tray, Butler turned away and walked through the crowd. Moving with special care, slow, strolling toward the stage where the Baby Boomers were belting out another sixties' favorite. "Three cats in the yard. Life used to be so hard."

For a moment as he passed behind their set, he was invisible to the eyes in the sky, the three hundred video cameras that dotted the ceiling of the casino, each one concealed in a small dark globe. Then, directly behind the bass player, shielded from the casino floor, Butler swung open the back of one of their Panasonic speakers he'd customized earlier in the day. He slid the rack inside. One tray crammed in already. Grand total of eighty thousand dollars' worth of chips. Legal tender in any of Morton Sampson's two dozen cruise ship casinos. He drew out the second rack of counterfeit chips and headed back to the blackjack table.

After he'd given the dealer his rack of phonies, Butler glided across the casino, heading casually toward the Atrium exit. He was only ten feet from the door when a woman howled from across the room. Annette's replacement standing inside the cashier's cage, one hand at her throat.

At the same moment, a man about Butler's size, a light-skinned black man, came sprinting down the hall, headed directly toward him. Butler held his ground and the man veered through the doorway and collided headlong with two white-haired ladies, spilling their buckets of quarters. The man stopped short, apologized, helped them scoop up a couple of handfuls of coins. Then Annette's replacement screamed again and the black man apologized once more and hustled off.

Next morning, Sunday, when the M.S. *Eclipse* docked in Key West for a seven-hour shopping tour, Butler was among the first wave of passengers down the gangplank. In gray jeans, long-sleeve blue work shirt, tennis shoes. Black sunglasses. Blond hair pulled back into a ponytail. Hands empty.

Positioned at the bottom of the ramp, the caramel-tinted man was studying the crew and passengers as they disembarked. Beside him was another man in tourist clothes and close-cropped hair. David Cruz, head of security. Butler saw a piece of poster board tacked to the bottom of the railing, the two men consulting it as waves of passengers made their way down the long gangplank.

No doubt a hasty sketch based on Annette's description, a rendering of the man who called himself Jack. Evidently she wasn't up to sitting out in the sun all morning, checking the three thousand faces of crew and passengers. Dizzy and weak, her eyes were probably still blurred. Four hundred thousand volts would do that.

Butler didn't try to strike up a conversation with anyone, didn't try to blend in. Just came striding down the ramp alone, even took off his sunglasses as he approached Mr. Sugarman. The man staring at him, taking a quick look at the sketch, then back at Butler, staring into his eyes. Cruz shifted his position, seemed to pick up his scent. But he kept coming down.

Both men stared at Butler. He was a tall, thin man. Annette probably gave them that much for certain. But the rest of it, his nose, eyes, the shape of his cheekbones, those things were always tricky to describe. Even if she was looking directly at him, trying to put precise words to what she saw, most of it would get lost in translation. The words were the weak point. Most people just didn't have the words.

Butler walked on by. The man called Sugarman giving Butler one last look then turning his attention back up the ramp. Searching for the next tall thin suspect.

Butler crossed the parking lot, went around to the driver's side of his Winnebago, unlocked the door and climbed inside. Four days ago he'd parked it across from Mallory Square in a place where he could easily observe the cruise ship's ramp.

Butler went back to the driver's seat and settled down, windows open, sunny Key West morning pouring in, the drowsy coconut breeze, that sweet stench of vomit that always seemed to bloom two blocks either side of Duval Street. He watched the shadows straggle along the sidewalk. His mind clear, only a mild ruffle in his pulse.

While he had a minute free, he opened the leather pack on his belt and unplugged the nine-volt batteries. Five of them. Simple store-bought coppertops, impossible to trace.

He tore open the wrappers on five new ones and snapped them into place. He rolled up the right sleeve of his shirt, checked the connections, blew a spray of dust off the voltage amplifier strapped to his wrist. Unbuttoned his shirt, followed the wires where they were taped to his flesh, running to his armpit, down his ribs, out a small incision through the shirt to the battery pack on his belt. He searched meticulously for any nicks in the coating of the two wires, one red, one black. But everything was fine. Everything tight and clean and fully charged. He rebuttoned his shirt, tucked it in, rolled down his sleeve, and settled back to wait. Feeling a flood of well-being. A radiance centered in his gut. He was moving down the master list. One through five were finished. The groundwork laid. Ready for number six, the big moment. Halfway there. The slow half done, the arduous half. Years in the making.

It was two hours later when the Baby Boomers finally appeared, towering over the Filipino crew that was spilling out the gangway. The band members rolled their equipment down the ramp. Sugarman and Cruz were there. A little slumped over now. Losing their enthusiasm.

The Boomers loaded the equipment into their Ford van. Butler watched them heave the speakers into the back with the other equipment.

Out Truman Avenue Butler stayed a car or two behind, fell a little farther back as they headed up U.S. 1. The boys were careful drivers, so it was easy to keep a car or two between them up the narrow stretch of overseas highway through the endless ticky tack of Sugarloaf, Cudjoe and Big Pine, Marathon and Grassy Key, Layton and Long Key, Matecumbe and Tavernier.

Two hours later, a hundred miles up the road from Key West, at the south end of the nineteen-mile stretch of asphalt that shot straight north through the southern Everglades back to mainland Florida, Butler took a position one car length off the bumper of the van. Bearing down. Saw the driver glance back in the outside mirror. Saw his eyes hold for a second, then let go.

Butler leaned over, snapped open the glove compartment, and

drew out the black plastic transmitter. He thumbed the switch, felt the unit hum in his hand. The sweet fizz of electrons. He raised the unit to the windshield, cocked the aerial toward the white van, leaned to his left, head out the window to check the oncoming lane. He waited till the road was clear for several miles, then drew his head back inside and pushed the red button.

But the van continued to drive smoothly.

Butler rattled the transmitter and pressed the button again. Still nothing. He tamped the plastic case against the dash, then aimed the aerial toward the van once more and mashed the button several times.

And it worked. The circuit breaker he'd duct-taped to the Boomers' steering gear last week was activated by the radio impulse, the circuit switch flipped, released the small bolt holding the idler arm to the relay rod, the bolt fell free onto the highway, skittered away.

A second later the van jerked hard to the right, then swerved left. Sixty miles an hour, a rudderless ship.

The van veered into the oncoming lane, stayed there for a hundred yards, then swung back to the right shoulder. Two more erratic zigzags.

"Shit!" His smile melting away. The thing taking longer than it should. The van slowing, fifty, forty-five.

Butler leaned to his left, saw in the opposing lane a distant line of traffic caught behind two transfer trucks. Heard the wail of the truck's air horn as once again the van swung across the oncoming lane, bumping along the opposite shoulder.

This time the front wheel slid over the lip of the drainage canal, caught. The van leaned, teetered on two wheels, then went over on its side, skidding along the embankment, hit the water and bounced across the surface like a skipping rock until it came to rest, heavy and dead, settling, the driver's side sinking four feet under water. No doors coming open.

Messier than Butler had pictured, but still workable.

The transfer trucks roared past. Cars screeched and slewed around him as Butler eased the Winnebago off the highway. A hundred yards behind him two cars collided, another plowed into the wreckage, spun twice around, and careened into the canal.

Butler got out, jogged across the highway to the Boomers' van. Somebody was there already, a black man in bright pink shorts and an aqua tennis shirt, nice new deck shoes. The man hesitated a moment on the bank of the canal, then lunged forward, splashed up to his chest, and went for the driver's door.

Butler waded slowly into the warm water, inched through the thick custard at the bottom. Water rose to his waist, then a few inches higher. He closed in on the van, peered inside the back doors, saw the jumble of equipment and the bodies lying akimbo. No one stirring.

While rubberneckers moved slowly past on the roadway, Butler hauled open the van's rear door. The lead singer's body was draped around the Panasonic speaker, his ear pressed against its cloth mesh as though some echo of music were whispering to him, consoling him in his pain. The man drooled blood, a flap of skin dangled near his chin. Everybody groaning, starting to come alive. Butler shoved the lead singer aside and scraped the speaker back across the floor to the rear doors.

He pried open the backing and took a good breath. The plastic wrap hadn't torn. The chips were still locked neatly in their slots. He drew the two trays out and stacked them, tucked them under his arm.

When he turned, a young man was standing in his way, waist deep in the water. Hawaiian shirt, no tan. Kinky blond hair, Nordic features. A few hours off the plane, taking his Minnesota flesh down to Key West to blister it. Giving Butler a cold glare.

"What the hell you doing, man?"

Butler sloshed forward through the canal but the man dodged to the right and blocked his way. He reached a hand out as if halting traffic.

"You're staying right there, buddy, till we get this sorted out. You look like a looter to me."

Butler smiled.

"Loot," Butler said. "Good choice."

The young man kept his arm stiff, hand out.

"Loot's from the Hindu *lut,* and the Sanskrit *loptram, lotram,* which means plunder. I'm sure you didn't realize it, but it's a very aptly chosen word in this context. An ancient military term. Originally it referred to spoils of war stolen from a captured city. Back in the sweet long ago. It's important to know the words, to know what you're saying."

The young man eyed Butler uneasily but stood his ground.

Butler shifted the trays of chips and lifted his right hand into view. Showed the helpful young man with the pale Yankee flesh the two steel prongs protruding from thick rubber tips on his pointing finger and the middle one. He spread the fingers into a V and made a careful fist to activate the charge.

Between the two prongs a blue spark sputtered.

One of Butler Jack's most useful creations. Parts recycled from three stun guns, the DC thyrister capacitor set at 25 pulses a second, the whole thing rewired, voltage doubled. Could put a three-hundred-pound mountain gorilla on its ass for half an hour. Take it anywhere. Zap them and they drop. Sometimes they dropped just looking at him, a hiss of current between his fingers. Like he'd risen from the underworld.

The blond hero stared at the crackling spark and sucked in a breath. As Butler stepped forward, the young man stumbled to his side, went down on one knee. Water to his chin.

Butler released the button, then pressed it again, gunning his engine for effect. One more time showing the good Samaritan the snap and sizzle of voltage writhing between his fingertips.

The man stayed knee-deep in the canal watching Butler as he approached. Butler stretched out his hand, brought the sputtering current to within a foot of the man's face.

"Come on, man." The young man's voice broke into a nervous yodel. "I didn't mean anything. Really. I had it all wrong."

Butler jabbed his fingers against the man's forehead and the current hammered him backward into the dark canal. With his mouth still open, the young man slid below the surface, a few listless bubbles rising from his lips. Eyes wide, their shine dulling quickly.

Butler felt the death. Felt the flutter of it in the air as if a hummingbird had whisked past his face. Standing there above the miracle of death, Butler invoked the image of the girl. The girl in the white dress. Pink and blue embroidery on her lacy collar. The girl in the white dress, on her swing on the wide porch. The angel girl. His uranium, his glowing core. The girl who powered him through all the desperate moments. Butler pictured her and once again she rescued him as she had rescued him for years. Her cool smile, the sprinkle of golden hairs on her arms, the delicate bones in her wrist. Her perfect blue eyes. Urging him forward. Urging him away from the dead canal water, back to the Winnebago. Back to his seat behind the wheel. The girl he would see soon. Number six on the list. When everything was in place. Almost there. His angel. His glowing core.

An hour later Butler Jack exited the Palmetto Expressway onto the Tamiami Trail, drove a few blocks east, and stopped at a Cuban market. Butler went inside, walked straight back to the storage room. There he traded the two trays of casino chips to a smartly dressed young woman for fifty-one thousand dollars in used twenties.

Loaves and fishes. Water to wine.

CHAPTER

2

"Cruise ships?"

"Yeah, you know, those big white things, like *Love Boat*. Gopher and the gang."

"Gopher?" Thorn said.

"*Love Boat*. It was a TV show. People always falling in love on this big white cruise ship." Sugarman looked out at the glassy flats. Cast his lure thirty feet out, the six-pound line melting against the still water with barely a trace. "Jeez, never mind. I forgot for a second who I was with. Only guy in America never heard of *Love Boat*. Mr. Pop Culture himself."

"Hey, I try to keep up. But it's hard."

"Yeah, without a TV, a radio, newspapers, I expect it is."

"I read books," Thorn said.

"Like I said, totally out of it."

Thorn picked up his paddle, realigned the canoe so they were facing away from the early afternoon sun.

For most of August and September Thorn had puttered in his downstairs workshop, trying to construct the canoe without benefit of blueprint or model. Just a vague image in his mind. The canoe had emerged after a month of trial and error. Bending the water-soaked slats of birch until they bowed. Stretching the canvas across the birch. Twice he'd misaligned the keel, cut the canvas short, snapped innumerable ribs. But finally it came together, everything flush, riveted tight, ready for its shakedown cruise.

Neither he nor Sugarman had fished from a canoe before, but they were getting the hang of it. No leaks. Well balanced. Of course, later on this afternoon would be the real test, returning to the docks at Flamingo. Five miles of open water.

Thorn's back muscles were burning already, a blister had broken open on his right thumb from the trip out. Sugarman soaked through his khaki shirt in the first ten minutes as they'd paddled through the cool dawn.

But they didn't complain. It was worth the effort to fish those southern Everglades flats, a place no powerboat could reach, not even the shallowest draft skiff poling with its engine tilted up. On those secluded shoals there were large areas with barely enough water at high tide to dampen the sand, closer to a beach than a bay. But some of the finger channels that webbed the sand were chocked with fish. Grouper and trout, redfish and snapper. Even a few tarpon were laid up back there.

"How the hell you get hooked up with a cruise ship company?"

"Out of the blue," Sugar said as he drew in line. "Last month the head of security for Fiesta Cruises calls up, wanted to know if I'd hire on for a month or two, work undercover. I asked him how he picked me, he wouldn't say. Just that my name wound up on his desk."

"You got a mysterious benefactor."

"Appears that way."

Thorn watched his lab puppy sleeping under the center seat of the canoe. Leaning forward, Thorn waved away a mosquito that had settled on the dog's nose. Add that to the list of good reasons for having a dog around—mosquitoes preferred their blood to humans'.

"Fiesta Cruise Lines," Thorn said. "That's Morton Sampson's company."

Sugarman swung his head around, peered at Thorn. "Jesus! How the hell . . ."

"Hey, I know a few things. He's famous. Morton Sampson, the guy with the missing daughter. Monica."

"You never heard of Gopher, *Love Boat*, but you know Morton Sampson."

"Handbills," Thorn said. "You remember. Someone dumped a stack of them in the ditch out by the highway. Back when they were looking for the girl, couple, three years ago. I used those posters to light the evening cook fire for about six months. Pretty girl. They ever find her?"

"No. Her old man must've spent a million dollars on posters, private eyes, TV ads."

"Damn good-looking young lady. It bothered me to light her up every night. But I couldn't just throw those things away."

Thorn watched a hawk strafe the mangroves to their east warding off some interloper.

"This new job," Sugarman said, "I get all the free cruises I want. Except it's wasted on me. I never had any aspirations to cruise. Big ship like that, it's like some skyscraper's fallen into the bay and floated off. And, man, the ships smell like damn Greyhound buses. Too many people been there, the upholstery, the rooms, everything reeks of body odor. Smell you can't get out. Every week the boat docks, passengers get off, cleaning crew comes aboard, dusts and waxes the floors, an hour later more passengers are lined up to get on. Thing never has a chance to air out."

"That what they hired you for? A body odor detective. Catch who's stinking up the place."

Sugarman looked up at the empty sky.

"I'm after a thief," he said.

Rover woke and began to whimper. Thorn reached over, lifted him up and suspended him over the side of the canoe, and a moment or two later the dog let go of a stream of pee. Damn good boat dog. When he was done, Thorn set him back on his pillow.

"This guy, he's been hitting this one ship for around fifty thousand dollars every month for the last seven months. The M.S. *Eclipse*. Uses a different approach every time. They think it's somebody in the crew, so they brought me in. Want to keep it all hush-hush. Bad for business otherwise."

"High adventure on the high seas."

"High seas is right," Sugar said. "Couple weeks ago I'm prowling the casino all night. Boat's tossing and pitching in that tropical storm Edgar. Twelve-foot swells. But does that stop the goddamn gamblers? No, nuh-uh. Room is full. They're pulling the slot machine arms like one set of robots making love to another set. They can barely stand up, but they're keeping at it. Place is smoky as hell. That's the worst part. Gamblers gotta have their cigarettes."

Thorn leaned forward and scratched Rover's ears. The puppy groaned with pleasure.

"Middle of that tropical storm, I notice this guy. I don't know why. He's dressed like everybody else, with his plastic cup full of coins, same as all the rest. But there's something about him. Way he moved, I don't know."

"Furtive gestures," Thorn said.

"Yeah, something like that. Guy had sneaky eyes. He wasn't looking around, glancing over his shoulder or anything. In fact, maybe that's what caught my attention. Just kept his eyes down. Dark glasses, baseball cap. He'd work one machine for a long time, a half hour or so, he'd move on to the next one. Going like that all night, one machine to the next."

"Yeah?"

"It was an accident I caught on. He left a quarter in the payout tray. I picked it up, and bingo bongo, I know he was pulling something."

"He was using slugs."

"No," Sugarman said. "Much better."

"I'm supposed to guess?"

"You'd never get it. Even after I had the thing in my hand, it was a few days before I figured out how he was working the scam. By then the cruise was over, the guy had disembarked, long gone."

Thorn picked up his paddle, sculled them away from the small island they were drifting toward.

"Don't you want to know what it was? The scam."

"I'm all atwitter."

Sugarman said, "He milled the edges off the quarters."

Thorn looked over at him.

"The rough, serrated edges, you know. Smoothed them off."

"And what the hell would that accomplish?"

"Exactly," Sugar said. "What difference does it make, grinding the edges off the quarters? The casino people had no idea, so they fly in one of their hotshot engineers, he meets us in Nassau, one of the stops. This kid, he looks like a movie usher, long greasy hair, some loser you'd find hanging around a video game room, but no, he's their resident electronic genius. Smug little bastard.

"So anyway, we sat around, dropping that quarter into machines. It registered like any other quarter. No difference. Bing, bing, pull the arm, you get two cherries and an apple. Nothing. Open up the machine, take it out, try it again on another machine. Same thing."

Thorn watched the puppy sleep. His paws jerked as he chased a rabbit through the tall grass of his dream.

"The video kid, he gets out his laptop computer, starts banging away, doing computations, analyzing the specs. The cruise people are yammering among themselves. So, I get up, walk around looking at the slots. I've been mulling this thing over for days, coming up with nothing, but then out of nowhere it hits me. I don't know diddly about the mechanics, except the little I just overheard as these guys were talking. But what I do know is the win rate is four percent on slots, but on that particular cruise the win rate went up to seven percent. Either a lot of people got real lucky, or somebody was rigging things.

"So without completely understanding it, I go back over and announce that I know how the guy pulled it off. They all look up. And I hear myself, I'm off to the races but hell if I know how I know any of this.

"I say, look, what if the milled quarter goes in, registers like the real quarter. But its weight is just enough different from a real quarter that maybe, for some reason, it doesn't register when it comes out."

"I'm not following this."

"See, the machines are set to pick up slugs or foreign coins. They have a very precise measuring scale for entering coins. So a scam artist couldn't adjust the coins too much, or the machine won't take them. But just milling the edges off, apparently that isn't enough to trigger the alarm."

"I guess I'm just dense," Thorn said.

"Okay, the crook comes in with a bucket of milled quarters. He goes up to a machine, starts playing. Puts them in, loses, loses, loses. His milled quarters are in the machine now, circulating among the real ones. Then he wins a small jackpot, four or five real quarters. He keeps on playing, feeding the machine the milled quarters, and he loses, loses, loses. Then finally when he hits another winner, this time in addition to the eight or ten real quarters he's supposed to win, one of his milled quarters is in line next to them and it slips out too. Only it doesn't register going out. Its smooth edges allow it to slip past the exit counter. The exit counter isn't so precise. If you catch the slugs going in, there's no need for the exit to be finely tuned.

"So what happens, instead of winning eight quarters he wins nine. Eight of theirs, one of his. Keeps feeding the milled quarters, and whenever he wins, his special quarters don't stick. So he keeps playing one machine long enough, he's got all his milled quarters back and he's milked most of the real quarters out of the machine too.

"Then he moves on to the next one and does the same thing. Careful to keep his customized quarters separate from the real ones. Very patient. Very low tech. No big jackpot or anything. But little by little over the course of an evening, he can walk out of there with a sizable take. Do seven thousand a day for the whole week of the cruise, he's got his fifty."

"Fifty thousand. It's this guy's magic number?"

"That's been his take. Poker or slots or roulette. Then last weekend he got away with eighty thousand bucks' worth of chips. He sells them somewhere, makes sixty, seventy percent of face value. So there it is again, hitting around that same figure. Fifty thousand. That was the trip one of the casino workers was killed, slashed open. His shirt was stolen."

"That's connected?"

"The bad guy used the shirt to impersonate a casino worker."

"Killed a guy for his shirt."

"Yeah, it looks that way."

Thorn stared out at the still water for a while. "How'd you figure it out? The milled quarter thing."

"That's what they wanted to know. All of them looking at me suspiciously, you know, like maybe I was in on it. But I couldn't tell him. I heard it come out of my mouth, babbling away like some part of my brain figured it out, while the rest of my brain didn't understand it. A gift from the gods."

Thorn nodded. He knew a little about those.

"Anyway, we tested it out. Went into the ship's machine shop, filed off the edges on fifty quarters, played them, and sure thing, they didn't stick in the machine. If they were in the chute next to a payout, they came out too. You keep playing long enough with money that slips out on its own, you could skim every quarter out of that whole casino."

"Impressive," Thorn said.

"It would've been," Sugarman said. "Except the guy got away. His face didn't come out on the video cameras. We checked and the guy kept his head down, very aware of being watched. Had on that baseball cap, big dark glasses. He was tall, that's all we could tell.

"The cruise ship people, they were happy I'd figured out the quarter thing, sure, but it didn't get them any closer to the guy. Then a week later he stabs this guy to death. So now it's serious. Not just money anymore."

Sugarman ran his finger through the water, seemed to be writing a word there.

"I had no idea how much money flows through those ships, the casinos. Hell, every Saturday those ships leave port with two and a half million in the casino bank. A week later they come back with close to three mil. All you need, the average passenger loses fifty dollars a day for a week, there's your half million. So somebody steals fifty thou, it's chickenfeed really, compared to what's actually on the stage coach."

"Chickenfeed? Hell, I'm in the wrong business."

"You're not in any business, Thorn."

Thorn smiled. "Yeah, well, thank God for that."

Thorn watched a small hammerhead sliding along the bottom.

They broke for lunch. Drank a couple of icy Foster's and swallowed down the peanut butter and jelly sandwiches Sugarman's wife had packed. Big gooey things that leaked around the edges.

Afterward, Thorn leaned back against the canvas seat in a half doze, listening to a distant osprey's shrill lament, his rod at his feet. He heard Sugarman casting, felt the gentle wobble of the canoe as he worked his line.

Thorn drifted down into the dusky light of a snooze. Picturing Rochelle's face. Her striking face behind the pages of a book. Turning pages. Reading in the bed beside her. Smelling her cinnamon scent. Hearing Rochelle breathe. The dream shifting suddenly to a conversation. Dreaming soundless words. A stream of them coming from Rochelle's mouth, one of her theories. She had dozens of them. A theory about dreams. Why we dream. Why we remember some, don't others. Something to do with physics. Thorn following her words, her idea, then things becoming more and more intricate until he was lost and found himself watching her lips shape the words, not hearing her theory anymore, just watching the stream of beautiful words coming from her intriguing mouth. Exotic words, wide exotic mouth. Rochelle.

Sugarman let out a whoop that jerked Thorn upright.

Sugar's reel was revving, and twenty yards to the east the silver water humped and surged and a monster snook flopped hard on its side, shook its head savagely against the six-pound line.

Sugarman rose to get leverage on the fish, but the canoe wobbled precariously and he squatted back down. For the next ten minutes, Thorn watched him fight that same impulse, until the snook made a sudden reel-melting run and Sugarman came to his feet again, hauled back on the rod, and tipped the canoe.

Everything went overboard. Their gear, the remains of their lunch. The puppy splashed around, then started swimming in delirious circles licking at the water as he went. Up to his knees in muck and soft sand, Thorn laughed and cursed, and after a moment's bewilderment, Sugarman joined in. The two of them wallowed about until they got the canoe righted, the provisions and the puppy back inside, Sugarman one-handing his rod the whole time, keeping the line taut on his fish. Thorn steadied the canoe while Sugar climbed back inside, then Thorn slid over the side and settled into his seat again.

Finally Sugar hauled the fish to the boat. While Thorn held the tippet high, they examined the brute. Close to forty pounds. On Sugar's light line, the snook might even be a world record if they wanted to take it back, weigh it on official scales.

"Gonna keep it?"

Sugarman gave Thorn a quiet look and pried the barbless hook from the fish's jaw, eased him back into the water, moved him gently back and forth till the fish recovered and glided away into the labyrinth of tidal channels.

As they were drying out in the sun, Sugarman lifted his hand and gestured at the deepwater cove twenty feet away. A pod of dolphin had rolled into the inlet. Thorn counted half a dozen circling the cove.

A moment later the water boiled with bait fish. For several minutes the dolphin worked together, herding what must have been a very large school of mullet tighter and tighter until they had them clustered in a thick mass. Then the dolphin moved in, the water churning briefly. Lunch.

"Damn mullet never had a chance."

"Makes you glad dolphin are on our side," Sugar said.

Thorn stared at the last flutters of water. "Only reason they're on our side is 'cause they don't know us that well."

They watched the dolphin move away, an undulating line.

"We ought to get out here more often," Thorn said, leaning back, stretching out his arms. "Blow out the arteries."

"Some of us got jobs, man."

"Go on," Thorn said. "Give me some more shit."

"Naw, it's too easy."

"Well, anyway, that explains where the hell you been these last few weeks. I was beginning to worry about you, man."

"It's good to be missed."

"Actually what it is, I'm running a little low on hair."

Sugarman scowled.

For the last few months Sugar had been grabbing handfuls of hair out of the trash can behind the Hairport Beauty Salon next to his office. Dropping the hair off at Thorn's so he could experiment with it in his bonefish flies. Thorn had discovered that pinches of frosted hair worked the best. The frosted stuff stood up to saltwater almost as well as boar bristle.

"You been kind of engrossed lately," Sugar said. "I didn't think you'd notice I wasn't around."

"You mean Rochelle. Engrossed with Rochelle."

Sugarman shrugged.

"Yeah," Thorn said, smiling. "I guess you could call it that. Engrossed."

Sugarman lifted his gaze to some clouds in the east. "By the way. Tell me something, Thorn. Why the hell'd you name that dog Rover? All the names you could've picked, you couldn't do any better than that?"

"It was Rochelle's idea. It's ironic."

"Ironic?"

"Well, actually she's got another name for it. Post-modern. It's a post-modern thing. Like an intellectual joke."

"Ironic I've heard of."

"That year of Harvard," Thorn said, "it gave her a peculiar sense of humor. Some of the books she reads, I can't pronounce their titles."

"Well, making your dog the butt of a joke, I don't know about that. Seems like bad karma."

"He doesn't mind. Rover seems to suit him fine."

Rover was curled in a ball in the shade of the middle seat.

Out in the center of the cove, a single dolphin rolled. Lingering behind to clean up the scraps. Thorn watched it surface and dive, surface again, its sleek gray hide blending perfectly with the water. It made one more round of the cove, then headed toward the bay to catch up with its buddies.

CHAPTER

3

"The wind's changing."

"I don't feel anything." Sugarman raised his palm into the still air, moved it around.

Gazing to the north, Thorn tried to find some sign he could point to, a riffle in the mangroves, some darkening of the waters, a swerving frigate bird. But the sky was the same impeccable blue it had been all day, the bay gleamed as bright and motionless as ice, no birds, just a quiver of breeze out of the southeast.

So here was another of those things Thorn knew to be true but could not find words for. There were turning out to be more of those as the years went on. The silence inside him teeming with inexpressible knowledge. Things his skin knew, his fingertips, a host of sounds and scents, visceral data he could decode but not describe.

"You're sure?"

"Yeah," Thorn said. "Switching around to the north. Going to be in our face pretty soon."

"I sit here, I'm looking the same place you're looking, and hell if I see anything."

"Birders call it jizz," Thorn said.

Sugarman turned his eyes, gave Thorn a skeptical smile. The yellow lab puppy lifted his head and stared at Thorn.

"Jizz." Thorn smiled. "It's all the little things a bird does, preening, fluttering around on its perch. The way it lands, the way it takes off. Body language. Birders can tell the jizz of one bird from the jizz of another. When they're too far away, or the sun's in their eyes, even with binoculars they can't see the bird's exact shape or coloration. To identify it, they have to recognize its jizz."

"Jizz," said Sugar suspiciously. "Jizz."

"Yeah, a tremor in the mangrove leaves, smell of the water. Something's different. It's like you and your guy on the cruise ship, his furtive gestures. Maybe you can't describe it, what exactly he was doing that caught your attention, but you knew it anyway. It's like intuition. You know something, but you don't know how you know it."

"Well then," Sugarman said, reeling in his line. "I guess we better pack it in."

Sugar set down his fly rod, took a minute to neaten his gear, then picked up his wooden paddle, let go of a long breath, and began to slice through the water.

In sync with Sugar's stroke, Thorn swung the canoe back to the north, toward that first set of mangrove islands a mile away. They glided across the windowpane, kept a smooth pace, Sugarman groaning slightly with each stroke.

Thorn watched a leopard ray approach from the right, saw it flash beneath them, just the tips of its wings waving as it skimmed flat across the sand. With his bare feet on the thin canvas floor, Thorn could feel the faint tickle of its passing.

Half an hour later as they left the protection of the last mangrove island and swung out into the open miles of Whitewater Bay, the wind was full in their faces, a twenty-knot breeze, and they had to jab their paddles in deep and pull hard just to move ahead a few feet at a time.

But still, that wind felt good. It was laced with clean, freshly filtered air that tingled in Thorn's nostrils. Dewpoint in the fifties, a few more grains of oxygen than usual, drier than anything they'd breathed since last March. Air off the glaciers. It popped open the sinuses like menthol, gave everyone an extra jolt of energy, the chattering pulse of a new season.

Off to the west in an upper limb of a slash pine, a bald eagle observed them as they labored across the sound. Approaching from the northwest was a wedge of dark, silver-tipped clouds. Whorls of white foam spun upward off the leading edge of the front like an extravagant pompadour, some ghostly Elvis about to wail.

Thorn watched Sugar's back. Watched him paddle, timing his own stroke to Sugar's, falling easily into Sugar's rhythm as if he were waltzing with a lifelong partner.

Sugar was in his early forties. Thorn's closest friend. Six three, a thin and handsome man with severe cheekbones, dark almost pretty eyes with long lashes, and caramel skin a half shade lighter than Thorn's constant tan.

Sugar's Jamaican father disappeared shortly after his birth and his Norwegian mother, a fragile blond teenager, stayed around Key Largo a year or two more before she too vanished. There was an overexposed photo of her in Sugarman's office, his only one. Not more than eighteen at the time, his mother sat on a ratty sofa, a cigarette in one hand, a can of Schlitz in the other, laughing at someone's joke. An attractive young woman, but with eyes already shadowed by harsh memories. Thorn had only one vague memory of her. She was kneeling in the sand helping Sugar and Thorn build a sand castle on a beach somewhere. He remembered her jittery manner, nervous as an April butterfly. Eyes always scanning the area as if she were searching for something she couldn't name.

After she ran off, Sugar was raised by two black spinster sisters who sang in the Key Largo Baptist choir and whose income came from running a tomato stand beside the overseas highway. Tomatoes and the dented hubcaps they retrieved daily from the shoulder of the rutted road.

The spring Sugarman graduated high school, he married Jeannie Frost, his cheerleader girlfriend of several years. She was fair and blonde, a devout Caucasian. Unconsciously, Sugar had duplicated his parents' mixed marriage, a fact Jeannie was fond of reminding him whenever they argued.

A year or two ago, after twenty years with the Monroe County police department, Sugarman grew so disgusted with the hamstringing bureaucracy, he dumped his shield on the Sheriff's Department desk and walked. His idea was to rent out his expertise to small businesses, install alarm systems, handle employee surveillance. But it hadn't worked that way.

What he discovered was that hardly any businesses in the Keys made enough profit to pay for a security advisor. Even the lawyers and doctors were just scraping by. Dropouts from colder climates, most of them worked only when they had to. Half-assed fishermen or drunks, more likely both. They all seemed to be running from some failed life back on the mainland. One thing was certain, it was rarely money that attracted people to that string of limestone islands trickling off the tip of Florida.

While Sugarman struggled as a cop and later as a capitalist, Jeannie devoted herself to self-discovery. She'd had a host of hobbies, none of which lasted more than a few months. But still, by God, she knew she was good at something. It was out there, all she had to do was find it—that self-actualizing activity. That's how she talked. Jargon she'd picked up from years of fifty-dollar-an-hour counseling sessions.

Back in August Jeannie had given up on her most recent fantasy, to be a Flamenco guitarist, and she'd sold her two guitars to a high school kid who lived across the street. By September, she'd decided what she'd really wanted all along was to get pregnant. Be a mother before her clock expired. Already she'd visited half a dozen Miami doctors, sent Sugarman to labs up there for sperm cultures, hemizona binding tests, hypo-osmotic swelling tests, some new unpronounceable outrage every week.

"Hell, I could tell her why she isn't getting pregnant," Sugarman said. "It's 'cause every last drop of my goddamn sperm is going into sterile plastic cups."

When Thorn and Sugar finally got the canoe back in the no-wake entrance canal, a narrow channel that shot straight to the docks, the wind died off and Sugarman seemed to get a fresh burst of energy. Thorn kept the rhythm, the canoe racing along, the only noise was the deep rasp of their breathing.

A seven-foot alligator surfaced beside them, swam along, escorting them back. Rover woke, leaned over the low gunwale and began to bark at the dark creature.

A few hundred yards from the docks, Thorn heard the roar of

an outboard engine behind them and swiveled in time to see a white fishing boat bearing down. He rammed the paddle in deep, drove the canoe hard to the right into the dense mangroves, and the boat blew past, not three feet away, forty miles an hour. Its huge wake pitched them sideways deeper into the branches, nearly tipped them. Thorn lunged for Rover, caught him by the scruff as he was about to tumble overboard, a succulent dollop. For the next ten minutes while they bailed, the alligator drifted nearby eyeing them eagerly.

At the docks they found the white boat tied up alongside the gas pumps. A man in a red long-sleeve flannel shirt and jeans was lounging against the leaning post, watching them paddle. His hair was tucked under a navy watch cap, big wraparound sunglasses hid his face. A black mustache so bushy it looked like he fertilized it. The man was tall, but with the pinched waist, wide shoulders, and compact physique of a gymnast.

As the canoe coasted closer, the man reached into his cooler and drew out a speckled sea trout and lobbed it into the basin a few feet in front of their canoe. The water exploded and the fish vanished below the surface. Thorn watched the wide pebbled backs of two large gators slide beneath the water to contest the spoils, churning up a mass of bubbles from their combat.

Without looking toward the boat, Sugarman paddled the canoe up to the dock, eased out of his seat, stepped out onto the slippery ramp, and hauled the canoe a few feet higher up. He steadied it while Thorn stepped out. Thorn set Rover on the dry part of the ramp, and the puppy shook himself hard and walked up to the shade of a cabbage calm and collapsed.

"Gators are going berserk," the man said.

His jeans were tight and a handful of blond hair curled out the neck of his flannel shirt.

Thorn climbed up the ramp, mounted the dock, and approached the man.

"Interesting word, *berserk*," the man said. He yawned, covered his mouth with a fist, then took it away and gave Thorn a faint smile.

"It's Norse. Combination of *bjorn*, which is bear, and *sark*, which is shirt. Bear shirt. What the Norse warriors wore as armor."

He leaned forward and opened the fish box again. Full of reds and snook, a year or two short of legal.

"Sometimes after guzzling too much wine, a Norse warrior would flip out, run into battle, bellowing like crazy, go crashing into the opposing enemy lines without his bear shirt. So that's what it means. Fighting without armor. Going berserk. Taking a risk and not giving a shit."

Sugarman was there now, standing a couple of steps from Thorn.

"I like words. I study them. Their histories. They each have one, you know. Like people. They come from some place, they change over time. A blend of different backgrounds. Like people, mating, reproducing. My mother gave me a lifelong interest in words."

Thorn shifted his feet. He felt something happening behind his eyes, a teakettle's whistle rising to full volume. His face felt chapped.

"That's a no-wake zone back there, asshole," he said. "You almost swamped us blasting by like that."

"Oh, really?" the man said. "Golly gee."

Thorn gave Sugarman a look and Sugar shook his head. Forget it. Another hopeless psycho wandered down from Miami.

The man reached into his fish box again and grabbed the tails of two undersized redfish and slung them out beyond the dock. Another gator had drifted in to join the fun, and the three of them splashed and jostled until the fish were gone. A few scales sparkled on the surface, some entrails. And then those too swirled down into the dark water.

The man straightened, moved to the edge of his boat, put one foot up on the gunwale. "How about you boys? Ever go berserk?"

The man grinned behind the mustache and hoisted himself up to the dock. He craned his head forward, squinting at Sugarman. With a huff, the man started toward him.

"Forget it, Thorn. He's mine."

Thorn stepped aside while Sugar held his position. When the young man shot his left hand toward Sugar's face, he caught the guy by the wrist and held him at arm's length. The guy twisting, trying to lever out of Sugar's grip. Thorn had watched Sugar handle himself in at least a dozen fights, but even in the ones where he was seriously overmatched, Thorn had never seen the look that was on Sugar's face at that moment. Not fright, not panic, something closer to horror.

Sugar stiff-armed the young man, held on against several wrenching lunges, but even though it seemed to Thorn that Sugar could easily take the man to his knees, he did not press his advantage, and used his free hand only to swat away the man's wild swings.

Behind the two fighters the gators surfaced. The man saw them and it seemed to give him a surge of strength. He grunted and dipped his shoulders and bulled Sugar backward toward the edge of the dock. Sugarman staggered and winced, but kept the man's wrist trapped in his grip. And Thorn saw the opening, a simple judo move, a swing-your-partner do-si-do, requiring only an easy pivot to toss the guy down the length of the dock. It was there, so obviously there, something he'd seen Sugar execute a few times before, but this time Sugar didn't take it. But seemed instead to be in a languid trance.

And the guy groaned, leaned forward, planted his right foot between Sugar's legs and they were locked in a tug-of-war joust. Sugarman's back to the water, the young guy pushing forward. Thorn watched as Sugar lost ground, an inch, another inch, but still he didn't use his free hand to strike the man, didn't do anything but hold on, keep the guy at bay, backing closer to the gators. That same look on his face. Horror and something else now, a dark confusion.

Thorn waited as long as he dared, and when Sugar's heels were a foot from the edge of the dock, he lunged, clapped a hand on the man's shoulder, and spun him around. Sugarman slumped forward, rested his hands on his knees, gasping for air.

The man faced Thorn, gathering himself, studying this new adversary. Two feet of humid air between them, a mosquito droning in Thorn's ear. The guy looked even fitter up close. Face crinkled with amusement. Everything a joke for this one.

The man summoned an exaggerated smile, the kind that beauty queens must practice before a mirror. Then slowly he lifted his right hand, spread his fingers into a V as if he were going to stab

Thorn in the eyes Three Stooges style. Something on the tips of those two fingers flashed like shiny false fingernails.

He curled the rest of his hand into a fist and a bluish white current arced between his two extended fingers.

"What the hell . . . ?"

The current sputtered and snapped. The man inched closer, stretching out his hand in a mild and exploratory gesture as though all he meant to do was test the softness of Thorn's cheek.

Thorn set his feet, balanced himself, and when the hand shot toward his face, he kept his feet planted, simply bobbed to his right, drew his chin out of range. The man stumbled to the side, then spun around, lowering himself into a crouch. Thorn followed him around like a matador sweeping after his bull.

After a moment of glaring silence, the man lunged again, knifed the right hand, this time at Thorn's chest, but Thorn fanned the blow away. The man struck again, and he struck once more and another time. And each time Thorn used the skills he'd practiced in the sweaty gymnasium all through September and October. Slipping, ducking, dancing to a wordless tune with his partner. Creating the other half to this man's ungraceful ballet, balancing him, smoothing out his jerky movements. Sending the younger man onward in the same trajectory his swing was taking him. Thorn didn't counterpunch, didn't try to hurt the guy, but looped him off again and again out of the sphere of Thorn's space.

Two or three minutes of that and the young man was exhausted. Not much of a fighter. Just had that one trick, that inch of current. The man moved out of range, stooped forward, rested his hands on his knees, lifted his eyes and stared at Thorn. Still that smirk. Thorn had smothered his best shots, but the man wasn't cowed.

Sugarman was standing upright now. Face drained.

"Okay," Sugar said. "That's enough. Let's switch off the juice, we'll sit down in the shade, talk this over. How about it? See what our choices are, where we go from here."

The young man lifted his eyes, focused on Sugarman, then straightened. He raised his fingers again, closed his fist, and once more the current hissed. Sugarman stepped back.

The guy turned and hopped into the rental boat, and with two yanks on his mooring lines, he shoved the Aquasport ten feet from the dock.

"I'll be seeing you around," the man called out. "Count on it. Both of you."

He shoved the throttle forward, surged up on plane and headed back up the channel.

Sugarman stared at the boat's wake as it sloshed through the mangrove roots. "Did I see that right? Guy had sparks shooting out his fucking fingers?"

"Yeah," Thorn said. "Must've been plugging his pecker into a light socket for the last week. Getting all charged up. Freddy Megawatt."

Sugarman stared down the canal where the wake was dying out. "You seen that before? That some kind of weapon you can buy in the store these days?"

"Not any store I been in," Thorn said.

Sugar was still staring down the canal.

"What the hell happened to you, man? That guy was half a second from kicking your ass into the goddamn water. Gator brunch."

Sugar shook his head, swallowed. Pulled his eyes away from the canal. "I was trying my best."

"Bullshit."

Thorn stared into his eyes. Sugarman shrugged it off.

"I don't know," he said. "I don't know what happened. He took me by surprise, I guess."

"That was weird, Sugar. That was fucking weird. You were out there, teetering on the edge. It looked like you halfway wanted to go over."

"I'm okay," he said. "Don't worry. I'm fine."

Sugarman wiped the sweat from his forehead. Dusted off the bottom of his shorts.

They rested for a few minutes in the shade of a cabbage palm, then in silence they pulled the canoe out, loaded it onto the roof rack of Sugar's Ford Explorer, lashed it tight. Put Rover in the back. Thorn giving Sugarman careful looks.

A few miles down the coarse strip of asphalt, Sugarman looked over, then back at the empty highway. Sky darkening now. Fast-moving front about to catch them.

"By the way, buddy," he said. "What the hell were *you* doing? Those moves."

"I was fighting. Saving your ass from electrocution."

"You know what I mean. What was that, judo?"

"Judo, yeah, and a bunch of other bullshit mixed with it. Aikido, other things. Hell if I understand the gobbledygook that comes with it. Last couple of months Rochelle and I've been going twice a week, taking classes from this woman she knows. You're supposed to blend with your opponent. Convince them they damn well aren't going to hurt you no matter what they do, and you aren't going to hurt them. This's the first time I had a chance to try it out. Seems to work."

"Work? Hell, I never saw anything like that. It was goddamn magical."

"I'm the only guy in the class, so they're always using me for the attacker. I didn't know if I'd learned anything or not."

Thorn smiled and looked out his window. That empty stretch of sawgrass and marsh, gray and brittle and rich with hidden life. The teakettle in the back of his head had cooled now.

Sugarman was silent, hard at work driving his truck. The highway clear ahead, the Glades brown and desolate around them. Rover rose up in the backseat, whined like he had to pee again.

Sugarman took a long breath. "I don't like Rochelle."

Thorn looked over at him. Smiled. "Is there a punchline?"

"It's no joke, Thorn. She's a tramp. You should dump her."

Thorn stared at his friend. Sugarman kept his eyes on the road.

"She's fucked every guy between here and Key West and now she's finally gotten around to you."

"What're you, crazy? What's going through your head, man?"

"I'm dead serious. It's been bothering me from day one. I think it's time you dumped her." Sugarman's jaw worked. He shifted in his seat, took a fresh grip on the wheel.

Rover stuck his head between the seats, sniffed at the arm rest, then tried to climb forward, be with the guys. Thorn turned him around and headed him back to the rear.

Sugarman stared out at the empty road, breathing deeply. Thorn's ears were hot. His throat had clutched up. So angry he wasn't sure if he could speak. He cleared his throat.

"Okay, listen," he said. "I like Rochelle. I like her a lot. She's not like anybody I've been with. We're comfortable together."

"Comfortable, huh?"

Sugarman glanced over at him, then back at the road.

"Yeah," he said. "Maybe not in the same way as Darcy, but yeah."

"Comfortable," Sugar said. "You're comfortable."

"That's right. Something wrong with being comfortable?"

"Just doesn't sound like your word, Thorn. Doesn't sound like one of your top-ten goals in life."

Thorn watched a white Winnebago passing them, big lumbering thing. Thorn watched the Winnebago dwindle in the distance.

"I don't know what you think you're doing, Sugar. But I think we better just drop it right here."

"No, Thorn. I'm not dropping it. I can't stand to be around the woman. I gotta tell you that. You keep hanging out with her, I don't see how you and me are going to stay friends."

"Hey, fuck you, Sugarman. This isn't even a little bit funny. I don't believe you're saying this bullshit. What the hell's going on with you?"

Sugarman drove the truck with great care. A mile. Another mile. Pressure growing in Thorn's ears as if he were strapped inside a plummeting jet. The stubborn silence seemed to gel around them. There were a dozen things that would break this trance. A joke, an apology. But nothing made it into his throat, and the hush deepened and took root.

Two hours later they were back in Key Largo standing in the deep shade below Thorn's stilt house, unloading his canoe. The silence felt ancient. Rover ran up the outside stairs and Thorn could hear Rochelle talking to the dog, asking it questions about its day.

Sugarman got into his Explorer, sat for a minute then sent his electric window down. He gave Thorn a long look, a last chance for one of them to break the silence.

Then he drove away.

CHAPTER

4

It was Friday the seventeenth, almost two weeks since their Everglades trip. Thirteen days without speaking to Sugarman. His office just a half mile up the road, his house a mile south. It was absurd. A childish stalemate. Endangering the best friendship Thorn had known, childhood buddies, high school teammates, a long history of fishing trips, hilarious midnight card games, two lives so intertwined Thorn could barely remember a day they hadn't laughed over some snippet of local gossip or a joke Sugar had heard somewhere and badly mangled in the retelling. Now look at them. Letting the icy silence build brick by brick into some insurmountable wall.

Thorn was tying flies in the shade of a giant sapodilla tree, his vise and workbench facing Blackwater Sound. A mile away the markers of the Intracoastal guided a steady flow of boats up and down the coast, and beyond that were a scattering of mangrove islands and the waters of Florida Bay and the Gulf.

Blackwater Sound was eye-flinching bright, a dazzling shelf of diamonds. The sunlight ricocheting off its surface, brilliant sparks flying. From the southeast a humid breeze flooded up out of the Florida Straits and rattled the seed pods overhead, made the pelicans and gulls bank hard to gain altitude as they worked their territories from one side of the island to the other, Atlantic to Gulf and back again.

Squinting out at the blaze, Thorn saw the stark silhouette of someone poling a skiff across the tidal flats. For a pulse-bumping moment he imagined it was Sugarman. But as the skiff grew closer, he saw it was only Calvin Jaspers up on the poling platform of his blue Hewes bonefisher.

The old man leaned into his long fiberglass pole, coasted ahead ten feet, reset the claw foot against the muddy bottom and leaned into it again, a good solid rhythm, moving along, heading toward Thorn's dock.

Calvin was a lean and dignified man of seventy-five with a thick tangle of white hair and high English coloring. He'd ministered to Ohio Presbyterians for thirty-five years. Now he was a bonefish convert, and Thorn's best customer.

For the last few years Jaspers had managed a fishing school fifteen miles down the road in Islamorada. Eight hundred dollars for a weekend of flats-fishing instruction by some of the world's best guides, room and board at The Cheeca Lodge, and all the frozen margaritas his lawyer and doctor clients could guzzle at the end of every sunburned day.

But about a year ago everything changed. Some contagious disease had swept through urban centers all around the country and apparently infected a large percentage of the professional class with the fly-fishing bug. In one year alone, applications for Jaspers' school quadrupled. For the last five months he'd been hustling seventy-five to a hundred fly-fishing wanna-bes through his school every weekend, and because most of them were beginners or hopeless bunglers, they lost a lot of tackle, brand-new flies snagged on the bottom, caught deep in the mangrove branches, or simply spilled overboard.

All summer Thorn had been tying flies as fast as his fingers could work, handing over dozens of Crazy Charlies and Bonebusters to the Reverend Jaspers every Friday afternoon. Clearing over three hundred dollars a week, the highest steady income Thorn had seen in his life.

He watched as Jaspers made his skiff fast to the cleats, straightened up and waved hello, and started slowly down the dock. He was barefoot and wore a long-sleeved khaki shirt, matching shorts, fishing pliers in a leather holster on his belt, a white floppy hat, and black wraparound sunglasses. As he approached, Thorn could see his lips were crimped into a strange and unfamiliar smile. The look of a man with ruinous news.

They exchanged hellos and Thorn handed him the green felt pad with a dozen of his latest creations. A weedless fly, small and light, meant to resemble the tiny shrimp that bonefish shot to the surface for. It was the most realistic fly he'd created in a long time.

First he wrapped a barbless hook with an iridescent pinkish thread—a few hundred tight turns to form the plump body of the shrimp. Near the eyelet he glued two silver beads bought by the scoopful from the hobby shop tray, beads intended for some summer camp bracelet. He dotted the beads with bright red marine paint to give the shrimp a goggle-eyed stare. Then used a half-inch spray of beauty shop frosted hair for a tantalizing hula skirt that concealed the razor-point hook.

The fly was pink and small with a frothy, tantalizing look. An easy gulp. Not as outlandish as the ones he'd been tying over the last few years, but a convincing fly, with just enough whimsy to mark it as Thorn's.

Calvin Jaspers took the felt pad from Thorn and stepped back from the workbench, away from the sapodilla's deep shade. He tilted the pad at different angles to the light, tugged one fly off, held it up as though he were checking a diamond for a smudge of inferior color. A moment or two later he hooked the fly back onto the green pad and held the pad down by his side and stared out at the bay for half a minute.

"What is it?" Thorn said.

Jaspers turned and his smile deteriorated.

"They're beautiful," he said.

"Glad you like them."

"Damn beautiful."

Thorn was silent.

"They're all the same," Jaspers said. "Identical."

"Small variations," Thorn said. "But yeah, I've been trying to perfect this style."

"I'm afraid I don't want them."

"Oh," Thorn said. "Okay."

"Don't you want to know why?"

"All right."

"These are exactly like the ones you sold me last week and the week before."

"That a problem?"

"Well, they haven't been catching fish, Thorn. None at all. First time that's happened with one of yours. I had close to a hundred anglers down two weeks ago, eighty-five last week, a dozen guides taking turns with them. Skunked. Every one of them, guides included. Two weekends on the water, sixteen hours a day. No bones. Zip, not a snapper, a jack, not even a trash fish. Damn embarrassing. They're beautiful flies though. Had a lot of comments on them."

"Thanks."

"But if they aren't catching fish, you know, they're worthless to me. Impractical."

"I understand."

Thorn stared out at a catamaran, its sail down, motoring along the channel.

"Hell if I can say why they aren't working. Damned strange. Anglers spotted plenty of fish, but just couldn't get anything to hit. So here's what I've decided. I'm going to have to give you a breather, Thorn. I'll stop back around, say the middle of December, see what you're working on. If it looks good, if it looks like the old stuff, we're back in business."

"Sounds fair."

The catamaran was towing an inflatable raft. A black dog was in the raft barking furiously at a flock of trailing gulls.

"Sorry, Thorn. I hate to drop this on you."

"It's okay. No problem. I'll see you in December then."

"No hard feelings?"

"None," Thorn said. "None at all."

He turned to go, then swung back around. "You got any explanation for it, son? You've always had such a magic touch."

Thorn glanced down at the custom vise that gripped the fly he'd been working on. "Maybe I've lost it."

"No, I'm sure it's just a slump. You'll get it back. Just keep swinging at those pitches."

"I'll do that, Reverend."

"You feeling all right, son?"

"I'm fine. Never better. Very relaxed."

"Well, maybe that's it," the preacher said. "Maybe that's the whole thing right there. It's possible, you know, for a man to feel too good for his own welfare, lose his edge."

Thorn waved a mosquito away from his ear. "That one of your religious doctrines?"

"Uneasiness is good," Jaspers said. "A man who doubts is a man who tests things, doesn't get sluggish. As I used to say, lazy faith is no faith at all."

"Hey, they're just bonefish flies, Reverend. A hook wrapped with colored threads, some feathers and fur. That's all they are."

The man smiled. "Sure, son. If you say so."

He hesitated a moment more with an odd look in his eyes, then turned and walked away. Thorn felt his smile wither from within, but out of stubbornness and recent habit he kept it there for a few moments more.

Upstairs, he found Rochelle hunched over her portable sewing machine. He stood in the doorway and looked at her for a moment. Last summer's sun still shone gold in the tips of her hair. A month or so ago, shortly after she'd moved in with him, she'd cropped her shoulder-length auburn hair very short, just barely enough to part. Now she looked like a penitent. A sexy penitent.

The new cut seemed to enlarge Rochelle's green eyes. It emphasized her cheekbones too. Her lips. Thorn liked to hold her face in his hands. He liked to kiss her that way, face cradled in his palms. He liked to massage her head, scratch her scalp, which made her hum and rock her head to loosen the muscles in her neck. He liked to feel the shape of her skull, molding his hands around it.

He couldn't remember liking to do any of that with other women. He'd been in love a few times and each time was very different. Every instance seemed to have nothing to do with the ones before. Of course the women made it different. Each of them distinct, and Thorn kept changing as well. That must've been why the pleasure he felt with Rochelle, the melting away, the angles of stimulation, the exact weight and complexity of his feelings, all of it was mysterious and unfamiliar. The rhythms of their conversations, the silences, the grammar of their touch. New cadences, new junctures of flesh.

Even with years of experience with other lovers, it was as though Thorn were starting fresh with her. All his education didn't help, made no difference whatever. Love, it seemed, was one of those things about which it was impossible to be wise.

Rochelle had finished making curtains for the west windows and was working on the east ones now. White Spanish lace. Simple and elegant, tossed easily by the sea breezes. They gave the room a soft, sleepy feel. A room to nap in.

He'd never had curtains before. No need, with a jungle of Florida hollies and seagrape, ironwood, gumbo limbo and strangler fig cloaking the perimeter of his property, any voyeurs would need a week of hard labor with a machete to get within peeping distance.

"What's wrong, Thorn?"

Rochelle's sewing needle was still, the machine humming before her. She was holding a hem of the white lace, poised to feed more of it through the guide. Rover was asleep, lying on his plaid mat near her feet. She wore an ankle-length dress in a blue paisley print, a scooping neckline that gave a generous view of sun-freckled flesh. A hippie costume making the rounds again. But underneath the dress, Thorn knew she wore black scalloped lace panties. A bra that was barely a whisper of fabric. That was Rochelle. A junk painting that the world saw, a sensuous masterpiece underneath. Scratch away that hippie dress, you found a woman who loved to rollick. A woman who'd refreshed Thorn's interest in the erotic, reminded him how to caper, how to laze away an afternoon, smooth his jagged brainwaves.

"You're not smiling," she said. "What is it?"

Thorn told her about Jaspers and her face softened. Oh, only that.

"Well, I like them. I think they're beautiful. Much prettier than the flies you've done in the past."

"You're not a fish."

"No," she said. "Would you like me better if I were?"

"I like you fine."

"If I were a fish," she said, making a sly smile. "You could mount me. Hang me on the wall."

"I don't mount fish."

"Sorry," she said. And she looked at him a moment more as if trying to decode this new disposition. Something she hadn't seen before. It had only been a month, living like this.

Thorn wished he could tell her how to deal with him, what to say to make this uneasiness disappear, but he didn't know himself.

"You could mount me anyway," she said quietly.

"I could," he said. "Yes, there's always that."

He tried to smile but could feel it turn sickly on his lips. "It's okay, Rochelle."

"Is this just a mood?"

"Yeah, I guess it's that."

"Well, then I get to have one too."

"Fair enough." He felt his smile coming back. "We could take a gigantic mood swing together. Get seriously cranky, go out on the porch, shake our fists at the sky."

Rochelle stood up, started over to him.

There was a breeze stirring the curtains. When they bloused out, the room changed, waves of light trickling across the walls.

He'd spent more hours in that room than any place on earth. Sitting at his fly-tying desk, he could hear the quiet ticking of the wood, knew all its creaks and groans and crackling as it weathered the years. He could tell the hour of the day by the shape of the shadows lying across the floor, could name the bird by the sound of its claws scratching across the wood shingles.

But just then those curtains and the tricks they were playing with the light made him dizzy and confused. Giving him a breathless vertigo that passed almost as quickly as it came.

Rochelle took him in her arms and Thorn fit himself against her. His hand rising to touch the back of her head, the soft bristle of her scalp. The embrace snug and familiar.

"Glass of wine?" she said, her mouth at his throat.

"I've still got work to do."

"You work too hard."

"I like to work. It's what I do."

He felt her body flush against his, so close it seemed they were seeping into one another. She smoothed a hand across his bottom, let it linger.

"It's almost happy hour," she whispered.

"Well, maybe just one glass."

Rochelle peeled slowly from the embrace, went to the wine rack. It was a simple teak arrangement she'd given him as a gift. The wine rack held ten bottles, mostly Cabernets, which was what she favored. She uncorked last night's bottle, pulled two glasses from the shelf. Hers as well. Long-stemmed glasses etched with a lacy design around the rims. Not the heavy squat things Thorn used for wine—a half cut above jelly jars.

They went out into the sun, leaned against the porch railing and gazed at Blackwater Sound, the harsh concussions of light against its surface. Another cool front had moved through overnight and the sky was scraped clean again. A frigate bird was suspended a mile up in the perfect blue, a winged dragon searching for prey. The sunlight was sharp and pure, cleaner than light ever was on the mainland. Temperature in the low seventies, a breeze from the north carrying a hint of evergreen.

"You're not one of those men who works so hard because he's got to leave an empire behind, some monument with his name carved on it."

"No, no empire. Nothing like that."

"Or maybe you use work to block out some dark, tormented interior life." Smiling playfully.

"I like tying flies. It's not complicated. I just like doing what I do."

Her forehead smoothed. Rochelle raised her glass. "Well, then. Let's drink to doing more of what we like to do."

"A worthy toast," Thorn said.

"And to spinning our cocoon against the poisons of the world."

Thorn hesitated, then lifted his glass to hers.

"To cocoons everywhere," he said. They clinked.

The noise woke Rover. He hustled out to the porch, giving himself an ear-flapping shake as he came. Lately Rochelle had started pouring out little puddles of wine on the bare planks for him to lap up, and now whenever he heard the tinkle of glasses, he came mooching around.

"What would you think," Thorn said, "about inviting Sugar and Jeannie over for supper one night this weekend?"

A strained smile played on her lips. "Sure, of course, invite them over. I like Sugar."

"You do?"

"Sure. Any friend of yours."

"Tonight or Saturday?"

"We've got martial arts Saturday, Thorn."

"Tonight then."

"Oh, God, I forgot," she said, topping up her glass, then his. "Sugarman called."

"Called? How'd he do that? There's no phone."

"My cellular. He called my dad, got the number from him."

"What'd he want?"

"I don't know. He didn't tell me."

Rochelle had a sip of wine. She lifted her free hand and pointed at the lazy arc of an osprey as it crossed overhead.

"Where's your phone, Rochelle?"

"In my purse. What? You're going to call him now?"

"I thought I would. Yeah."

"He's left by now."

"Left?"

"He was going somewhere, just wanted to tell you good-bye, I think. This was a couple of days ago."

"Couple of days?"

"Three maybe. Four, I don't know. Since I've been living here, I've been losing track of time."

"Four days ago. And you just now remembered?"

She narrowed her eyes. Set her wineglass on the railing, turned to face him full on.

"Yes, I forgot," she said precisely. "I'm sorry. But, Thorn, you don't even own a phone, no clock, no calendar, now all of a sudden you're worked up at me for not being a good personal secretary?"

"I'm sorry."

She turned away. And when he put his hands on her back, she was stiff. It took a full minute massaging her shoulders, her neck, before her muscles relaxed, and she closed her eyes, let her head slump forward. Made a small croon of pleasure.

The bay still dazzled, boats left their luminous signatures across it. The sky was an empty, perfect blue, and butterflies making ditzy gyrations around the geraniums at the far end of the porch. A glorious day. A beautiful, alluring, and highly intelligent woman groaning beneath his hands.

But Thorn was not there. Thorn was not anywhere.

CHAPTER
5

Irma Slater. That's what she called herself. The ugly name she'd plucked out of the air. Grating, off-key, a handful of sour notes. Irma Slater. She'd considered Earlene, Eunice, briefly toyed with Brunhilda. But no one would believe those. Even Irma was pushing it, not a name you heard anymore. Someone born in a tarpaper shack, had pine twigs for toys, illiterate and malnourished. Ozarks, Appalachia, one of those hill women who looked twenty-five years older than she was. Washed clothes against the river rocks. Lucky to get out of the hollow once a year.

The young woman known as Irma Slater was having her Friday evening fish sandwich at the Mangrove Bar on Sugarloaf Key, seventeen miles up the road from Key West. Feeling the usual salty crust on her arms and throat from the day's accumulated sweat. She wore a blue denim shirt, washed so often it was fragile as cobweb, faded pink Bermudas, and a pair of rubber flipflops she'd picked up for seventy-nine cents at the Price Mart.

Hell, if she amortized the cost of her five identical outfits over the three years she'd worn them, frayed cotton panties included, her whole damn wardrobe probably worked out to something like point zero zero two cents a day. Maybe she should sit down, do the math, have the exact number ready. A good conversation killer.

Add in all the money she'd saved these last three years in the Keys, no makeup, jewelry, perfume, manicures and facials, no panty hose or bras, purses or cashmere sweaters or Armani suits. Throw in the hundreds of sad, hollow afternoons of impulse shopping at Neiman-Marcus she'd missed out on, and she'd probably saved enough money to put a dozen kids through college. Buy each one a Ferrari.

As it was, she'd saved four hundred and eighty-seven dollars and seventy-five cents in the last three years. Hid her stash in a Tampax box under the lavatory. Her nest egg. Her run money. In case she had to leave in a hurry, hit the road again, bus tickets, a few weeks' food until she got established somewhere else.

And it was a damn good thing she'd learned to be thrifty, because on what she made at Sugarloaf Retreat she barely had enough to cover her seven fish sandwiches a week. Coffee for breakfast, skipping lunch so she could splurge on Heineken instead of Busch at dinnertime.

It was the seventeenth of the month, middle of November, less than a week till Thanksgiving, the tourists just beginning to trickle down the highway again, shed their sweaters. Tonight, like every night, she sat on the corner bar stool, her razor pen, her drawing pad lying beside her dinner plate. An empty space on either side where the waitresses gave their drink orders. Jesse called her spot the cockpit.

Jesse was the bartender, chief bottle washer, and owner of Sugarloaf Retreat. Kinky gray hair in a ponytail. He was in his midfifties, from Indiana, retired real estate broker who'd scored big in shopping plazas, retired early, bought this broken-down motel. Now he spent his days roaming the ten acres of his bayside property in a red thong bikini, no shirt, barefoot. Nights he played bartender, and as a concession to the tourist crowd, he put on a flowered shirt. Like most everybody else in the Florida Keys, Jesse was going through a very public second childhood.

Reason he saved the cockpit for her was to help her ward off the bozos—the turkeys who slugged down a couple of courage beers and came sidling over to hit on the lonely lady with the short blond hair. Between the waitresses coming and going and Irma

Slater's sour tongue, the bozos were usually back with their buddies in less than a minute.

"Hello, pretty lady," they'd say. Some variation.

Beautiful, gorgeous, ravishing, luscious, stunning. Heard it all her life. First words she remembered. Beautiful face, gorgeous sunny golden hair. Grown-ups always touching her curls as if to check that she was real. Touch, touch. And even when they didn't speak the words aloud, they said it with their eyes, said it with the change in their voice. Beautiful, gorgeous.

The boys were the worst, and later the men, the ones who winced but kept on staring as if her beauty caused an ache in their guts. A painful affront, a challenge. They stared at her as if she were a museum goddess. Marble, granite. Cold stone. That's how they treated her. Left room around her as they circled, marveling. While she waited for the inevitable—for one of them to break out of the orbit, move in, mutter the words, beautiful hair, a knockout, all that. As though she hadn't heard it before, hadn't already come to despise them for what they said, despise herself for making them say it.

In the process she sank away inside that museum goddess. Became a woman no one knew, no one cared to know. They saw the sculptured face, the large blue eyes, the sharp cheekbones, the figure that swelled and narrowed in extravagant proportions. You should be a model, they said. You should be an actress, they said. So she could get paid to be gawked at. Yeah, right.

She found she could go anywhere, do anything, the doors always swung open for her. The doors inside those doors. It was hers, the ripe world, the plums. The gorgeous sweet secret heart of things was laid out before her. Hers for the selecting. All she had to do was show up, point an elegant finger at what she desired.

And as though that weren't enough, there was the money. The cash, the lucre. Tainting everything, infecting it. Formidable wealth. Born with it, surrounded at every turn. Lavish house with Miami's most expensive vistas, childhood vacations to Paris, Zurich, hundred-thousand-dollar cars to chauffeur her to tennis classes and cotillion. Wealth so abundant there came a time when she was no longer sure where the money started and she began, no longer clear on which passion she aroused in those who professed their love. Which were the playthings, which the players.

Hell, yes, she knew there were a thousand worse calamities than being rich and beautiful. Tortures so grievous she had no inkling. Wars, famines, grinding poverty, abuse of every kind. She wasn't so far gone she confused her plight with real tragedy. Even at its worst, her misfortune struck her as no more than bitterly ironic. A mild irritation chafed to a bleeding sore by all those daily reminders of how blessed she was.

Severe enough, however, to bring her there, to Sugarloaf Retreat. Grievous enough to cause her to rename herself Irma Slater. Irma Slater. A name as harsh and unattractive as she could invent. All because she had concluded finally that she could no longer trust anyone who knew her by her real name.

Not even David Cruz.

She'd known David in high school. They'd dated, nothing serious. He was Cuban, wanted to be a cop. So far out of her league, he was a joke among her friends. Though David never seemed to mind. She liked him, had a soft spot, but lost touch when she went off to boarding school her sophomore year.

Five years later, a college girl then, the summer of her junior year, home from Sweetbriar, she bumped into him at someone's goofy barbecue. He was a cop by then. Living his dream. Hair cut short, looking cute and strong and very different from all the others. And he seemed immune to her beauty, to her father's wealth. Looked at her, seemed to peer past the surface, searching for who was down there. They talked. And he spoke to the hidden person, the invisible one, coaxing that part of her into view. They went to supper at the big bright, raucous Cuban restaurant he liked. A place her other friends used to mock as being too bright and raucous and Cuban.

Back in Virginia, she wrote him. He answered. His letters full of specifics, anecdotes about his days on the streets of Miami. He was funny. Earnest. He was doing what he'd dreamed of doing and he loved it. Sharing this with her. Her letters were glib. Acid stories about the Miami yachting crowd she'd always mingled with. Pen-and-ink caricatures of the Virginia prissies.

By Christmas her senior year, she and David Cruz were making secret plans to marry. And then a month before graduation, a month before she was to return to Miami, throw it in her parents' faces that she was becoming a cop's wife, a commoner, her mother dove into the Atlantic from the upper decks of a cruise ship. Her bloated corpse recovered two days later.

A mother she barely knew. Her fragile heart, her migraines, her long voyages into speechless depression had kept her in her darkened room most of her married life.

Home for the funeral, she slept over at David's apartment. Lying in his bed, snuggled against him, she felt his tension, knew something was wrong. Not the same David he'd been at Christmas. What is it? she asked him. What's going on?

I took a new job, he said. Head of security operations. You did? Not with the police anymore? You quit being a cop! That's right, he said. I'm moving into the corporate world. Safer, he said. Safer, yes, she agreed. That's fine, off the streets, fine. As long as it's what you want. Sweetheart, he said. Your father, he said. He said, Your father gave me the job. Assistant security chief for the whole company. He knows about us. He knows we're engaged. I didn't tell him, I promise, but he knows. He knows? How could he know? Look, he said, this job, it pays very well. This is a real job. I could provide for you this way, give you things you're used to. Your father, he said. Your father, he said.

She got out of bed. She dressed.

It's okay, she told David Cruz. It's fine. You did the right thing. The only thing you could. My father's a determined man. He's going to throw down a yellow brick road in front of me no matter what.

You're mad.

No, she told him. I understand. I love you.

I love you too. You're sure? Everything's okay?

Of course, David. Of course it is.

Another soul stolen. Fuck him, fuck all of them.

Back at school, she went about her business. Finished hanging her senior art show. A hundred black-and-white ink drawings, minimalist, some no bigger than postage stamps, scenes of Florida. A beach ball lying on an empty beach. A tumbled umbrella, an elaborate sandcastle ruined by the tides. Gulls in broken formation.

Intricate drawings, her Japanese period. Deceptively simple but with thousands of precise razor strokes. Her major professor named the show "Florida Dissonance."

The weekend of her show, she told her roommate she was going to the grocery for a jug of wine, then drove her Saab to a mall on the edge of campus. Stared out the windshield for half an hour, watched darkness settle, watched the parking lot empty. Then she took a long breath, gripped her hair and yanked out a hunk, scattered it around the interior. She drew a razor blade from her purse, pressed the cold metal against her fingertip, bore down. She milked the wound, wiped the blood on the steering wheel, the dash, the door handle. Left the keys in the ignition, walked away, caught a bus. It was April.

Of course, disappearing wasn't that easy. Her father went on a mad campaign. The papers took it up. The magazines. He made the national TV news four nights in a row as his daughter lay in cheap motels in Virginia, Carolina, Georgia watching him. Foul play. Fearing the worst. FBI in on it. His wife dead two weeks ago, now this. Hinting there might be some connection.

Some good leads developed. A Hispanic man seen lurking at the mall that afternoon. Father pleading with her abductors to let her go, get in touch, something. A huge reward. Her father choking up for the cameras, a thing he hadn't managed at her mother's funeral. Married over twenty-five years, but at the graveside her father smiled, a cordial host. Now look at him. The cameras, the lights. Dark circles under his light blue eyes, he's choking big time. Drama king.

As she drifted south, entering Florida, and finally into the Keys, the posters met her everywhere. She ducked her face, tucked her hair under a baseball cap. Wore Salvation Army blouses, men's trousers, big round sunglasses. Took buses.

A dozen times a day, she swung between euphoria and panic. Had trouble breathing, her chest too tight. None of it as easy as she'd imagined. So isolated. So disoriented, which, she supposed, was why she was drawn back to Florida, something familiar, the Keys, a place where she and her mother had been happy for two weeks together years earlier. The only mother-daughter trip they'd ever taken. Staying in a bayside motel, snorkeling over the turtle grass, reading side by side, feeding the snappers. Sharing the quiet together.

Four months into her exile, August, her photo faded from the papers. The posters on the telephone poles were tattered and bleached. Continuing the slow, secret slide down the Keys, she stopped at every joint and dive and funky outdoor tavern she could find, searching for the place she and her mother had spent their two weeks together. Every night she collapsed in a different mom-and-pop motel. Numbing herself with tequila, taking boat bums into her bed, dancing every night to jukebox music. Finally one August evening on Sugarloaf, seventeen miles from the dead end of Key West, she found the motel. New owner. Things run down. But the ghosts still hovered. She stopped. Checked in. Felt a warmth sweep through her.

A month later, down to her last six dollars, she accepted the job Jesse offered. And this place became the best home she'd had. Sugarloaf Retreat, eighty motel rooms, a netless tennis court, a dolphin named Sweetcakes in the lagoon. Jesse had grown up watching *Flipper,* and this was part of the fantasy, migrate to the Keys, sun and ocean breezes, perpetual summer, star in one of the canceled TV shows of his youth.

She worked as a maid. One of two, the other being a Guatemalan grandmother with no English. They made beds, swept, vacuumed, swished the toilets, the usual. Cleaning up the remains of other people's pleasures. Got paid cash. No social security numbers, no withholding. Jesse didn't ask. Her free time, she fed snappers off the dock. Tossing them shrimp, bits of bread, just as she and her mother had years ago. Her drawings enlarged, relaxed. Still dense with detail, but more open, more available, a deeper breath. Three fishing poles leaning against the wall of the bait shop, a desiccated shrimp on one of the hooks. A flats boat staked out fifty yards from a tangled mangrove island. Each twist of mangrove root rigorously accurate.

She became Irma Slater. Brash and ballsy. Kept the guys at bay. Liking this new woman who took no shit, knew how to give it by the bucket. This spitfire who could tell them to fuck off and sit there staring them in the eye until, by God, they stalked away. Or else if the moon and mood were right, take them back to her motel room, strip away the Kmart clothes, have her way. But even then, the minute the words came from their lips, beautiful, gorgeous, all that, she would spring the trapdoor beneath their feet. Let them drop.

Irma Slater taught her how to do all that. Tough Irma. Happy Irma. A no-nonsense woman growing inside her, filling the hollows. No games, no bullshit. Just took her pleasures when she wanted, shut the door and locked it the rest of the time. Irma looking at the world, seeing the rough, simple things. Drawing them honestly in pen and ink. No hokiness. No gimmicks or intellectual interference. Irma Slater, not looking for love. A long way past that.

Her first month at Sugarloaf, Irma Slater buzzed her hair, sheared off fifteen years of blondness. Got right down to the scalp, a burr. Found that her skull had some interesting ridges and knobs, little plateaus she'd never known were there. The buzz cut didn't make her ugly, but it helped. The men steered wider arcs. This close to Key West, they assumed she was butch. Though that didn't stop all of them. She did her hair twice a week. Kept it to a pinch, that was it, a fine blur of yellow.

For three years she'd been doing the Sugarloaf shuffle, the same strict ceremony every day. Irma Slater becoming solid inside her. A woman of simple tastes. In the cockpit by six, broiled yellowtail two hours out of the water. A plate of conch fritters on the side, two beers. For the next couple of hours, she'd watch the sun tick lower until it flattened against the Gulf, then watch its golden fire leak away into water and clouds, watch the pelicans darken to silhouettes. Then the moon would rise and some nights it coated the black water with silver as if a giant parachute of lace had drifted to earth. Irma briefly considering watercolors, acrylics, oils. But decided no. A greater challenge to continue with ink. The white page. Make that silver lace visible through the magic of omission.

While she dawdled over the second beer, she hummed along to the ten-year-old country tunes playing on the jukebox. At eight or nine, warmed by the Heinekens, the fritters, the yellowtail, she'd pace the quiet hundred yards along the seawall to her motel room. Take a quick shower, crawl naked inside the sheets, flip on the light, and forge on through the next chapter of the biography of the week. Whatever the librarian was pushing. Submerge herself in Truman's life, Monroe's, for an hour or two, fill herself up with someone else's tragedies, conquests, their inevitable last days. Fall asleep listening to the clicks and baby babble, the sweet gasps of Sweetcakes ten feet beyond her open window.

In these last three years, three barefoot, liberated years, the euphoria had flattened out, become a steady, reliable hum of pleasure. A Zen calm. Watching the next moment, the next after that. No expectations, no aspirations. Breathing and eating, sleeping and fucking, working and reading and drawing, satisfying Irma Slater's spartan needs. Building her nest egg. Her crisis fund. And in those three years she'd filtered out most of the residue. Not cured, not by a long shot. But a start, a damn good running start on some kind of deliverance after all. Self-pity in remission. Penniless and anonymous. What more could she want?

That Friday night she was down to the last sips of her second Heineken, a small crowd accumulating along the railing beside the canal. Motel guests, snared by Jesse's gaudy neon sign. A couple of Japanese girls taking flash snapshots of the pelican sleeping on the tallest piling. At the picnic table a family of blond giants from Minnesota ate fish sandwiches and sipped Cokes. She watched a flats boat skim off the dark bay, come surfing in on its following wake. The jukebox throbbed with Hank Williams, the moon a smiling sliver in the east.

She was lifting the last conch fritter to her mouth when a man filled the waitress's station to her right. Jesse gave her a look, see if she wanted help. She grimaced that she didn't as she munched the fritter. Since coming to Sugarloaf, she'd made it a part of her training to learn how to handle the bozos, defuse the lust that she still sometimes inspired. Her figure decoded inside the shapeless shirt.

"I'm waiting for my boyfriend," she said, eyes on her beer. "He's Italian and the last guy he caught putting the moves on me is in the trunk of a '55 De Soto in a Dade County canal."

The man didn't move. He was tall, she could sense that. Standing quietly, making no attempt.

She drank down the last of the beer.

"Abracadabra," the man said quietly. "Abracadabra."

She kept her eyes down.

"It's a beautiful word, don't you think? So full of magic."

She turned her head, took a glimpse of this one.

Tall with blond hair down to his shoulders, wavy and clean. Light blue eyes that held to hers. Eyes with a deep spark. In faded jeans and a crisp white button down shirt. Wide shoulders, narrow hips, a deep chest. His skin was pale, more white than cream. In his early twenties. A mouth poised on the edge of a smile. Only a degree or two off Hollywood handsome. Nose too prominent, a half inch too much forehead. Interesting, you'd call him, worth a second look. A third. Irma was vaguely curious. The moon in the right phase. Her cowboy for the night, perhaps.

"Abracadabra," the man said. "It's from the Hebrew *ab,* which means father, and *ben,* which is son, and *ruach acadash,* which is the holy spirit. Do you like words? I do. I like words. My mother gave me a lifelong interest in them. I study them. We become friends. Words in my mouth, saying them, the feel of them, bringing them alive, and them bringing me alive. Do you have words like that, words you enjoy feeling in your mouth? Words that bring you alive? Abracadabra. Father, son, and holy ghost."

The young man smiled at her and leaned closer. "Look, I know this isn't a normal way to begin a conversation, discussing etymologies. But these things are on my mind, and you should say what's on your mind. Don't you agree? Anyway, the fact is, since we're old friends, I thought we could jump over the formalities anyway. Get reacquainted."

Irma changed her mind. She slipped down from her stool, picked up her pad and razor pen, and stepped away from him. Feeling the tidal pull of his voice, the dark undertow. Resisting it.

"Are you fleeing? Have I scared you?"

"I don't scare that easy."

"Don't you remember me?"

He was a yard away. Composed, his eyes on hers as if this were the end of a pleasant date, warming up to the kiss.

"My name is Butler Jack. In that order, Butler first, then Jack. I've found I have to explain it because some people, they hear my name, they think there's a comma between the words, like I'm saying it backward. But that's frontward. Butler Jack. Ring a bell?"

"No," she said.

He showed her a charming smile. "Come on, don't fool around. Sure you do."

"I don't know any Butler Jack, frontward or backward."

"Oh, stop," he said. "You don't need to keep pretending."

"You have me confused with someone else," she said. "I'm Irma Slater."

"No, you're not. You're Monica Sampson. Daughter of Morton Sampson of Fiesta Cruise Lines. And I'm the kid who was in love with you. Butler Jack, the one who sent you love letters. Long letters full of poetry. I'm finally here. I've come to get you like I promised."

CHAPTER

6

The woman known as Irma Slater coaxed herself back to her stool and settled there. Took a casual sip of the warm slosh in the bottom of her bottle. Felt the fish sandwich turn, grow fins, swim upward.

"Your daddy made number forty-one on the *Forbes* list last year. Did you know that? Only a dozen Americans above him. Closing in on some of the lesser Saudis. And I was very sorry about your mother. I would've gone to the funeral, but back then, four years ago, I was at sea. Working the cruises. By the time I got back to port, the funeral was long over. She was a beautiful woman, your mother. Not up to your standards maybe, but striking just the same."

Irma drew a clumsy breath. She glanced across at Jesse. He was washing glasses, bobbing up and down, focused on his work. She steadied herself with a hand against the bar. Looked closely at this guy. Hair off-blond, a tinge of red, or maybe that was the lights. His eyes darting around, interested in everything, the people coming and going, Jesse working behind the bar, Butler's gaze returning to her with a crinkle of humor as if he were absorbing this place, amused to find her in such a spot.

"You're making a mistake. You're confused."

"You haven't changed that much, Monica. Sure, your hair is

different. Oh, I understand why you cut it. It isn't just for the disguise, is it? You wanted to get rid of all those years hanging down your back. All those memories. But does that really work, Monica? Can you shave your head and get rid of the past? I don't think so."

"What the fuck do you want?"

"Want," he said. "Now there's another interesting word. We use it all the time, but what does it really mean?"

Irma felt the blood burning her face as if she'd been slapped hard on both cheeks. Fight and flight battling to a standstill in her veins.

"On the one hand, if you *want* something, you *desire* it. But then of course *want* also means *lack*. You desire what you lack. What you want is what you're wanting, the thing you're missing. The things that would complete you."

"Look," she said. "Save the bullshit. I'm satisfied with my vocabulary like it is."

"Electricity works like that. It seeks what it's missing. Positive charge seeks negative. Negative ions seek positive. What nature wants is to get even, get back to zero. Everything neutralized. But of course that never happens. There's always a negative charge floating around, or a positive one, looking to stir things up. Wanting the thing it doesn't have, that last little thing that would make its world complete. Everybody's searching, right down to the subatomic particles, we're yearning for something, some little bitty thing."

"I'm leaving," Irma said, and started to rise. But he rested a hand on her forearm. Didn't restrain her exactly, didn't force her down, but his touch disarmed her just the same. He was staring at his hand against her flesh, studying it. His skin awake against hers, more than simple touching, like he was taking a reading of her radioactivity.

"You remember," he said, "when you used to sit on the porch of your big house. Pink and blue dresses, lace around the collar. You'd sit on the swing and look out at us, standing around in the distance, holding our paper plates, waiting in the chow line. You sat there in the swing on your porch and you brushed your hand through your thick gold hair, very casual, like we weren't there, like we weren't all watching your every move. Do you remember, Monica? Remember the swing I'm talking about? Remember looking out at us, the children of your father's employees, the annual Thanksgiving cookout? Do you remember that?"

She gave him nothing.

"How about the ice turkeys? Those sculptures sitting in the middle of each picnic table. A turkey carved out of ice, each one filled with silver dollars. Fifty, sixty silver dollars in every one. Remember that?"

Irma kept her face empty.

He took his hand from her forearm. She looked down at the place where it had been, half expecting a welt.

"While we ate, the ice melted in the sun, the heavy coins dropped into the silver trays. *Ping, ping.*"

"My name is Irma Slater," she said.

"And one day, you came down off the porch. You sat at my table. None of us knew what to say. Everybody went dead quiet. That ice melting. You sat there with the napkin in your lap, looking down at the plate of hot dogs and sauerkraut. Your bare arm right next to mine.

"Remember? Remember telling us not to grab the money? You said your daddy was playing a trick. Trying to humiliate us, make us snatch the money from the weaker children. We should just let it sit there. Not take it. Not fall for his scheme. Don't give him the satisfaction."

Irma looked out at the dark horizon, the spray of stars.

"None of the others listened. They kept on grabbing. Not me. I sat there and watched the silver dollars fall onto the trays and I didn't try to snatch any of it away from the other boys. I didn't surrender to your father's game.

" 'It's a war,' you said. 'You're on one side or the other.' "

Irma swung around and peered into his eyes. The color of the Atlantic on a gusty day, turquoise stirred to a milky blue.

"You might recall my mother. She worked in your father's office. His private secretary. Took his dictation, made decisions he didn't have time for. Remember her?"

She slid the beer bottle forward a half inch, a pawn taking the center of the board. Using up some time, once again looking out at the darkness, the red heartbeat of a channel marker. Feeling the fish in her belly slide back down into the acid juices.

"So what is this? You want money? A handout? Well, you've come to the wrong damn place."

"I remember the angle of your neck when you sat on the porch, the way you cocked it to one side, how you kicked your feet to make the swing move, the way you'd move your eyes over all of us. You gave us dreams, Monica, fantasies. All the boys. Even some of the men. They'd talk about you, say things I can't repeat.

"You remember our correspondence?"

Of course she did. A letter from him arriving one spring afternoon on blue stationery, a lock of his blond hair inside. Using the sweeping, flamboyant phrases of romance novels, he'd pledged his undying love. Asked for hers. She'd answered the letter. Not even remembering which boy he was from the employee picnic, but going ahead, trying out the vocabulary of courtship, a twelve-year-old's fantasy. She put the lock of hair in her jewelry box. Waited for his next letter. Answered it immediately. Then came several more. And finally the ring.

A two-carat diamond Scotch-taped to the sheet of stationery. "Be mine forever," the note said. "Pledge your troth to undying love." She wrote back and gave him her unqualified yes. She wrapped yarn around the ring to make it snug against her finger. Wore it to bed. Woke one morning to find her mother standing above her holding her left hand, examining the stone. It was his mother's ring. He'd stolen it from her. It went back. No more letters allowed, no more contact of any kind. Her mother more angry than she'd ever seen her. Monica went away to summer camp. Fell in love with a fourteen-year-old boy across the lake. Larry something, a swimmer. Forgot about the episode entirely.

"I remember," she said.

She felt sand flies chewing on her legs. The bay rippled with crimson light as though it had been sheened with kerosene and set ablaze. She inhaled the familiar sulfurous scent that rose on windless nights from the surface of the lagoon. A pungent mist. Fish guts and seaweed with a tinge of swamp gas.

"My father sent you," Monica said. "You're here to drag me home."

"No, I'm a free agent." Butler edged up to the bar, leaned a hip against it. "But the truth is, Monica, your father knows you're here."

She swung around, stared into his eyes.

"Yeah," he said. "Your friend over there, Jesse."

"What about him?"

"Ask him. Ask him where he got the money for his new sign out front. All that neon doesn't come cheap, you know."

"You're lying."

"A man called one day, my mother spoke to him. He wanted to report that he knew where Mr. Sampson's daughter was hiding out, but first, he had to know what the reward was up to. There were a lot of calls like that, but the difference was, this one was real. This guy knew where you were."

She stared across at Jesse. He was looking at her now, his eyes working back and forth between her and Butler Jack. She drew a breath, pulled her eyes away from him and rubbed at the clot of tension forming at her temples.

Butler Jack touched her shoulder. "That little girl on the swing, she was very wise. What she said when she sat down at our table. The little girl who didn't want any part of that money. She had everything in the world, but there was still something missing, something she wanted very much, something she was yearning for. Positive ion searching for its other half."

She stared out into the shivering darkness.

"I still don't take the money," Butler said. "It falls on the silver plate in front of me, *ping, ping, ping,* but I'm not tempted. I've chosen my side. You changed my life, Monica. You changed everything. And now I'm here. I'm a warrior for the cause."

"What the hell do you want with me?"

"You know, it's amazing," Butler said. "Here we are like this, side by side, talking about the past, about all these memories. Re-united after all these years. I thought I was ready. But look at me. Look."

He held up a quivering hand.

"How long has he known? My father."

"Years," he said. "Since the first month you arrived here."

She took a breath, another. Felt a moth flutter inside the membranes of her heart. "Okay, so why hasn't he done anything? Why hasn't he shown up?"

"I don't know, but I can tell you one thing. Right after you disappeared, stock in Fiesta Cruises went up forty percent and it's stayed there ever since. Might be a coincidence. Or maybe it's from all that sympathy and free publicity he got. I don't know. Makes you wonder though. Makes you think. A man like your father, he has to calculate every move, there's money riding on everything he does. Lots of money."

She eased off the stool, Butler stepping aside.

"One last thing before I go," he said. "I guess you don't watch TV or anything. I guess you haven't been keeping up."

"Keeping up with what?"

"What your father's been doing. His major life changes."

"I don't give a damn about my father."

"Oh, but it's interesting, Monica. It bears on us. You and me."

"There is no us."

"Oh, yes there is. You and I, we're related now. Two years ago your father married my mother. She went from private secretary to wife and TV star. Morton and Lola. Cute couple. Which makes us brother and sister. Family."

She felt as if a corpse were breathing on her neck. A bleak chill sneaking through that humid air, finding her, lifting the flesh on her back, her arms.

"I'm parked in the lot," he said. "Right out front, big white Winnebago. When you're ready to join me, that's where I'll be."

"And why would I want to do that?"

"Because he's coming. Your father is coming to get you, take you home. Get you psychological help."

"I don't believe you."

"So wait and see. Take your chances. I'll be out in the lot when you need me."

He smiled at her and turned and walked away. When he was just beyond the swimming pool, Jesse was at her shoulder, patting her roughly on the back as if she'd choked.

"You okay, honey? You look shaky."

She couldn't look at him. Fizz in her veins, blood churned to useless foam.

"Who the hell was that? An old boyfriend or something?"

She stared at the water, the bar lights quivering there.

"Look, let me buy you another Heineken."

Jesse went back behind the bar, opened her a new beer, and set it down on the polished mahogany in front of her.

"You have a history with that guy?"

"Apparently I do."

"I thought so, way you were talking to him. I could sense something going on there."

Jesse rubbed a damp rag across the glossy bar. She was silent, staring at him. Finally Jesse looked up, saw what was in her eyes. He opened his mouth, then shut it.

"Does my father know?"

"What?"

"Jesse, don't make the last thing you ever say to me a lie."

"Hey, hey. Irma, what're you saying to me?"

"He gives you money, but what do you give him, Jesse? You keep him informed about my eating habits? What I'm reading. Weekly progress reports?"

"Jesus," he said. "Jesus."

"It's true, isn't it? You son of a bitch."

The family from Minnesota was standing by the cash register, father giant holding the check, waiting. Burning a laser hole in Jesse's flowered shirt.

He kept staring at her as she turned away. The jukebox was cranking up again. Something sappy about truck stops, big rigs rolling, lonesome women, cheating men.

CHAPTER
7

Rover lay on top of the sheets between Thorn and Rochelle. Barefoot, in his cutoffs and gray T-shirt, Thorn was propped up on a pillow, reading, working his way through Jack London's stories about Alaska, something he'd read as a boy. He'd been doing that lately, revisiting stuff he had strong memories about. Most of it turned out to be disappointing, corny or flat, making him wonder about the rest of his childhood, what else he'd gotten wrong back then. Thirty years later still coasting on those questionable judgments.

But these London stories remained strong. Cold and foreign. Taking him off somewhere he had no real desire to visit, but was still glad to know about. Lying on his bed, an eighty-degree breeze stirring the moonlight around, the fronds clittered just beyond the new curtains. Less than a week till Thanksgiving and just those two cool fronts so far, nothing below seventy this fall. That was fine with Thorn. Far as he was concerned, man wasn't meant to live north of Fort Lauderdale. Look what happened when he tried. He wound up having to kill his dog, eat it, wrap himself up in its fur to stay warm.

Rochelle, in an oatmeal-colored chemise trimmed in satin. The chemise showed her long tanned legs, hinted at everything else. She was doing needlepoint, a garnet and gold square with words emerging. He couldn't read them yet, but suspected it might be on its way to saying "Home Sweet Home." With Rochelle there was no way of knowing. She might be doing Home Sweet Home for the same reason she named the dog Rover, another of those post-modern things. A joke on herself. A new challenge for Thorn, an intellectual woman, not just smart like the others had been, but this one a student of rare and formidable subjects.

Rochelle had already finished her book for the night. A novel with Gothic overtones set in the world of newspapers written by a journalist. She said she liked it. Said it was scary and provocative, unadorned prose. A speed-reader, Rochelle could gulp down a few hundred pages in an hour, books on quantum mechanics, on natural herbs, biographies of statesmen, historical novels, books on psychology, dog-training manuals. Every night something new, as though she were cramming for some extraordinary final exam.

"Another couple of weeks when we're done with all the home improvements," Rochelle said, "what in the world will we do with all our spare time?"

He bent the corner of a page, closed his book, looked at her. She kept her eyes on her needlework.

"I have a couple of ideas."

"I know about your ideas."

She leaned over and kissed him on the ear. Touched a cool tongue to the sensitive whorls.

Thorn set the book aside. But Rochelle drew away, smiled at him from a safe distance. A smile that fiddled with his thermostat.

"How do you feel about paint?" she said.

"Paint?"

"Latex, acrylic. You know, paint."

"Are we still talking about sex?"

She chuckled. Or was it a giggle? He could never find the exact word for her laugh. Girlish but husky. That was Rochelle, a woman of tantalizing contradictions. The hippie dress, the black lace beneath. A woman who could discuss particle theory and was teaching herself needlepoint.

"How do you feel about painting some of this wood? Brighten up the inside of the house. It's like a cave in here."

"You don't like weathered wood?"

"Well, it's a little raw. It looks unkempt."

"That's the point."

She glanced at him, then went back to work.

"Are we arguing?" she said.

"I think it's called a discussion."

"Now don't forget, Thorn, you're the one who said you wanted to spruce things up. Don't make me out as some Good Housekeeping Nazi."

Thorn gazed up at the bedroom ceiling. "You have some particular color in mind?"

"Well, for the outside, I was thinking a buttery yellow might be nice, maybe a hunter green on the shutters. If we wanted to live dangerously we could try a salmon inside, mauve. And brighten up the ceiling with a quiet white."

Thorn kept staring at the exposed beams. Ironwood trunks. Heavy with sap. It had taken an entire afternoon for Sugarman and him to winch those beams in place.

"Everything is optional," she said. "I'm not campaigning."

Rochelle's parents owned a couple of frozen yogurt shops, one in Key Largo, the other down in Plantation. Rochelle kept their accounts, though she hadn't been going in to work much in the last two months. She brought the books home now, only stopped by once or twice a week to visit her parents. They seemed to like Thorn okay. Though most of the time they smiled nervously as if expecting him to erupt any second, spew molten rock.

Since dropping out of Harvard a decade ago, Rochelle had a history of choosing her men unwisely. Hanging out with drunks and cowboys even after they'd bloodied their fists against her. She told Thorn she'd thought of it as a challenge, breaking broncos, something like that. A certain thrill, stirring her competitive instincts. If she could just hang on a little longer, keep from getting bucked off, the guy would calm, learn to mind his manners, and the two of them could ride off together.

A week or two ago, standing in her parents' living room, Rochelle announced that she'd finally found the right guy, the one she'd been looking for all along, and her mother and father just kept smiling nervously at Thorn.

Rochelle had grown up in Key Largo, but she'd never aspired to be an island girl. No waitress-in-training. No shrimper's wife. She'd had citified ambitions that sent her off to Harvard full of brash idealism. A mathematics major. But things had not gone well. In her first semester she'd been seduced by the chairman of the math department. A married man in his fifties. Thorn hadn't heard all the details. But there was some kind of scandal, and Rochelle came back to Key Largo bitterly subdued.

Eventually she'd reconciled herself to the limited culture of the Keys. She had her books, she had the diary she worked on for an hour or two every morning. But still she seemed restless, cramped.

For Thorn Key Largo was exactly challenge enough. He had no desires this island and its waters couldn't fulfill. But he knew Rochelle was struggling. And he suspected that she was using him, their relationship, to heal some wounds she hadn't even admitted yet. That would've bothered him, made him worry about the healthiness of their affair, except he supposed he was guilty of doing the same thing. Both he and Rochelle were dedicated loners. Both of them tired of being by themselves.

"Yellow with green shutters," Thorn said.

"You'll like it," she said. "It'll be homey."

He pronounced the word to himself. Homey. Thinking about it. Like *comfy* or *cutesy*, it wasn't a word he remembered using. *Homey.* It wasn't a word Darcy would've used either, except with an ironic twist.

But then he couldn't keep using Darcy as the measure for all things. After all, the earth spun on, gravity and ultraviolet rays worked their relentless magic. This year Thorn was creakier than ever, moving slower, his flesh less resilient. He was spending a lot longer in prone positions than he had five years ago. Eyes harder to focus. Slower to wake up. Major arteries narrowing. Maybe it was damn well time to admit he was no longer a kid, time to start including those words in his vocabulary, *homey, comfy*. Grow up, live like the big people did.

"I don't want to come in here," Rochelle said, "some female whirlwind, change everything around. Tie you up in my apron strings. You want to keep it just like it is, fine. I have no problem. I'm not trying to put my stamp on you."

"I know," he said.

She leaned over and they kissed. Thorn touching the back of her head, the soft burr. The kiss lingered, became something more, Thorn firming. He drew in her lavender scent, and something else, a pumpkin flavor, warm, nutmeggy. All those aromas her skin had absorbed from a day of cooking. Another thing to get used to, a woman who cooked, who liked it, was damn good at it. Considered it a pleasure. Dishes he'd never heard of. Fattening Thorn up, his stomach tightening against the waistbands of his shorts for the first time in his life.

She pulled away, drew a breath. She gave him a smile and shucked off the chemise. Her body always surprised him. It seemed too lean to support the weight of her breasts. Thin arms with such strength. Stronger than any woman he'd known. Hardly any hips at all. Dancer's legs and delicate feet.

Thorn stripped out of his cutoffs, his T-shirt, reached out for her and they sank back into the kiss. Her fingertips tracked down his arm, left a trail, her hand finding his, taking hold, lifting it. Breaking off the kiss, so she could bring his hand to her mouth. She pressed her lips to his fingers one by one like a mother kissing away her child's hurt. Then drew each finger into her mouth and washed it clean. Took special care with his thumb.

With her eyes on his, she guided his damp hand across her mouth, down her chin, her throat, pressed it flush against her chest. Held it there until he could feel the agitation of her heart.

She eased his hand down her stomach, brushed his palm across the fine dusting of hair around her navel. Touched his pointing finger to the wrinkled depression, then lower and lower, until finally his fingers were snarled in her dense pubic hair.

She released him and on his own he moved to the warm slush between her legs, lingered there, explored, then drifted lower to her thighs, slick as silk, and came back to the dampness. Driving the breath from her lungs, driving it from his own.

It was quicker tonight. The prelude hurried, the unspoken hunger greater. Across the room a breeze bellied out the lace curtains, and Rochelle was suddenly on top of him, steering him inside. Then they were folded together, notch to notch, the flawless match of seasoned partners. The waltz, the tango, there seemed to be no step they couldn't do. Nothing unique about the method, nothing new, but still it was different. The grind of her hips, their heated kiss, their bodies flush. A frantic need. So easy, so uncomplicated, so comfortable.

Irma Slater had been lying there for an hour, maybe two, immobilized on top of the bedspread, eyes closed, taking deep breaths, trying to evaluate, digest. A whole new set of conditions. A paradigm shift, they called it. The old laws faulty, finally crumbled under their own erroneous weight. Turns out the universe was not at all how we thought it was. Sorry. All bets off. Shore leaves canceled till further notice. At least until we come up with an entire new set of natural laws.

She listened to Sweetcakes out in the lagoon. Heard the dolphin's hard clicks, blats of breath, water surging. Familiar sounds, but nothing felt familiar anymore. All of it was cockeyed, skewed, sliding away from her, the ground tilting as if the subterranean plates had buckled. A new slant. Lying there, gripping the bedspread with both hands, trying to hang on, ride this out. The bed sailing through the dark.

Her muscles shuddered, an eerie purr working in her blood, as though somewhere nearby a colossal tuning fork set on her personal wavelength had been struck a powerful blow.

She knew she should rise. Throw her clothes in a bag. Dizzy or not, she should get the bloody hell out of this room. Her cover blown. She should flee. She should damn well grab her four hundred eighty-seven from the Tampax box where it was hidden and fly into the night. And this time do a better job of disappearing.

Sugarloaf Retreat, three years. All a lie. A flimsy stage set. Jesse whispering into her father's ear, her father whispering back. If this is what she wants, let her have it. Let her play. Money passing. Now she was certain Morton had visited, spied on her from afar. Yes, that's her, that's my daughter. And for whatever reason, he'd let her carry on her pathetic charade. Not free. Never. Not for a second. The same puppet, same puppeteer.

She stared around at the darkened cell where she'd spent these last three years. In all that time she'd not personalized the room in any way. It was exactly as it had been the morning she'd checked in. Over her headboard hung a gloomy oil painting of a New England beach in winter. In the bathroom was a calendar turned to some January ten years ago. The only other decoration a framed photograph of a family of beavers constructing a dam.

On the wobbly bedside table was a green ceramic lamp and copper ashtray she'd never used. Crammed in on the other side of the bed was a deal desk whose drawers contained a Gideon Bible and some faded postcards showing Sugarloaf Retreat seven years ago. Not much had changed since then.

By the door sat a Danish modern chair with torn red cushions. And the carpet was so ancient that years of tracked-in sand had turned its bright gold to the color of wet cement. The walls were sickly green. An orange water stain on the ceiling directly above her bed shaped like Kentucky. Same stain she'd looked up at seven years ago.

For this was the room where she and her mother had slept side by side. A girls' getaway before Monica left for college. Her mother so different during those two weeks in the Keys. Relaxed, alert. Chatting breezily with a motel worker as she and Monica fed schools of snappers from the dock. A groundskeeper with dark hair and a perpetual cigarette between his lips. In the evening he started bringing her mother cans of Pabst Blue Ribbon, and the three of them lounged on the lawn beside the bay, watched the sun set fire to the water and clouds, watched the stars. He knew the names of the constellations. Had stories to tell. It came as a shock for Monica to realize she had never heard her mother laugh until then. Never seen her tipsy. Monica going back to the room to sleep. Her mother coming in later, stumbling, laughing to herself.

One night not making it back till dawn. Monica remembered sitting up in bed.

"Mother, is this why we came? Did you know Al was going to be here?"

"Sweetheart," she said. "I knew somebody like Al was going to be here."

Monica fantasized that the three of them ran off together. A gardener, smelling of cut grass and whiskey and tobacco. A man with strong hands, a shifty smile, and a blatant appreciation for her mother's slender body. A man who made her mother grin.

At the end of the second week, Morton Sampson made a surprise appearance. Claimed he missed his two girls. But his big smile was skewed. He moved in. Monica was banished to an adjoining room. For hours she kept her ear pressed to the connecting door, but heard nothing. Absolutely nothing.

The next morning her father took them fishing in the motel's rental boat. He anchored only a few feet offshore, cast his baited hook to the same fish that Monica and her mother had been feeding for two weeks, their pets.

Her mother did not speak. Hid behind her sunglasses. Morton caught a dozen fish, made a production of cutting them open and cleaning them on the boat, throwing their guts overboard. Hands covered with slime, the knife flashing. Her mother looked everywhere else.

When he decided he'd made his point, her father drew the anchor, puttered them back to the dock. Monica stepped over the pool of fish blood to climb from the boat but stopped short. There was too much blood on the deck, far too much. She swung around and saw the glint of the fillet knife at her mother's feet, the slick of red spreading across the white deck, the gaping slit. She screamed.

As her mother was lifted into the ambulance, Morton took Monica by the elbow and drew her roughly aside. "While we're at the hospital you have a job to do."

"What?"

"The boat," he said. "It was delivered to us unsoiled, we'll return it in the same condition. In this family we clean up our own messes."

"No way," Monica said. "I won't do it."

He looked into her eyes and for the first and only time he let her see that part of him which must have provoked her mother's vicious headaches.

"You were her accomplice, Monica; this is your reward."

A moment later his smile returned, the savage mist cleared. He gave her his sweet daddy look.

Morton spoke to the owner of the hotel. Left Monica in the man's charge. He provided brushes, hoses, sponge, detergent.

Monica climbed into the boat and went down to her knees, staring at her mother's blood. The manager's wife came out, stood for a moment watching her.

"Get out of there, child. We'll take care of that."

But Monica took hold of a brush, bent to her work, scrubbed at the streaks. The manager's wife staying for a while then going back inside. As she worked Monica scuffed her bare knees against the rough deck, tore them ragged. Scrubbing for hours, her mother's blood mingling with her own, hosing it away. The fish scales, the slime. Down on her knees in the brutal afternoon sun, the smell of her mother's blood, the stickiness.

When she was finished, Monica located the manager's wife and asked the woman where she could find Al. Thinking he should know, imagining that he would confront her father, stand up to him, whisk her mother away.

"Al's clipping somebody else's hedges now," the wife told her. "Don't worry about him, honey, the Als always make out."

That evening they drove home in her father's Cadillac. Her mother bandaged and detached. A man was hired to bring her mother's car back to Miami. The headaches resumed immediately.

Now Irma lay on the bed and listened to Sweetcakes splash. And seconds later the dolphin splashed again. Worked up. Showing off. Very peculiar for this time of night. Another splash. A dozen hard clicks. Begging for food.

She rose, padded to the window, nudged a corner of the curtain aside. And saw them. Two men down by the lagoon, the dolphin performing for their benefit. One man tall and heavy. Moonlight glistening on his bald head. She recognized the shape of that skull, the slump of his shoulders.

The other shadow was Jesse, the gray ponytail, the shlubby body. The bastard hadn't given her a day's head start. Hadn't let ten seconds go by. Or else Butler Jack was right. He had come for her, to pluck her out of her life, take her back with him, have her fucking head examined.

Jesse and her father were huddled. Didn't look like an argument. Her father never argued, never had to. Got his way with
charm and happy faces. Not a mean bone, as far as the public knew.
Slid people where he wanted them to go, made them love going
there, think it was their own idea. Smothered them with good,
good, I like that. Very good. Got his way. Always, every single
time, he got his goddamn way. A nice man. Everyone said so.
Amazing that such a nice man had built such an empire. Simply
amazing.

Two men of business in the moonlight twenty yards away,
having a talk as if Irma Slater didn't exist, as if they weren't the
least concerned she might walk out, shotgun them both in the
back. If only she had a shotgun.

She let the drapes settle.

She opened her drawer, scooped out her clothes, dumped
them in her college knapsack. Went to the bathroom, got the Tampax box. Shook it. Took a long, disbelieving breath. Opened the
flaps. The box was empty. Her nest egg gone. Saved dollar by
dollar for these three years. She dug her fingers inside it, then bent
back to the lavatory cabinet. In a panic now, peering under there,
but no, there was only that one Tampax box.

She turned and slung it back into the bedroom.

There was a double-hung window in the bathroom. She pried
it open, pushed out the screen, wriggled through, stepped into the
parking lot. A transfer truck blew past on the overseas highway.
Someone was playing a radio nearby. Boom chucka. Silver clouds
had muffled the moon. What breeze there was smelled like deep
fried grease, air that could clog an artery.

She sifted down a row of rental cars, found the white Winnebago parked at the edge of the lot near a stand of Australian pines.
There was no light on inside, no movement.

Hesitating there, outside the Winnebago. She hated the idea
of throwing herself on the mercy of some guy. But she had to
consider the practicalities. For all she knew there'd be a manhunt,
roadblocks, helicopters with spotlights. Morton milking this for its
market potential. With only one narrow road out of there, the sea
on both sides, there was nowhere to duck. And no way in hell she

was going to hitchhike in the dark, face into random headlights and hope.

Across the parking lot, she heard Jesse's voice. Saw him coming around the west wing of the motel.

And Irma Slater rapped on the door of the Winnebago.

Maybe Butler Jack would have a shotgun, or know where to get one.

CHAPTER

8

The Winnebago was dark, Irma bumping her shoulder, her shins, hands out like a sleepwalker, cursing. Heavy curtains blocking all but a trickle of light from the parking lot. She had no idea of the layout, never been in one of these before. Very cramped, with an odor like motor oil, something metallic.

Butler Jack stood at the curtains, staring out. She joined him and saw the lights blazing in her room. Someone in the bathroom window, examining the broken screen. She saw his bald head, the fringe of white. Her father craning out, looking left and right. Morton Sampson.

"I'm gonna kill him," she said. "I want to kill that bastard. It's the only way I'm ever going to get away."

"Slow down," Butler said. "Maybe we can find something worse than that."

She stepped away from him, stared warily at his profile for a moment. But she was no judge of lunatics. For all she knew she might be one herself. She went back to the window. They watched for a while longer. The lights in her room switched off. Irma hoped her father remembered that room. Hoped it made his heart squirm. Remembering Al. The man who could make Morton Sampson's wife smile.

They waited. No helicopters came. No police with their bloodhounds. Another quiet night in Sugarloaf. They waited at the window, watched the empty lot. It unnerved her. Surely Morton Sampson wasn't going to lose his precious Monica again so easily. Give up without a good struggle.

At midnight, they saw him duck into the rear seat of a white Lincoln, Jesse bending low to have a word or two, then the car slid out of the parking lot, headed up the road toward Miami.

"Well, that's that," Butler said. "So now it begins. We move on to number seven."

"What?"

"I have a list," Butler said. "We're at number six, moving on to seven."

"What the hell are you talking about?"

"With a list, you can't get sidetracked. You know where you are. Moving down the list. There are so many distractions, so many ways to get lost. But with a list, you always know. Like the ten commandments. All written down. Very clear."

She peered at him through the dark but couldn't see his face. It sounded like some kind of put-on, but she wasn't sure. Not sure about anything at that moment.

She let him steer her to the bunk bed, and he told her she had the top. She climbed up. A simple cot, thick canvas stretched between two boards, a mattress pad. She patted the area to get her bearings, felt something silky spread on the top sheet.

"Lingerie," Butler said. "A nightie. I guessed the size."

She groaned and lay down on the top sheet, arms stiff at her sides. Ready to claw out his eyes if he tried anything. Irma pissed. But going along for the moment.

Butler rustled around in the dark, then got into the bunk below her. He sighed, then a few moments later sighed again. She could feel him lying there, awake in the dark. Deepening the silence. Reminding her of pajama parties from her youth. Hours of aimless chatter and giggles that suddenly dissolve into quiet. Everyone still awake, eyes open, listening.

She stiffened. She thought she felt him touch her back through the canvas, follow the shape of her body, his fingers trailing across her butt. But the touch was so light she wasn't sure. She said nothing.

She held the lingerie, rubbed it against her cheek, as slick as oil. Hadn't touched any satin in years, not since Irma Slater took over things.

"Fornication," he said. "It's from Latin *fornix*. Which is an architectural term that means arched or vaulted."

She was silent, eyes open in the dark.

"Combined with *forno*, which means oven. Which is where the word furnace comes from. The Romans at the time of Christ used arched brickwork in the underground parts of buildings, and because that's where prostitutes worked, in the basements, the word gradually was associated with illicit sex. But it's interesting, isn't it, all those other words floating around in there, furnace, underground, vaulted. Heat, excitement, basements, tombs, the shape of female anatomy. Death and sex, heat and hell. It's all there."

She leaned over the edge of the cot, stared down. "I'm no prostitute."

"I know that."

"I'm not that little girl either. The one in the swing."

"Now there you're wrong," he said. "People are the same as words. They have all those things floating inside of them. Their histories. Nothing disappears. The ice sculptures melt, but they're always there. The little girl in the swing. You can try to escape, but you can't."

She lay back against the cot, looked up into the dark. "No sex, Butler. End of debate."

He was quiet for a moment. She could hear him breathing. "Well, we're talking about it," he said. "At least the subject is broached. It's important to talk. Put things into words, that's important, don't you think? Giving voice to the hidden world."

She lay still, eyes open, waiting. He was silent beneath her. The parking lot was quiet. Just a breeze sifting through the Australian pines, that ghostly moan. It wasn't right. Not like her father, the man who'd put up a million-dollar reward. She lay for a long time, listening. Hours. She heard Butler's breath slow and begin to flutter. Still she lay awake. Hours.

And then she was dreaming and her dream was filled with eyes. Human eyes, unblinking. They were watching her. Watching Monica sleep. Haunted eyes, sad and hungry, those ludicrous over-sized eyes from roadside black velvet paintings. Her black velvet father watching her every moment. Morton Sampson, and her mother Irene, black velvet Irene, and Butler Jack, his milky blue eyes, others she couldn't name. Everyone watching her, seeing her. Feeling their eyes, floating out there in dream space. She did not wake, knowing somehow that they were not dangerous, but still she felt their eyes like breath against her skin. Felt them every moment of the night, eyes through the dark, those eyes, those sad eyes.

Even with his eyes closed, even in the total dark, he could see her glowing above him. Butler Jack couldn't stop trembling. The glow of her. The power. He'd been wrong to believe it would be the same. The little girl had power, yes, her image in the swing, the white dress, the wide porch, all that. She had power, but it was nothing like the woman who lay in the cot above him. This one glowed. The uranium more unstable than he'd imagined. So close. He could reach out his arm. Her body molded above him. The heat she threw out. Butler sweating, his bones aching. His erection.

She was here.

None of it mattered now. None of the humiliations mattered. The pains he'd endured. The intricate work, the plotting. She was here. Monica lay above him in the dark, her body floating a foot away. The night glowed with her. The air was rich. Giving him a strength he'd never known. He was a warrior. A Viking. He could wade through a thousand armored soldiers. Slaughter them all. Berserk.

Before dawn on Saturday Thorn rose, dressed in the shadowy living room, and left the house without waking Rochelle. He drove to Sugar's concrete-block house in Largo Sound Park. The sun beginning to tint the low mountain range of clouds with the purples and sulfurous yellows of a week-old bruise.

Sugarman's house was locked up, blinds drawn, no car in

the drive. Cal Higgins from across the street was having a cup of coffee in his front yard, watching his dog pee on the neighbor's trees.

"Haven't seen them since last week," he called over to Thorn. "Crack of dawn Monday, I think it was."

Next door Mrs. Miranda came out to her porch. Pink housecoat, front half of her hair in curlers. Thorn went over. Mrs. Miranda shook out a Camel, lit it, and talked around the smoke. Saying she thought the two of them were getting a divorce.

"A divorce!"

"They didn't tell me in so many words. But both of them been hinting around about it for a week or two. Then one morning she drives off in that Jeep, it's full of her things, baggage, a TV set, lamps, her macramé collection. Half hour later he leaves in a taxicab, hanging his head. Now to me that looks like she was setting up shop somewhere else. Going their separate ways."

Thorn stared at Sugar's house.

"Usually he tells us when he's away," she said. "Leaves a number where he can be reached. But I guess he was in a hurry this time, embarrassed or just forgot. He was working the cruise ships, you know, but a couple of days ago he let it slip that he was quitting that job."

"Quitting?"

"Yeah," she said. "Tell 'em to shove it."

"You know all Sugarman's business, don't you?"

She squinted at him through her acrid smoke. "I see what I see."

Thorn drove a couple of miles up U.S. 1 to the strip shopping center where Sugar's office was wedged in between an inflatable raft store and a beauty shop. The red-haired beautician opening up next door had no idea where he was. Gone for at least a week as far as she knew.

He went back to the VW, climbed inside, stared out the windshield at the big plastic alligators and sharks hanging in the window of the raft shop, the air-conditioning stirring them. He stared at the heavy door on Sugar's office. It was constructed from thick planks of mahogany, Thorn's office-warming gift. Some leftover wood from rebuilding his house. Sugarman loved that goddamn door. And Thorn remembered vividly the couple of punch-drunk days they'd spent dovetailing it together.

Under ordinary circumstances Sugarman never would've left the island without giving Thorn his full itinerary. And for twenty years he'd consulted with Thorn over the slightest tremor in his marriage. But then, circumstances were no longer ordinary between them. Sugarman had seen to that. Pushing Thorn into that impossible ultimatum. An act so completely unlike his mild-mannered friend that the more Thorn had considered it, the more obvious it became that Sugarman was concocting this feud. Pushing Thorn away. Pushing him, it seemed, safely out of range.

Thorn started the engine, continued to stare at the bright floats in the window beside Sugar's office. With a growl, he revved the tinny engine, sucked down a long breath, then jammed the shifter into first, popped the clutch.

The wheels mashed against the curb and the car stalled.

He started it again, drove it up against the edge of the sidewalk, the engine groaning and complaining as if it had been babied too much lately, Thorn letting it get flabby. Just like he'd been babying every fucking thing, letting it all go soft and dopey.

Thorn revved it higher, worked the clutch, and finally the car lurched forward, scraped and bumped over the curb, kept grinding forward until it rammed into Sugar's office door. He threw it in reverse, pulled back. The mahogany was barely nicked.

Thorn thumped back down into the lot. Sat there a moment revving the engine, goosing it higher and higher. The red-headed hairdresser from next door threw open her door, stuck her head out, a cigarette in her mouth and a portable phone pressed to her ear. She was in her aqua smock.

Holding the throttle flat to the floor, Thorn gave her a nod and shoved it into first again, popped the clutch, and the car lunged forward, slammed over the curb. This time he angled the wheels properly, and the edge of the bumper battered the center of Sugar's door. Cracked the thing down the middle, top to bottom. He backed up, parked the car, took care to get it neatly between the lines before he turned it off. The beautician was yammering into the phone as she craned for a view of the door, half of which still dangled on its hinges.

Thorn pushed his way inside, went through the reception area into Sugar's office, flipped on all the lights and began to search. He found no notes in Sugarman's calendar, no tickets, no reservation slips, nothing. Not even any papers strewn about his desk. Only a neat stack of magazines, *Time* and *Newsweek, People,* a month or two out of date, dentist's office stuff. Perhaps Mrs. Miranda was right. A divorce, gone their separate ways. A not-so-sudden dismemberment of their union, a decision that had been in the making for years.

Stubbornly Thorn worked his way through the drawers, top to bottom. Finding nothing the least bit unusual until he reached the next to last one. There, tucked beneath a stack of typing paper, was a five by nine black-and-white photograph. He drew it out.

Two people sitting on a broad porch somewhere, wicker furniture. A pretty blond woman, late forties, a boy beside her. Mother's arm over the blond boy's shoulder, hugging him to her. The shot had the graininess of a telephoto lens. A hazy surveillance photo. Thorn was about to set the photograph aside and move on but something in the woman's eyes snagged him.

He drifted across the office, carried the photograph over to the bookshelves. He stood there for a moment studying Sugarman's shelves, ran his eyes back and forth along their length, and there it was. He held the photo out, positioned it next to the snapshot of Sugar's teenage mother.

It was the eyes. The older woman was fleshier, cheekbones softened, hair swept back in a more stylish wave. But the haunted eyes were identical. The woeful shadow, the faraway focus. Thorn moved back to Sugar's desk. Took a couple of deep breaths, trying to absorb this.

He was just easing down into Sugar's chair when the young patrolman appeared, inching forward in a tense squat, steering himself around the edge of the fractured door with his service revolver leading the way. His eyes snapping onto Thorn's.

"You're dead if you twitch," the young cop said. "Keep your fucking hands in view."

Thorn stood up. "Hey, look it's okay, Sergeant."

"Shut up, and keep 'em where I can see them."

"Look, I'm the owner's friend. We do this all the time. Bust into each other's place. Like a joke we play on each other."

"Keep your motherfucking hands up where I can see them."

"It's true. Ask anybody around here. Thorn and Sugarman. We're famous for doing shit like this."

The kid was sweating, inching forward toward Thorn. He could see the enlarged veins in the cop's wrist. Guy fully pumped. When was it that all the cops got younger? Suddenly moved down a generation from Thorn.

"Look, there's no reason to get all . . ."

The kid tightened his stance, aimed down his barrel.

That's when Thorn felt the prickle in his nostrils, a sneeze rising inside him, coming on with such abruptness he didn't have time for a word of warning, just squinched his eyes, shot both hands high, and threw back his head, felt the spasm shake him hard, echo in his ears. Thinking as it happened that this was how it was going to end for him, killed by a chance sneeze. And thinking how that was the way it should be. Same way his life had consistently worked, some stray mote or insect wing floating out of the swirling chaos, microscopic debris sucked into his nostril and bing, Thorn becomes splatter on the wall. No more Thorn. Shot for random sneezing. Thorn's God guided by the same unwavering perversity he'd always used. Sneeze, bang. One long loaded crapshoot from birth to death.

He heard the roar of the gunshot and somewhere nearby a scream. When his eyes cleared, Thorn saw the beautician huddled behind the cop. An aqua-smocked angel. The young patrolman, white and shaky.

Over Thorn's shoulder something toppled to the floor. He swung around and watched a shattered fragment of Sugar's one and only trophy tumble off the shelf beside his desk. The slug had split it in two and gouged a five-inch hole in the concrete block.

"Christ, he's going to be pissed," Thorn said, coming back around. "He averaged 205 that summer. Never bowled better."

The cop holstered his pistol, kept his hand on the butt as though his flesh had melted, bonded forever to that steel.

* * *

Two hours later Rochelle bailed him out. Breaking and entering, resisting arrest, criminal mischief. Thorn managed only a sketchy explanation. Got carried away, he said. That's all. He waved off her other questions and they drove home in silence, had a quiet lunch. She didn't ask him any more. Gave him a wide berth as she went outside to work in the yard.

Thorn sat for a while at the round oak table and stared at the curtains billowing with an easterly breeze. He got up, circled the room, touching her things. Cooking utensils, microwave, vases, dried flowers, a photograph of her parents. Her sewing basket, her portable Singer. Her rings and jewelry, her black-faced watch, her wind-up clock, her four different styles of tennis shoes lined up neatly beside the bed.

To quiet the racket in his head, Thorn went to the bedroom closet, got down his fly reels from a high shelf. Took them outside on the sunny porch.

He removed them from their boxes, stacked them on the floor. He went back inside, got his screwdrivers, some cleaning stuff. Back in the sun, he chose the Orvis to disassemble first, laying out the parts beside the railing. Began carefully dusting each of the twenty-eight pieces with a small paintbrush. On a few of the parts he had to use the edge of an oily rag to flake away the salt scum, a few freckles of rust. It'd been a damn long time since he'd had this reel opened, done any kind of upkeep.

His wooden house, his several reels, his skiff and ancient cabin cruiser all needed constant tending. Thorn had surrounded himself with high-maintenance possessions. The absolute worst thing you could do for stuff like that, reels, boat motors, or wooden houses, was let them sit. But that's just what he'd done lately while he and Rochelle explored the dark side of the moon.

On the north perimeter of his property, she was kneeling in the fishtail ferns, weeding. First time, as far as Thorn knew, anyone had ever pulled a weed on his five acres. He wasn't sure how she knew which ones were weeds, but she was working hard. Sweating profusely, on her knees, snipping with hand shears, tugging up vines, uprooting crabgrass, making huge piles. She'd already finished the south side, working with furious concentration.

Everybody irritated today. Everybody teetering. Like some frightful phase of the moon.

Thorn dusted off the drag assembly, the knob spring, the drag click ball, the knob retainer. When he had them as clean and shiny as he could get them, he started on the spool cover. Focused, working that shiver out of his hands.

Finally Thorn began to reassemble the reel. He set the click pawl spring against the spindle. Slid on the O ring assembly, tightened the retaining screw, pressed the spool drive plate to the compression spring. Done it a few hundred times, could manage in the dark if necessary.

Not seeing it until now, that of all his reels, he'd chosen this one first. Staring down at his hands, at this Orvis, which was a present from Sugar on Thorn's thirtieth birthday. Given to him during a raucous party that commenced at sunrise and didn't end till two days later. The house swarming with people. Thorn and Sugarman and dozens of their closest. Kids and dogs. Somebody even brought a butchered pig, laid a spit and roasted it.

Thorn had never owned a reel so fine. It must've set Sugar back a month's salary. But here it was, over a dozen years later, and that reel still sang as sweetly as it had on its first afternoon. And while it had broken the spirit of countless heavyweight fish, it had never once seized up.

Holding the reel in his right hand, Thorn's eyes drifted up and he looked out at Rochelle, then out at the bay again. He felt a nettling sting behind his eyes. As he raised his hand to rub them clear, the reel slipped from his grip and broke open against the rough boards of the porch, its clockwork spilling through the gaps in the planks, all those tiny disks and springs and nuts falling in a bright rain down into the dust below.

CHAPTER

9

Thunder shook the Winnebago, and the dream she was having abruptly vanished. Something about eyes, lots and lots of eyes floating in a gray mist. She pushed herself up on her elbows, blinked away that haze. The light inside the van was tinted purple. A thunderstorm rolling over, its gusts rocking the big van.

"Good morning, sleepyhead." Butler smiled at her, then swiveled back to his work.

He was stationed at a workbench across from the bunks. Wearing a pair of gray jeans and a white tennis shirt. A blue bandanna clenched his hair into a ponytail.

He was hunched forward over the long desk, some kind of high-tech soldering gun in his right hand. She craned forward to see, and it looked like he was melting dots of silver onto a circuit board. As he worked he peered through a jeweler's magnifier on a band around his head. Taking one look through the lens then glancing up at what appeared to be a blueprint tacked on the wall before him.

Scattered around the walls above his workbench were dozens of black-and-white photographs. She swept her eyes around the compartment and saw more photos on the walls, on cabinet doors, on the door of the small fridge, the shelves. Rows and rows of children. Several hundred of them. All those eyes, dark, empty. Asian boys, Hispanic girls, European, African. Some naked, some in loincloths. Bellies swollen, flies walking on their eyes. All staring into the camera lens with matching expressions as though they'd been posed by the same manipulative photographer. Come on, kid, gimme that sorrowful, hopeful, hungry look.

Outside there was a white flash then the immediate cannon blast of thunder as if the lightning spike had struck one of the tall pines a dozen feet away.

She climbed down from the bunk, came over to him. He was bent over, touching another careful dot of silver to the circuit board. She glanced around the room, scanning the faces in those photographs. Feeling a cold tingle move up her neck.

"I was an only child, just like you," Butler said, continuing with his work. "My mother and I, alone together. I never met my father. Don't have any idea about him. But it didn't matter. It was just me and Lola."

"Look . . ." she said.

"No, let me finish. You need to know about me. What you're getting into."

She heard the eighteen-wheelers sizzling past on the wet highway fifty, sixty yards away. The never-ending flow of goods to Key West, Saturday traffic pouring down from Miami. She took a seat on the edge of the bottom bunk.

"There I was, her only son. But I couldn't do anything right for Lola. She wanted baby Jesus as a son. Albert Einstein wouldn't have been smart enough for her. Nothing I did made her happy. She'd stick a book in front of my nose, no matter what it was, I'd read it, drink it down and it would stay in my head. Every word. But was that good enough for Lola? No, sir.

"I'd quote the book back to her, give it to her word for word, but she'd just shake her head, unhappy, like I didn't understand. I'd fallen short again. Nothing was ever right for Lola Jack. Fall down on the playground, get a little tear in my brand-new pants, Lola wouldn't hit me. She wouldn't get out a strap or anything like that. She'd squint at me like I was the devil and I'd just farted poison gas. Just stand there and scrutinize me and not say a word. And I remember how at times like those the lights seemed to get dim, how I'd begin to whimper and grovel and she'd just stand there and look. Never hit me.

"Though I wish she had. I wish she'd beat the ever-loving shit out of me. So I'd know where I stood. But she didn't. Lola was too good for that. She was white and pure and Christian. Sang in the Presbyterian choir. A soloist. Wonderful voice. White dresses, white hats, white gloves. Going to church every chance she had. Good Lola. Bad Butler."

He kept his head down. One part of his brain glancing up at his blueprint and then adding another silver dot, the other part talking. Talking.

"We were poor. Always struggling. Barely enough money for food, clothes, rent. Lived in a terrible neighborhood, murders out in the street. It took her twenty years, but Lola finally worked her magic on your father. Got him to notice her, promote her. Got him to marry her.

"And that was what she wanted all along. Her plan. A big tall rich man. Somebody to swoop her up and take her off to the penthouse for bottles of champagne and caviar and scintillating talk with his pals. She used to tell me how she was selling herself short all those years. She deserved better. But then she found a buyer worth her stock. That's Lola. Now that's who she is, my mother. Living at the top of the pyramid, eating baked Alaska and escargot while the world starves.

"But, you know, Monica. I'm not angry. I'm actually grateful to her. Grateful she pushed me away, taught me self-reliance. Because what I found out was, a person doesn't need his mother's love. A person like that can accomplish a great deal if they stay focused. If they use every second to advance their cause. If they have a list and follow it, an outline. If they know where they're going, why they're going there, what it's all for. And that's been me. I've had my list, my commandments, I've followed it, and I'm here now because of it.

"Some people might call me compulsive. Overcompensating for a joyless childhood. I have no friends. I don't have hobbies. I don't go to the movies, I don't listen to music. I don't play sports or any of that. I don't go to restaurants, I don't travel except for work. I don't stand around and gawk at sunsets or stare at the stars. But I don't feel deprived. Not a bit.

"You look around at the great men, men of major accomplishment. You look at them and you tell me how much stargazing they did. How much music they listened to. No. The great ones had a mission and they carried it out. They stacked up the hours of work one after another, stacked them up higher and higher until they'd built something that changed for all time how the world works. Changed the goddamn gravitational field of the earth. They didn't handicap themselves playing by the pathetic rules they found around them. They invented new rules. There are men who altered forever the way human life proceeds. Their names are written in granite outside important buildings.

"Those men didn't whine and groan and worry about whether their pretty mother loved them or not. They set themselves an impossible goal and they accomplished it. And that's exactly what I'm doing, Monica. That's who I am. That's who you're with. That's who you were talking to out there on your front porch, your swing. That's who you were writing to, those love letters long ago. Pledging your undying love."

She glanced around at the dark paneling, the cheap red curtains, the linoleum. Rain pelted the roof, fat subtropical raindrops. The air inside the van was thick with the vanilla scent of rain.

"Who are these kids, Butler? What's going on here?"

Butler set aside his magnifier. He stretched his arms out to the side, yawned and stood up. He came over to her, patted her on the shoulder. A wide smile erupting.

"My children." He motioned to the photo of a small girl staring forlornly into the camera. The child sat on the dusty ground, her hands cupped in her lap. "That's Lucy."

He pointed a finger at the photograph next to Lucy and the one next to that. "And that is Ben Aram. And this is Belinda."

"You're a photographer?"

"Oh, no," he said. "These are my children, the kids I sponsor. International Rescue Foundation. I started with Lucy, then I added two more in Rwanda, some more after that from Sierra Leone, Senegal. That was a couple of years ago. It grew."

Monica stood and moved close to one of the walls of photos.

"Twenty dollars a month," he said. "Twenty a month buys them food and clothes, covers their housing costs."

She circled the small space, scanning the photos. Hundreds of them, all those haunted eyes. Distant lightning fluttered through the windows.

"And you're doing this, sponsoring all these kids, because of me, what some little girl said all those years ago?"

He beamed. "It's the groundwork. The beginning of our campaign."

She shook her head and turned away from him.

"So," Butler said. "We'll eat breakfast while we drive up to the airport. Later on we have to find time to go shopping. Buy you a new wardrobe. Bright colors, plaids."

"And why would we do that?"

" 'Cause we're going on a cruise. Everybody dresses that way on cruises. Garish stuff. Like golfers on hallucinogens."

He continued to grin at her. Eyes full of mischief.

"What cruise?"

"Twenty-fifth anniversary of your daddy's cruise lines. A very big deal."

Butler stepped over to his workbench, scooped up something, and came back over to her. He held out both hands, a small compass in each one. She frowned at him. The grumble of thunder rolling away toward the Atlantic.

"Can you tell which one of these is accurate?" She glanced at them. One pointed in the same direction the Winnebago was headed. The other put north ninety degrees off the first.

"It's a trick question," Butler said. "Neither of them is. True north is that way." He pointed toward the rear of the van.

"So?"

"Magnetic north," he said. "I've altered it."

Butler was smiling, looking at his two compasses.

"Oh, I know it doesn't seem like any big deal," he said. "After all, how often does anyone consult a compass in their daily life? But, you know, in certain circumstances if your compass reading was off just a degree or two, it could be a major problem. And in that case, the person who knew exactly how much distortion had occurred and which direction true north was in, well, that person would be very much in demand."

"I'm not going on any cruise," she said.

"Oh, you'll love it," he said. "The water, the sun, all the planned activities."

"Look, Butler, I appreciate your help last night, hiding me. And I'm glad something I said made a difference to you. But this is as far as it goes."

She looked into his pale blue eyes.

"Your father will just find you again, wherever you go, he'll track you down. And he'll do the same thing again. You're never going to be free of him if you keep running."

"The world's a big place. I can go somewhere, start over. He's not that powerful."

"Trust me, Monica. When we're through with him, you'll be free of him forever. This cruise will do it. When it's over, Morton Sampson will be powerless over you or anyone else. Somebody will have to sponsor him. Twenty bucks a month. Rice and beans."

Butler's smile was relaxed.

"We need to go up to Baltimore today," he said, "finish off a final detail, then we come back and board the ship late tonight. I have our tickets already. Everything's set. IDs, passports, credit cards, everything. We'll have a few hours on the plane, it'll give us time to talk, find out about each other again. Give you time to get comfortable with this new situation. You ever been to Baltimore, Monica?"

"No."

"Well, we're about to change that. We're about to change everything. But we got to start moving. Our plane leaves in a few hours, we're getting short on time."

Butler walked to the front of the Winnebago, sat down at the driver's seat. He was smiling as he started the engine, shifted into drive, and pulled out to the edge of the highway to wait for a break in the traffic.

She looked at the side door. She could step out, walk away. If he tried to follow her, she'd find a way to flee. Run over to the dock, steal one of Jesse's rental boats, scoot up the islands, get out, catch a bus. There were ways.

"How about passion, Monica? You know the word *passion?*"

She found herself saying yes, she knew it. Staring at the side door while Butler waited to pull out on the road.

"But do you really? Do you know what you're saying when you say it? Do you know what's coiled up in the word, hiding inside it, the other words you're bringing alive when you say passion?"

His voice was growing softer, fading, and without meaning to, she stepped toward him.

"*Passio* is from the Latin. It means suffering, especially that of Christ. Isn't that interesting? Also it's derived from *passus* and *pati,* which mean to endure. So when you say you feel passionate about something, you're saying all these things at once. That you're suffering, like the agony of martyrs, but you're enduring that suffering. That's what passion is all about—enduring desire. That's why it aches so much. Why it hurts to desire something. You have passions, don't you? Something you ache for, something missing in your life, something you're wanting? Don't you, Monica? Don't you?"

"I'm not that little girl, goddamn it."

"Give it time," he said. "Give it time."

For a while she stared out her window at the watery distance, Butler humming to himself. She reset the angle of her seat, leaned back. Idly picked up the headset lying on the console and slipped it on. There was a swivel-down microphone attached to it, like a hands-free telephone. She cocked the mike down so it was an inch from her lips and suddenly Butler snatched the headset off her head.

"Jesus! Be careful."

"What the hell?"

Butler continued to drive with his left hand and held the headset out with his other. He squeezed the earplugs close together, then brought the microphone near his lips.

"Hello," he said.

And a crisp blue spark shot across the inch of space between the earplugs. Monica pressed her back against her door.

"Holy God, what is that thing?"

Butler drew the plug out of the lighter socket and set the headset on the dash.

"Just one of my toys," he said. "Something I've been fooling around with."

"You consider that a toy?"

"Oh, it is at the moment," he said. "Nine volts is all. It'd give you a buzz, but wouldn't knock you out or anything."

"Still," she said.

"I'm sorry. I shouldn't leave these things lying around. I'll be more careful now that you're here."

"Good," she said.

She rested her hand on the door handle. Soon as they hit Miami, first traffic light, she was out of there.

CHAPTER

10

While Butler drove, she dumped Special K into plastic bowls, poured in milk. Across from the kitchen sink was a photograph of an African child dabbing rice into his mouth with his fingers. Monica looking at the boy or girl, the eyes too big for the head. Tummy bloated, face shrunken.

She went back to the front, set Butler's cereal on the console, and took the passenger seat. He looked over at her and smiled his thanks, then cut his eyes back to the road. A careful driver. Not in a huge hurry, obeying the road signs.

She ate a few bites, placed the cereal on the dash. Beside the bowl lay a dagger with a black grip and fancy chrome filigreed hand guards. She reached out and picked it up, rubbed a thumb across the blade. Very sharp. She put it back on the dash, felt him looking at her. She stared out her window.

In Miami she'd find a job. Waitressing. Motel maid. It didn't matter. Save up as fast as she could. Get bus fare to Taos, San Diego, some other planet, and go.

She shifted in her seat, looked forward out the windshield. "Did I really say that thing?"

"Which thing?"

A line of cars stretched in front of them, crossing the Seven

Mile Bridge. The sky had cleared, bright water spread in every direction, ten shades of green.

"The thing about war. One side or the other."

"Your exact words," Butler said. "I never forget anything. I have one of those brains, I read a book, I can say it back. I hear a speech, a song, anything, it stays inside there. All the words in order. I have to be careful what I learn because I'm never going to forget it. A gift and a curse rolled into one."

"I know about those."

He smiled to himself, steering with one finger for a moment.

"That thing you do, those definitions, what the hell's that about?"

"Etymologies, not definitions. The histories of words."

"All right, etymologies."

"Oh, I guess it's because of Lola," he said. "She was hellbent on making me succeed. Thought vocabulary was the key, so she had me study dictionaries. I'm glad she did. Now I understand what I'm saying, the words inside the words. I'm grateful to her. Otherwise I'd just be skimming the surface like everybody else."

"So you've been stealing from my father, using the money on those kids."

"That's right."

"Great," she said. "Fucking great."

She shook her head, couldn't help but chuckle. "But you know, what I said that day, Butler, that was just some spoiled kid making a smartass crack. What the hell did she know? She was twelve years old."

"It doesn't matter. What's true is true. Whoever speaks it, however old they happen to be."

The storm had blown out to sea. A mile or so to the east dark funnels of rain were tearing loose from the thunderhead, while closer in the sun took back the shoreline. She watched a trio of pelicans skim close to the water. Near shore a Jet Ski crashed back and forth across a cabin cruiser's wake.

"Now let's talk about you," he said.

She watched the thunderstorm plow to the north. "There's nothing to talk about."

"You have no politics," he said. "No career. I mean, yeah, you went to college, you studied things, you did your drawings. But the truth is, Monica, when you disappeared like that, you were running away from things, but you weren't running *toward* anything. That's the fact. Isn't it?"

"You don't know me. Stop pretending you do."

"Am I wrong?"

Butler kept his eyes out there on the traffic. Smiling away, cocksure. Monica let the silence answer for her.

"Those ice turkeys," he said. "Those silver dollars dropping out. The kids at the tables trying to act polite, but still grabbing. The way they whooped as the coins fell. That was your daddy's little training session in capitalism. No adults there to make sure the money was spread around evenly. The money went to the quick and the strong. That's his idea of charity—make them scramble, make them dive into the dirt and thrash and jostle. Teach them the American way. You were only twelve years old, Monica, but you knew that was wrong. You saw it and understood immediately."

She drew in a breath, puckered her lips, and blew it out.

"You know it's possible, Monica, it's possible to know things when you're young and not to understand them until you're older. It's possible."

"So what do you want? I'm supposed to become your partner, Bonnie and Clyde?"

"Robin Hood and Maid Marion, I like them better."

"What do you need me for? You're doing fine already."

"We'll steal some money from your father. Once you have your share, you can decide what you want to do. Stay with me, go off on your own."

"I'm no goddamn thief. I work for my money."

"You'd be doing something good. You'd be contributing to the welfare of thousands of children. Lucy, the others. Fiesta Cruise Lines had a three-hundred-million-dollar profit last year. The money I've been taking, it's like a scrape on the knee."

Monica looked back at the wall lined with photos. He was right. She hadn't been running toward anything. Just away. Always away.

"Jesus," she said. "This is nuts. This is totally fucking crazy."

"Yeah," he said. "I knew you'd like it."

He smiled at her, just a glance. But it felt like he was looking past her eyes. Getting in there where nobody but David Cruz had ever been before. Just that spooky split second.

Two hours later they were at Miami International. They left the Winnebago in an outside lot, took a shuttle to the terminal. In an airport boutique she found a ginger-colored linen dress and suede oxfords, a thigh-length burgundy sweater for the Baltimore fall. Butler drew out a roll of twenties, paid for the clothes. She changed in the store, put the work shirt and torn shorts into the shopping bag.

Their seats were in the last row of the plane, old smoking section. The window seat empty. Butler in the middle, his blond hair loose down his back. Monica on the aisle. Look at them, anybody would think they were a young married couple on vacation. An hour into the flight people began lining up next to her seat, waiting for the bathroom. Butler kept on talking to her like he hadn't noticed them.

"Multiply it out," he said. "Twenty dollars a month, it doesn't sound like much, but you take on twenty-six hundred kids, that's a big nut. Over fifty thousand monthly."

She cut her eyes to the large black woman waiting for the bathroom a foot away. She lowered her voice. "You probably shouldn't be talking about this."

"Those kids, they're an addiction for me now," Butler said. "You know that word? Addiction?"

She sighed. "Spare me, okay."

The black woman went into the bathroom and a businessman in a crisp white shirt and red tie took her place. He smiled at her and Monica gave him back a stinger look.

"Addiction is from the Latin *addicere, dicere*. Means to sentence. To adjudge. In Roman law it meant you were bound over to judicial review. Eventually the word went off another way. Started to mean attached to, or devoted like an adherent, a disciple. Amazing how many words have God hidden in them. God or Christ. Religion.

"So anyway, addiction is the right word for it. These kids are my sentence. They're my devotion, my punishment. Helping feed all those kids. Like the children out in your father's yard, the workers' kids, families barely scraping by. I'm giving them the silver dollars in that ice turkey, no tricks, no humiliation. Twenty bucks a month, do with it what they will."

The businessman caught enough of Butler's spiel to roll his eyes at Monica. You wanna come sit with me, honey, shake loose from the wacko, you're more than welcome.

She leaned toward Butler, keeping her voice low. "Fifty thousand a month?"

"Been at it for seven months now. Over three hundred and fifty thousand so far. Your daddy knows I'm out here. He's got people looking for me full time."

"But they haven't caught you?"

"I'm smarter than they are. And I know the M.S. *Eclipse* inside and out. It's a carbon copy of the ship I worked on for years. I know every cranny. One cruise a month, I walk on just like any other passenger. Nobody recognizes me because they don't know who they're looking for. Every five days the ship takes on two thousand new passengers. What're they going to do, memorize every face? Check for repeaters? Anyway, I use different names, wear a disguise, keep to myself. Don't wander the decks unless I have to. It's not hard."

The businessman shook his head, giving up on her. He stepped aside for the black woman, then slipped into the toilet.

Butler had a taste of his apple juice. Patted his lips.

"There's violence involved," he said. "You should know that."

She was silent.

"Just so you know," Butler said. "I do whatever it takes. I have no compunctions."

"Well," she said. "I'm not big on compunctions myself."

"The Latin stem of *compungere* means prick sharply or sting. It's where we get pungent. So compunction literally means a pricking of the conscience. That feeling when you've done something wrong. That's how you know what you're doing is right. You don't get pricked."

Monica tore open a packet of pretzels, shook out a handful.

"The last few months," he said, "I've been setting things up. Sooner or later no matter how good I am, law of averages says they'll catch me. So I'm going to make one big score, disappear for a while. I've been using the cruises to plant my devices. Sneak around at night, three in the morning, I can go anywhere I want. That and dry dock."

The passenger in front of her, an older lady, reclined her seat all the way. Getting interested in the conversation.

"Devices?"

"I started out in the Coast Guard. Flew choppers for two years, spotting Cuban rafters in the Straits. I was studying electronics the whole time. After that I became an apprentice engineer for Fiesta. Lola got me the job but I worked hard. I earned my pay. I was about to make chief. I was on my way up, learning things, how the ship works. All its systems, its vulnerabilities. Every ship has them. No matter how many backup systems they have, there are always weak spots, entry points."

Butler turned his head and smiled at her.

"What happened? Why aren't you still with them?"

His smile collapsed. "I got screwed is what happened. I got screwed big time."

He pulled a magazine out of the seat flap, fanned through the pages. Fanned through them again, stuffed the magazine back.

He smoothed his hands over his face, until a faint smile appeared. He folded his hands into his lap.

"Sorry," he said. "Sorry."

"I've never been on a cruise," she said. "Daughter of the great Morton Sampson, but somehow I managed to avoid it. Never had the desire."

"Oh, it's fun, you'll like it."

"Fun," she said. "I'm not even sure what that is anymore."

"There's some disagreement. Could be Middle English for *fonne,* which means fool. Or Latin for cheat or hoax. Either way, fun is rebellion, breaking the rules."

"Not from fungus? You're sure?"

He looked over at her, nothing on his face. As though all the muscles below the tissue had dissolved. His lips moved like he was translating her words into a tongue he understood. The man was smart in flashes. Had a sexy streak. But there seemed to be dead spots too, air pockets.

"A joke," she said.

"I know that."

He raked his long hair away from his face. A striking man, but not handsome in any classic sense. A man who grew on you. The blue eyes, the sharp nose. Lips so perfectly formed they looked stenciled. Reminding her of some painting Monica had studied once in the foggy long-ago.

The businessman came out of the toilet, started chatting up the flight-attendant in her kitchen cubbyhole. Letting her know what a big-time traveler he was, knew all the frequent flyer lingo.

She looked back at Butler. His eyes were closed, cheek against the headrest, face turned her way. She remembered what painting it was. A course in religious art Monica's junior year. Dali's *The Sacrament of the Last Supper.* An early Dali, before he got surreal. No clocks melting over branches. This was a simple blond Jesus with a cheap dye job. Beardless and fleshy. A man who'd clearly enjoyed his final meal and now had risen to give his after-dinner speech. Dark eyebrows that clashed with the orange-blond hair. A celestial light rising behind him. His right hand was lifted and his pointing finger was raised, the second finger uncurling as though he were listing a few things for his disciples to remember later on. Or perhaps he was about to make a V with those two fingers. Victory.

Maybe she had the details a little off, her memory fuzzy. But she clearly remembered the hair color. A cheap dye job, the powder-white skin, a bland, unworried look. Dali's Jesus. Half saint, half huckster. Some air pockets there too.

"Those organizations," she said. "Like the one you're sending your money to, they're famous for ripping people off. A dollar of every twenty might get to Lucy. The rest buys fancy houses, Mercedes for the administrators."

He opened his eyes. "You're cynical."

"I'm realistic."

"You have to believe in something," he said. "I believe my twenty dollars is getting through to Lucy."

"Believing it doesn't make it true."

He looked at her, smiled indulgently, patted her arm. "Sure it does, sweetness. Sure it does."

"Look," she said. "I haven't decided what I'm doing. I'm going along with you to Baltimore, but I haven't made up my mind what I'm doing next. I may just get out in Baltimore, start over from there. So don't get your hopes up."

"Fine," he said. "Take your time. No pressure."

She stared down at the hand resting on her arm, at the silver prongs on the tips of his first two fingers.

CHAPTER
11

In Baltimore they got a cab, sailed north for half an hour, then five miles from the Bethlehem Shipyard at Sparrow Point, the highway gridlocked behind a three-car pileup. Giving Butler a chance to study the countryside as the car crept along. Little squat houses of red brick smudged with coal dust, duplexes and triplexes and octoplexes. Graveyards and junkyards and thrifty gas stations. A half-assed Penney's Mall, Fabric Warehouses, National Guard Armory, lumbermills, more junkyards, a couple of chemical plants.

The cold air smelled like mineral spirits, a chemical fog hovering over the dismal marshes, not a bird in sight. A raw wind out of the northwest, rust-colored sunlight. They'd shipped all the industry to Mexico and Taiwan, and this was all that was left behind, that wretched air. Probably some twenty-dollar-a-month kids around there. A lot of them. He decided he would have to look into it.

By the time the cab pulled into the Bethlehem Shipyards it was almost two in the afternoon, and they'd run up a fifty-dollar fare. He told the old black driver to wait. Might take as much as an hour, but if things went smoothly, he'd be back in half that. Told Monica she'd have to stay there too. She was too damn attractive for this place, people would notice. Remember later.

"What kind of business you in," the taxi driver said, "you don't mind my asking?"

In the rearview mirror Butler Jack stared into the man's eyes. Then he turned to Monica and extended his right hand toward her, displayed the silver prongs, the rubber cups attaching them to his fingertips. Rotated his hand, let her examine the Velcro cuff holding the wires in place, the small button in the palm of his hand, like that practical joke buzzer. Shake hands, get a buzz. Slowly he curled his thumb and two fingers into a fist, kept the two fingers spread. Pressed the buzzer and activated the sputtering charge. A little exhibition. Just so she knew.

"Never mind," the old man said. "You go do your business, whatever it may be, I'll be sitting right here when you come back. You can count on that."

Butler lifted his hand and pressed the sizzle of voltage to the old man's neck. Monica gasped and watched the man stiffen and slump forward against the wheel.

"Jesus Christ!"

"It's all right," Butler said. "He'll be fine. Sleep for an hour. By then I'll be back."

"You didn't need to do that. Holy shit."

"You shouldn't curse. It doesn't reflect well on you."

Butler got out, unzipped his gym bag, drew out the blue jumpsuit. He slipped into it, put on his baseball cap. Leaned back into the cab and told her good-bye.

Carrying the gym bag, Butler headed down the broken asphalt drive past twenty or so Indonesians huddled in coats too thin for the weather. They were waiting by the employment shed, day laborers, prepared to lick the grease off a hot griddle if that's what it took to get their dollar.

The Indonesians eyed him as he walked past the checkpoint, the guard looking up from his desk inside the little hut, seeing Butler was a white man in a blue jumpsuit and a baseball cap, waving him on through. Weren't many places on earth you couldn't walk into with that uniform, a tool kit in hand.

Butler ambled past three warehouses with high-up windows, most of them broken. Past the machine shops, the welding pit, around a curvy lane and out into a patch of dreary sunlight.

The five ships were sitting side by side, each one settled onto enormous wooden chocks. An oil tanker, and four cruise ships. Cost over a hundred thousand to haul a ship that big out of the water. Add in another million lost from taking it out of service for a few days, and that's why the shipyards operated twenty-four hours a day, always crawling with workmen.

Picking his way across the power cables and water hoses, under the spotlight scaffolding, the dock slick with oil and mud, Butler didn't draw a look from any of the other workers. Passed through gangs of them smoking, worked his way out to the last two docks where the *Statendam,* a midsize cruise ship, was perched. Beside it was a monster ship, twice its size. The *Juggernaut,* a Liberian-registered supertanker, one of the half-dozen largest crude oil carriers sailing the earth. Longer than two aircraft carriers end to end, four hundred thousand tons of steel, every spare inch of the ship was hollowed out so it could carry more oil.

Empty out the crude that ship carried, you could coat every beach in Florida an inch deep, you'd still have enough black sludge left over to fill all the swimming pools in Miami.

Once a week the *Juggernaut* loaded up at an offshore facility near Freeport, sailed around the tip of Florida to the Galveston refineries. Butler had her schedule, a printout of her weekly course chart. Knew the route she'd sail back down the East Coast from Baltimore to the Bahamas. Had the mile-by-mile global positioning bearings, Loran coordinates, everything.

A ship as big as that, you'd think it would take a hundred men to keep it operating. But nine was all it carried. Four of them on duty at any given moment. The others doing sack time, playing gin rummy, their dicks in their fists.

Because the *Juggernaut* sailed the same short hop every week, they could get by with a very low tech bridge. Magnetic compass, speed log, position reference system, all fed through a digital auto-pilot. Ten years behind the techno-curve. A four-hundred-thousand-ton, single-hull floating tar pit operated by poorly paid Chinamen, only a couple with any piloting skills. The whole operation guided by a navigational system only slightly more sophisticated than the one on the *Pinta,* the *Niña,* the *Santa Maria.*

Everybody raised hell about the damage off-shore drilling could do; well, they should get load of the *Juggernaut,* seven days a week cruising a couple of miles offshore, a hull that would rip like paper if it brushed a reef.

Butler Jack took the gangway down to the floor of the dry dock. A dozen men in heavy coats standing around looking up at a welder on a crane showering sparks around the enormous props. The welder in his late teens, early twenties.

Butler stood next to a man in a bomber jacket.

Guy took a look at Butler but didn't say anything. Sparks flying all around them. Man was in his late fifties, baggy eyes, a day's beard.

"The shield around the propeller shaft spring another leak?"

"That's right," the man said.

"Third time it's been in for that," Butler said. "Maybe this time they'll get it right."

"Don't count on it," the man said.

The man kept looking up into the shower of sparks. "What job you on today?"

"Little soldering is all," said Butler. "How 'bout you?"

"Backing up the kid. He scrapes a knuckle, they send me into the game."

The man rubbed his palm across the gray bristle on his cheek. Then looked back up into the bright rain coming from the welder's torch. "When that kid finishes the one spot weld on the shaft shield, they're dropping this piece of shit back in the water. You got some work to do onboard, you better quit your gawking, shake a fucking leg."

Butler went up the gangway, flashed his badge at the Chinese man up there who was playing security guard, and blew on past. All the regular seamen were probably down on the Block trying to find some hooker to take their money. Butler worked his way to the bridge, no bigger than the closet in a cheap hotel room.

He was ten minutes into swapping out the units when the security guard walked onto the bridge.

"You not on list. I look, not see name."

"Look again," Butler said.

He set the old circuit board aside and slid the new one into the narrow slot, had to tap it into its notch with the butt of a screwdriver.

The Chinese man moved behind him. "You follow me down the stair, we wait in crew cabin. Talk chief later."

"Go suck on a won ton, Charlie Chan."

Butler set the clamps on the ends of the board, blew some lint away from the contact points. Goddamn ship was a disaster. Dirt and grime everywhere you looked. A wonder it made it back and forth the few hundred miles it had to travel every week.

The Chinese guard got his bony arm under Butler's chin and popped him up straight. He switched into Chinese, laying into Butler with a string of weird warbles as he dragged him backward.

Butler twisted his head to the side just enough to see an inch or two of naked flesh exposed at the guy's cuff. He reached up and pressed the prongs to the skin and triggered the voltage and the man was flung sideways against the chart box. Took a bad gash on the forehead.

Butler turned back to the console, spent another ten minutes wrapping up his work. Even with the interruption he'd be on and off, back at the cab in less than half an hour.

He took the inside stairway, dragging the Chinaman down fourteen flights to the bottom deck. It took him a couple of minutes to locate the water treatment plant just forward of the engine room. Like the rest of the *Juggernaut*'s equipment, this was ten years out of date. Evaporative filtration system working off the heat from the turbines. Butler had read about the units but this was the first one he'd seen.

He tried three hatches before he found the one he wanted. A reservoir bin that probably held a thousand gallons of freshly filtered water. Butler took hold of the Chinaman's ears, straightened him up, and slammed his skull backward against the bulkhead. Once, twice, three times, another time till there was a bloody print. Butler wiped the bulkhead clean with the sleeve of his jumpsuit, then heaved the guard onto his shoulder and crammed him through the hatch door.

He leaned in, watched him float. Reached out, turned him facedown. Then Butler shut the reservoir door. Cranked it tight.

Nobody would check on the reservoir bin, not in a hundred years. At least not until they got a whiff of something rotten trickling out their faucets. By then it'd be a week too late.

At the bottom of the gangway, back on the docks, he pulled the *Juggernaut*'s old circuit board out of his gym bag, dumped it into a trash bin, then nodded to the welder in the leather jacket as he passed by. The welder looked away, staring up into the shadowy underbelly of that gigantic ship, into that cold fire raining down.

When he got back to the cab, Monica was staring out at the dreary day. The cabbie was still sleeping.

He opened the back door and sat down beside her. "You could've run."

"I know."

"Why didn't you?"

"Should I have? You planning to zap me with that thing?"

"Not if you're good."

He smiled at her and she gave him one right back.

God Almighty, it was turning out better than he'd ever imagined. That was the way it always went. Imagination was never as good as the real thing. In your head the imagined thing was always fuzzy and vague, but the real thing, when it came along, it was always full of gristle and bone and the stench of fact.

"Well?" she said. "I believe you mentioned something about a cruise."

Butler held her eyes for a moment more, then lifted his right hand, held his fingers in a V and let the current flash.

Monica was riding this out. In the cab with Butler Jack driving. Back to the Baltimore airport, the unconscious cabbie slumping against the passenger door.

They stopped at lights. A half-dozen times she could've thrown open a door, run. Exits everywhere. But she was there. She was riding this. Doing something, causing it to happen. Thinking of her father. Of the fish he gutted while her mother watched. The blood on the deck of the rental boat. Her mother's blood. The ice turkey, the silver dollars dropping.

Going to sting him, make the bastard squirm. If the opportunity presented itself, she might even let him know it was his daughter doing it, give him a glimpse. All she wanted was her four hundred eighty-seven dollars back, her nest egg; the rest of it could go to Lucy and her starving sisters.

After it was done, head west. See what was beyond the horizon. Start over, get it right. Santa Fe, El Paso. Whatever looked good from the bus window. Find a motel that needed its sheets changed. Maybe get out her pen, draw some cacti, some iguanas. See what she could do with sand.

They were back in Miami by seven that Saturday evening. Butler drove the short hop over the Dolphin Expressway downtown, parked the Winnebago at the Bayside Market, and handed Monica a roll of fifties, told her to have fun, shop till she dropped. He said he had a couple of last-minute things to do, he'd meet her at Sammy's later, then ducked away, a hip hop in his step. A man in overdrive.

Monica wandered into the flashy mall. For a half hour she window-shopped, feeling disoriented, a mild whirl behind her eyes. Finally, she pushed open the door of a shop and stepped inside. She began to shop.

"Can I help you?" they said.

"Can I help you find anything?"

"Anything I can do, let me know."

In her years as Irma Slater, Monica had forgotten the hollow thrill of shopping. She stood before three-way mirrors for the first time in three years, the clerks assuring her she was utterly gorgeous in that green silk sheath, the turtleneck tunic, that long cotton sweater with a soft, jacquard texture, she felt lost. A three-year time warp. Even if she'd wanted to stay up with changing styles, living in the Keys prevented it. People seemed to leave behind on the mainland whatever fashion sense they had. Keys chic was little more than grunge in the sun.

Finally, two hours into it, so weary of the exercise, so out of shape as a consumer, Monica wound up snatching this and that, plunking it all down on the counter, a handful of bras, a half-dozen panties, three pairs of shorts, some deck shoes, trying nothing on. An orgy of impulse shopping.

She carried her bags to Sammy's, a neon and chrome hamburger joint on the top floor of the marketplace. They gave her a table by the front window, a view of the Intracoastal. Something loud and Cuban on the jukebox. She ordered a fish sandwich, a draft beer, double order of fries. Sat and waited for Butler.

From her seat she could see the top decks of the cruise ships. The sleek white monsters glowing in the distance. She dipped her fries in ketchup, wolfed them down. Drank her beer.

She felt good. She felt fine. It was time to be gone from Sugarloaf, from the slow, unvarying weather of the Keys. The lazy clocks, the mellow, coconut breezes. It was time to test herself against the jangle of the city, the quick-draw pace. She still found it hard to believe she was here, just a few minutes away from boarding one of her father's ships. It was nuts. She felt foolish and dizzy and wildly dislocated. But she was going to do it. It gave her a delicious thrill. Steal from her father, give the money away to charity. Wow.

She believed she was ready for the challenge. Irma Slater had toughened her, taught her everything she knew. Now, by God, it was up to Monica.

CHAPTER
12

"I'm perfectly satisfied you can do the job, Mr. Sugarman. I won't accept your resignation."

"How do you do that, not accept a resignation?"

"It's easy." Sampson smiling.

"Look, Mr. Sampson, what you need is a couple of dozen professionals and a complete overhaul of your security system. If you want to catch this guy, that's the only way."

They were midship on the Verandah Deck of the M.S. *Eclipse*, standing near the flickering light of one of the three swimming pools. Sugarman in a pair of khaki camp shorts and a navy polo shirt. Deck shoes. As close to yachting clothes as he had. Jeannie would take one look and probably shake her head, his shoes clashing with his shorts, shorts with his shirt. She could tell when things clashed. One of her major skills.

He was taking occasional peeks over the railing at the dock ten stories below. Nearly ten o'clock Saturday night, and still the supplies were arriving. An endless stream of food and liquor rolling up the gangway. A week's groceries, fourteen thousand pounds of beef, seven hundred fifty pounds of veal, nine thousand of vegetables, nine hundred gallons of milk, seven hundred pounds of coffee. He'd gotten to know one of the chefs, heard the litany a dozen times now. Ten thousand pounds of fresh fruit. A thousand bags of tea.

No possible way for Sugarman to know which of the hundreds of people streaming on and off the ship were legal. Stop every one, check them for wigs or disguises, verify their IDs, run background checks, the ship would never get loaded. So it was hey, if you got a dolly full of tomatoes or Chivas Regal, come right on aboard. Hang around, shoot the shit, have a look around if you like. Hide in a closet, pop out later if you're so inclined. Stick a knife in someone's belly, steal their shirt if it strikes your fancy. Hell, he knew what the guy looked like, he knew where he was going to be, and he still couldn't catch him.

A mile to the south the sleek Miami skyline was a rainbow of flashy colors. One building neon blue, the one beside it green with flecks of red, one a banana yellow, another vivid orange. Along the docks the other half-dozen cruise ships looked like they'd been drizzled with luminescent frosting. Long strings of Christmas lights twinkling on each of them. All six would be at sea by happy hour tomorrow. Fifteen thousand lucky souls with nothing to do for a week but drink and eat and stare at the moon. But none so lucky as those on the *Eclipse*. They would do their drinking and eating and staring with the incomparable Lola Sampson as their shipmate.

Sugarman gazed down at the brightly lit dock, watched another stretch limo drop off more of Morton Sampson's friends. Getting a jump on the festivities. A couple of rising rock stars, news anchors, business moguls. You name it, if they had ten million in the bank, they were invited to the party. Celebrate Morton Sampson's unceasing success. Meet the lovely Lola.

"All I'm saying is, Mr. Sampson, things have uglied up. This guy we're dealing with, he's raised the ante. Killing a guy for his shirt. It's impossible to predict what somebody like this is going to do next. And on our side, what do we have? We got a couple of security people, average age fifty-nine. David Cruz, he's fine. A good kid. But his staff, people he's got working for him, hey, between the bunch of them, we got a grand total of three years' law enforcement experience. I mean, come on, the best these folks can do is break up a fistfight between a couple of cardiac patients. I think we better face it. It's time to bring in the big people."

"And you expect to accomplish this before we get under way?"

"I think we have to delay the cruise till we can bring security up to strength. That's the only way you're going to be able to ensure the safety of the two thousand passengers."

"Who do you have in mind exactly, these big people?"

Sugarman glanced over at a couple of Filipinos mopping the teak deck nearby. Cutting looks at Mr. Sampson. The head boss, husband to the gorgeous Lola, staring like the man was God the father himself. And Sampson looked the part, all right. White ducks, bright new boat shoes, crisp guayabera with epaulets. Bald on top but with thick white sweeps of hair on the sides. Face nicely tanned. Great teeth. Showed them a lot. Proud as hell of his super teeth.

"Look, if you're a hundred percent serious about catching this guy," Sugar said, "you're talking FBI. Major leaguers. They have the training, the computers, the manpower. They can do in ten seconds what it would take me a year."

"We're sailing in international waters, Mr. Sugarman. The FBI has no jurisdiction. We're on our own out there. I don't believe the Coast Guard has an investigative branch."

"Okay, so I don't know anything about jurisdiction, but I know you need professionals. And a bunch of them."

"Is this how you conduct your business? Things get a little difficult, you walk off the job, leave your clients in the lurch?"

Sugarman shook his head helplessly.

"Mr. Sugarman. I want to impress something on you. This is the most important cruise in the company's twenty-five-year history. We've been promoting this cruise for months. A week of *Lola Live* broadcast from onboard the ship. And you expect me to delay departure? Risk a public relations nightmare? No. No. That's simply impossible."

"I'm just telling you what I think. It's time to bring in the heavy hitters. I'm not getting the job done. We got a guy who's targeted this ship. He knows what he's doing. He's a slick bastard and he's dangerous. He's beating us. He'll keep on beating us unless we do some serious reevaluation, top to bottom."

Morton Sampson smiled, patted him on the back, a comforting touch. Dad ready to forgive his wayward son. Console him in his hour of desperation. "My wife speaks highly of you."

Sugarman nodded his gratitude.

"Yes, Lola has taken an unusual interest in your well-being. In fact, she was the one who brought you to my attention in the first place. The article in the *Miami Herald,* that incident with the fish. Saving the state from an environmental calamity."

Sugar brushed a patch of hardened salt off the railing. "That wasn't me. It was my friend, Thorn. I was just along for the ride. And it wasn't that big of a deal."

"That's not how the papers had it."

"The papers write about you all the time, Mr. Sampson. How often do they get it right?"

Sampson watched a laughing gull swoop down out of the darkness and land on the radio tower that slanted off the bridge. Radar dish, antennae. The bird began to hop from one vital instrument to another. Sampson glared at the creature until it seemed to feel the heat of his look and threw itself into squawking flight.

Sampson cleared his throat and brought his cheerful smile to Sugerman. "Lola convinced me that if we wanted to solve our problem, and do it discreetly, we should bring in somebody from the private sector. And your name was first on our list. It remains first."

"Well . . ."

"You wouldn't want to disappoint Lola, would you, Mr. Sugarman? She has such a high regard for you."

"I appreciate that. I do. But the fact is, hey, I haven't accomplished diddley."

"You figured out that slot machine scam, didn't you?"

"Yeah, but not in time. The guy got away. I mean, I just can't do this by myself. The ship's too big. Too complex. There's too many passengers, too many crew, too many places to hide on board. There's just no way one person is going to catch your thief, Mr. Sampson. It would be sheer luck if I were to do that. I wish I could tell you otherwise, but there's no way."

Another limo drifted up. The onslaught of dollies continued.

"We stand here, Mr. Sugarman, in one direction a spectacular panorama of the city. And out there the Atlantic is waiting. On every side we are surrounded by extraordinary beauty and luxury. On the deck of a four-hundred-million-dollar state-of-the-art vessel. It would only be natural for you to assume that the owner of all this is a very fortunate, very wealthy man. And you'd be right, of course."

Sugarman smiled, held his tongue. Sampson's eyes were glowing, focused on something in the shadowy distance.

"I'm sure you've heard of the Peter Principle, Mr. Sugarman."

He studied Sampson a moment, searching for a flicker of amusement. Any giveaway this was a joke.

"The Peter Principle," Sugar said.

"The notion of rising to your level of incompetence. Being promoted to a stage beyond your abilities."

"I didn't know it had a name."

"Yes, it does. And the idea isn't just for people. It works for corporations as well. A corporation can also rise to its own level of incompetence. It can grow too strong for its own good. As odd as that sounds."

Sugarman nodded.

"Get musclebound," Sugar said. "Like a weight lifter."

Sampson brought his eyes back from the horizon. He settled another smile on Sugar.

"Good," he said. "Yes, musclebound. I like that."

He played with the thought for a moment, then put a hand on Sugar's shoulder.

"Yes," he said. "A man who started off large and strong and because he was large and strong, he could handle more weight than other men could. He could heap things on his back, more and more, shoulder limitless quantities. And in that way he enlarged himself to greater and greater proportions, worked his muscles relentlessly until he could carry more weight than almost any man on the face of the earth."

"Until he got so big he couldn't move anymore."

"That's right," Sampson said. "Exactly. Until he lost his limberness, his flexibility. Paralyzed by his own strength."

"You're telling me Fiesta's in trouble?"

Sampson was staring down the three-mile lane of water that fed to the ocean. He didn't look paralyzed. Didn't look the least bit musclebound or incompetent.

"Do you have any idea," he said, "what it would do to Fiesta Cruise Lines if it became known that a violent act had taken place onboard one of my ships? A murder. Can you guess what would happen to stock values if the general public began to believe that my ships were not safe? Robberies, murders occurring monthly. No, Mr. Sugarman, this is exactly why people come on cruises in the first place, to avoid such dangers. If they wanted risk, if they wanted crime and violence they would simply stay in Miami."

He smiled at his joke. Sugarman liked him. He wouldn't necessarily take a bullet for the guy, but he liked him, liked him a good deal. The man was a positive thinker. He looked you in the eyes, didn't flinch, listened to you until you'd had your say, treated you evenhandedly and then, by God, the man put his Yes up against your No. He could probably make you cheer or salute or do some other serious gushing if he set his mind to it. The guy knew how to inspire, knew how to rally the troops. But he was no game player. All of it was right out in the open. His personal stock of charisma against whatever you could muster.

"Let's say those same newspapers who brought you to my attention, Mr. Sugarman, let's say they got hold of such a story. A murder on the M.S. *Eclipse*. Oh, they would send one of their smart, derisive young reporters over here. He'd tear around, talk to people. No matter what I tried to do, it would come out, our plight, our misfortune. All of us would be smeared. The cruise ship lines, even you, Mr. Sugarman. Think how it would affect your own future business opportunities to be linked to such a high-profile debacle."

Sampson's eyes flicked over to the Filipino moppers; the two of them saw him watching and slammed it into high gear.

"And imagine, if the company were in a ticklish financial position, say for instance its cash flow was sluggish, its creditors growing leery. Can you picture what would happen if there were a drastic drop in traffic, the flow of revenue was suddenly constricted?"

"So what is it? You been building too many ships lately? Spending all your money getting bigger?"

Sampson smiled thoughtfully. "I see why Lola is so high on you."

"Maybe you should go public, sell some shares, get the cash rolling in."

"Oh, I've had offers to buy a significant stake in Fiesta. Good offers, solid offers. Even Bergson waved a few million in front of me."

"Wally Bergson?"

"That's right. Bergson swooped down a few months ago, backed a dump truck full of money up to my house, ready to drown me in cash. He wanted to add Fiesta to his universe."

"Probably the last thing in Miami he doesn't own fifty-one percent of."

"But I wouldn't do it. I still won't do it. And I'm not about to put myself into a position where I *have* to do it."

"So you're content to lose fifty thousand a month? A crew member now and then? Like that's a reasonable cost of doing business."

"If that's what it takes to keep afloat, yes. But, Mr. Sugarman, you are going to save me from all that. You're going to catch this outlaw. And you're going to do it discreetly."

Giving Sugar that passionate smile. That overpowering Yes.

"Okay, look," Sugarman said. "I'll make you a deal."

"Good, good, now we're talking."

"I'll re-up one more tour. But after this cruise is done, no more. I'm giving my notice unless you agree to bring in some serious backup for me. And I mean professional law enforcement people."

Sampson put out his hand and Sugar gripped it. Dry and big and strong. But not squeezing hard. Not one of those. Not needing to impress anyone, mash the small bones. Just a good, firm handshake.

"Fair enough," he said. "We'll talk again at the end of the

week. I'll consider your position. In the meantime, eyes like a hawk, Mr. Sugarman. Eyes like a hawk. Let's catch this son of a bitch. Let's string him up."

He let go of his hand and clapped Sugar on the back, gave him a quick shoulder hug, and left him standing there.

Sugarman didn't believe in luck. Bad luck maybe. But good luck, no, that was something you made happen. A product of a thousand small things you'd done already, things hard to calculate. Training, habits of mind, good wind, focus, groundwork. He didn't believe the gods were running the show. He'd experimented with that for a few years when he was young, going to church, prayer meetings, the whole nine yards. Got down on his knees, spoke to the spirits he heard flying around in the night air. But nothing happened. Knees got sore. Spirits kept flying.

At the time he thought maybe he didn't know how to pray. Too difficult, too philosophical for him. More the thing for people like Thorn. Thorn was somebody who could get down in the philosophical muck and find an acorn now and then. Not Sugarman.

Now what he believed in was blind chance. The pinball universe. If you worked at it, had some hand-eye coordination, practiced your skills, you got a couple of whacks with the flippers, keeping the balls in play, maybe a hip nudge now and then, but basically, gravity was going to beat you. Flip all you wanted, eventually chance and gravity were going to steal your balls.

Ten minutes after leaving Sampson, on the way back to his cabin, six flights down, blind chance bounced him in the right direction. He heard an argument down a forward passageway when he was headed aft. For no particular reason, he stopped, listened. Two guys going after each other in chop suey English. Nothing he needed to get involved with. But as he was turning away, he sighted a tall thin man cutting across the corridor down a different hallway on Riviera Deck. Just a blink, but he caught the long blond hair, the narrow waist, wide shoulders. Hawaiian shirt, white pants, straw hat.

Sugar dodged behind a bulkhead. Waited a second then took a peek around it down the long hallway. Empty now. He felt the flurry in his chest like a tattered sail beating in the wind. His legs weak. Not sure what he would do this time if he faced off with the guy. If it was who he thought. Same feeling he'd had on the docks that day, the guy jumping across, coming for him. His legs drained. Doe in the headlights. Nothing he'd ever experienced before.

He sucked down a couple of breaths, stepped out, headed down the corridor.

Far as he remembered, there was nothing down there but a fire station, the media room. A few hundred cabins, the cheap ones without portholes, a curtain hanging over a square on the wall so you could imagine you had a window if you needed to. The guy he'd glimpsed wasn't dressed as crew. None of the paying custom- ers were supposed to board until tomorrow morning, no outsiders should be on the ship at all except for Sampson's innermost circle, and all of them were hanging out seven flights up on the Verandah Deck, popping the Dom Pérignon in the suites with the panora- mas.

Sugar paced slowly down the narrow hall, tried the doors of several cabins. All locked. The cleaning crews had made their final rounds already, scrubbed the brightwork to a glimmer.

Which left the fire station and the media room.

He went to the fire station first, turned the handle, swept open the door, and stepped in quickly. He succeeded only in flush- ing a moth from its perch, the brown wings careening right into Sugar's face, big as a viper bat. Sugar ducked and swatted at the thing, knocked it to the floor. Round one to Mr. Reflex.

He checked out the room completely, found nothing, shut the door, went forward a dozen feet to the media room. This time he opened the door slowly, stayed in the hallway, and peered into the eight-by-eight space. A swivel chair set before the small control panel where the movies were downloaded from satellites, the Mu- zak selections made, the many messages from the bridge or the cruise director were relayed to the PA system or to the TVs throughout the ship.

On the far side of the control board, he saw a switch plate swung open. He ducked farther back into the hallway and peeked through the crack in the door. No one hiding there. He stepped inside and moved over to the control panel, bent to look. Only a bundle of wires. Some kind of meter or radio unit attached to them. Nothing he recognized. Then he noticed a small pair of wire clippers sitting on a shelf inside the panel.

Apparently their thief was up to something else this time. A little sabotage maybe. Pipe a porno movie into every TV. Distract the crew with a professional blowjob while he ripped off the casino, walked off with his monthly fifty thou.

When the decking creaked behind him, Sugar stiffened, took a careful breath, gathered himself. Then wheeled around. He made it halfway round before the forearm clenched around his throat, yanked him upright, dragged him several steps backward. The man was strong, flattening Sugar against his chest. His hoarse breath in Sugar's ear.

"Okay," Sugar muttered. "Be cool. Okay? Nobody's done anything wrong here yet. Nobody's in trouble at this moment."

Adrenaline flooding his bloodstream, everything revving.

The man said nothing, maneuvering him into the center of the room. Then Sugarman heard the crackle of electrical current and glimpsed out of the corner of his vision the bluish flash of naked voltage.

"Know where electricity comes from?" The man's dry lips touched Sugar's ear. "The word, I mean, not the thing itself."

He didn't answer, kept himself tense against the man's considerable strength, making minor adjustments, exploring the possibilities of twisting free.

"No? Well, I'll tell you. It's from the Latin *electrum,* which means amber. Amber, the yellow fossil resin. That seems kind of weird, doesn't it? Amber, electricity. Weird until you know the facts. That when you rub amber with your hand or a cloth, you get an electrostatic charge."

Sugarman managed a grunt.

"It's interesting, isn't it. Amber, rub, electricity. Yellow, fossil. All those other words floating around in that one word. You rub loose some electrons, they've been just sitting there, hidden away, doing no one any good. Until one day somebody discovers it, rubs it and pow. It's got a whole new life. A reason for being. Like you and me, same thing. The two of us, we rub against each other, static discharges, a whole new thing happens."

He stroked his fingers lightly against Sugar's cheek then brought his hand around so Sugarman could see. Holding it inches from his eyes, the voltage sputtering.

"I told you we'd meet again."

"Why don't you turn that off? We can talk this over."

"Nothing to discuss. You're on one side, I'm on the other."

"Look, you don't need to be doing this. You're a decent kid."

"You don't know me, old man. You don't know a fucking thing about me."

"You're wrong," Sugar said. "I know who you are. And I know we can settle this. You need money, I think I can get you what you want, you don't have to keep doing this. Causing violence."

"You offering me a deal?"

"Yeah, a deal. Fifty thousand a month, like you've been getting. Neat and clean."

"A deal like with a contract, lawyers, dotted lines?"

"If you want it like that. It can be arranged."

"Maybe I like the violence."

"No, you don't."

"Like I said. You don't know a thing about me."

The current shut off. The hand moved out of view. Sugarman felt the arm at his throat relax a half notch. Sugar sucking in a decent breath. He could go creative, stomp the guy's instep, try an elbow, a gouge. Let his legs soften and drop dead weight against the man's grip. But he did nothing. Just hung there. The doe, the headlights. Knowing it was crazy. Knowing what was behind those headlights, the hurtling tons of steel. But standing there instead, risking it for a few more seconds. All the reasons for fighting neutralized by all the reasons for giving in.

A second later he felt something touch his neck, two cold spikes. And he gasped, set his feet, and wrenched to his right, but the vulnerable moment had passed. The man was prepared and Sugar didn't break the hold, didn't even weaken it.

"Time for closure, bro."

A blast of heat roared up his spinal column and Sugar saw a shimmer deep inside his eyes. And he felt his body shudder then sag in the stranger's arms. Felt himself crumple to the floor. Mind still bright alive, head full of pulsing light, but his body gone. Lying there, eyes unseeing. Legs bent underneath him in an unnatural pose. Synapses chattering.

Wouldn't you know.

Just when Sugar had begun to figure out a few of the major life issues. These last few years growing more secure in his views, his few codes guiding him through a series of nightmarish moments. Guns going off. Splattered in blood. Amid all that he'd managed somehow to keep his feet moving.

To know where he should go next, all he had to do was turn around, find his tracks across the snow, the sand, the dirt, whatever, turn back around, hold to that same course.

But at the moment Sugarman couldn't see the footprints anymore. Couldn't see shit. A fuzz like TV snow inside his eyeballs. Sounded that way too, like one of those white noise machines some people needed to sleep.

Thinking all this as his disinterested body drifted in the empty air, thinking that maybe he was hearing the meltdown of his own circuits. His nerve networks dissolved, his ganglia and neurotransmitters, synapses, all those fragile filaments broiled. His solids turning to liquids, the liquids to gas. As though this were what it sounded like, the thing that came for you. Not shrieking ghouls in black coaches, not God rumbling at the windy gates of heaven, but this simple electric noise. Rising up from inside your own body and reaching out for you and bringing you down into the depths of its terrible buzzing.

CHAPTER

13

That Saturday night the martial arts class was squatting in a circle on the wrestling mat on the gym floor at Coral Shores High, a dozen women and Thorn. It was late, around eleven. Rochelle on one side of him, a large woman named Randy on the other. Everyone in the circle was staring at Thorn. Everyone except Rochelle, and she was looking off at an exit sign in the west corner.

Twenty feet away Rover sat primly watching the spectacle, his leash tied to one of the bleachers. Thorn wiped the sweat from his forehead, brushed his hand on his gray gym shorts, then rubbed his mouth against the shoulder of his T-shirt. He'd just finished describing his fight with Freddy Megawatt on the Flamingo docks two weeks ago. Midway through every class, Paula Parkins asked one or two of them to tell how their training was affecting their daily lives. Mostly the women spoke about the confidence they'd acquired. Once or twice somebody had recounted a physical application, rebuffing an unwanted advance in a bar, around the office. But nobody had described a fight.

Paula Parkins was scowling at him through the dense silence.

"I was afraid of this," she said finally. "It's exactly why I was reluctant to let you join this class in the first place. If it weren't for Rochelle's persistence, I wouldn't have."

"Look," Thorn said. "It worked like it was supposed to. I put the guy down, convinced him to give up. Nobody got hurt."

"That's a total distortion of the philosophy of this course."

"It is?"

"Tell him, Rochelle. Tell him what he did wrong."

She was still staring at the green exit sign above the gym door. Thorn had spent a lot of torturous hours in this room a few decades ago. His two years on the wrestling team, getting bent double by guys stronger and quicker than he was. Leaving practice every day with his face swollen, abrasions on his cheeks that reopened the next afternoon. Major pain.

Rochelle said, "You could have just walked away, Thorn."

"I could've?"

"Yes," Paula Parkins said. "You didn't need to fight. You elected to fight."

"Elected? Jesus, this guy almost ran us over in his boat. I just barely caught Rover from going overboard, an alligator out there about to gulp him down."

Rover heard his name and thumped his tail twice.

"So because he splashed you with his boat and ruffled your dog, you felt you had to punish this man," Paula Parkins said. "And you used the skills I've taught you to do that."

She was only an inch over five feet but weighed almost the same as Thorn. Wearing her white judo suit, a pink belt. She was in her late forties with long brown hair. Never wore makeup, didn't do her nails. None of that falderal.

She'd spread her feet, arms dangling at her side. Looked like she was ready to sling him against the far wall.

"I was angry, yeah," Thorn said. "But I didn't hurt the guy. I put him down a couple of times is all."

He glanced at Rochelle. Still focused on the exit sign.

"You were exercising your competitive macho ego," Paula said. "That's a grotesque misuse of everything I'm trying to teach in this class. It's heresy. You fought when you didn't have to. You used what I've shown you to humiliate a foe."

"If I'd wanted to humiliate the guy, I would've punched him in the goddamn mouth. Broken a tooth."

"And now you're arguing with me. Now you're cursing and challenging my authority in front of my class."

"Okay, all right. All right. I'm sorry."

"We'll take a five-minute break," Paula said. "And, Thorn, as of this moment, you're no longer a member of the class."

In one corner of the gym among the purses and street shoes a phone warbled. Several of the young women got to their feet and went over to see if it was theirs. Rochelle was still reading the exit sign, another hour and she'd have it figured out. After a moment Janice Hardy came back with Rochelle's phone.

Rochelle took it, pressed it to her ear. She said nothing for a moment, then she extended her arm to Thorn. Eyes on his. "It's for you."

Her voice was empty.

He held the phone to his ear and said hello.

"Thorn?"

It was an older woman he didn't recognize.

He said yes.

"He gave this emergency number. And your name." Her voice was low. Barely above a whisper.

"Who is this?"

"Sugarman," she said. "He's been hurt."

Her voice was frayed, a ragged breath tearing at the words. "He's on the M.S. *Eclipse* docked in Miami. There'll be a ticket at the gate in your name."

There was a fluttery static on the line. Solar disturbances. A stray voice speaking to someone else about leasing a car.

"Hurt how?"

Rochelle was on her feet, staring down at him. Several of the other women had reassembled, the circle forming again. Ready to start throwing each other around with nonviolent ferocity. Paula stood near the exit door, fists on her hips, waiting to purge the room of his masculine presence before going on. Only Rover was looking Thorn's way, and he seemed slightly ashamed.

"How was he hurt?" Thorn said quietly.

"His heart." She paused. He could hear her swallow. "He might not make it."

"Who is this!"

Rochelle moved in front of him, a desolate smile on her face. The woman on the phone was breathing hard. Twice she started to say something, then cut herself off. He heard her draw a deep breath.

"Who is this, goddamn it!"

Bleakly Rochelle reached out a hand for her phone.

"This is Lola," the voice said. "Lola Sampson. Sugar's mom."

Thorn came to his feet. And the line turned to static.

Out in the dark parking lot Rochelle leaned against the passenger door of his VW. Thorn looking past her at the steady flow of cars heading toward Key West. Rover sniffed nearby tires, practiced lifting his leg.

"You're leaving?"

"I've got to, I don't have any choice."

"Why? Because you get a phone call?"

"Sugar's been hurt. It's serious."

"They told me this was going to happen. They warned me."

Thorn stared out at the traffic. All day, all night, a ceaseless parade of rental cars.

"Who warned you?"

"My friends, my parents. Everybody saw it. But I said no. He's finished all that Hardy Boys stuff. He's settled down."

She began to weep, raising a hand to stiff-arm him if he tried to embrace her. She spoke through her tears.

"I should've seen it. The way you live. You were just indulging me, saying what I wanted to hear. Just keeping things smoothed over. That's who you are, isn't it, Thorn? You're going to be a boy the rest of your life. Doesn't matter who you're with, you're going to go off on your adventures whenever you get the urge. Treat me just like you did the wonderful Darcy Richards."

Thorn drew a quick breath, felt his right hand rise from his side. Rochelle glaring at him, her chin jutted out as if she were daring him to strike. His hand dropped.

"Don't talk about Darcy that way."

Rover stood between them now, the headlights entrancing him. Thorn saw a couple of her friends from class waiting by their car across the row from them.

He had to work for the words, his breath deserting him. "I don't have any choice, Rochelle. My friend's in trouble. He's been hurt."

"Of course," she said. "You don't have a choice."

"Rochelle, I'll be back tomorrow, the next day at the most."

"Don't forget, Thorn, I've seen what happens. I know how the story goes. One thing leads to another."

"What're you asking me to do, stay here, ignore my friend?"

"I wouldn't ask you to do that, no."

"Well, what?"

"I'm not asking you anything, Thorn. You have to go. You don't have a choice."

"This is crazy, Rochelle. I don't understand."

"No," she said. "How could you understand?"

"I'm coming back, goddamn it. I'm coming back."

"You can't come back," she said. "You were never here."

His hand twitched again. The traffic poured past on the overseas highway. The puppy sat down by Thorn's foot, leaned lightly against his leg.

"Go on," she said. "Do it. Do what you really want to do."

"I love you, Rochelle. I'm not going to hit you."

"There's different ways to hit, you know."

She stood there a minute more, chin out. Things tearing inside Thorn's chest, like strands of muscles stretched beyond their limit. Breath hurting, a dark flicker inside his eyes.

After a long moment Rochelle swung around and marched away toward her friends. Rover jerked his head and watched her go. Then he stared up at Thorn, waiting for a command.

Rochelle's friends huddled around her. A couple of them glanced in his direction as they comforted her. For months now he'd played the rapist with these women, let them hurl him across the wrestling mat. Performed his role even though it made him feel unclean, gave him an occasional nightmare.

Week after week as he attacked them, they exposed themselves, the murderous dread and fury in their eyes. The same look Rochelle had given him just now.

Acting out the rapist's part, watching their eyes harden, Thorn had come to know the savagery they expected from his race.

And finally in the last few sessions, to his horror, some Pavlovian dribble of hormone had entered his bloodstream and called up his own lurking rage. He'd felt his throat tighten as he grabbed their arms, felt some hot tangle of passions rise unbidden inside him as he threw his body at these women. Felt the ugly growl of the animal inside.

Perhaps Paula Parkins was right. Maybe Thorn was doomed to be a sexual simpleton forever. Driven by a need to test his virility. A man who could never be domesticated by lace curtains or lavish meals. His sexual wiring was faulty. Doomed to be attracted by nothing more consequential than a woman's slope of belly and swish of hair, her childbearing advantages. Driven forward by some grim and shallow need to replicate himself, pour his seed into the most fertile ground available. Unable to anchor to any enduring bond. Adrift in a sea of biologic impulse. No matter who lay beside him at the moment, no matter what promises he made to her, a part of him would always be listening for the next bugle call.

As he peered through the parking lot at Rochelle and her friends, Rover sniffed his sweaty ankle, gave it a tentative lick. Thorn looked down at the dog. Rover was wagging his tail as he cleaned the salt from Thorn's ankle. A good dog. Damn good dog.

Thorn stepped away from Rover, opened the door to the VW, dropped inside. He nagged the car to life, slammed the door, backed out of his space. Rochelle didn't look his way.

Heading across the lot, Thorn glanced once into the rearview mirror. Rover had joined Rochelle and her friends, licking the sweat off their ankles now.

CHAPTER

14

As Thorn accelerated over Jew-
fish Creek onto the dark stretch toward Miami, the steering wheel
tore loose from his hand and jerked hard left. He wrenched it back
in line but it shimmied wildly in his grip. Must've knocked the
VW's front end seriously out of line when he'd bashed Sugar's
office door.

In five minutes he was breathing hard. His T-shirt soaked,
hands slippery on the ridged plastic wheel. The car was trying
desperately to merge with the opposing headlights.

After some grueling experimentation he found that below
forty, things were bearable. Over forty he had to use both hands
and half his weight to wrestle the car into a wobbling line.

For the next hour he pushed the VW to fifty, then on to sixty,
battled the sultan of swerve to a standstill. By the time he reached
Cutler Ridge, it was after midnight and the muscles in his arms
were failing, sharp spasms were breaking out in his lower back. And
he still had another thirty miles across town to the Port of Miami.

And now there was something else. Traffic. It was Saturday
and even the highways in the outskirts of the city were packed.
He'd read somewhere that on weekend nights, two-thirds of the
drivers in Miami were crocked. He could see why. You'd need a
good buzz to navigate those highways at that time of night. As

many cars were doing twice the speed limit as were doing half of it. Drunks and dopers, geriatrics and teenagers stupefied on puberty, tourists who'd apparently arrived from some part of the world where driving was a branch of warfare.

Car after car came hurtling up to Thorn's bumper, blooming large in the rearview mirror, then, with inches to spare, they bounced out to the passing lane, roared past, then cut in a foot from his front bumper. Some new game being played. Everyone in on the rules but Thorn.

He hung on to the wheel, dragged it to the right. The car steadfastly determined to veer across the median, turn ever tighter counterclockwise circles till it ran out of gas. At least it gave him something to do, something other than thinking about Sugarman, replaying the voice on the phone line, the look in Rochelle's eyes, any of it. He tried to stay focused on the three lanes in front of him, on his hands clenching the wheel. The tick of the next second.

A minute or two later while he was scrambling to remember which combination of highways was the most direct route downtown, his front right tire blew. The tension in the steering wheel abruptly vanished. The flat equalizing things, letting him steer with one hand for the first time in an hour. But a minute later he heard the rim grinding against the asphalt, saw sparks whisking past.

He took the first exit he came to, Kendall Drive. Into the concrete heart of Miami's condo district. Thumped down the ramp and pulled into the first gas station that was open. A minimart, six pumps out front.

He drew up to the side of the grocery, parked in the shadows. He hammered the wheel, cursed the gods, then cocked his arm, aimed his fist at the windshield. A dark-haired woman in the passenger seat of a bright yellow Corvette next to him gazed over, smiling. Knew just how he felt. Thorn lowered his fist. Gloria Estefan doing a raunchy salsa on the Corvette's speakers.

He didn't have a spare tire. Didn't have a nickel in his gym shorts. He dug through the coins in the ashtray. He'd spent his last fifty cents on the toll back in Cutler Ridge. All that remained were seven pennies, a paper clip, and a bonefish fly he'd tied about seven years ago. A Crazy Charlie. Quirky thing that used to knock the bonefish dead. The guy that tied that fly seven years ago had been fifteen pounds lighter, twice as hard. A man who never let blown tires defeat him. Never sat in minimart parking lots, slamming his knuckles into safety glass.

Thorn opened the door, stood up, shook the kinks out of his arms. To his right coming out of the minimart was a heavyset man in a metallic shirt and black trousers. He had a bottle of wine tucked under his arm and was opening a pack of cigarettes. Thorn watched him crumple the cellophane and let the wind take it. He was headed toward the Corvette, whistling to himself as he smacked the pack of cigarettes hard against his palm.

Thorn beat him to the sports car by five steps, ducked inside, slammed the door and locked it, shot the window up. He had the engine started as the guy reached the car. The man hammered his fist against the hood, yelled at Thorn in Spanish, and grabbed hold of his aerial.

Thorn buried the accelerator, smoked the big tires backward, narrowly missed the pumps. The guy shouting at him, slinging his pack of cigarettes as Thorn fishtailed onto Kendall. Not much of an arm.

"Don't worry," Thorn told the woman. "I'm a safe driver."

He ran two red lights, hit eighty before he had to slow for the entrance to the Palmetto Expressway. He glanced over at her.

"Hell," she said. "I thought we'd never get rid of that dork."

Twenty minutes later they were at the Port of Miami and Thorn was convinced he'd done the Corvette guy a favor, kidnapping his date. The woman's name was Sherry. She was a waitress with three kids. Fired from six jobs in the past two months. She'd been drinking white wine from a plastic cup when they left Kendall, and by the time they reached the docks, she was glubbing it direct from the bottle. She guessed she had a drinking problem. But then who could be sure when something was a problem? Look at the French, look at the Russians, all the shit they drank, and those people lived forever. She just liked the taste of the stuff. And it made everything sharper, clearer. Gave her good ideas. It also, by the way, made her want to dance. She knew some great dance places. You could rub against ten people at the same time in one of them. Forget South Beach. That was all transsexuals and trendy wanna-bes. Give her Tobacco Road. Good old-fashioned boogie, tight little dance floor, smoke so thick the visibility was down to a foot. Sherry's kids were home with Mom. Sherry was worried about her daughter. Fourteen and with aspirations to be a stripper. Had knockers out to here, took after her mom in that department. The girl said she might as well get paid for having such giant headlights since everybody stared at her all the time anyway.

"There're cabs over in that far lot," Thorn said as he swung into a space and shut down all those horses.

The M.S. *Eclipse* was brightly lit. The gangway down. A little activity at the bottom of the ramp.

"You going on a cruise, honey, and you're not inviting Sherry? Your old friend, all the things we been through. 'Cause look here, I can be very romantic, you know. Cruises make Sherry incredibly horny."

Thorn told her good night and jogged over to the ramp. He could hear Sherry shrieking at him fifty yards away.

"I'm a friend of Lola's," he told the red-faced security guard at the bottom of the ramp. The guard was chewing thoughtfully on a pink drinking straw. He craned his head and listened to Sherry's curses, then grinned at his cohort, a supple young Latin man with a manicured mustache. The Latin guard grinned back. Then both of them gave Thorn a long look. In his gym shorts and sodden T-shirt. Must've smelled like a mildewed jock strap.

"Well, well, Hector, if it isn't another friend of Lola's."

"Lola has a great many friends," the young Hispanic said.

"Whole fucking world is a friend of Lola's. She's in their living room nine o'clock every morning, yes sir, Lola's their old buddy."

"Look, I spoke to her a couple of hours ago. She called me, told me to get up here."

"She called you, did she? The two of you had a fine chat."

"Yeah, Lola telephoned him to get up here. His friend Lola."

The Greek chorus plays Miami.

"You got any ID, perchance?" The red-faced guard twiddled his straw with his tongue. He had an old-time Boston brogue, like the baaing of an Irish sheep. Another place, another time, Thorn might've invited him out for a pitcher of beer. Swap lies.

"Call Lola, ask her if she wants to talk to Thorn."

"That your name? Thorn?"

"Kind of fucking name is that, Thorn?" The Hispanic kid was trying hard to sing harmony with the cop but was half an octave off. "Not any kind of fucking name I heard before. How about you, McDaniels?"

All three of them turned to watch the Corvette roar out of the lot, clip a parking barricade, and disappear into the night.

"You see," McDaniels said. "Here's how it is, old chum. Everybody and his retarded brother-in-law wants to go along on this cruise. We been getting you dumb fucks all day long. Please, mister. Please, mister, I'll do anything. Down on their knees, willing to perform unnatural acts if that would get them on board. But the problem is, see, you got to purchase a ticket before you go for a boat ride. And the tickets are gone. Sold out weeks ago. So it doesn't matter if you had yourself a holy psychedelic vision telling you Lola Sampson wanted to see you. You don't have a fucking ticket, you can take a fucking hike."

"She said she was leaving a ticket for me."

McDaniels grinned painfully. But the kid's face went soft and he turned and slunk away behind the cop, went over to the bulletin board that was set up beside the gangway. He plucked an envelope off the board and brought it back to the cop.

Sheepishly he held out the envelope to the older man.

McDaniels snapped out a hand, gripped the young man's slender wrist, drew the envelope close, then, still clenching the kid's wrist, the cop reached into his breast pocket, drew out his glasses, and peered at the writing.

"Thorn," McDaniels said. He seemed older now. Aged fifteen years in a few seconds. The pleasant flush of arrogance draining away, leaving behind a tired man who was paid to do grunt work for the monied few. "Thorn," he said again. "All right. Well, I'm still waiting to see some ID."

Thorn told him he didn't have any. Smiling coldly at the man now, pushing it. Telling McDaniels that people like Thorn ordinarily didn't trifle with ID, because most citizens of this planet were perceptive enough to recognize who he was without showing them a little card with his photo on it.

"Is that right? You're a celebrity, that's what you're telling me? I'm supposed to know who you are?"

"Hey, Barney, there's a note on the envelope there. Says don't delay Mr. Thorn. Says send him straightaway on board."

McDaniels cut his gaze to his partner, burned him with that look. There was going to be hell to pay for this, and the supple one was about to start coughing up.

"Well, Mr. Thorn, enjoy your cruise." The cop looked his way, took a healthy chew on his pink straw. "I guess we'll be seeing you at the party."

"Lucky me," Thorn said.

The ship's hospital was two floors below the waterline. Behind the nurse's desk sat a young Asian man reading a paperback romance novel. Lavish script emblazoned over the image of a long-haired man without his shirt, his damsel sinking into quicksand, clutching his thighs for salvation. The Asian man behind the desk was slender and had a small mouth. He glanced up at Thorn and rubbed his eyes. A rough reentry into the shabby world.

He took a peek at Thorn, then lifted off his chair a few inches to get the full view. He let himself down and squinted at Thorn's face.

"You need see doctor or nurse, they no duty now. Come back tomorrow you sick."

"I'm looking for a man named Sugarman."

The Asian man tried to repeat the name but failed.

"Sugarman. Sugarman."

"Oh," he said. "You here for stiff? You from coroner office."

Thorn stared at him, felt his head nod.

"Got two stiff tonight. You take your time getting here. What, you very busy with shooting on street?"

"That's right," Thorn said. "Murders, lots of them. Bodies stacked up."

"America terrible place. Miami bad. Very much murders."

The man stood up, came around the desk. Green surgical pants, a dirty white T-shirt.

Thorn followed him out of the infirmary, down a short hallway to a shiny steel cabinet. The silver box was humming. Thorn had seen them before, portable meat lockers. He knew the sound of the tray sliding out, knew the sterile chemical odor, the dizzy jolt when the bloodless body came into view.

The man swung open the door. Both trays held cadavers, soles facing out.

"Have heart attack on last day of cruise. Too much party."

He rolled out the first tray and held the sheet aside so Thorn could view the naked body of an elderly woman. Thorn shook his head. The man pushed her back and slid out the bottom tray. It was a black man. Six two, slender build. Thorn stared at the corpse's face for a long time before he was certain it was not Sugarman. This man was seventy, seventy-five with a white mustache.

"Neither of these," Thorn said. "Younger. A black man."

"What say name again?"

"Sugarman. Sugarman."

The man worked it in his mouth like a glop of peanut butter.

"Ah," he said. "Slugger man."

"Right," said Thorn. "Slugger man."

He nodded wearily, finally unraveling Thorn's abysmal enunciation.

"Where is he?"

"He upstairs. No room here." The man waved at the locker.

"Where?"

"In spa," he said.

"Where?"

"He go spa," he said. "Spa. No room here, he go spa."

Thorn couldn't locate the elevator, so he climbed the eleven stories to the uppermost deck. The ship was a garish blur around him. Tinsel-flecked mirrors, tacky neon, carpets and walls in feverish shades of fuchsia and iridescent purples as gaudy as the lipstick of hot-tempered whores. There was music oozing from the PA system, some processed gruel with echoes of Mancini.

Thorn was angry by the time he reached the spa. Angry and frazzled and ready to chew flesh. Somewhere in a back room of his consciousness he'd decided that when he finally tracked down

Sugarman's murderer, he would take him back to Key Largo and make it his life's work to torture the son of a bitch, keep him just above the waterline for the rest of his days.

The New Horizon Spa was a few feet away from the railing of a seven-story atrium, a hollow core in the center of the ship that glowed with golden neon. You could perch at the railing on any of seven floors, spy on your fellow passengers above, below, across from you. On the other side of the canyon, a glass elevator rode up its tracks, empty.

There was no one at the front desk of the spa. Thorn hammered the bell, called out several hellos but nobody answered. He went behind the desk and pushed through a mirrored door into what appeared to be the spa's business office. The room was lit but unoccupied.

He went back outside and headed down the darkened hallway toward the men's locker room. Showers, dressing rooms, saunas. A coed weight room at the end of the hall. He looked in every room and found no one. Then swung open a door marked MASSAGE. Four rooms in a row down a short hallway. Thorn threw the first door open, switched on the light. A padded massage table, a small desk with oils and fluids. A mirror and a clothes rack. No one there.

In the third massage room, he flipped on the light, drew in a breath, and stepped back into the hallway. Sugarman's body lay on the massage table. He was wrapped from his feet to his chin in silver foil. His face gray, eyes shut tight.

CHAPTER
15

"Nice view," Butler said.

Monica stepped into the cabin, Butler across the room, holding the heavy curtains aside so she could admire the Miami skyline bristling with light.

After they returned from Baltimore, Butler changed clothes, putting on white slacks, a blue Hawaiian shirt, and a Panama with a jazzy colored band. Ready to reggae. Their passports said they were married. Mr. and Mrs. Oliver Jackson. Canadian. She'd asked him where the hell he'd gotten the head shot of her, and he'd smiled mischievously and refused to answer. Clearly a photo taken while she was at Sugarloaf. Then she remembered an old couple with a camera a couple months back, their weird request to take her picture. It spooked her, every detail of his scheme so carefully worked out. On the other hand, it gave her some perverse comfort. They were going to pull this off, not get caught.

"Will there be anything else, sir?"

The Filipino valet stood in the doorway. It was almost one in the morning. They'd had a difficult time finding anyone to help them with their bags. Butler with a heavy Nike athletic duffel, four suitcases. Monica carrying the five shopping bags filled with new clothes. The two sullen cops at the gangway had tried to ignore them until Butler got nasty, showed them his first-class tickets, told the cops he was a Hollywood director, Monica the star of his latest hit. The younger cop believed he recognized her, wound up asking for an autograph. Monica batting her eyes, signed an index card. Finally the older one motivated himself to locate a valet, call him down. Chop, chop, the red-faced man said into the phone. Get down here chop, chop.

The Filipino handed Monica the door keys.

Butler Jack didn't turn from the window, saying "Aren't you going to show us the room, point out all the amenities? I believe that's customary."

Monica told the valet they were fine, he could be on his way. She found a five in her new purse and with a final darting look at Butler Jack, the valet shut the door.

"Look at that," Butler said. "Squandering all that money on electric lights when there's a billion people on this planet who'd kill for a pot of rice. Five percent of the earth's population gobbling up seventy-five percent of its resources."

Monica set down the shopping bags and surveyed the room. Gray tile on the floor, the curtains and bed done in a matching flowered print of rich greens and golds. The overstuffed blue tweed sofa was stacked with burgundy pillows. Walnut covered three walls and trimmed the sliding glass doors that led out to a spacious balcony. In the bathroom white marble topped the teak vanity. Three vases of fresh gladioluses were stationed around the room.

"Know how much all this luxury is setting us back?"

"I don't care," she said. "We're here."

"Six thousand dollars apiece. Twelve thousand total for a measly six days at sea. Do you know how many Lucys could eat for a year on twelve thousand dollars?" He turned from the window and stared at her.

"I still haven't heard the plan, Butler. I want to know what the hell we're doing before we get any farther along."

"Tomorrow," he said. "Don't worry, it's all written down. My list. I'll go over it with you before things get hot and heavy."

A smile reshaped his face. "It's romantic, isn't it. Being on a ship."

"We're still tied up at the dock. It doesn't start being romantic until we're under way. Or so I've heard."

She sat down on the edge of the bed and watched Butler's lips sneak into another smile.

"Know how Florida got its name?"

"Spare me, Butler."

"Ponce de León discovered the peninsula in 1513 around Easter time, the time of year when Spanish churches are filled with flowers. *Pascua florida* means the flowering season, or Easter. So there you go again, God, religion. Florida was named for the season of rebirth. Death and resurrection. A holy state, a state of second chances. All those retirees getting their second chance. Just like you and me. We're getting ours too."

Talking to Butler Jack was like trying to have a conversation with a used car salesman. It didn't matter what topic you started with, he'd find a way to circle back to the sales pitch.

"It's incredible, when you think about it. That we're here like this, together again after all these years, overcoming so much. Your mother, my mother, interfering like they did the first time. They didn't understand. But look at us now."

He did a little bounce and smiled at her.

Holding her eyes for several moments, another mood seemed to seep into him. The smile drifting away, Butler steepling his hands at his chest. His eyes flickering.

"I waited for you," he said quietly. Coming across the room to sit beside her on the edge of the bed. "I waited."

Monica was silent. Butler snuck a hand onto her thigh. She looked down at it.

"And you?"

"I'm here," she said, "aren't I?"

"But you *waited* for me, didn't you?"

"Waited."

"You said you would. Remember? You wrote it down. I still have the letter. It's in my bag. 'I will wait for you always, forever, till the end of time.'"

Monica swallowed. She needed a beer. Something stronger. Two or three. A fleeting memory of her nights at Sugarloaf, the fish sandwiches, the mindless routine.

"Did you, Monica? Did you wait like you said?" A rising strain in his voice. Butler stood, stepped away from her. Monica looking up at him.

"You mean sex? Am I virgin? Is that what you're asking?"

"I waited for you," Butler said. "I gave you my pledge, and I kept it."

"I'm tired, Butler. I need to sleep."

"Did you? Yes or no."

Staring at him, Monica tried to hold her face in a neutral mask. She managed it for a while, but then she felt it slip, a tic in her lips that must have revealed it all. She saw it register in Butler Jack's eyes, saw the sparkle crumple, a shadowy fog rise.

"It was him, wasn't it? That cop."

"Cop?"

"You know who I mean. David Cruz."

She stood up, felt the air burn her throat. "What the hell do you know about David?"

"It was him, wasn't it? That bastard spoiled you. He took it from you. Your innocence."

"I don't know who the fuck you think you are, but I've had enough of this shit. Is that clear? You and I, we don't have a relationship. We were kids. We were fantasizing. Playing a game. That's all that was. If you thought it was more . . . well, I'm sorry for you. But anything I said then, any promises I might have made, they were childish babble. Do you understand me? We were twelve years old. Children. You'd have to be crazy to hold on to something like that. Believe it meant anything."

"Is that what you think? I'm insane? A psychopath?"

"Look, I came along with you. I'm here. But I'm not some virginal twelve-year-old. Is that clear?"

"You said you'd wait. You wrote the words."

"Well, I didn't wait, goddamn it. I didn't wait."

Monica suffered his fierce glare as long as she could, then gave him a firm good-night and walked to the bathroom. Shut the door and locked it. Five minutes, ten, she stood before the mirror. Hearing nothing out in the cabin.

Staring at herself, the goddamn eyes, the perfect fucking nose, the flawless skin. That face that had inspired Butler Jack, pushed him over some impossible edge. That face, that fucking face. Look on her and die. Look on her and grow stupid, infantile. Medusa. A Gorgon, snakes for hair.

When she opened the door, Butler was gone. She stepped into the cabin, went directly to her purse. Grabbed it up. To hell with this. She would get off this ship right now, get far away and regroup. Hide. Start over. She'd been crazy to go along with him. Crazy to get involved.

But she'd been so disoriented. Irma Slater evaporated, a vacuum left behind. And the photographs, those starving kids, his campaign against Morton Sampson had stirred her, given her a wicked thrill. The idea of hurting her father. Striking back. A little justice for her mother's sake. But that seemed like temporary insanity now. Sheer craziness.

She searched the room for anything she might take along, one of her new outfits. But there was nothing she wanted. She hurried to the door, wrenched the handle. Yanked. Yanked again. But he'd done something to the lock. The door was frozen.

David Cruz was doing push-ups. It was how he handled stress. Lately he'd been doing a lot of them, up over a hundred at a time. Dipping to his chest each time, head tilted up, marine style. Naked, of course, that was the best way. Felt sexy, his member flopping against the rug each time. Like fucking, only more pure, nothing but that piston grind, up and down, up and down, so later, during sex, when he couldn't count, when he couldn't do anything but feel the feel, he could go for an hour, up and down, a pile driver, one of them called him, a derrick, said another. Up and down.

He was proud of his body. Proud that everything was still as firm as a teenager. Firmer than most. Look around him, he could find guys his age, lots of them with the sagging bellies and flabby muscles of old men. Not David Cruz. Something drove him. The sexiness factor was one thing of course but there was something else. Something he didn't like to consider. But it was true. The class factor. He had a blue-collar body. Coal miner, day laborer. Those guys weren't hard by choice. It was their job, their grind.

Even though David Cruz had escaped that world, riding high as head of security for a major corporation, making over a hundred thousand a year, he was still a blue-collar guy. A day laborer by his codes. Did the push-ups so he wouldn't lose touch, wouldn't turn away from his roots. Seventy-five, eighty, ninety, a hundred push-ups. Going over a hundred, seeing how high he could reach, feeling the joy of it tonight, the compulsion to break higher, the stress of his job, this goddamn thief who was targeting one of his ships, making David look bad, forcing Morton to bring in an outsider, David feeling threatened, feeling the pressure in his gut, the knotting. A hundred and twenty, up and up, breaking every record he'd ever set. Going to break two hundred tonight. He had enough stress lately for that. Enough stress to break a thousand. Smacking his chest to the rug, feeling his member swing, feeling it firm up slightly.

Sometimes push-ups were better than sex. Cleaner, neater, took him higher most of the time. Better than sex with everyone but her. The one whose name he would not say. The one he'd failed, the one he couldn't protect. Sex with her had been something different. Something interplanetary. Long and complicated. Beautiful and hard and sweaty. Athletic and soft. Everything. The one he couldn't name taking everything he had to offer, showing him things she knew, then the two of them stumbling into new territory, discovering a few things neither of them had suspected. Weird. Sex with her was better than push-ups, better than going over two hundred. Better than a hundred thousand dollars a year. Better than his leased Lexus, better than any single thing or group of things he'd ever known, imagined, dreamed of, hoped for.

He had lost count, in the two hundreds somewhere, moving up and down, a pile driver, a maniac, a madman, an incredible machine locked in the On position. When someone hammered on his door.

Butler Jack was plummeting in a crashing plane. Strapped in, no escape. The pressure immense, skull-cracking pressure. The scream of air, the shriek of blood trying to move through his shrunken veins, a terrible darkness rising up all round him like chemical smoke, the eerie sway of the world, gravity sucking him down, the earth's core magnetized, G-force tripled as Butler Jack sliced through the air, down and down.

He had finally summoned the nerve to ask her the question. To verify that she was indeed still his soulmate. The uranium. So sure of the answer, so certain.

But she hadn't waited. She'd broken her promise, the words on paper, her handwriting. "Forever, till the end of time." Those were her words. On paper. And Butler Jack had glowed when he read them, glowed ever after. The glow of her inside him lighting his way. Moving him through the shadowy world. For years. Through the hard years. Always her smile, the sprinkle of golden hairs on her arm, the heat of her body drawing him forward. Giving him the power, the wattage. Always her. Now as he walked down the narrow hallway, the glow was sputtering, shadows rising all around him, closing in on all sides. And the pressure, the incredible plummeting pressure.

This man. This man had waylaid her. Laid himself in her way. Laid between her legs. This man, this fucking man who Butler Jack knew, the security chief, Morton Sampson's top cop. Laid in her way. Took her, spoiled her, dirtied her with his own greedy needs.

He knew this man, David Cruz. Knew him on sight from his years on board the M.S. *Comet*. Knew he was inferior. A man of the body. A man who walked and sat and talked with such physical certainty. Butler Jack had known people like him all his life. They were common. The physical ones. The ones who trained their bodies to do what their minds could not. The ones who lifted and carried and packed and loaded. The ones who feasted on gravity, defying it, growing strong to deny its hold on them. He hated these people and these people hated him. Hated him on sight. They recognized Butler Jack. He was strong but he did not earn it. Did not lift weights or do the machines, any of it. He was strong because his father and mother were strong. He was strong because he could think strong. Because he could outmaneuver, outfox, outcerebrate.

David Cruz had stained her. Soiled her. He had befouled her. Forced her to break her hallowed vow to Butler Jack, forced her to lie, to betray her own words. But what irony it was. What wonderful dark twisted fortune that David Cruz should turn out to be his mortal adversary. How perfect it was that this man who was one of those being paid to track down Butler Jack would find him now. Would find him at his door.

Cruz never used the security peephole. It was a matter of pride, a belief that he could handle whatever gremlin or monster stood on the other side. He had his training, his years on the street. A black belt in alley warfare. Box or wrestle, gouge or pull hair, whatever it required. David Cruz was a man of simple pride. His hand-to-hand skills were good enough, he could take on anyone, be fairly sure he'd have a better than even chance of winning. There were always those men out there, faster, trained in some evil art from the Orient, they might be able to get the better of him. But there weren't many of those. And even with them, David Cruz would be willing to take the gamble. Good skills versus evil art. He'd always wager on the good.

When the knock came, he grabbed a pair of boxer shorts, stepped into them as he moved to the door and drew it open.

The blond man who stood before him in white slacks and flowered shirt had his left hand upraised. In it he held a black-handled dagger by the tip of the blade like a crucifix, holding it lightly as if he meant to flick it into David's chest.

Cruz took a half step back. A strategic retreat. Fighting room. Dodging distance.

The man stepped into the room. His face slack. Mouth dead. Only in his eyes was there any suggestion of what the fireworks inside his head might look like. One summer in Spain David Cruz had watched the Pamplona bulls. Watched them bleeding from the picadors, their heavy neck muscles slashed, their eyes taking on the glazed ferocity he saw before him now. Knowing they were doomed, only a matter of moments before they were gone, but with some final savage need to sink their horns in flesh, take a few lives with them. Dangerous beasts.

David kept his eyes hovering on the man's chest. An opponent's eyes could trick you, the legs as well. A feint, a crafty head fake could put you off balance, enough of an opening to sink the blade. But if you watched their chests, kept your eyes locked there, the knife in your peripheral vision, you could decode their real movement, anticipate the strike.

"You bastard. You filthy fucking bastard."

David didn't reply. He circled clockwise, watching the chest. The knife still held upright like a priest moving down the aisle at mass.

"Innocence," the man said, his voice roughened with rage. "You wouldn't know, you ignorant asshole, but it's Middle English, from Old French, and before that Latin. From the verb *nocere,* which means to harm. With the prefix *in* meaning *not*. Not to harm. To keep innocent. White and virginal. But you harmed her, David Cruz, you lay with her. You destroyed the innocence."

"Lay with who?"

"You know who. Monica. Monica is who."

They tracked around the tight oblong between Cruz's bed and his dresser. David's hands up and open, ready to fend off, to wrestle, punch, whatever lay open to him.

"Monica Sampson?"

"You know damn well who I mean."

"You're the one who kidnapped her? You're him?"

David wanted badly to look at his face, wanted to shift his eyes from the man's chest, but he disciplined himself, checked the impulse. Heart fired up now, more at the mention of her name than at the knife.

"What did you do with her? Where is she?"

"What did I do with her?" The blond man cackled. "You're the one who did her. It was you, David Cruz. You, you worthless wretched bastard."

David thought he saw the knife move. A whir of silver light. He dodged to his right. But when he looked again the blond man was still there, the knife in his hand, same position. Smiling now. The upper hand. David spooked, not sure what he'd seen. Not sure where to look now. The after-image of the silver light still burning in his eyes. But it was nowhere.

It wasn't his method to go on the attack. He was a counter-puncher by nature. But her name coming from this man's lips, the silver light, brought him up to the balls of his feet. He felt himself leaning forward, off-balance, a surge of anger richening the mix-ture in his lungs.

David broke the circle, stepped back, held his ground. Stared into the man's eyes briefly. Saw the same bleak and depraved look as before. Moved his eyes back to the chest, saw the knife holding steady as the man raised his right hand, extended it out to his side as far as he could reach, as if he meant to give David a roundhouse slap. And the silver light came again, off to the right, out of his peripheral vision. David hesitated briefly, then swung his head, squinted at it. An inch of current, its crackling buzz. Not under-standing what the hell he was looking at.

And in that instant he felt the first swipe of the blade, the warm wetness on his bare chest. Felt the second slash across his cheek and neck, a numbing trail, and the third clipping his wrist as David cranked up an arm to defend. A fourth slash down his ribs, the man ducking under his arms somehow, quicker than he looked.

He chopped at the blond man's neck but the blow glanced off his collarbone. He lashed out two quick fists, neither of which connected, as the man bent and bobbed, eluded the next blow and the one after that. David felt the weakness growing in his legs. The slick of blood on his chest and arms. A shallow trench opened from his throat to his bellybutton. He knew that without looking. Knew he was dead unless he ended this quickly, could hold his wound closed, get to the infirmary.

Not sure where to look anymore. The knife jiggling in the man's left hand, the buzz of current in his right. David backing away, feeling the bed behind him. The blond man closing in.

It was a story he'd heard somewhere. A street cop's advice to every homeowner. You find a burglar in your house. You've got a gun in your hand, you don't know if the burglar's armed or not. What do you do? You ask the burglar a question. Any question, how is your mother doing? The premise being that people always freeze when asked a question but rarely do when told to freeze. How is your mother doing? The burglar freezes, and you shoot the motherfucker. Keep on shooting till you're empty.

Only difference, David Cruz had no pistol.

"How is your mother doing?" he said, a croak in his voice.

The blond man stiffened, held. And David Cruz ducked and lunged, smashed his shoulder into the man's solar plexus, heard him retch. Clenched an arm around the man's waist, drove him backward, slamming him against the wall. Legs pumping, hands reaching up and finding a grip on both the man's wrists. Spread-eagled his arms, pinning him to the wall.

The man wriggled but wasn't strong enough to break this hold. And David Cruz drove a knee into the man's crotch. Drove another one and another one. The man screaming but unable to move. Another knee and another. The blood from David's wounds slathered everywhere, making his grip slippery. Giving the guy wiggle room with his right hand, the electrified one.

David kneed him again and again. The screams. The man weeping now. Face twisted.

The man wrenched that right wrist, strained it. The ugly crackling of the current again. And David Cruz felt the cold touch of voltage against his arm. His body tossed sideways. Falling to the floor. On his back. Legs spread. He was immobilized but dimly awake. Knowing what was coming. Knowing it from somewhere a great distance away, a promontory, a place like the one David Cruz had climbed at boy scout camp many many years ago. North Carolina. Seven mountain ranges. Count them. See thirty miles away. That's where he was at the end, lying on the floor of his cabin, but at the same time returning briefly to North Carolina, becoming again that boy, a boy looking out at David Cruz on the floor of his cabin on the M.S. *Eclipse.* The young David Cruz learning to be good, learning to be true and honest and fair, but even then, even as a boy he had known somehow that violence was coming for him, coming from a long inevitable distance away, somehow always known, as he knew now, watching through the dim mist as a man kicked at the crotch of his adult body, kicked at it and kicked at it. David Cruz, the boy, seemed to be watching all of this as it unfolded, watching from some safe distance away. Seeing the bad man kneel above David's adult body and begin to work on his flesh with a sharp blade.

CHAPTER

16

Thorn stood beside the body, a pale light angling in from the hallway. He reached out and touched a fingertip to Sugar's forehead. Clammy.

"Sugar."

Fighting off the tremble in his hand, Thorn peeled back the silver blanket to feel for a pulse. And jerked his hand away.

Sugar's bare flesh was coated with some kind of slime that gave off an aroma as sickly as overcooked broccoli. Thorn stepped back from the chrome massage table. A clot was forming in his throat.

He leaned forward, dabbed a finger against Sugar's nearly hairless chest, scooped up a glop of slime. Turning to the wedge of light from the hallway, he held up his finger. The stuff was green, strands of it dangling like shredded spinach.

"Seaweed," croaked the voice behind him.

Thorn staggered into a table, knocked over a bottle of oil, which crashed on the floor and broke. When he swung back to the massage table, Sugarman was up on one elbow, tucking the silver blanket back around his body. Face puffy and strained.

"Boy, was I out." His voice frail, Sugar taking shallow breaths. "Dreamed I was in that canoe. Stroking, stroking. Getting nowhere. Paddling like a maniac, the thing stuck dead in the mud. Terrible goddamn dream."

He lay back against the table. Took several shallow breaths.

"Jesus, you're alive."

"Maybe. I'm not sure."

"What the fuck happened to you?"

Sugar closed his eyes, worked on getting his breath.

"And what the hell is that stuff you're covered in!"

"Seaweed. A purgative."

"Man, oh, man. You scared the everloving shit out of me."

Feebly Sugar tucked the blanket into place. "What they do, they microwave the seaweed, get it piping hot, a lady slathers it all over, wraps you in this thermal blanket, turns out the light, leaves you to cook for an hour, sweat like a son of a bitch. It's to get rid of the toxins. I must've been full of them. Must've had twenty pounds of toxins floating around inside me."

"You sound like death on the half shell."

"At least I can talk."

"Well, you sound terrible."

"You come all this way to give me shit?"

Thorn sat down on the swivel stool beside the table. "Someone called, said you'd been hurt. You might not make it."

"I was probably fibrillating at the time," he said. "But they de-fibbed me. Hit me with those paddles, you know."

"You had a heart attack?"

"Kind of."

"Talk to me, Sugar."

He opened his eyes, stared up into the half-light, sighed, eyes drifting closed. Lying there sweating inside his foil blanket. With his eyes shut, he told Thorn the story, breath coming hard. Stopping every sentence, gathering himself, going on.

A few hours ago, headed to his cabin, he'd seen a guy duck in a room. It looked weird, so he followed. Guy got around behind him somehow. Same young guy they ran into on the docks in the Glades. He zapped Sugar with that thing on his fingers. After he was knocked out, the guy apparently rearranged him so one hand touched the bulkhead. To ground him. Then he put his current against Sugar's right nipple, making the voltage run from his right nipple across his chest to his left hand.

"Through your heart."

"Exactly. Guy was trying to rattle my pulse out of sync. And he succeeded, but somebody walked by, started screaming. Guy ran. They got a nurse down there. She de-fibbed me. Did some CPR and brought me back. Though my ribs, man, it feels like Muhammad Ali's been using me for a heavy bag."

"This fuckhead tried to electrocute you, you're lying there joking about it?"

"I'm too weak to get mad. My heart's not up to it."

"Jesus. I walked in here, I thought you were dead."

"Well, I believe I may have paid a brief visit to the great beyond. And let me tell you, place isn't all it's cracked up to be. Organ music is for shit."

"Man, oh, man."

"Nurse told me a fibrillating heart looks like a bunch of squirming worms. Muscles all separated into strands, jumping and jiving all out of sync."

Thorn felt his own heart quiver.

"Know what I found out? Fiesta's policy for heart attacks?" His eyes were open now, staring at Thorn.

"You're working yourself up, Sugar. You should just relax."

"Normal procedure on cruise ships, the med staff does what they call a scoop and run. They get the body back to the infirmary quick as possible so none of the paying customers see it and get upset."

Thorn told him again to calm down.

Sugarman saying, "But that's not how you're supposed to treat a heart attack. The golden minutes, all that shit. You should put the paddles on right away, crank up the joules. Seven, eight minutes, no oxygen in the brain, after that you got brain damage. But no, Fiesta can't spoil the party, so they scoop and run. Spend the golden moments hustling the body back to the hospital. Got to keep the good times rolling. Can you believe that shit? Public relations versus medicine. PR wins. I got to talk to somebody about that."

Sugar took several long breaths.

"Guess I was lucky the ship was in port, all the passengers off. They treated me right where I was, got me de-fibbed. After I stabilized, they took me to the infirmary, put me on an IV, the whole thing. Couple hours later my blood pressure is back, everything fine, so I snuck out, came up here. Felt so goddamn bloated from the IV, decided to indulge myself. Though I gotta say, I'm still feeling puny. Room's moving around a little."

"Puny! Sugar, you had a fucking heart attack. You should be putting fluids in, not taking them out."

"Yeah, yeah. But, man, I was so puffy I couldn't make a fist. Felt like I was stuck inside the skin of a dwarf."

"You idiot."

"Dizzy as shit too. First-class headache. But all in all, not bad considering I was probably dead for half a minute."

Thorn stood up, lay his hand on Sugarman's shoulder.

"Listen, Sugar. This person who called me . . ."

"Yeah."

Thorn stepped back, waved the thought away. "Hell, it was probably a lie. Somebody's idea of a stupid fucking joke."

"Let me guess," Sugar said. Lying very still, mummified in that aluminum. "Lola Sampson."

"How the hell . . . ?"

"She's the one found me. Walking by in the hallway with one of her Hollywood friends. Lola giving the tour of the lower decks. The woman stopped, saw what was happening, and screamed. Lola ran back but by then the guy was loping off down the hall."

Sugarman eased up, blinked three times, gathering his wits. Gave Thorn a woozy half smile. "Time to hose off this goop. I must've sweated out every damn toxin I ever absorbed in my complete and total life."

Sugarman boosted himself to a sitting position, caught his breath then edged off the table, hugging the silver blanket around him. He shuffled toward the door, a delicate old man.

"The woman on the phone," said Thorn, "the one who said her name was Lola, she also claimed she was your mother."

Sugarman halted.

"That was her name wasn't it, your mother? Lola?"

"That was her name, yeah. Lola Marie Sugarman."

Thorn came over to him.

Sugarman swiveled, looked into his eyes. Smiled quietly.

"I've known it for years," Sugar said. "Where she was, what she was doing, all of it."

He turned and padded out the door. He went down the short hallway with Thorn dogging him into the shower room. Sugarman peeled off the shiny blanket and stepped out of a pair of paper diapers. He stood there for a moment, the slime oozing off him.

"Ten, twelve years back, when I was still on the force, I got a wild hair and ran her name on the computer. She'd dropped Sugarman and was using her maiden name, but with a little work I found her. A secretary for Fiesta Cruise Lines. Sampson's personal secretary. Worked her way up from clerical assistant."

He stepped over to the shower.

"And your father? You run his name too?"

"Didn't bother. Could care less."

"So you've talked to her, worked it all out?"

"No," he said. "I never been a big believer in wallowing in the past."

"You traced her, spent time looking for her. What for? To practice your police skills?"

"I wanted to see what I could find out. When I learned what I did, I dropped it. She had a decent life. Everything was fine for her. I didn't need to rush in, upset everything."

"You didn't even want to hear her story, why she ran off?"

"She was barely twenty years old at the time, for christ sakes, her husband leaves her, she's got this screaming kid, no job. How's her story going to be any different from the other ten thousand versions of what I heard already?"

"How come you never told me any of this?"

"I didn't tell anybody."

"That's who I am? Anybody."

"Hey, buddy, you're a hell of a lot more than anybody. You're my boon companion. But it wasn't something I needed to talk about. It was information, pure and simple. She's alive. She was working for this guy in Miami. Big deal. I'm glad she's doing okay."

"More than okay."

"Yeah, I guess."

"So that's your mysterious benefactor? Person who got you the job with Fiesta."

"Right."

"Why would she do that, get you hired? She's gotta know it's you, her son."

"She must have her reasons."

"And why would she tell me who she was?"

"I don't know. That comes as a surprise."

Thorn shook his head. "Man, I don't believe you. Your own mother. Never said anything."

Sugarman turned on one of the showers, kept a hand in the spray till it warmed, then stepped into it and began to rinse. Thorn turned around, looked at himself in the mirror, straightened a few hairs, then mussed them up again. Turned back around.

"I feel like a pervert standing here watching you shower."

"You look like a pervert. Those gym shorts, the T-shirt."

"It was what I had on when I got the call."

Sugarman stepped out of the shower, went over to the towel bin and pulled out a fresh one, started patting himself down.

"I don't think you've been honest with me, Sugar."

Sugarman sawed the towel across his back. "Yeah? How's that?"

Sugar opened a locker, took out a pair of khaki camp shorts, a blue tennis shirt, and deck shoes. Thorn watching him. Feeling the throb in his arms from fighting that steering wheel for over an hour.

"You've been lying to me, right from the get-go."

"I have?"

"That bullshit about Rochelle. Insulting her. Pushing me away like that."

"That wasn't bullshit. She's not the right woman for you."

"Look, Sugar, I was in your office. I dug around, trying to find out where the hell you were, I came across a photograph."

Sugar sat down on one of the benches, rolled his head like he was working out the neck kinks. Watching Thorn as he did it.

"This photo," Thorn said. "It was a shot of Lola sitting on a porch somewhere. You know the one I'm talking about?"

He stopped rolling his head, held Thorn's eyes.

"The boy sitting with her, one she had her arm around, he looked familiar to me."

"How'd you do that, get into my office?"

Thorn said, "This boy looked a lot like our friend on the docks a couple weeks ago, Freddy Megawatt. A younger version. Guy that tried to kill you. Tried to kill you twice now."

Sugarman disengaged from Thorn's gaze.

"Freddie Megawatt," Thorn said. "This guy is your brother, isn't he?"

The air leaked out of Sugarman. He leaned forward, rested his elbows on his knees.

"No," he said.

"You're lying. He's your fucking brother."

Sugar tipped his head up, gave Thorn a vague nod. "Half brother. Same mother, different father."

Sugar straightened, holding himself erect, the slightest of wobbles.

"That day I was studying the casino videos of the guy playing the slots, even wearing a disguise, his head down like that, it hit me. I ran that damn tape over and over. Just that quick glimpse of the guy's profile. But I thought I recognized him."

"And you recognized him again that day out on the docks."

Sugar gave another small nod.

"And you were gonna let that fucking kid roll you over the side, feed you to the alligators."

"I was fighting him," he said. "I wasn't giving in."

"Bullshit."

"Look, I'm tired, Thorn. I need to lie down."

"Is that true, Sugar? Because the kid's your little brother, you couldn't lift a hand? You've been hired to capture this fucker, but instead you've decided you're going to let him take you down? You're gonna throw the fight?"

Sugar rose and took a minute or two to pull his clothes on, step into his deck shoes. He walked over to the bank of mirrors, rubbed his hair dry with the towel, then scrunched it for a minute, achieving absolutely no result Thorn could see.

He looked at Thorn in the mirror. Coughed, wiped at the corner of his mouth. "Go on home, Thorn. You did your good deed, you answered the call. Now you're free to leave."

"Fuck that. I'm not going anywhere till I know what the hell's going on in your head."

Sugar rubbed his cheek with the back of his hand. He held himself still as if waiting for his heart to catch up to the moment.

"Come on," he said. "I need some fresh air."

Thorn followed him out of the spa, through a hatch that led to the railing of the Sports Deck. Facing north into the thick city lights. A breeze lifting Thorn's hair, rearranging it. A couple of small fishing boats heading out the long channel toward the absolute darkness of the sea. Sugarman leaned heavily against the rail, drinking in the air. Head bowed.

"I've been an asshole," Sugar said. "The horseshit I said about Rochelle. I'm sorry. But that day on the docks, when he came out of nowhere like that . . . After you whipped him, I saw that look on his face when he said he'd see us later, both of us. It hit me. The shit I'm in, it's my personal self-created shit. All my doing. I don't have any right dragging you into the line of fire. You got a good thing going, your life is healing up. Rochelle's fine. It was never Rochelle. I'm sorry."

Thorn was silent.

"His name is Butler Jack. He uses Lola's maiden name. Jack. He's twenty-three years old. Just a kid. Young enough, he could be my own son. I mean, yeah, he's fucked up. He's dangerous. But he's my goddamn flesh and blood. What the fuck am I supposed to do?"

"He tried to kill you, Sugar."

"I know that."

"He's tried twice."

Sugar shook his head solemnly. "I know it's stupid, Thorn. It's crazy. I should just treat this kid like any other crazed fuck comes dancing down the boardwalk with a weapon in his hand. I don't know what it is. Something cramps up in me. I looked him in the eye, and all of a sudden I get jelly in my gut, I'm standing there, my dick is waving in the wind, arms wide open. Go on, stick your sword in my belly. Open me up. I don't know what it is."

"You want to die? You want this kid to do the honors?"

"I'm telling you, I don't know what it is. I keep thinking about it, what's going on with me. I think, well shit, maybe Butler Jack is the guy I would've been if Lola had stuck around and raised me. That's me I'm looking at. A version of me."

"What bullshit."

"Yeah," Sugarman said. "I say it out loud, it sounds crazy. But that's what happens. I cramp up."

"You need to see a goddamn shrink. And quick."

Sleek clouds knifed past the heavy moon. There were party sounds coming from somewhere a deck or two below. The tinkle of glasses, quiet laughter. Jaunty big band music.

"So this cruise, they going to cancel it now? Search the ship and root out this kid."

"No," Sugar said. "Going ahead as planned. Two thousand people coming aboard. Some tonight, the rest tomorrow, sailing for six days. Sampson won't hear of shutting it down. Show must go on."

"Even knowing there's a killer roaming around."

"Even knowing that."

Thorn watched the city lights shivering in colorful streaks across the dark water. A lone gull sailing low, heading out to sea.

"I'm going to need some clothes," he said.

"What?"

"I saw a boutique on my way up to the spa. Just as long as they got something besides Banlon and Sansabelt slacks."

"Forget it, Thorn. This isn't your fight."

"If it's yours, Sugar, it's mine."

For a moment more Sugarman continued to stare out at the lights. He blinked. Blinked again.

Then he raised his left arm and settled it over Thorn's shoulder. They stood like that for a moment or two. Then Thorn turned to face him, opened his arms, and stepped into the embrace.

CHAPTER
17

Monica slid open the glass door and stepped onto the balcony. It was a ten-story plunge to the dock. No one walking around down there anymore. The two cops had called it a night, the gangway blocked off. She leaned forward as far as she could but saw no lights in the adjacent cabins. She called out but her voice was torn to pieces by the steady offshore breeze.

She came back inside, did a thorough tour of the room. The phone cord was snipped. She found a few electrician's tools in Butler's bag, but nothing she might use to pry the door or pick the lock. The only thing close to a weapon was in the minibar, a corkscrew inside a bamboo holder. She opened it up, gripped the bamboo in her fist, lining up the spiral point so it stuck out between her middle fingers. It might defend her against a sleepwalker, but she doubted it would slow down Butler Jack. She pitched it back on the shelf and went into the john.

Nothing in the medicine chest, nothing beneath the sink. Just two drinking glasses on an inset shelf. She picked up one of them. Raised it above the sink and let it drop. The longest shard was two inches long. Worse than the corkscrew.

She went back to the cabin, dragged the desk chair over to the door, and cocked it against the knob. One good shove would probably break it in half, but hell, what did she have? She circled the cabin again, but everything she touched was bolted down. She stared at the bed, considered the king-size mattress. With some struggle she might be able to lean it and the box springs against the door. She lifted an edge, then let it fall.

Maybe she was overreacting. Butler had stalked off in a rage. He'd jiggered the lock, trapped her there. But that didn't necessarily mean she was in danger. By the time he returned, the storm might have churned itself out. She could apologize. Claim he'd misunderstood, that she'd waited after all. When he was asleep she could sneak off the ship. Get the hell out of there.

She went out to the balcony again. Took several deep breaths, leaned against the railing and gazed at the city lights. The flashy skyline of Miami's downtown. Butler was right about that much. The men who built those monstrous skyscrapers were obsessives. She knew about their kind. Growing up, she'd watched her father's relentless labor as ship after ship in the Fiesta navy was constructed and put into service. The planning, the focus. The complex engineering, the rivet-by-rivet labor.

It took people like him, the Morton Sampsons, men capable of brutal concentration, to build such things. People willing to sacrifice everything, their families, friends, their own leisure, so the grand structures of the earth could rise. Like the men she'd studied in college, painters, the great masters. Men driven by fanatical fixations. Madmen, social misfits.

To leave a lasting mark on the world, it seemed you had to sustain a passion so intense that every other aspect of life was subsumed by it. Everything those men did collected around one powerful core. Their homes, their families, their mistresses, even their gardens and their pets, every detail of their lives seemed chosen to serve their greater need.

Each was powered by some unfathomable hunger. Like Butler Jack, an impossible ideal at the center of his whirlwind. A vacuum with Monica Sampson's face. As if it were some law of nature, the deeper the lack, the emptier the core, the more fierce the passion that swirled around it.

It was no consolation that Monica had inspired in another what she'd been unable to achieve herself. Sure, she had her drawings. But they were a pleasure, not a need. Done for her own amusement, no spiritual passion burning there. The only thing remotely close to a craving she'd known was her desire to escape the easy, privileged life mapped out for her.

Back inside the cabin Monica paced the floor until at last she came to rest on the edge of the bed. She tried to push the fear away, tried to get back the easy rhythm in her pulse. But there was a cold sweat building on her flesh. Just on the edge of her consciousness, a feverish panic. This was all wrong. She had no business being there, a week at sea with Butler Jack and her father and a few thousand of his worshipers. And David Cruz. Hearing his name on Butler's lips had made her light-headed. That Butler knew David, knew about their romance from years ago. Jesus H. Christ.

And the door locked. Monica, a hostage.

All of it coming bitterly clear to her in that moment. So stupid not to have seen it before, not to have felt the manipulation, the neat little trap Butler had set.

He'd located her somehow. To render her vulnerable he'd probably sneaked into her room at Sugarloaf, stolen her nest egg. When he was ready to move, he'd telephoned her father, informed him where she was hiding. All that bullshit about Morton spying on her, Jesse in on it, that was just to motivate her, alienate her from her friends, pry her loose. Jesse didn't admit it. He'd been aghast when she confronted him. And after Morton took a look around the place, he must've thought it was a hoax. That's why he hadn't stayed around, called in the Royal Canadian Mounties.

Butler timing it all just right. Luring her on his trip, getting her on board. Didn't even have to resort to violence. Just seduced her, talked her along. Had her passport waiting. Jesus, how outrageously naive she'd been. Butler had kidnapped her without her even knowing. He was going to trade her for money. Collect the ransom Morton had offered years ago.

She stood up, took several deep breaths. She began to inspect the room again. Had to get out of here. Had to escape before the ship left port tomorrow afternoon. Eyes roaming, coming to rest on the fire sprinkler mounted above the bathroom door.

She pulled the chair away from the door, positioned it beneath the sprinkler. On the bureau she found a glass ashtray with a book of Fiesta Cruise Line matches. She snatched them up, climbed the chair, and scratched one into flame beneath the sprinkler head.

The flame tickled at the plastic seal but nothing happened. Four matches later, still nothing. She climbed down and began to search. Complimentary postcards in one drawer, a plastic laundry bag in another. In the top drawer of the bedside table she found a Gideon Bible. She looked at it for a moment, riffled the pages. With a grunt, she gripped the first half-dozen pages from Genesis and ripped them free. She rolled them into a tight cigar, mounted the chair again, and lit the end.

She held the feeble flame to the sprinkler head, the pages withering to black flakes, ashes falling to the floor around her, but it didn't even scorch the seal. She tore more pages out, rolled them into a cylinder and wadded a couple inside the open end, lit the torch, stabbed it close to the sprinkler, held it till she could feel the sting of flame against her fist.

She worked all the way to Psalms before the matches were used up. Tossing the Bible to the floor, she stepped down. Cheap-ass paper. The flimsy stuff probably couldn't reach a kindling temperature sufficient to melt ice.

She went back out to the balcony, looked out. Fighting back the rising terror. She stared down at the ten-story drop to the dock. She supposed she could rip the sheets into strips, let herself down. But with only two sheets and a bedspread she couldn't make it more than two or three decks.

She went over to the door, hammered her fist against it. Hammered till her hand was swollen and sore. She called out. She yelled help. She yelled fire. Fire, fire, fire. Her voice swallowed up by the deadening acoustics of the ship. One in the morning by now, two. Someone on the crew might hear her if they happened to be directly outside the door, but if it was Butler instead, things could turn ugly. He might tie her up, gag her. Or worse. She'd have to pretend she was still compliant. Pretend she didn't suspect his plan.

She drew a breath, blew it out. Turned around and went across to the sliding door and pulled it closed. She sat down on the edge of the bed, steadied her breathing, held her hands up before her face, tried to still the jitter. Put herself in a trance.

Thinking now that her best chance might be to use the one reliable skill she'd always had. An awful thought, but that was perhaps the best weapon she had. Monica got up and set the lights low. She stood before the mirror and undid the top three buttons on her dress, spread the fabric to show her cleavage. She made a pout. Then she lay down on the bed, propped herself up on the pillows, cocked up a provocative leg, experimented with different smiles. She watched the door.

It was after ten on Sunday morning when Monica jerked awake. Nearly noon before her pounding finally got someone's attention in the corridor, a crew member with limited English. She called out for him to find someone to open her door. It was stuck. Stuck, the man repeated. Locked, she said. The crew member told her to turn the bolt. She said it was stuck. Would not work. Get an engineer. Get somebody to open the door.

For an hour she waited, fretting that he had misunderstood. Her gloom deepening. Finally at one-thirty the engineer arrived. He investigated the problem for a few minutes, then had to go back and find the proper tools. At three forty-five the door finally swung open.

A young Italian in a blue jumpsuit and yellow hardhat stood in the hallway, smiling proudly. The dismantled lock lay on the floor at his feet.

"I never saw anything like this," the young Italian said. "Someone plays a bad prank with you. He is destroying the lock completely."

"I need to get off the ship," she said.

"Too late," the Italian engineer said. "She is leaving now."

Monica wasted a minute waiting vainly for the elevator then ran down eight flights of stairs to the A Deck gangway. But the young Italian was right. All exits were sealed. The *Eclipse* was under way.

At four on Sunday the nineteenth of November the big hawsers were thrown clear and the M.S. *Eclipse* drew away from the docks. Its turbines murmuring pleasantly as the ship crept down Government Cut toward the Atlantic.

Thorn stood at the forward railing of the Sports Deck wearing one of Fiesta Boutique's high-fashion outfits, a red and white striped polo shirt and a pair of baggy green swimming trunks. Thorn the Christmas tree. All he needed was an angel for a hat.

He was following Sugarman's orders. Fitting in, just another passenger. Eyes open, looking for Freddy Megawatt, Butler Jack. Tall, well-built guy. Long blond hair, though of course he could be wearing a wig, a disguise. Not likely he'd be expecting to see Thorn aboard. But just the same he should keep his back covered. Stay vigilant.

Thorn watched as Miami slipped past, the luxury islands on the north side of the ship, big Mediterranean bungalows inhabited by a new crop of movie people and their bankers, and to the south were the cargo islands full of orange containers and gawky cranes that lifted an endless stream of stolen Land Cruisers and Mercedeses onto departing ships. Reggae music was piping out of the overhead speakers, played by a band one deck below. Most of the rest of the two thousand passengers were assembling along the railings, umbrella drinks in hand, cameras ready, a festive hubbub. A few waiters in outfits even gaudier than Thorn's wriggled through the crowd with trays of conch fritters and barbecued shrimp.

South Beach was coming up fast with its tropical sunrise colors, pink and aquamarine, its zany architecture. Once when Thorn was young, Kate Truman had taken him on an educational excursion to view the strip of Art Deco hotels, and a couple of times since he'd revisited, catching it at other moments of its cycle. Decline, decay, rejuvenation. Deco was a style Thorn had never developed an affection for. Too self-conscious, a silly sci-fi look with a coldly industrial tinge. So clearly a fad. Hot today, look out tomorrow.

As the ship moved beyond the mouth of the channel, he was surprised to feel the same tease of pleasure he'd always known at the outset of any journey to sea. Mingled now with the heady relief of knowing Sugar was alive, of being back in his orbit.

He found himself enjoying the tousling breeze, the tantalizing exit from the civilized world. He listened to the band doing its best to crank the party into happy mode. Loopy and rambunctiously gay island music. Not bad really, though he'd never decoded the lyrics to any reggae yet. As they eased past the final channel markers and beyond the pilot station and settled into the rhythms of a five-foot sea, he kept his face into the wind, sensed the land slipping away behind them.

An hour ago he'd called Rochelle ship-to-shore.

"I'm going on a cruise."

"How nice for you." Her voice slack.

"Nassau, Jamaica, Cozumel, and back. Six days."

She was silent.

"I thought maybe you could fly to Nassau," he said, "meet the ship on Monday. We could have a romantic interlude."

"Fly to Nassau?"

"A cabin to ourselves. Lots of room. Everything's paid for."

"Is Sugarman okay?"

"He was attacked, but he's recovering. A little groggy and weak still."

"He's okay, but you're going on this cruise anyway?"

"The guy that attacked him is on the ship somewhere. We're searching for him."

"So what is it you have in mind, Thorn, we're going to have this romantic interlude between gun battles?"

A few strained seconds went by.

"How's Rover doing?" he said.

"He walks around the house. He sniffs the bottoms of the doors like you're hiding behind them."

"And you?"

"I'm not a dog," she said. "I know you're not here."

"You're sure you don't want to join me?"

Rochelle breathed into the receiver. "Of course I do. But I can't."

"Why?"

"We need to talk," she said. "When you get back."

"Rochelle? Look, I'm sorry you're upset. But we can fix this. I'm sure we can."

"I'm moving my things back to my apartment," she said. "I think it's best."

He groaned and felt something heavy sink inside him. "You don't need to do that, Rochelle."

"I've decided. Don't even try to talk me out of it."

"All right," he said quietly. "If that's what you want."

"No, Thorn. That's what *you* want. You just don't know how to say it."

Thorn perched on the edge of his queen bed, stared at the blank TV set across the room, hearing the echo of silence on the line. Missing his chance. Abstaining. Things being agreed to, things unraveling forever in the grim hush.

"You're a loner, Thorn. We're both goddamn loners. It had no hope, never. We were stupid. We conned ourselves. The only thing we have in common is we're both cripples. One functioning heart between the two of us."

Rochelle's voice trembled as if a crack were opening up along a familiar fault line. The habits of grief and mourning replayed yet again. Thorn had had this conversation before as well, had it too often, but never on a phone. Something about the electronics flattened out her voice, kept the shrill parts suppressed. He couldn't see her eyes. Couldn't move with her around the room, perform that brutal waltz of recrimination and remorse, the final slashing of the cord. He was speechless, holding that dead piece of plastic in his hand, pressing her flattened voice to his ear. An ache hollowing out his gut.

"Have a good cruise," she said.

A buzz of static rose and fell.

"You too," he said. "You too."

A second went by, another, a final chance at something, then she clicked off.

Now Thorn leaned against the railing, stared out to sea. He refused yet another pink drink. Waved off the platter of conch fritters and barbecued shrimp. Kept his face into the breeze, watching the blue water grow steely, the disorganized chop turn to steady rollers. The big ship plowed into the Gulf Stream with the ease of a giant harvester moving through new wheat. With the Atlantic a ten-story drop below, it felt more like gliding along in a hot air balloon than riding a boat at sea.

A mile or so to the south another sleek white cruise ship raced along in vaguely the same direction. Probably another reggae band playing over there, kettle drums banging, the plink and plonk of xylophone and steel guitar. More fritters and umbrella drinks. More rented gaiety.

He was considering one of those pink drinks after all when behind him the PA system sputtered, squawked, and the reggae group abruptly died. Thorn could hear the real band continuing to play in the distance. Some of the passengers near him swung around and stared up at the speaker as a man cleared his throat, tamped on his microphone.

When the man began to speak, Thorn recognized the voice instantly, and in that moment he knew that this neatly organized planet they were sharing had just come badly unhinged from its axis.

"Hello, hello. Welcome aboard the *Eclipse* where the party never stops. Now, before we get any farther along, we need to spend a few moments on an important vocabulary lesson. To paraphrase the Good Book, in the beginning was the word and the word was *Jack*."

The sound system screeched and buzzed and the reggae band momentarily returned. While the man struggled to get control of his equipment, a couple of white-haired ladies in pant suits, one pink, one green, nudged in next to Thorn.

"What's going on?" one of them said.

"This isn't normal," said the other. "Vocabulary lessons? We've never heard anything like that and this is our seventeenth cruise. Isn't that right, Del? Seventeen."

Del nodded. Seventeen, yes.

The speakers blared again. There was a harsh flutter.

"Jack," the man said, the static dying out. "Jack is from Middle English *Jakke* and possibly from the Old French *Jacques*. Before that it appeared as the Latin *Jacobus* and the Greek *Jakob*. As a name it indicates a common man. One who does odd or heavy jobs. Lumberjack. Steeplejack. Jack of all trades. It's also a playing card, of course, its value just below the queen. Otherwise known as knave. As a verb, *to jack* can mean to lift, also to hunt or fish with a jacklight, which is illegal. Hence, if we follow the back-formation process, a jacker is a knave who lifts something, which means he steals it, and therefore, a hijacker is one who steals goods from a vehicle on the king's highway, that is, in transit. Or by association, it has come to mean seizing control of any moving vehicle, especially in order to reach an alternate destination. Hijack. Interesting, isn't it? All those other words living inside that one word. Hijack. Common man seizing control."

A woman on the deck below laughed like a giddy toucan. Thorn saw a man nearby guzzle the remains of his drink as if it might be his last. And then the PA whooped and blared and went into electronic meltdown, a series of painful blaps and crackles until finally it fell silent.

A moment later, a big-band orchestra played a few mushy bars and a woman began to sing. It was a moment or two before Thorn could tell, but apparently this was a recording of the cruise line's theme song. "Wish you were here to join our fiesta. Fiesta Cruise Lines where every minute is a party." The woman's earnest contralto belting out the jingle.

As Thorn was assuring Del and her fellow cruiser that he had no idea what was going on, his gaze ticked across a woman at the railing twenty feet away. She was staring out to sea, not joining the nervous fuss going on around her. A still point in the agitated throng. He took a step her way, then excused himself to Del and her companion.

As he drew closer to the young woman, he saw she was in her mid-twenties, her yellow hair shorn to a half-inch burr, a cut even shorter than Rochelle's. She was wearing a T-shirt a size too large, the jersey was a tangerine color with white tie-dyed stripes. White jean shorts with a fringe at the cuff and a pair of sandy espadrilles. The tangerine T-shirt was baggy but it failed to completely conceal her body, a physique so lush it might have been conjured up by some moonstruck boy in the throes of adolescence.

Thorn moved through the jittery crowd, some of the younger men growing boisterous, groups clustering, talking anxiously. Thorn settled in beside her, mirroring her posture, forearms braced against the rail, his face jutting into the breeze. He turned his head and peered at her profile and realized what it was that had tugged at him from twenty feet away.

" 'Ah, the snotgreen sea,' " he said. " 'The scrotumtightening sea.' "

She didn't turn to look, but he felt her stiffen.

"It's James Joyce, the Irish writer. From *Ulysses*. A book I never actually finished."

He could see her trying for a peripheral glimpse of him.

"You can go ahead and look at me," he said. "I've been glowered at before."

"You ever been pitched off a moving ship?"

Thorn eased closer, whispered near her ear. "You're the daughter, aren't you? The one who disappeared."

Slowly her face came around and she squinted at him. Her lashes were long and blond, eyes a powder blue. Though she had the eyebrows of a brunette, dark and thick with a slight arch above her right eye that gave her a skeptical look. She wore no makeup and he could tell her milky skin was the kind that can never hold a tan. He couldn't put words to what it was about the blend of mouth and nose that gave her such an earthy cast. By normal standards, the sharp cheekbones, the straight nose, the sulky lips all suggested a regal pedigree. A spoiled heiress who could summon and dismiss the likes of Thorn in a snap of the fingers. But he detected something else lying just below the surface, some firm muscularity that gave her features a fierce and slightly reckless edge, the look of a woman who has learned the lessons of hardship.

"You have me confused," she said precisely, "with someone else."

"I don't think so."

She pushed off from the rail and headed into the crowd. Thorn held his place and called out to her. "I used to set fire to you every night."

She halted. Kept her back to him for a time, then took a deep breath and turned to face him. From two yards away she regarded him, her mouth clamped tight as though she were stifling a curse. Then she rejoined him at the railing.

"The wanted posters," Thorn said, "the ones with your photograph on them. I used them for months to start my evening cooking fire. I hated to do it, such a face. But apparently someone got lazy and dumped a stack of them in a ditch outside my house. The posters turned out to be good kindling, so I spent a lot of time looking at that photograph. More than I needed to, I suppose."

Behind her a handful of middle-aged couples had gathered in earnest debate about the hijack announcement. One man calling it a tasteless prank, another convinced it was the beginning of some shipboard fun, one of those special planned activities Fiesta was famous for.

The blond woman lowered her eyes and consulted the back of her hand for several moments, then lifted her gaze again and noted unhappily that Thorn had not moved.

"Where have you been all these years?" he said.

Her lips parted, searching for the words.

"It's you, isn't it? Monica Sampson."

She winced at the name, then glanced around to see if they'd been overheard. "Who are you?"

"My name is Thorn."

She ran her eyes over him. Didn't seem to think much of his outfit. He watched her consider him, watched an idea take form slowly in her eyes. A careful smile materialize.

"And what cabin are you in, Thorn?"

He smiled back and gave her his cabin number.

"What would you say if I stopped by later, we could look out your porthole, watch the water slosh. The snotgreen sea. I understand it's very restful."

The words were right, but the tone was a half step off. Thorn had met his share of assertive women. He'd had his fanny patted more than once. He was used to it by now, though it struck him as oddly disappointing that women gloated over this new freedom when it seemed they'd done nothing more than appropriate the worst hunting habits of men.

As Thorn was fetching for something bright to say, Monica manufactured an alluring smile, and languidly, she raised a hand to his face and gave his cheek a backhand stroke as if to check for stubble.

A moment passed between them, she continuing to eye him in her parody of a sultry babe, Thorn smiling, mildly charmed, but letting her know with his eyes that he wasn't buying her silliness for a second. Finally she gave him a small private smile and helpless shrug, as if to say at least she'd tried.

A half second later her eyes strayed from his to something in the distance behind him, and the last shreds of her contrived erotic charm evaporated in an instant.

Thorn swung around and saw a group of people working through the crowd. Sugarman led the way, looking haggard, his face sheened with sweat. Behind him was a pretty blond woman with her mouth hardened into a grimace. Trailing her by a step or two was a tall bald man with shocks of white hair on his temples. He wore a white silk shirt and even whiter slacks and he seemed to be fighting a losing battle to keep his smile in place.

Thorn stepped into view and without breaking stride Sugarman waved him along.

"Wait," Thorn said, and turned back to Monica. But she was no longer there.

He hesitated a moment, searched the crowd, but when he didn't see her, he tucked in close behind the white-haired man and followed. The sea of passengers parting, several of them calling out as the group passed. Hailing them by name, Lola and Morton Sampson, asking if this was a prank, what were they supposed to do, what the hell was going on?

The bald man gave a hearty laugh and waggled his hand at the crowd like a candidate driving past in a parade. Thorn tagged behind the troop down a narrow outside stairway. Around a tight corner and halted before a hatch door where the red-faced security man from last night was standing guard. When McDaniels caught sight of Morton Sampson, he tore the red drinking straw from his mouth and gave two quick raps on the hatch door, their clever secret code. The hatch promptly swung open.

Thorn hustled along behind the group, past the guard into the cool half-light of the bridge.

CHAPTER
18

Blaine Murphy was assistant chief engineer for the M.S. *Eclipse*. Short, curly reddish blond hair, held the all-time sit-up record of eight hundred and fifty-three at the Coast Guard Academy. After finishing up there, he'd served two years hauling Cuban rafters from the Florida Straits, then he jumped to the private sector and now was zinging his way up the pay scale with Fiesta. Normal time frame for making chief engineer, getting the hell out of the control room and up to the bridge, thirty months. Blaine's goal was to beat that by six.

Every second of the day, focused on that. Nine decks away, up in the sun, the wheelhouse, chart room. Chuck his gray jumpsuit. Don those starched white uniforms, gold buttons, rub the captain's shoulder. Best of all, step up, take command, grip the controls in his own two hands.

Moving swiftly, ahead of schedule, Murphy had outlasted, outengineered, out-ass-kissed every new Coast Guard jock they'd thrown at him so far. For the time being he manned the control room, where it was his job to monitor the computer screens, keep the ledger up to date, make careful notations in the log book, the history of every alarm and the corrective procedures taken. One eye constantly flicking up to the video screens that surveyed the engine room and boiler room from several different angles.

Blaine Murphy's domain, the control room, was jammed with long sleek console panels and tall switchboard stations, a wall of dials and meters and gauges, all of them numbered. A cross between a high-tech recording studio and the NASA command center. The room hummed constantly with current, and the regular throb of the engines one deck below vibrated day and night through the gray tiles. The walls and tabletops and panel covers were done in a boring beige Formica. If Blaine could've chosen the motif, he would've used scarlet Scotch plaid. His favorite pattern for shirts, pants, slip covers, hell, for anything. Red Scotch plaid. Jazzed things up nicely, kept the pulse cranking.

In his two years in the drab confinement of the control room, Blaine had overseen the repair of dozens of pieces of malfunctioning equipment on all sectors of the *Eclipse,* from its propulsion systems to its water treatment plant, alternators, navigation devices, voltmeters, bow thrusters, refrigeration, the incinerator. Every crucial operation on board was wired through that room. The heart of the ship, center of power. If something failed or was about to fail aboard ship, Blaine Murphy was the first to know.

Still, with so many repair functions automated, there wasn't that much knuckle-busting work. Change a circuit board now and then, a chip, minor dial adjustments, flip a breaker switch. Two men was all it required to oversee every fuse, every junction box in that small floating city. The heavy, complex labor was almost always performed in dry dock, or back at port. But once or twice a month Blaine was called on to troubleshoot, patch together some crucial circuit or piece of machinery, bypass a broken valve, rig a gasket out of cardboard, do whatever jury-rigging it took to keep the systems up and running while the *Eclipse* was out at sea. Those were the occasions when he scored his points, made the small ratchets ahead in his career. In two years his repair record was spotless, batting a thousand. Ingenious, resourceful, and well trained, Blaine Murphy had never had a single breakdown he couldn't get up and running in half a day.

So when the man's voice came out over the PA system, a voice that wasn't Captain Gavini's or the cruise director's or anyone's on the crew, Blaine began to prickle with excitement. He'd heard the rumors about some ongoing problem with security. Casino thefts, a recent suspicious death. Someone apparently preying on the *Eclipse*. But to his great frustration, Blaine had not been consulted in the countermeasures. So when the voice finished his weird pronouncement and immediately thereafter the white phone on the central control panel rang, a call from the bridge, Blaine knew his expertise was finally being solicited. He was about to be brought into the loop on the most important voyage the *Eclipse* had ever taken.

It was not the captain on the phone, but one of his Italian stooges. Chief Officer Rudolfo Vincetti wanting to know what Blaine could tell them about that voice. Pudgy Vincetti.

"I heard it," Blaine said. "What exactly do you want to know?"

"Did it originate in the media room? The captain wants a response immediately."

Blaine told him to hold on. He moved across the room to the bank of power switches. Everything from the refrigerated morgue to the two hundred slot machines was wired through that giant circuit breaker board. He ran his finger down the row of switches, found the media room toggle, then went back to the phone and told Vincetti, no, the voice could not possibly have originated there. The media room was off-line. Typically, not turned on till two hours into the voyage when the stream of public announcements formally began. Blaine heard Vincetti repeat the information to the captain, and Gavini replied in Italian.

Blaine waited, absently watching the screens of the engine room. The Asian sweathogs down there with their ear protectors, their blue jumpsuits grease-stained already, moving like dwarfs in the catacombs. Then seeing someone else walking in a strange bowlegged gait down the narrow metal grating between the big turbines. This man wasn't one of the midget Filipino or Malaysian mechanics. This guy was tall and thin, lugging a nonregulation tool bag. He thought for a moment it was Robbie Dorfman, the junior assistant engineer on this watch. Half an hour ago Blaine had dispatched Robbie down to the engine room to answer a call, and he hadn't reported back. But this guy was taller than Robbie. Didn't move like him. Blaine was angling closer to the TV screen, squinting, when Vincetti's voice rattled in his ear.

"Captain also wants you to check on NFU for port rudder."

"What's the problem?"

"He wants you check it. See if any difficulty exists."

"Is this an exam or something? You're not going to tell me what the hell I'm supposed to be looking for?"

Vincetti said something to him in curt Italian. Blaine was pretty sure it was a curse. Calling him a shithead, probably, or something similar. The Italians were fond of shit curses. Shit on your sandwich, they'd say. Shit in your marriage bed.

He smacked the phone against the console, went over to the NFU control board. The navigational function unit relayed electronic messages from the autopilot up on the bridge down to the hydraulic power modules in the engine room. The NFU box was a way station for the flow of data through the navigational process.

Week after week routine procedure rarely varied. A few miles out, the captain turned on the autopilot with its preset destination encoded. He entered the desired ETA and sat back for the next several hours, letting the unit calibrate course heading, factoring in tidal differentials, wind speed, taking the ship along its course. The computer's job was to absorb all the electronic garble flowing through the various sensors and decide any necessary course adjustments and speed settings. Normally the captain took the control of the ship only as it approached the shipping lanes or harbor.

The NFU box was simply one of several monitoring devices along the track between bridge and rudder. If Gavini suspected trouble with the NFU, it probably meant he was having difficulty reconciling the actual course with the preprogrammed course. If the NFU unit was defective, bad things could happen. Worst-case scenario, you could find yourself sailing north when you'd instructed the autopilot to take you south.

But the fact was, in two and a half years, Blaine had never seen a single defect in the ship's navigational equipment. Once the autopilot was set, Gavini could damn well sit back and light up his pipe. And this time, just as he'd thought, there was no indication in the NFU box that anything was operating at less than a hundred percent. The unit was alive, green light lit, normal functioning.

He returned to the phone, told Vincetti everything was normal, and Vincetti relayed the information to the captain and Murphy asked again what the hell was going on. Without a thank you or good-bye, Vincetti hung up.

Blaine Murphy slammed the phone down. He stood staring at it for a moment, feeling the blood heat his face. "Fucking wops. Fucking third-world wops."

He sat down in his swivel chair, brought it around so he could glance at the video screens again. For half a minute, Blaine stared at the image on number-two screen without absorbing it. Some blob obscuring the normal view.

He sat up straight. Then rose from his chair and marched across the room, craning up at the monitor. He stood just below the screens and peered at number two. Something he'd never seen before was filling the screen. A solid mass, a blurry pale shape suspended an inch or two from the video lens, blocking the camera as if somebody had hauled himself ten feet off the floor and was holding the palm of his hand in front of the lens. Whatever the hell it was, the object was vibrating from the beat of the engines like everything else down there.

Blaine had a small degree of control over the engine room cameras, so he went back to the main control board and toggled the camera to the right, then abruptly sent it left. The movement nudged the object hanging in front of it, sent whatever the hell it was into a small pendulum swing.

He repeated the process, toggling right and left, then did it again and one more time, swinging the object into wider and wider arcs. He pushed away from the control board, skipped back over to the screen, grabbed a swivel chair from behind the radio panel, and climbed up for a closer look.

On one swing to the right, Blaine made out what appeared to be a coil of electrical cord, three loops, four, on the next he was staring at what looked a whole lot like a fucking human eye.

He yelped, jumped down from the swivel chair, ran back to the control panel, rocked the camera back and forth, getting a rhythm that sent the object into ever wider paths. Four, five, six times, then running back to his swivel chair, climbing up and bringing his face close to the screen. Getting right up there into the halo of electrons until he was certain what he was looking at.

Blaine Murphy felt his throat clamp, the fluorescent light in the room yellowed, and his body swayed on the chair. Suddenly he was feeling very ungainly.

He drew a careful breath. Gingerly he let himself down. Blaine had never had a fainting spell before. Never even come close as far as he knew.

He sat back on the swivel chair, lowered his head to his knees. A rush of nausea flooded his throat. He knew he should get to the phone, call security, call the bridge. Protocol, protocol. And he'd do that, sure he'd do that. As soon as the dizziness passed. As soon as he got the image out of his head—Robbie Dorfman's face swollen up, tongue peeking out, the noose at his neck.

"Gives you the collywobbles, doesn't it, Blaine?"

Blaine jerked upright, lost his balance, had to lunge to his right, grab the console to keep from tumbling out of the chair. A man was standing on the other side of the control panel. Tall and thin, his blond hair grown out long in the three years since Blaine had seen him last.

"What the fuck you doing in here?"

"What's wrong, Mr. Sit-up Champ, you having some technical difficulties down here? Something you can't fix?"

"You! You did that. To Dorfman."

Butler Jack smiled sadly. Glanced over at the number-two screen: Dorfman's mouth was smushed against the video lens, a corner of his tongue.

"I could tell you what's wrong with the NFU box, and for that matter with the entire navigation system. Hold your hand, lead you through it step by step, show you all the trapdoors, the tricks, the little surprises. You could pass the info on to Gavini and win yourself some more brownie points. You'd like that, wouldn't you, Mr. Sit-up. Add to all the points you got stacked up already."

"A fuckup like you, Butler, what could you show me I don't know already?"

"Well, I guess we're about to find out, aren't we? And, Murph, you be real careful now, you hear? You don't want to wind up like our friend Dorfman."

Leaving him with a tricky smile.

*　*　*

Thorn could see that Lola had passed on to Sugarman her best features. Her delicate nose, her long lashes, and narrow lips. The exquisite cheekbones of a Scandinavian princess. As they gathered behind the center console, the captain greeting each of them, Lola gave Thorn a brief but empty smile.

She wore a sleeveless jumpsuit, sand colored. A string of shiny black beads at her throat. The diamond on her slender hand probably exceeded the combined net worth of everyone in the room. Excepting, of course, Sampson himself. She was tanned and fit and seemed to have lost most of the nervous flutter Thorn remembered from his youth. She moved with the studious ease of someone born to this role. A bland nonchalance that probably fooled her TV audiences. But Thorn knew a little of her real history, and he could see in the way her eyes warily clicked over the men on the bridge that she was on constant lookout for anyone who might call her bluff.

Hovering beside Lola was a gaunt young man in his mid-twenties in jeans and black high-tops. His wavy black hair hung to the middle of his back, almost obscuring the red script lettering on his silk athletic jacket. LOLA LIVE. He had the weary eyes of someone used to the headier climate of the Pacific time zone. He checked out everyone on the bridge, his smile becoming lazy and indulgent as if he'd seen all this a few times before, seen it done far better on a half dozen different movie sets.

"This is my fault," Sugarman said. "Yesterday before I was attacked, I saw something, it looked like some kind of radio unit planted in the media room. I forgot about it till our friend started giving us his lecture."

He held up the bundle of wires and transistors.

"That should stop his sermonizing for a while."

"Don't be so sure," Sampson said, cutting a quick glance at his wife. He was holding a squat leaded glass. A few dwindling cubes and the ragged remains of a lime wedge.

Thorn watched as the first mate, a stocky red-haired man, moved from his station at the port-side console and leaned close to whisper something to the diminutive captain. But the older man shook his head and waved the first mate away.

"It is my belief," the captain announced, his English shaped by the ornate constructions of the Mediterranean, "that we should immediately return to port. Were it any other occasion as one so momentous, I would have done so already. But I felt it was necessary to advise you of my decision before executing it."

"Not on your fucking life," Sampson said.

Lola grimaced and swung away, crossed her arms across her chest, and stared out the port side bank of windows at the empty spread of sea.

"Sorry," Sampson said. "I'm sorry, but I'm upset. Forgive my language."

"I agree we should turn back," said Lola, still facing away from the group. "We never should have gotten under way in the first place. I was against it. But I was overruled."

Sampson rattled the ice cubes in his glass, drained off the last sip. Once again the first mate stepped away from his controls and leaned close to Captain Gavini but the small man shook his head brusquely.

"Where's David Cruz?" Sampson turned his strained grin on Sugar. "I want him up here. I need someone on my side."

"I sent a man for him," Sugar said. "He'll be up in a sec."

The captain said, "I am fully aware of the gravity of such a decision. But the passengers' safety must be my primary concern, and for that reason I am ordering the ship to come about and return to Miami immediately. We should be docking in three hours."

"You've got to be kidding. Because some prankster gets on the PA system, we're turning about. It would take more than one person to hijack this ship. Don't you think, Captain?"

"I'm returning to port immediately, sir. I cannot take such a chance."

Sugarman nodded.

"Captain," the first mate said. "I'm sorry, sir. But you've got to look at this."

While the captain and the mate bent close to study the green screen of one of the radar units, Sugarman stepped over to the starboard windows. He steadied himself with a palm flat against the deeply tinted glass.

"Holy shit!"

A buzzer began to pulse on the center console panel. Thorn leaned toward the flashing red light, saw a black identifying strip fastened below it. Anticollision radar.

The captain had stepped quickly to Sugarman's side and now barked out a command in Italian. The first mate cranked back on a silver handle that looked like a throttle lever. Two other officers who'd been waiting outside in the chart room shot through the door.

"Dead slow," the captain shouted. "Dead slow, goddamn it."

The alarm buzzer continued its grating alert.

Thorn hustled over to Sugarman's side, peered south out the window. Less than a mile away the sister cruise ship he'd noticed earlier was moving along an intersecting course. The *Eclipse* seemed to be on a heading that would ram the other ship's port side in a matter of minutes.

"Sir, the autopilot won't shut down," the first mate said. "I can't override it. Rudder angle, course heading, everything's holding firm."

Captain Gavini bumped the mate out of the way and gripped the black-handled joystick in the center console and dragged it backward. The VHF radio sputtered and an angry voice shouted, demanding an immediate response from the M.S. *Eclipse*. No one moved to answer. The officers jostled each other as they moved up and down the panels, trying combinations of switches. Cursing.

"Shut down power. Complete shutdown."

One of the second officers lifted a clear plastic lid over a large red button and flattened his palm against it. Another of the officers snapped up a microphone on the port console and spoke quickly. "Engine room not responding, sir. Control room dead, sir."

"Use the manual phone," the captain ordered.

The second officer picked up the receiver on the side of the control board and gave the crank several turns.

"Dead," he shouted at the captain. "Line's dead."

The other second officer was bent over a screen on the starboard panel. "Rate of turn at five degrees per minute, Captain. Six degrees now, seven. Turning sharp, Captain."

"Mother of God," Sampson said.

Hurrying to his side, Lola asked him what it meant.

"Rate of turn more than five degrees a minute can tip the ship. We keep turning like this we'll flip on our fucking side, sink like concrete."

"Go to batteries," the captain said. "Electrical shut-down."

"Can't do it, Captain. Nothing's responding." The first mate stood behind the control panel. Arms at his side, staring bleakly at the array of switches and LED lights that had begun to wink on and off. There was a moment of stunned silence, then the blare of the small overhead speakers mounted in each corner of the bridge.

"Wish you were here to join our fiesta. Fiesta Cruise Lines where every minute is a party."

Butler Jack's off-key voice filled the wheelhouse.

"Where every minute is a party."

They'd moved so close to the sister ship that Thorn could make out the faces of the passengers lining the rail, some of them waving their arms, some scurrying away for cover, a few with videocams catching every second of this.

"Got it back, Captain. Controls are hot."

The first mate pushed the joystick and the LED numbers flickered to life and began to change quickly.

"Starboard rudder full," Gavini said. "Push it. Push all of it. Bow thrusters, stabilizers, everything."

"We need to move the passengers to the starboard rail, Captain. As many as possible. Ballast. You need to make an announcement."

"No announcements!" Sampson shouted. "They'll panic."

"Too late for that," Gavini said. "Starboard rudder full, do you hear me, Mr. Vincetti! Eight degrees, nine, whatever it takes. Bring it around. Stabilizers on."

"We'll tip, sir."

"Do it, Vincetti."

It was probably his imagination, but Thorn thought he could feel a mild shudder in the giant ship, a faint noise that sounded like distant prop wash. He watched as the officers in their white uniforms standing outside the bridge of the sister ship flapped their arms. He could even make out their gold braids.

Then the *Eclipse* rocked hard to port. Everyone on the bridge fumbling for a handhold. Lola was slung sideways, falling to her knees before the kid in the silk jacket grabbed her arm and helped her up. Shouts came from the deck below. Screams. A coffee cup slipped off the console and crashed to the deck.

"Eight degrees, Captain," the first officer said.

The kid and Lola climbed up the inclined floor and held to the teak rail mounted next to Sugar and Thorn. The alarm buzzer continued to throb.

"It takes a mile to turn this thing," Sugarman said quietly.

"We haven't even had the fire drill," one of the second officers moaned. "No one knows where to go. Life boats, preservers, none of it."

"Shut up, Hugo," the red-haired man said.

Thorn watched the distance between the two ships shrink, five hundred yards, four. The *Eclipse* began to register the jarring wake of the other ship.

"Nine degrees, Captain."

"Bring it down."

"Down, sir?"

"Starboard rudder half. Bring it down to five degrees. We're clear of them."

"Clear, sir?"

The captain was no longer consulting his instruments. He'd planted himself at the forward window and was dead-reckoning their course. Several more agonizing minutes passed before the alarm buzzer shut off and it was clear the ships would not ram. The gap had stopped narrowing the moment the captain spoke.

"Jizz," Thorn said to Sugar.

Sugar nodded. "Guy's got a good eye. A good feel."

"Thank God for that."

The sister ship peeled off slowly to the south, while the *Eclipse* eased north. At their closest point only two or three hundred yards had separated them. But it had seemed very close. Very very close.

"We have full instrumentation, Captain."

The overhead speakers crackled again, and everyone on the bridge pivoted to stare.

"Well, so much for our little demonstration," the voice from the speaker said. "And now our party has begun. For the time being, let's all just try to relax, get on with our merry cruise. But I hope my demonstration has made it clear to you—Butler Roger Jack is the captain of this ship."

Morton Sampson cocked back his arm and slung the heavy glass at one of the overhead speakers. It shattered against the pale gray wall.

Sugarman stepped over to Sampson, put his hand on the man's shoulder, and gently turned him around. Though his smile was still lingering faintly, Sampson's face had gone whiter than his hair. A dull haze filled his blue eyes as if he had been staring into the sun.

"We need to talk," Sugar said. "Right now."

CHAPTER

19

Butler's testicles were swollen three times their normal size. He could barely walk. They throbbed. Two tennis balls pumped tight with blood. He was sick. Vomiting for hours in David Cruz's cabin. Puking through the night, there with the corpse, watching the sun rise. His testicles pulsing with every beat of his heart. Writhing on David Cruz's bed, legs spread, building up his courage to press ice to his balls, ice in a wash cloth.

Then later, twisting against the sheets, trying to scrub away as much of the blood from his hands and arms as he could manage. Unable to move. Depressed and in agony. Certain the plan was finished, destroyed. Unable to sit up, walk to his cubbyhole to transmit his messages, get things going.

He spent the day in David Cruz's cabin. The deadbolt on. People knocked, called out Cruz's name, but Butler made no move. Lying in his painful sweat, balls aching, growing ever larger. In the mirror they were becoming grapefruit. He was hungry and sick. Paralyzed on David Cruz's bed. Until finally late in the after-noon the mooring lines were cast off, the ship pulled away, set off to sea. The party beginning, but Butler lay on the bed moaning. Sick and aching. Everything wrong. Everything lost. Years of planning. Because of his balls. Because David Cruz had kneed him. Because his balls were about to explode.

But then an hour out to sea, things miraculously eased. The pressure abated. He could stand. He could move. Still suffering but it was endurable. As if some heavenly power had interceded on his behalf. As if his plan had found favor. The sea parting. His balls stopped throbbing. Celestial morphine. He could move. He could walk, take awkward steps. He could trek to his designated spot, broadcast his message to the masses. Tell them his name. In the beginning was the word and the word was Jack. Hijack.

His balls were huge and bluish black and they bulged in his pants, but they were shrinking back to tennis balls. He could move. He spoke to the passengers, told them who was in control. The plan moved forward.

Then his quick visit to the engine room and the control room. Robbie Dorfman. Blaine Murphy. Just to say hi. Hi, Blaine. Hi, Robbie. Making a couple of minor adjustments in the operations of the ship.

And the lurching of the ship as Gavini averted disaster.

It was working.

At a little after six o'clock Butler unlocked his cabin door and stepped inside. Monica was gone. Bowlegged, he walked directly to the bathroom. He stripped off the thick rubber tips on his fingers, the Velcro, the wires and battery pack of his zapper. Peeled out of the gray jumpsuit he'd found in David Cruz's cabin, took off the bloody clothes beneath, bundled them in a Fiesta laundry bag. Butler got the water as hot as it would go and held the dagger under the hard stream, watching the flecks swirl down the drain.

Then he stepped into the shower, scoured away the red smears on his arms, the blood caked in the curly blond hairs at his wrist. Wrung out the wash cloth. When he was done, he dried off thoroughly, moving the towel gingerly against his nuts. He washed his hands in the sink, washed them again. He squeezed out some toothpaste and brushed his teeth, rinsed with mouthwash then brushed a second time. Flossed. Shaved with a disposable razor, dried his hair with a towel, fluffed it by hand, combed it out.

Experimented with a part on the right side, but didn't like the look and parted it as usual in the middle.

He had to stand on the lid of the toilet to examine his testicles in the mirror. Golf balls now. The blue-black shine of a crow, a yellow tinge beginning to appear.

He selected a pair of roomy white shorts, knee length, stepped into them carefully. Put on a black button-down shirt, long sleeves to conceal the wires. He reconnected the zapper. Fastened the battery pack to his belt. Put on white Top-Siders. Through the whole exercise he kept his brain in short focus. The thing before him. The toothbrush, his hair, the shorts, the zapper.

When he was dressed he stood before the mirror and studied himself, tried to detect anything unusual in his face. But there was no hint of his new condition. He went into the cabin.

Monica had betrayed him, but the glow had not died. If anything, it had intensified. A flare on the surface of the sun. Her treachery combined with the pain in his testicles was fueling him. He was soaring now to yet a higher pinnacle, his energy level shooting heavenward. In pain, yes, but he was infused, flushed, supercharged. Surprised to find it so. She'd been his guiding light for half his life. And in an instant he was finished with her. The booster rocket falling away, Butler soaring on. Free.

Inside the cloud of pain he felt a clean, pure current of joy. Blood surging. A great wave of confidence growing. After the near collision with the other cruise ship, Butler Jack had hobbled through the *Eclipse,* tip to stern, eavesdropping on the anxious talk. Women sobbing, children with their numb looks. A disaster narrowly averted. Almost everyone had witnessed it or knew someone who had. And still no one from the crew had explained anything to them. The captain remained silent, Lola and Morton were mute. What was happening?

Butler roaring inside. Holding it in, his power over these people, these privileged, extravagant people. Their destinies in his hands. Supreme commander. His power on graphic display before all of them. His mother, his lost Madonna, all those who had thought him weak and incompetent.

Now he stood, legs spread wide. Butler listening to the spellbinding chant that filled his veins. It was working. It was working. It was working. Every detail going off as he'd planned, the timing perfect, the broadcasts. All of it perfect.

He had killed David Cruz. Blood everywhere. Carved him open and sank his hands into the cavity of his enemy's chest. Electricity in one hand, steel in the other. Splashed with the man's blood, awash in it, smelling it, inhaling the dying breath of his foe. Touching the man's heart.

It was ambrosia. An exhilaration that rippled through him still as if a thunderbolt had fired across the sky and Butler had shot his hand out and seized the lightning, snapping it from the clouds. Filled with it now, its bright white juice.

With a groan, Butler squatted over his athletic duffel. Worked his way through three or four of the zippered compartments before he found the list. He unfolded the piece of paper and took it to the dresser and spread it out. He read it over once, his mantra, then turned and snatched up a pencil from the desk and scribbled a final line. Watching himself from afar as his hand formed the words. Butler Jack hovering over the moment. Dislocated. There, not there. The transfusion of strength holding steady. Butler adjusting to its heady power, second by second learning to modulate it, bathe in its glow while smoothing off the ragged edges, the frantic rush. He'd always had energy, always had drive, but this was different. This was a new realm.

Butler sat on the desk chair, refolded his list.

He went to the dresser mirror and looked at himself. Reached out, touched the cool glass. Left a smudge over his eyes. Maybe he was insane. Maybe he had stepped across that threshold. Lost connection. But no. He knew the words. He knew all of them and they did not describe this power he felt. This strength.

Insane was from the Latin *sanus,* for healthy. *In* meaning not. Not healthy. Or *mad* from Old English *gemaedde.* Meaning foolish, vain, boastful. Ruinously imprudent. But Butler felt healthy, knew he wasn't foolish or boastful. And no *psychopath* either. Psycho for mind and the Greek *pathes,* or *pathos,* was suffering. A suffering mind. Or *crazy* from Middle English *crasen,* which meant shatter. Break into many pieces. A cold word of Scandinavian origin. None of those described him or the white-hot juice circling his veins. The intensity.

Butler put the list back in the duffel.

Standing in the middle of the room, his heart clanging. A terrible burn in his belly. Like hunger, only greater. Like the accumulated appetites of all his children, two thousand of them, their bellies swollen from starvation, their teeth gigantic and useless in their shrunken mouths, two thousand of them, while around him, on board the *Eclipse,* this ship of shame, two thousand others glutted themselves, ate meal after meal, seven a day, gorging until their bellies bulged with fat, grease dripping from their mouths, crumbs on their lips, licking the butter from their fingers, sucking away the sugar, the sour cream, the meringue. Consuming, stuffing, squandering. Dazed by excess. Filling themselves with the stolen bounty of the world.

Sitting this close to his mother, Sugarman was tongue-tied. An awkward kid, a whole shitload of things he'd always wanted to say, always wanted to know swelling up inside him, practically choking off his breath. At a distance it'd been easy. What he'd said to Thorn, not needing to get involved with her life, all that, it was true. He'd been pretty nonchalant. But this was the first time he'd been in this proximity, and he was having trouble finding anywhere to put his eyes.

In the walnut-paneled conference room, Capri Deck. Down some stairs from the bridge, sitting around the long shiny table. Burgundy leather on the chairs. Sampson, Thorn, Lola, Gavini. Sugarman having to explain who the hell Thorn was. Telling them he was his investigational assistant. Fetching for something more impressive, but the words wouldn't come. Tongue-tied. Everyone looking at Thorn in his silly outfit, the red striped shirt, baggy green shorts in some kind of material that made wax-paper noise when he moved. Thorn, uncomfortable from their scrutiny, said, "I'm working undercover."

Sampson leaned forward, staring at Thorn. "Why wasn't I told about this person?"

"He's my associate," Sugarman said. "My partner."

"And this is Rafael," Lola said, nodded to the long-haired lad in the jacket. "My cohost."

"Charmed, guys," Rafael said. He made a gun of his hand and fired a greeting shot toward the head of the table. Clucking his tongue as he did it. "You know, I was thinking. We should make an announcement, see if any of the passengers had their videocams going during that near miss. We could go with it tomorrow on *Lola Live,* a kind of America's Scariest Videos. I bet we'd get a bump in the ratings. Perk us up for the rest of the week. The buzz it would start."

"He's out of here," Sampson said. "This is a security meeting, not a TV matter."

"Hey, now. I don't see . . ."

Sugarman brought his hands up, formed them into twin six-shooters and aimed them at the kid, then swung them toward the door. "You're outgunned, buddy. Now go. Outta here. Now."

When Rafael was gone, Sampson cleared his throat, put on one of his corporate smiles, stood up at the head of the conference table and asked Sugar where David Cruz was.

Sugar said he didn't know. He'd sent McDaniels looking.

Lola's arms lay on the table extended before her, fingers laced, eyes down, like she was praying. Sugarman trying not to stare at her, but having trouble shifting his gaze anywhere else for long.

Rhoda Metzger, the ship's doctor, a prim woman in her fifties, was invited in to give a brief report on the injuries suffered when the *Eclipse* made her hard left turn. Too early to tell for sure, people were still arriving at the infirmary, but so far there were two cracked ribs, a half-dozen sprains, a broken arm, five passengers requiring stitches.

Sampson moaned quietly, then said, "Well, I suppose it could be worse."

The doctor glanced at her watch. "Will that be all?"

Sampson told her she was free to go. She made a motion to the door then swung back around. "Someone needs to make an announcement. Reassure the passengers nothing's wrong. There's a great deal of anxiety floating around the ship at the moment, Mr. Sampson."

"I'll do that at dinner. Now thank you, Doctor. You may go."

When the door shut behind her, Gavini began to discuss the navigational system. He was convinced there was some kind of malfunction in the autopilot circuit board. Under normal circumstances dropping speed below ten knots would automatically shut down the autopilot. But that hadn't worked, nor had the emergency stop button functioned properly. He believed there was an insect in the system.

"Bug," Sampson said. "You mean bug."

"I have my engineers testing the hardware at this moment," Gavini said. "We will find this insect very soon, I am sure of this promise."

"Are we currently on course?" Thorn asked.

"Certainly," Gavini said.

"So we're going on to Nassau, not turning back?"

Sampson eyed Thorn. Worked up a small smile on his behalf. "That's correct, Mr. Thorn. We're going on as scheduled."

"Look," Sugar said. "It isn't any damn bug in the system. We're bullshitting ourselves if we think that. Our friend had this whole thing rigged. He knew exactly how close to come to the other ship. Knew exactly when to give back control to avoid a collision. This isn't an engineering glitch. This is a very carefully orchestrated scheme."

Sampson was still on his feet, presiding. Giving Sugar some of the leftover smile still lingering on his lips. As he stared back at Sampson a tingle of recognition went through Sugar's head. He played with it for a moment without success until it whisked away and was gone.

"Well, as for me," Sampson said, "I tend to side with our captain. Maybe our culprit has found a way to tamper with some of the computer programs, plant a couple of devices like the one you found. He may have discovered a way to temporarily override the systems, but it's nothing more serious than that. Pranks. Once the engineers track down the intrusions, we'll be fine. What you should be focused on, Mr. Sugarman, is how we root out this person."

Sugarman shook his head.

"You're forgetting," he said. "I found that transmitter in the media room and I yanked it out of there, but that didn't keep him from speaking over the intercom or the PA, did it? The guy's got a plan. He's got backup systems. He's been on this ship once a month for the last seven months. Maybe more that we don't know about. We shouldn't underestimate him."

There was a loud knock on the door and Sugarman got up to open it. A compact young man with neatly trimmed coils of red hair stood in the doorway. He was wearing the gray overalls of the belowdeck engineers. The young man glanced around, saw the distinguished gathering, and took a half step back.

"Blaine Murphy, sir," he said to Sampson. "Assistant chief engineer. I need to speak to the captain, sir."

"This is my fault," Lola said.

"Lola, please."

"It is. It's my fault."

Sampson pointed a finger at Murphy, executed a little turn-yourself-around-and-get-the-hell-out-of-here gesture, and the man stepped back outside and shut the door.

With her eyes down, Lola said, "I should have seen this coming."

"How could it possibly be your fault?" Gavini said.

"Lola is simply distraught, Captain. She's been looking forward to this cruise for months. Working very hard organizing it, inviting the luminaries. She's—"

"He's my son," she said. "His name is Butler Roger Jack. He served on the M.S. *Comet* for several years. I believe you knew him, Captain."

"Your son, Butler Jack?"

"Yes, that's right."

"I remember this boy." Gavini frowned at the recollection.

"I'm sure you do," Sampson said, finding another smile in his collection. This one merry and bright, a tinge of irony.

"I don't always remember my crew. But I remember Butler Jack. I fired him."

"Yes," said Lola.

"Why wasn't I told that Mr. Jack was your son?"

"We didn't want preferential treatment," Lola said. "We wanted him to succeed on his own merits. Or fail."

Sugarman came back to the table, took his seat.

"Why'd you fire him?" Thorn asked.

"An incident," Gavini said. "He exercised very poor judgment, put the ship at risk. Caused extensive damage."

"What happened?"

"Is this relevant?" Sampson said. Still on his feet, but the authority draining away fast.

"Mr. Jack was sent down to the engine room to make a minor repair to the plumbing system. We were coming into port at the time, I was at the helm. We were making our final preparations dockside, using the bow thrusters to ease into our space between two other ships. It is a tight maneuver, but routine, one that I have performed hundreds of times. Mr. Jack selected that moment to confuse the main water shutoff valve with the hydraulic valve. He turned off all the ship's oil hydraulics. Leaving me unable to steer the ship at a crucial moment of the docking procedure."

"The *Eclipse* rammed the *Transcendence* broadside," Lola said. "Caused a great deal of damage."

"Three and a half million dollars' worth," said Sampson. His smile dimming by half. "When you add time out of service, personal injury suits, lost bookings."

Lola pushed her chair back and stood. She stared across at her husband. "They need to know, Morton. We have to start telling them the truth."

Another hard knock sounded at the door.

Sampson sank into his chair as the door swung open, his robust smile was gone. A sickly counterfeit lingered.

McDaniels stood in the doorway, breathing hard. His face was sheened with sweat. He tried to speak, but his breath wouldn't come.

"What is it, McDaniels! What's wrong?"

He pressed a hand to his chest and raised his right hand to call time for a minute.

McDaniels was assistant security chief under David Cruz. A retired marine sergeant, he had a serious oral fixation on a drinking straw. The man chewed on the goddamn thing every waking hour. Probably slept with it too. A couple of months back when Sugarman told him he looked unprofessional as hell with that straw in his mouth all the time, McDaniels explained that he'd survived in Vietnam because of a straw like that one, stayed out in a swamp three days, leeches sucking him dry, Viet Cong camped ten yards away, that straw his only lifeline. Sugarman told McDaniels he was free to chew on the damn thing all he wanted.

Blaine Murphy, the assistant engineer, hovered behind the old Marine.

"Come on, Barney, what's wrong?" Sugar could see McDaniels' usual ruddy face had turned the shade of sour milk.

"David Cruz," he said, a catch in his voice. "He's dead. I never saw anything like it. Butchered. This is bad, sir. Bad."

Something inside Sugarman's chest turned over.

"Make that two killings," Murphy said, stepping through the door. "Robbie Dorfman. He was hanged. In the engine room."

Lola sat down heavily. Mouth open. Her hand rising to her throat as if she meant to strangle herself.

"David Cruz was murdered?" Sugarman felt himself lose hold, begin to drift. Becoming a wistful spectator on the moment.

"That's right. Slaughtered."

"Cruz," Sugar said. "Oh, my Jesus."

Sampson continued to grin obscenely at the far wall. Running a finger back and forth across his lips as if grooming his smile.

"Well, I'd have to agree with Lola," Thorn said. "Seems like this might be a damn good time to start hearing a little truth."

CHAPTER
20

"He steals the money and gives it away to charities," Sampson said. "Some misplaced altruism he got God knows where. Thinks he's Mother Teresa or somebody. Lives like a bum in a rundown Winnebago. Hardly spends a nickel on himself, donates everything to those hunger organizations. Now I ask you, how were we going to throw this boy to the wolves? Call in the police, the FBI. Tell me. How am I going to do that, my wife's son? Not to mention what would happen if the papers got a hold of it. Yes, the boy's disturbed, a tad unbalanced, yes, no doubt about that, but he's still a good kid. I watched him grow up. I watched Lola raise him. He's eccentric, sure, but basically a good kid."

Gavini was shaking his head. Staring around the table at these people, these stark raving lunatics. That's how it looked to Thorn too. Annual board meeting of Zombies International. Everybody looking lifeless, paralyzed. Sugar's eyes particularly strange, like they'd rolled inward, gotten a glimpse of something harrowing, and rolled back out, dulled. Sugar in shock.

Lola stared up at a portrait on the wall. An English squire in red jodhpurs holding up a string of dead rabbits. McDaniels with his straw, munching full speed. The kid, Murphy, full of idiotic zeal, eyes shifting around the table, silly smiles coming and going on his lips. Couldn't believe where he was, at the big people's table.

Thorn said, "He's killed three people, tried to sink a couple of cruise ships, seriously injured a few dozen passengers. He's attempting to hijack the *Eclipse*. In my neighborhood we don't call that a basically good kid. We call that a killer, a goddamn maniac."

Sampson's mouth came open, but he caught himself and sucked back his angry words. He drummed his fingers against the table and somehow managed to dredge up a patient smile. Thorn had met a couple of people like him before, people who had an array of calculated smiles they used to manipulate difficult opponents and deflect awkward truths. It was a kind of madness to respond to calamity with such smirks and grins. A response so totally inappropriate that it kept adversaries off-balance, unable to strike full force.

Sampson settled back comfortably in his chair. "Now let's try not to get ahead of ourselves. We don't know for certain it's Butler who's responsible for these deaths. We've had some serious tensions among the crew members. Fights, assaults. And we don't know Dorfman's mental state. He might have been suicidal, a drug user, who knows? These events could be completely unrelated to Butler. Then again, perhaps the boy is being coerced, someone exploiting his knowledge of the ship's systems for their own nefarious plan."

"Oh, fuck that," Thorn said. "You heard him on the PA. He wasn't under duress. He's getting off on this. And I wouldn't put any store in this feeding-hungry-kids-bullshit either. Sounds to me like this is about revenge. Getting even with the people who fired him. Show them what he can do."

At the end of the table Blaine Murphy raised his hand, kept it straight in the air.

Sampson's smile withered a fraction. "What is it, Mr. Murphy?"

"Butler was down in the engine room walking around. I saw him on the closed circuit video just before I discovered Dorfman's body. Afterward he came into the control room. We talked. He as much as said he'd done Robbie. Butler had a grudge against him. Made a lot of threats when he was fired."

"You talked to him?" Sugarman said.

"Yeah, he kind of issued a challenge. Catch-me-if-you-can kind of thing."

"Great," Thorn said. "A fucking game."

"Somebody should get down there." Sugarman looked around the table forlornly. "One of the nurses, somebody."

"There's no hurry," Murphy said. A chipper look for each of them. "Dorfman's dead. I checked. He's completely dead. I cut him down. Had to drag him all the way back to the control room. The Malaysian mechanics were too spooked to keep working with him hanging there in the engine room."

Sugarman shook his head, speechless. The same glaze on his eyes Thorn had seen on the Everglades docks, as if he could not look at this square on, his brother's depravity.

"A grudge," Thorn said. "What kind of grudge?"

"Butler Jack and Dorfman were working together when their ship rammed the *Transcendence*." Murphy bobbed his head at the Captain. "Butler tried to put the blame off on Dorfman. But Dorfman told the truth, that Butler Jack fucked up. I mean, screwed up. Sorry."

Sugarman sighed then closed his eyes and gathered a few breaths. Opened them and gave Sampson a long look.

"Let me get this clear," he said. "You and Lola, the two of you knew all this when you hired me. You damn well knew Butler was pulling these robberies, giving his money to the poor. You knew who I was looking for, but you somehow forgot to tell me?"

Lola looked across at Sugar. Her eyes blank. "We wanted someone who could frighten him a little but somebody we could count on to be gentle. I can see this was a mistake. One more in a long series."

Gavini was gripping the end of the table as if he meant to rip off a hunk of mahogany and march around the table, bash everyone senseless. There was a long moment of strained silence, looks passing around the table. Finally Sugar lay his palms flat on the tabletop.

"All right, here's what we have to do," he said.

"Good, good," Sampson said. "A proposal. Let's hear it."

"Captain Gavini shuts down the engines. Pulls the plug, whatever it takes. Go to batteries. Give Butler absolutely nothing to play with. Then we gather the passengers and crew in one location. I suppose that would have to be in the Starlight Room. Required attendance. Explain to them what's taking place, say anything you like, but give them the general outline of the situation. We're going to need everyone's help to apprehend this guy. And while you're talking to them, Thorn and McDaniels and I will go room to room. The whole ship, however long it takes. We'll root him out, find any accomplices he may have. And we'll hold them in the brig until we get back to Miami."

Sampson gave a hearty laugh.

"Good try," he said. "But I think not."

"I disagree, Morton," Lola said. "It's a good plan."

"My vote as well. A sound strategy." Gavini came to his feet. "Hold the passengers in one place. Search the ship."

"Now, now. Captain, relax. Please, sit." Sampson beamed at the captain until he sat back down.

"All right, I agree, Mr. Sugarman's idea has its virtues. It's simple and straightforward but I'm afraid it simply isn't possible. Don't forget who we have on board. Two top network anchors for starters. Dale Jenkins and Brandy Wong. Both major stars of the American media. We've got Rad Tracy, one of the hottest young actors in Hollywood, his parents and agent, and there's Beverly Mitchell and Her Three Ho's, who I don't need to remind you have two platinum albums. Not to mention Sally Ann Meadows, Billy Dee. The complete cast of *The Happy Bunch.*

"All of them on *Lola Live,* starting tomorrow morning. Live broadcasts from the Sun Deck. Everything's set. Satellite time, everything. We've been running national ads for the show for the last two months. There's just no way in hell we can turn the ship around, head back in. It would be an embarrassment of disastrous proportions."

"Two murders isn't an embarrassment?" Thorn said. "Hey, what kind of idiot are you!"

Sampson snapped his eyes Thorn's way, a twisted smile coming and going. "As things stand at the moment, I can speak to our guests, do some damage control, give them an explanation that will soothe things. But if we go public, make a show of it, I guarantee you, Brandy Wong or Dale Jenkins will be on the phone ten seconds later, and there'll be network helicopters hovering over us within an hour. Spotlights, an escort of Coast Guard cutters, the entire world media circus would descend on the *Eclipse*."

"Good. Let's do it." Thorn pushed his chair back.

"No, absolutely not. As satisfying as it sounds to go from cabin to cabin and flush him out, it's simply not possible. We will handle this internally. And we will handle it discreetly. There will be no departure from our scheduled activities."

Murphy raised his hand again.

Sampson leaned forward, his joviality running on fumes.

"Sir, if I may say so, I think that's a terrific plan. I'd only like to add one thing. I can help you capture Butler Jack. He's not nearly as smart as he thinks he is. If he comes on the PA system again, I can track him down. I'll toggle through the circuits, cut them off sector by sector. I could shut his voice off and on real quick, so we can find the exact spot where he's broadcasting from and we can nab him."

Sampson gave the boy a long and careful look.

"You can do that?" Sugarman said.

"Sure I can. I know this ship better than that jerkoff any day of the week." He looked around the table. Even a social dimwit like Murphy could read the strained silence. "Sorry," he said. "But it's true. If Butler makes another peep, I can tell you where he is. A minute, two minutes, that's all I'll need."

"All right, good," Sampson said. "Then it's settled."

He clapped his hands together, gave them a good dry rub. Once again brimming with pigheaded optimism.

Gavini rose.

"Mr. Sampson," he said. "I do not approve of this in any manner whatsoever. This is my ship, my command. My decision is final in all matters. We have had two homicides, sir, we must turn back immediately. There is no compromise on this issue."

"It's your ship, Gavini, but it's my navy. Next month look whose signature is on the bottom of your check."

The captain held Sampson's eyes for a few moments, then muttered something in Italian and looked away. "I cannot agree to this, sir."

"Oh, now, don't be a bad sport, Captain."

Gavini stalked toward the door.

"Wait a minute, Gavini."

The captain stopped and did a neat little aboutface.

"What about a compromise?"

"And what would that be?"

"You continue to pilot the ship till we reach Nassau tomorrow. Once we're there, we'll put the passengers ashore and then do as Mr. Sugarman suggests, go room to room."

"We should turn back now," Gavini said.

"A compromise, Captain, that's all I'm asking." Sampson cranked up a collegial smile. One potentate to another.

"All right, then," the captain said. "We will sail to Nassau. But we will not leave port again under my command until this assassin is found."

"Agreed."

The captain gave Sampson and Lola a stiff bow then left.

Lola lifted her chin, aimed it across the table at Sugarman. The two of them locking eyes, communing like long-ago lovers.

Thorn said, "And by the way, what the hell's this vocabulary business about? He trying to be some kind of comedian?"

"My fault again," Lola said, shifting her gaze from her son, looking at Thorn, some of the leftover heat still in her eyes. "When he was young I urged him to look up words he didn't know in the dictionary. I told him it was the path to success, a good vocabulary. So he memorized it. He sat down and memorized the entire dictionary. Took him a year to do it, but he learned everything in *Webster's Third Collegiate*. Every word, every pronunciation, everything."

"Very literal guy."

"Very smart," she said. "IQ close to two hundred."

Murphy made a throat noise and rolled his eyes.

"You should've given him a goddamn Bible," Sugarman said. "Maybe we wouldn't be here today."

"I did," said Lola. "He memorized that too."

"In the beginning was the word," Thorn said, "and the word was Jack."

Lola nodded.

"When he was fifteen," she said, "Butler refused to attend school any longer. He would sit in his room and pore over the dictionary and the Bible. He stopped speaking to me, wouldn't talk to anyone. Totally withdrawn. I became alarmed. Morton was kind enough to recommend a psychiatrist in New York City."

Sampson cleared his throat. "Lola, please. I don't see how this . . ."

She cut him off with the slightest tilt of her head and something she did with her eyes that only Sampson could see. The big man rocked back in his chair with his lips clenched in an excruciating grin. It was clear that the balance of power between these two had a public face and a private one. What Thorn had glimpsed was a half second of the private, and in Lola's nearly invisible gesture there was more clout than in all of Sampson's bullying charm.

Lola shifted in her seat and glanced around at the gathering. A tendril of blond hair had broken loose from her intricate French braid and hung along her neck.

"I took Butler to Manhattan to meet Dr. Weiner," she said. "A dour man in a pinstripe banker's suit. We had a two-hour appointment, but near the end of the session Dr. Weiner came out to the reception area and said he had canceled the rest of his schedule for the day. Devote it to Butler.

"Later, I could hear the two of them laughing. Long hilarious guffaws. I got up, went over to the secretary, and asked her if this was normal. And she told me that wasn't a word they used around there.

"I went for a walk, had lunch, took another walk while the doctor and Butler talked. By six that evening I was wrung out, a nervous wreck. His secretary left. I couldn't hear anything behind the office door anymore, so I knocked. But the doctor called out that they were not finished. So I waited. I sat out there till ten-thirty. Then all at once I began to have an overpowering premonition that something was wrong.

"I got up, went to the doctor's door. Knocked. But there was no answer. I knocked again, then I swung the door open. The room was completely dark. I stepped inside and I heard only the bubbling of Dr. Weiner's aquarium.

"I fumbled around for a light switch but couldn't find it. I called out the doctor's name. By then my eyes were adjusting to the darkness and I could make out something in the corner of the room where the aquarium stood. The shape of a man. He seemed to be moving very strangely, writhing from side to side. Nearly in a panic, I patted the wall for the light switch. And finally I found it.

"I flipped it on and I swung around and there was Dr. Weiner. The dour man in his pinstripe banker's suit had his hands around my son's throat and he was holding Butler's head beneath the surface of his aquarium. Butler's eyes were wide, looking across at me, bubbles from his mouth."

Thorn looked over at Sampson. The man was gazing up at the acoustic tile ceiling. His grin hardened into a death mask.

"I ran over, grabbed something heavy from the doctor's desk, a glass bookend, and I hit him with it. I hit him several times before he finally let Butler go and fell to the floor."

"Should've sued the bastard," Sampson hissed. "Wrung out his last dime."

Lola looked around at them.

"That's it?" Thorn said. "End of the story?"

"Yes," she said. "He was trying to kill my child."

"Do we know why?" said Thorn.

"Is there a good reason for trying to kill a child?"

Thorn shrugged. He could think of a couple.

"No," Lola said quietly, not meeting his eyes. "The doctor refused to discuss it. Butler and I returned to Miami the next morning."

"I'm still missing something," Thorn said. "I mean it's a colorful tale, but what's the point? Butler was assaulted by a shrink, so that's supposed to explain why he's killing people? Some kind of emotional scarring or brain damage or something. This makes it all okay?"

Lola frowned and said, "I'm relaying this to let you know that my son is exceptional. He has something. Charisma, a gift, an intensity. People react to him strongly. He can push people very hard. Over the edge."

"Great," Thorn said. "So we'll carry earplugs. Have our mirrors ready so we don't have to look him in the eye."

Sugarman was on his feet, his breath ragged. When Thorn saw his twisted scowl he realized Sugar had heard a different message in Lola's yarn. A mother willing to claw and scratch, do whatever it took to rescue her son. One of her sons anyway.

"Come on, Thorn, McDaniels." He steered his eyes away from Lola. "You too, Murphy. Let's get busy."

Thorn followed McDaniels out the door. He had to trot to catch up to Sugarman. "That was my first committee meeting."

"What?"

"My first meeting. People around a conference table hashing things out. I'd heard about them, but that was the first one I'd seen."

"Consider yourself lucky."

"I was expecting pie charts, graphs, overhead projectors. I thought at least I'd get assigned to a subcommittee."

Sugar turned into a stairwell, moved limber-legged down the stairs. Murphy and McDaniels falling behind.

"And hey, guess who I saw?"

Sugar gave him a quick look as they rounded another landing.

"The girl in the posters," Thorn said. "Monica Sampson. She's on the ship. I saw her this afternoon. She was leaning on the rail."

Sugarman stopped abruptly. Gave Thorn his full concentration. "You're shitting me. Monica?"

"It was her all right. I spoke to her. She even flirted with me. Very nice looking woman."

"Oh, man, oh man. What the hell do we have here?"

Sugarman shook himself and started back down the stairs. They swung around the next landing and Thorn nearly leveled a cabin boy with a stack of sheets. For a guy who'd just had a heart attack, Sugarman was moving.

"That's some brother you have. Two hundred IQ."

"Lucky me, I get the dumb father."

"Do we know who Butler's father is?"

"I know Lola lived with a guy for a while a few years after she split up with the illustrious Mr. Sugarman. Some white guy. Real estate developer or something, that's all I found out. Two years or three they were together, never married. He pulled a fraud scheme, ran off with a pot of money, a lot of debts. Nine months later Lola's got a new baby boy."

"A pattern with her. The men in her life running off."

"Running off or driven off."

"So what's the plan? Where're we going in such a hurry?"

"You're going down with us, see where the control room is, get oriented, then you're heading back up to the Starlight Room. Sit at your assigned table. Eat supper, keep your eyes open. I wouldn't put it past this guy to show up, try something right out in the open. Make a big splash. I'll stay with Murphy, see what he's got in mind about catching the guy."

"Supper? You want me to eat supper at a time like this?"

"Yeah. And keep an eye out for the girl. Monica. You see her again, take her into custody."

"Custody?"

"You know what I mean. Detain her. Don't let her sneak off. Okay? We need to talk to her. Showing up at a time like this, it's weird. Gotta be connected."

"When do I get my gun?"

"There aren't any firearms. We're naked."

"You're joking. No guns on the ship?"

"Sampson doesn't like guns. He's forbidden them."

"Even his security staff?"

"That's right. No guns."

"Maybe we can dig up a harpoon somewhere."

"Just eat supper, be normal. If he shows up, don't try any-thing unless somebody's in danger. Follow him if you can. But stay clear, no confrontations unless it's unavoidable. I'll try to meet you back at your cabin at eight, eight-thirty. We'll see where we stand then."

"How about two-ways? Hand radios. Some way to stay in touch."

"It'd be better if you just tried to blend in, Thorn. Be a pas-senger. Nothing to give you away. You'll be more useful that way than walking around with a radio squawking on your belt."

Blue ear protectors hung on a rack outside the engine room. They put them on and Sugar led Thorn on a quick inspection tour down the greasy grates between the huge turbines. Even with the ear guards on, the room was painfully loud. Thorn could feel the vibration of the enormous engines like small fists pummeling his flesh.

Sugarman pointed up at a length of cord knotted to a steel overhead beam. It was yellow nylon and it hung beside a video camera mounted on the wall. The cord had been sawed off a foot below the knot. Sugar made a choking sign with one hand. Where Dorfman was hanged.

Small Asian men in blue overalls and yellow hardhats cruised up and down the ramps carrying tools and buckets and dragging hoses behind them. The endless maintenance of engines that never rested.

Outside they hung the mufflers back on the rack and Sugarman led Thorn to the rudder room. The walls and stationary equipment had been painted a serene sky blue. It was a small space with oversized levers and pumps and oil pressure tanks that ran the two giant rudders.

"The steering system is operated by oil hydraulics," Sugarman said. "Oil-filled lines under pressure."

"And that?"

Thorn motioned at a large wheel mounted on the wall above the hydraulic valves. It was twice as large as a car's steering wheel and was backed by a sprocket that was looped with the largest bicycle chain Thorn had ever seen. Links the size of golf balls. The second sprocket was hidden below the floor.

"Manual steering," Sugarman said. "A throwback to the old tramp steamers. Sampson wanted it installed. It's the nautical equivalent to lake pipes on a hotrod, more show than function. Something only another seafaring buff would appreciate. Apparently Sampson's a nut on nautical lore."

"You know this ship pretty damn well," Thorn said.

"I've been spending a lot of time here, yeah."

After a quick tour of the sterile control room, Sugarman led Thorn back to the stairwell and told him to go on to supper. To keep his eyes open. If Thorn needed him, this is where he'd be.

"Sugar," Thorn said quietly. "He's killed three people we know about, so tell me you're over your goddamn case of self-restraint. If you have to go one-on-one with him, you're not holding back, right?"

"He's my brother," Sugar said. "That hasn't changed."

In profile, Sugarman's face was unbearably worn, beaten down, a man who had haggled with death, struck a bargain and been released. But also a man whose resurrection was only partially successful.

"Well, fuck it," Thorn said. "He's not my brother."

CHAPTER
21

$\mathbf{M}$onica eased inside her cabin.
She shut the door soundlessly and stood for a moment, fighting off
a shiver of dread. Across the room the heavy curtains were drawn,
the cabin dark.

She stepped forward, listening for any sign of him. But the
music playing on the PA in the corridor was filtering into the
room. A Jimmy Buffett jingle extolling the boozy life. She held her
ground, waited for her eyes to catch up to the dim room.

Then another step. And to her right she saw the slim line of
light showing at the bathroom door.

What she wanted to do was walk over to the bed and collapse.
She was weary beyond belief. Going the whole day without seeing
Butler Jack. Then the goddamn public address comes on, Butler
into his hustle, playing his word game. She'd barely digested this
when the guy Thorn comes out of nowhere, he's in her face making jokes, knows her name. She's hurrying away and the other
cruise ship almost collided with them. Butler behind it somehow.
She was sure of that.

She looked down at her hands. They were jittering so badly
that if she tried to take a swipe at Butler, she'd probably whiff. She
edged to the closet, rolled the doors aside, then moved to the
bathroom door. Holding still for a moment, she tried to peer

through the crack but could see nothing. The room was quiet. To the left just out of view a light burned.

She nudged open the door and stepped back. There was some kind of movement, the flicker of a shadow passing before the light, or maybe just her own reflection. She drew a deep breath. Felt the prickle of hairs erect on her arms.

Monica didn't know if she was brave or not. All her life she'd found a way to dodge even minor squabbles. As Irma Slater she'd been ballsy when she had to be, blown off a few cowboys who'd hit on her. And in her daydreams she'd screamed out brutal curses at her father, even slammed a fist into his nose more than once. But those were fantasies. So she didn't know. Facing danger, she might be valiant, or she might curl up like some worm and sob.

In a crouch, Monica stepped into the bathroom.

It was empty. She swung around and swept the shower curtain aside. Water dotting the tile. She stooped, leaned to the left to let the light shine on the shower floor. A smear of blood on the silver drain.

She forced herself to draw a breath. Felt a cold ribbon of sweat trickle down her ribs. She went back into the cabin, walked across to the heavy green curtains, reached out slowly, brushed them aside. No one. She stepped through them to the balcony.

It was after seven, the ocean empty and dark except for a faint ripple of iridescent purple light at the western horizon. The moon was swollen almost full as it drifted up from the black sea. A half-dozen tattered clouds flew past it. The brightest stars were already showing, the weaker ones kindling into view. The air was silky, touched with something sweet, a wisp of jasmine or someone's subtle perfume from the deck below. A night to bask in.

She turned and went back inside the cabin and made one more careful circuit, checked beneath the bed this time, but the mattress was perched on a solid support. The closet, the drawers, opening them one by one but finding nothing. She drew the spread back, stood looking at the clean, flat sheets as if he had some kind of black magic and could turn into smoke, glide about, flatten himself between the bedsheets.

Monica was losing it. She knew that. Losing it, toes curled

over the edge of the cliff. Taking a long look down. Picking her spot.

She went into the bathroom, relieved herself, rinsed her face with cold water, and went back into the cabin. She walked over to Butler's bags, kneeled and snapped them open. The four Samsonite hardsides Butler had brought aboard were almost empty. A couple of changes of clothes, shorts, sandals, tennis shirts, a shaving kit, that was it. Clearly intending to leave the ship with more than he'd come with.

She moved to the duffel and unzipped it.

The main compartment was filled with gauges, fuses, batteries of every size, bundles of multicolored wire, several small circuit boards wrapped in plastic baggies, pliers and the soldering gun she'd seen before, some other tools, several coils of coaxial cable, and a plastic box with a dozen slide-out trays. The trays contained springs and tiny bulbs that might have been transistors, another tray of what looked like microchips, and round flat batteries like Martian coins. A host of other arcane hardware as if Butler had harvested the goodies off dozens of computers. There were also three thick manuals with light blue covers. M.S. *Eclipse* printed in large block letters on each of them. She fanned through them, saw dozens of schematic drawings. Diagrams, lines connecting with other lines, the intricate electric pathways, the plumbing, the fire alarm system, steering mechanisms. She laid the manuals aside.

For the next few minutes she investigated every flap and zippered pocket in the big bag, found some receipts from electrical supply stores, a tight roll of fifty-dollar bills, an accordion holder with a few dozen photos of the starving children. She counted out ten fifties to replace her nest egg and tucked it in her pocket. He owed her that. It was only fair.

She didn't know what else she was looking for. A weapon would be good. Or some clue to his sanity, or evidence she might be able to use against him later. She'd handled the wedge of paper several times, but not till she was rising did it snag her attention. She bent back down and plucked it from the jumble.

The white page was folded into a tight square like a junior high love note. She took it over to the small desk, switched on the lamp, and carefully unlocked the folds, spread it open, flattened out the well-worn creases against the green ink blotter.

It was the list Butler Jack had mentioned, his plan of action. There were small pencil checks beside the first seven numbers.

1. Master tools of trade. Polish manners.
2. Select needy subjects. Tithe.
3. Locate her.
4. Study her.
5. Larcenous cruises. Plant wizardry. Dry dock.
6. Intersect with her. Final dry dock.
7. *Eclipse.* Take control. Dance the dance. Rogue wave.
8. Dispatch passengers.
9. *Juggernaut.*
10. Fifty-eight million dollars.

By the time she'd reached number ten, her hands were shaking. But it was the last one that sat her down on the edge of the bed. Took the air from her lungs. He'd scribbled it hastily by hand, barely legible.

11. Sacrifice her.

Blaine Murphy was trying to explain the ship's electrical layout, rattling out a string of numbers and incomprehensible terminology, ignoring Sugarman's pleas to slow down, simplify, until finally Sugar had to clap a hand over the kid's mouth and whisper in his ear to shut the hell up and listen for a goddamn minute.

When he took his hand away, Blaine Murphy's face was bloated with rage, but he kept his mouth shut.

Sugar explained that he and McDaniels were idiots. Idiots, absolute total morons. Okay? No need to try to impress them with his mastery of the subject matter. This wasn't a job interview, a final exam, anything like that. So he should put it in terms a couple of five-year-olds could understand. Murphy nodding. Yes, yes. Sure, all right. I was just excited.

Murphy stepped away, put some space between them, then started over.

Eleven decks. Each deck divided into four fire zones. The point was, if the ship caught fire, the steel doors could be closed to trap the blaze, keep it from spreading, so the worst that could happen was that one-fourth of one deck might burn. But that one-fourth would be cut off from the other three-fourths. By dividing the electrical circuitry into sectors, it made it possible for the ship to have a fairly serious conflagration and still stay operational.

"Conflagration, meaning fire," Murphy said.

Sugarman nodded.

Murphy was being cute, going very slow. Enunciating his words, pausing between sentences, but Sugar didn't interfere. Let him have his fun.

Eleven decks, four fire zones. Eleven times four equals forty-four electrical zones. A circuit breaker for each of them right over there on the wall.

So if Butler Jack tried to use the main PA system again, Blaine would simply work down the panel, one to forty-four. A quick off and on. If the PA turned to dead air for a couple of seconds then they'd know which zone Butler was broadcasting from.

"Show me the zones, a chart, whatever you have. How big is each one?"

"I'll show you, but it's easy enough to picture. Take each deck, everything on it, bow to stern, divide it into four. A, B, C, D. That's how big."

"Fuck," McDaniels said. "It's still a needle in a haystack."

"No, no," Murphy said. "When we know where he is, I'll spring the fire doors, cut off that section. Trap him where he is, so we can search that area for however long it takes."

"What if he's using his own energy source? Batteries, something like that, a transmitter like the one I found, breaking into the circuitry in one place while he's stationed somewhere a good distance away, radioing his message. He could do that from anywhere, his own cabin, a broom closet somewhere on a different deck entirely."

Murphy stepped safely away from Sugarman. He still wasn't over having his mouth covered like that. Probably reminded him of the old days in high school when they used to dunk his head in the toilet. The pug-nosed little know-it-all.

"To be able to speak through the entire ship, he'd need to splice into the main trunk lines. A small hand-held transmitter, battery operated, something like that, it wouldn't have the juice to do it. No, he's got to be right there where he's entering the system. Trust me. Don't worry. This will work."

Blaine Murphy sat down behind the central control panel. Took an expansive breath. "I don't care what Lola says, Butler Jack isn't so smart. Weird, yeah. Fucked up, I'll agree with that. But smart, no, nuh-uh. You heard what he did with the hydraulics, that screw-up at the docks with the *Transcendence*. That's Butler. That's who he is. That was a simple operation. Shut off the water pressure. A monkey on a leash could've done that. But Butler is a screw-up, plain and simple. Now that I'm involved, I promise you, Mr. Sugarman, we'll nail his ass in no time."

Sugarman looked at McDaniels. Behind Murphy's back the old marine made a jackoff motion with his right fist.

"I hope you're right, Murphy. I hope you're right."

Thorn ordered the salmon, baked potato, asparagus. Black forest cake for dessert. He talked to the honeymooning couple from Manchester, England, who sat across from him. Thorn wasn't absolutely sure, but he strongly suspected that the young brunette had her hand inside her new husband's fly most of the way through dinner. The way she kept twisting toward him, the guy's eyes going loose several times during the main course.

To Thorn's left was a tall dignified woman in her seventies who kept looking at her wristwatch. She told Thorn she was Garvia Hazelton and she was waiting for the eight o'clock casino opening. Between glimpses at her watch she informed them all that this was her forty-first cruise and at the moment she was six hundred and seventy-seven dollars in the black. Started out fifteen years ago a few months after her husband died. She'd permitted herself to gamble forty dollars in quarters that she'd taken from her husband's nightstand jar. On that cruise, just a few quarters left before her forty ran out, she won an eight-hundred-and-fifty-dollar jackpot. She took that as a sign, a message from her husband. Pulling strings on her behalf from up above. So she put that cash away in an envelope and had been using that seed money for the last fifteen years. Still the same envelope too. For luck. She showed it to Thorn, from a Red Lion Inn in Missoula, Montana. It still looked very fresh.

"He's up there rooting for me," she said. "Don't you think?"

"Absolutely," Thorn said. "No doubt about it."

On his other side was a family of four from Miami. The father was a lawyer. Maybe Thorn had seen his ads on TV. No, he hadn't. Really? How was that possible? He was on five times every day, before the evening news, before *Hard Copy*. He was the guy who sat on the edge of his desk, nice blue blazer with gold buttons. Not one of those others with their rolled-up shirt sleeves and phoney-baloney suspenders. Now did he remember? Thorn told the man he didn't own a TV, that might explain it. The kids leaned forward to take a gander at this guy without a TV. The mother was also a lawyer. She did real estate closings, specialized in condos. She asked Thorn where he lived and he told her and she said Key Largo had several fine condo opportunities. She gave Thorn her card.

Their kids had the worst table manners Thorn had ever seen. Twelve, thirteen years old, a boy and a girl. Both had mops of green hair, shaved bare on the sides. Both kept their faces about two inches from their plates all evening, ate with their hands, breaking off pieces of fish, shoveling them in, using their fingers to scoop up their mashed potatoes, first two fingers like they were taking the boy scout pledge. Sucking the potatoes off, digging up another wad. Their parents frowned, tried to get them to use silverware, but the kids ignored them, giggling, making a show of their little trick. The mother tried to negotiate. If you use your silverware, you can stay in the game room till eleven tonight. But the kids had decided they were going to stay in the game room till eleven anyway, permission or not. The parents shook their heads. They probably had better success with juries.

He found himself wishing Butler Jack would show up with an assault rifle. Thorn could take cover behind the lawyer family, scream insults at the guy.

He was finishing up his black forest cake when someone at the head table switched on the microphone, tapped it a couple of times. Flashbulbs began to pop from all around the dining room. A small group in the back of the room started to chant: Lola, Lola.

But it died out quickly. She acknowledged them with a discreet wave. Lola had changed into a cocktail dress that was tight and sparkled so brightly it was as if she'd oiled her flesh and rolled in crushed chandeliers. Her hair was down, brushing her shoulders. She had exchanged her black necklace for a slender string of diamonds. Sugar's mom, twinkling inside a cloud of fairy dust.

Morton Sampson moved behind the glass podium. He'd selected a pale yellow jacket over a pink shirt, white pants. A burgundy ascot at his throat. He had reset his smile for public consumption. It was at full bloom, splitting his cheeks as he began to introduce their illustrious traveling companions. Sampson started with Brandy Wong, the network anchor. Brandy rose and waved. Her black hair was in a pixie cut, and she wore an emerald cocktail dress. After a round of applause and more flashbulbs, Sampson had a short, obviously scripted conversation with her. He asked Brandy if she knew where in the world Dale Jenkins was hiding out. Dale was the anchor with the rival network and he hadn't shown up tonight for the inaugural banquet. Sampson suggested that maybe Brandy had nudged Dale overboard. Which earned him a polite titter.

"Oh, you know Dale," Brandy Wong said, projecting her small voice to fill the banquet hall. "He's probably in his cabin watching the evening news, rooting for his vacation replacement to screw up." It got a laugh and a few dozen flashbulbs.

When Sampson was through with her, he apologized for the afternoon's rough ride.

"I'm afraid the captain on the M.S. *Holiday* wasn't paying sufficient attention to his course heading. Fortunately our own good Captain Gavini reacted in a split second. Because of Gavini's excellent navigational skills, the *Eclipse* got through the mishap with a minimum of difficulty. However, Lola has asked me to make amends for any discomfort caused by this incident by announcing tonight that for the remainder of the cruise all alcoholic beverages will be provided free of charge, courtesy of Fiesta Cruise Lines. Drinks on Lola."

An enthusiastic murmur circled the dining room. A few shrill whistles.

Thorn hung around for the two platinum album lady and her

three backups. They were all about fifteen years old, very skinny with metallic red hair, and all four of them seemed bored or seasick. Apparently the lawyer's kids were fans of the group because they started singing one of their songs in croaky, adenoidal voices. Thorn took that as his cue to leave.

Sampson was speaking again, Thorn moving into the hallway when Butler Jack's voice broke in. Thorn halted, circled back into the Starlight Room. For half a minute Sampson tried to talk over Butler Roger Jack. Gripping the edge of the podium, bumbling about, smiling still, struggling to continue his roll call of prestigious guests, but the puny amplifier he was using was no match for the PA system's volume. Finally he gave up and just stood there listening with the rest of them. Somehow he managed to hold on to a ghastly smile, his mouth open, showing lots of teeth, as if he were all set to gnaw on a particularly juicy chicken bone.

As her son spoke, Lola rose from her chair, took hold of Morton by his shoulders, and guided him back to his seat.

CHAPTER

22

Thorn hustled down the ten flights to the control room, while Butler's beguiling voice filled every corner of the ship. Tonight his riff was on the word Roger. Butler Jack's middle name. Continuing, he said, his etymological autobiography.

Roger was from Old English *hrothgar* or something like that, Thorn huffing too hard to hear clearly. It was composed of elements meaning fame and spear. In other words, an acclaimed warrior. And as every boy knows, the pirate flag with its skull and crossbones was named Jolly Roger. A term rising in part from the mid-seventeenth-century usage of Roger as a coarse expression for penis. And Jolly as a variant of sexual intercourse, "to make jolly with." The pirate's flag named in memory of those ruffians' fondness for rape.

Roger also formed the basis of the word *rogue*. Rogue as in scoundrel or rascal, one who is playfully mischievous. Or a wandering beggar, or vagrant. Like Christ or Buddha or St. Paul, the roving pauper saints. Or rogue as in a solitary animal, especially an elephant that has been driven away from its herd and which in its isolation develops vicious and destructive tendencies.

Thorn stopped for a moment to catch his breath. He'd always had a fondness for words, liked to play with them now and again, an aimless pun. And he felt himself drawn uneasily into Butler's quirky sport, his compulsive whirl of language. Not exactly warming to the guy, but his interest tweaked. He probably needed to race down to the pharmacy, pick up that pair of earplugs.

Butler Jack was going on with it.

Rogue as in an organism that shows an undesirable variation from the standard. That is, an organism which marched to its own strange drummer. Or rogue wave, that unpredictable marvel caused by volcanic eruptions on the ocean floor. A rogue wave. Rolling along like a fifty-foot wall. Separated from its brother waves. A nameless tidal surge that wanders like a holy beggar, appearing out of nowhere like a pirate ship or a rogue elephant, to dash against unsuspecting travelers.

Thorn had halted on the landing of the Crew Deck. As he was getting back in motion, Butler Jack's voice flickered off the air for a second, two seconds, then resumed midphrase. Thorn drew a quick breath and broke into a sprint down the last stairway.

Overhead Butler Jack bade good night to the passengers and distinguished guests. Now they had a wee bit more information about the man they were dealing with. This rogue, this pirate, this wandering, unstoppable warrior rising up from beneath the sea. He would speak to them again soon. He wouldn't say when, but it would be momentarily. For now, Roger, over and out.

"Verandah Deck," Blaine Murphy said. "Sector B."

"Shut the fire doors," Sugarman said.

"Done. He's trapped."

"Where is that? What's there on Verandah, sector B? Passenger cabins?"

"VIP suites," McDaniels said. "The fucking hotshots."

Sugarman wasn't about to tell anybody, but his heart was doing something funny. Speeding up, slowing down, a pulse line like the stock market during uncertain times. The beat of a spastic drummer. With his finger against his throat artery, he listened in. Three quick, two slow, five fast, then one and a pause. Fluttery. Feeling the weakness in his legs, no blood down there, no oxygen. Not thinking straight either, having to work to concentrate. Feeling his shirt tight against his chest, running a finger around his collar to loosen it, but finding it was already loose.

Probably wasn't anything medical. Probably came from being in hot pursuit of his own brother. That together with being in such close proximity to his mother. And learning that he'd been hired so he would be meek and mild when he captured her favored son. The woman willing to risk losing one son to save the other.

Sugarman's heart doing a skip and a flutter and three quick beats, a jazzy bongo playing in his chest. A slap-happy metronome making him light-headed. Making him want to sit down, put his giddy head between his giddy knees.

Thorn showed up as they were boarding the elevator. Thorn out of breath. Standing next to him now, giving him a look as they rode upstairs in the elevator. His buddy Thorn, staring, as if he saw in Sugar's face that something was wrong in his heart. Making his diagnosis without benefit of blood pressure cuffs, any of that. Just Thorn looking at him, reading his pulse. That jizz thing again. The jizz of his jazz.

Sugar felt himself sinking way inside his head, getting a little weird. His thoughts turning to mush, to garble. Maybe it was a contact buzz from listening too long to Butler Jack. Butler Roger Jack. The guy's voice echoing in his head. Ricocheting around, shredding his normal thought processes.

Murphy and McDaniels stared at the overhead lighted numbers, the elevator car moving slowly, stopping once or twice to take on passengers but McDaniels waving them off.

All that knowledge Butler Jack had poured into his brain. Fact after fact, shoveling it in because his mother had urged him to. Butler Jack's mother. Sugar's mother. Improve your word power and you'll succeed. Good advice, well meant, sound, even if the kid was using it in a fucked-up way. Advice Sugar wished she'd given him. He hadn't gotten much either way. The spinster sisters who'd raised him were dedicated to clichés. Do unto others. That was about the extent of their moral direction. Sometimes they'd say only that much of it, do unto others, and it sounded like encouragement to bully.

"You okay?" Thorn asked him.

Sugarman nodded. But he could feel the collar on his gray

tennis shirt tightening like a noose. He could feel the hot sap rising inside him. One flutter, two flutter. His heart tap-dancing to some jive-ass crazy tune. Black man, white man. One with rhythm, one without. Which was he? Both and neither. One, flutter, two three four flutter. Feeling his knees unlock, legs go limber, feeling the oxygen spew from the balloon. Butler Jack's voice an echo. The distant other half to his own.

But he stayed on his feet, swayed out the door, followed behind Murphy, the pug-nosed little white kid. The kid without rhythm. White boy, black boy. One flutter, two flutter. Which was he?

"You sure, Sugar? You don't look good. You're sweating."

"You're not sweating, Thorn? You're a cucumber, are you?"

Following Murphy till they reached the dark steel door that blocked off the corridor, and Murphy ducked into a nearby fire room, diddled the switch, and the door slid aside.

"We're going in, Murphy. You close it behind us. Stay here till we call out for you to open it again."

"Can't I go, sir?"

"No, you can't. Now give Thorn your nightstick."

Murphy looked down at the black leather sap wedged in his belt. That was all they had. Four saps with three saps. Truncheons. He remembered that word too. His own vocabulary lessons, reading adventure books, James Bond. There was a truncheon in there somewhere, probably gold-plated or with a little transmitter inside, one of those James Bond high-tech tricks. No mother to stick a dictionary in front of his nose. James Bond would have to do for Sugarman. Sap, cudgel. Blackjack. That was it. Blackjack. Use a blackjack on the white Jack. Beat him gray. One, two, three, four, flutter. Beat the sap.

Everyone was staring at Sugarman.

"Give Thorn your truncheon," Sugar said.

And he did it.

Thorn saying "Truncheon?"

Thorn and McDaniels stepped through the door. Sugarman behind them. Two beats, one flutter. Hop, skip, and jump. Maybe his heart had been doing that all his life. Maybe he was just now noticing. Just now becoming attentive. There were other things like that. If you look for it hard enough, you sure as shit find it. If you worry over it, guaranteed it'll crop up. Maybe that's all this was. Maybe it was the normal way a heart beat when you were half black, half white. One chamber with rhythm, one without. Out of kilter, wobbling, one short leg, one long. Maybe it had always beat this way. Maybe Sugarman had always been light-headed, always had shirts that fit so goddamn tight across his chest they kept him from getting a full breath down.

Thorn stayed behind Sugar in case he fell over backward. He looked like he might. Tottering like some lofty pine gnawed to the core by beavers. Wobbly, unstable. Leading the three of them down the hallway, using his passkey on each door, very systematic. Kicking the door open, the three of them rushing in with their billy clubs raised.

Making a quick inspection, closet, bathroom. Then on to the next one. They'd done seven rooms already. There looked to be a couple dozen left. These rooms had balconies and much nicer furniture than Thorn's. Lots more space. The ship was laid out like the class system in miniature. Rich above, poor below. Even if you weren't rich, you could save up, pretend for a week.

Funny thing to Thorn was, up here, on the top deck, the ship swayed a whole hell of a lot more than down in the bowels. Every swell and trough registered. Even on tonight's gentle sea, the floor had a steady rock. In any kind of rough weather the rich folks were going to get banged around a hell of a lot more than the folks riding steerage. Which, all in all, seemed fair. Mild payback.

McDaniels was chomping on his straw. As they worked down the hallway, running out of rooms, the drumroll rising, the man was devouring that strip of plastic.

Sugar continued to sweat. Kept running a finger around the inside of his collar. Clearing his throat over and over.

"Maybe you should sit this one out," Thorn said. "You're quivering like a six-foot pile of lemon custard."

"I'm fine, Thorn. I'm fucking fine."

Sugarman's face was damp, eyes fogged. His gray tennis shirt had soaked dark across his chest in a pattern that looked like the round face and ears of Mickey Mouse.

They were down to the last three rooms. Sugarman used the passkey, stood aside for McDaniels to push open the door. Sugar first, rushing in. Thorn second, McDaniels trailing.

Dale Jenkins sat in the desk chair across the room. Posed for the camera. Handsome man, black hair, thick with just a sprinkle of gray at the curly temples. A tough, muscular face that had looked on more than its share of atrocities, dodged shrapnel, been sprayed with gore. Even Thorn had seen this guy. Seen him while Thorn sipped beers at bars, the relentless TV running. He'd seen Dale Jenkins out on battlefields, the elder statesman of TV journalists bouncing behind the tanks across the desert sands. Looking natural in field jacket and helmet. Once Thorn had seen him trapped in an Arab hotel room while the tracer bullets filled the night sky outside. Dale Jenkins. More than a haircut and straight white teeth. The guy had that old-time, no-bullshit, understated delivery. Things look bad, he'd say. But the spirit of the people is strong.

The kind of reporter who knew how to get out of the way, shut up, let the camera do its work. A word here and there. The right word, the right here and there. As a boy Thorn had watched with Kate Truman as a president was murdered, the film running over and over, the convertible, the young wife. And Dale Jenkins had been there with his dry, roughened cigarette voice. The nation's uncle. Holding back his fury, his grief, explaining in basic, practical words what was unfolding. A young man, a young president, struck down by an assassin's bullet. Thorn had watched him fight his own emotions so he might console a country. Twenty-eight, twenty-nine at the time. Now in his sixties. Distinguished and solemn. Even in death, sitting naked in his chair. Even with the long ragged wound opened from his throat to his navel. A second incision going from nipple to nipple. His bloody crucifix, his last cross to bear.

On the table before him sat a microphone. Wires stretching from the mike to the ceiling. A square piece of ceiling panel had been removed, the wires patched into a thick black cable up there. Dale Jenkins was slumped toward the microphone as if delivering his final report. Things look bad. Things look very bad.

McDaniels had to puke.

Sugarman spun around and flew back into the hall, Thorn

following. He slid his passkey into the next lock. Threw the door open. Searched the cabin. No one home. He jostled past Thorn, back into the hall, put his key in the next lock. And at that moment, ten feet away, the big steel fire doors rumbled and began to roll back into their pockets. The other set, the one Blaine Murphy was guarding a hundred feet down the hallway, rolled open as well.

Sugarman yelled at Murphy. What the hell was he doing!

"I didn't do anything!" the kid yelled back. "I didn't open them."

"Well, shut them," Sugarman called. "Close the fucking doors."

Thorn could see Murphy duck into the emergency room down there and then dart back out a few seconds later.

"They don't work!" he called. "They're dead. Doors are dead."

Sugarman took two steps toward Murphy, staring at the boy, transfixed, then broke into a run. Thorn rushed after him. Sugar was halfway down the hall before he staggered and crumpled to his knees. He continued to hobble forward as though he were slogging through deep sand, holding a hand out toward Murphy, the hand with the blackjack, waving it at the kid. Making a strangled noise, a warning. Look out. Look out.

Thorn reached Sugarman's side just as Blaine Murphy went down. Twenty feet away the tall man with swishy blond hair materialized behind the young man's fallen body. Butler Jack with sparks at his fingers. In his other hand was the glint of a knife, its blade smeared dark.

"You didn't think I'd see this coming?" Butler Jack roared. "You idiots are so fucking predictable. Trying to trap me with fire doors. You can't stop me. Not you. Not anyone."

Dropping to his knees, Thorn crouched over Sugarman, rolled him onto his back.

"Sugar?" he said. "Are you all right? Sugar?"

Sugarman's eyes were open. He was staring up at the ceiling. Thorn pressed his fingertips to Sugar's throat, felt the ragged pulse, a few strong beats, a long pause, a few weak ones. He lifted his head and watched as Butler Jack spread his lips into a triumphant smile, then turned and jogged away down the hall.

CHAPTER
23

McDaniels had a meat cleaver
sent up from the kitchen. He wedged his sap into his belt and,
gripping the cleaver in his right hand, he stood guard just inside
the infirmary door.

Dr. Metzger roused Blaine Murphy from his electric shock,
asked him a few questions, name, date, birthday, to be sure his
brain wasn't terminally scrambled, then gave him a sedative that
put him almost immediately back to sleep.

Lying in the bed beside Murphy, Sugar was hooked to an IV,
an array of monitors. He was dozing too. He'd had a mild arrhyth-
mia. Nothing to worry about normally, but for someone who'd
just suffered a heart attack it could be extremely serious. Metzger
stomped around, shaking her head. She pointed her finger at Mc-
Daniels, jabbed it at Thorn. She was absolutely appalled to discover
that Sugarman had gotten a seaweed wrap, then gone chasing
around the corridors of the ship.

"The man had a goddamn heart attack yesterday. Do you
understand what that means? What kind of friends are you to let
him risk his life like that? It's crazy. Absolutely criminal."

A while later Lola came down, stood awkwardly beside
Sugar's bed for a few minutes, but didn't touch him and didn't
speak. She seemed to be posing for the benefit of someone who

was not there. Demonstrating concern, heartfelt distress as if it were a part she'd studied but until now had not had a chance to perform.

When she left, she walked blindly past Thorn and McDaniels, a measured anxiety showing on her face. Ten minutes later, Sampson bustled in, gave Thorn a nod, and went immediately into the doctor's office and closed the door. Thorn could hear Metzger cursing several times, but nothing more.

When Sampson came out, he shut the door behind him. Thorn catching a quick glimpse of the doctor slumped forward, her head in her hands. Thorn stepped in front of Sampson. The man's smile had died, but its twisted carcass lingered on his lips. He eyed Thorn for a few seconds.

"Get out of my way."

Thorn leaned close and said, "You did this."

"Get out of my goddamn way."

Thorn took hold of Sampson's pink shirt just below his ascot. He twisted the silky fabric and lifted the man onto his toes and drove Sampson backward across the room. Knocking over a chair as they staggered toward a wall. Thorn slammed the big man against it, knocked the breath from him, and held him there. Sampson squirmed but couldn't break Thorn's grip.

"You goddamn idiot," Thorn hissed. Bringing his face close to Sampson's. "Dale Jenkins, Dorfman, Cruz. This is your fucking fault. Pretending nothing was happening, sailing on with this maniac roaming around. You thought you could keep the party going, nobody would notice. Now look. Look at this shit."

Sampson calmed himself. Though he was jammed against the wall, Thorn throttling him, Morton Sampson brought the parts of his face into harmony around a serene smile.

Thorn gave him a final rattle and let go. He stepped back a half yard. Measured a straight right hand to Sampson's chin. But he didn't throw it. Felt instead the tremble in his arm as his warring impulses fought to a standstill. Too much aikido training. Too much nonaggressive propaganda.

Sampson edged by Thorn, nodded to McDaniels on his way out.

"I think he's sweet on you," McDaniels said when Sampson was gone. The young Hispanic nurse chuckled.

Thorn walked back to check on Sugarman. Still asleep. When he returned to the waiting room, Brandy Wong was there. She carried a silver tape recorder and without preamble she launched into her interrogation, asking Thorn and McDaniels what was going on, who was this fellow on the PA, what kind of trouble was he causing? Was this man related in any way to the near collision this afternoon? The two of them looked at her politely but said nothing as she swept around the room. She kept at it for another few minutes. McDaniels went to work on his straw and Thorn looked off down the hall toward Sugar's room.

Brandy Wong made a little huffing noise that was supposed to devastate them and moved on to the nurse. Standing in front of her desk and asking her who'd been injured, why was everyone gathered down here in the infirmary? The nurse stared at Brandy Wong and smiled as if the woman had made a mild joke. The TV journalist glanced around at the three of them, growled something under her breath, then backed away. She stood for a strained moment in the doorway in her bright green minidress then spun around and stalked off.

"I guess she didn't recognize you," McDaniels said. "You know, you being a celebrity and all, I thought the two of you would have one of those rich and famous conversations I've heard so much about."

"Sorry," Thorn said. "I was crazed last night. It was a stupid thing to say."

"Yeah, well, I was pretty much of a jerk myself."

"Well, we're what's left of the army now, you and me."

"I think we're about to be decommissioned."

"Fuck Sampson, we'll do what we have to do."

"It's not about us anymore," McDaniels said. "The Feds. Coast Guard, FBI swat teams, you name it, any guy within two hundred miles who owns a flak jacket will be here in an hour or two. We're about to get the full treatment."

"I don't think so. Sampson's not going to let it leak. Dale Jenkins, any of it. You heard him. He gonna keep playing make-believe. Ride this out, maybe it'll all disappear. Hell, if that reporter doesn't know what's going on, then nobody does."

Thorn went back in to see Sugarman. He was breathing nicely. Heart going, neat, regular mountain ranges on his monitor. Nothing for Thorn to do. The nurse came in, took Sugar's pulse, looked at the monitors, and announced that his vital signs were just fine. She told Thorn she was going off her shift now. The doctor would be spending the night in her office if anything came up. Just knock.

Thorn asked her if he could take Sugar back to his cabin.

"Why would you want to do that?"

"It's next to mine, an adjoining door. I could watch him."

"Dr. Metzger would kill you."

"But can he be moved? Is he in any danger, his heart?"

"He'll be safer here."

"I'm not so sure of that."

"If he were my friend," she said, and put a hand on his arm, "I'd leave him here."

The mirror light in the bathroom was on in Thorn's cabin. Nothing else. He left it that way. Lay down on the bed and picked up the phone, held it up to the halo of light and punched in Rochelle's apartment number. He set the phone down as he listened to the half-dozen electronic linkages being made, the double clicks and buzzes and vacuums. Satellite to dish, dish to phone lines. Up to the stars and down again.

It was one-thirty in the morning and Thorn was readying an apology for waking her when the phone snapped up on the first ring.

A man's voice saying yeah, okay, talk. A dog barked steadily in the background. Thorn thought for a second he'd gotten the wrong number, but then he recognized Rover. The dog yapping like he'd treed a squirrel. Thorn asked for Rochelle.

"This another old boyfriend?"

"Not exactly."

Rover continued to bark. The same furious yelp over and over. Something new. Thorn gone for only a couple of days and a new Ice Age had started.

"She doesn't want to speak to any more of you assholes. Okay. That's what she's decided."

"Tell her it's Thorn."

The guy took the phone from his ear and snarled out Thorn's name like a dare. Rochelle's voice sounded in the background. The phone fumbled around, fell on the floor, and was picked up. Rover continued to bark.

Thorn settled his head against the pillow, pulled the blackjack out of his waistband, laid it on the mattress beside him.

Rochelle said hello.

"I called to check on you."

"To check on me."

"That's right."

"I'm busy," she said. "Call me some other time."

But she didn't hang up. Thorn listened to her breathe into the receiver. She sounded winded. A crying jag, rough sex. Maybe both. Abruptly Rover stopped barking. Another noise, a yelp, a whimper.

"Are you all right? That guy . . . Everything's okay?"

"Wonderful," she said. Voice husky, frayed. "Absolutely wonderful. I'm back in the saddle again. Don't worry about me. So glad you found a moment free to call."

"Rochelle . . . wait."

The connection clicked off.

Thorn set the phone aside. With his head against the pillow he stared up into the darkness for a few seconds and felt his eyes drifting closed.

"Trouble at home?"

Thorn jerked upright, snapped up the blackjack, and whirled toward the voice.

"Hey, hey! Don't hit me."

The young woman, Monica Sampson, was crouched beside his bed, shielding her head with both arms.

"What the . . ."

"A steward let me in," she said, lowering her arms. "Told him you were my husband, I'd lost my key. They're very trusting around this ship."

She stood up, eased to her left into the slat of light. She held his eye for a moment then raised her hands and began to slowly tug her jersey out of her shorts.

"I snuck in here," she said. "I looked all around, through your drawers, your closet. You travel pretty light."

She moved out to the foot of the bed. Undid the button on her shorts. Pinched the zipper and started to inch it down.

"Was that the little wife?"

"I'm not married," he said. "Not even close."

"Good," she said. "I don't do married men. It's a rule. My only one."

She tugged the shorts down over the swell of her hips. Stepped out of them.

"What were you looking for in my drawers?"

She let the shorts fall and stepped out of them.

"What men always keep in their drawers." She smiled. "A gun."

In one motion she whisked the jersey over her head. No bra. White bikini panties. Amazing shape. Gravity had not yet discovered her.

"Why did you think I'd have a gun?"

She lay down on the bed beside him, took the sap from his hand, gave it a look, a suggestive caress, then laid it between them.

"Because you're with them," she said. "You're part of the ship's security."

Thorn was looking at her face, keeping his eyes there. Tempted, but fighting it. "Why do you think that?"

"This afternoon. You went off with them. Morton and Lola and the security guy. I've been asking around. The black guy, his name is Sugarman, the head security guy."

"Sugarman, yes. He's a friend."

"So you're security too."

"Not exactly."

"But you carry a weapon," she said. She lifted the leather sap and let it flop back on the bed.

"What're you doing here, Monica?"

"I need security," she said. "A lot of it."

"Doesn't everyone."

She cocked an arm, rested her head on her hand, reaching out to him with the other.

"I'd settle for a weapon," she said. She touched his cheek with a finger. It was cool and seemed to be trembling, or maybe that was him. "A gun would be good. Would you do that, let a close friend of yours borrow your gun for a while? Personal protection, just until we get to Nassau."

"There aren't any guns."

She traced the stubbly line of his jaw, came to his chin, drew a tingling line down to his Adam's apple. He reached out, took hold of her arm, and laid it firmly on the bed between them.

"Sure there are. There are always guns."

"Not on this boat. No guns. These are all we have. Meat cleavers, truncheons."

She took her hand away. "You're kidding me. No guns?"

Thorn shook his head.

She blew out a breath that she seemed to have been holding for hours. She eased away and lay on her back and one arm snaked up slowly to cover her breasts, as if the drug she'd been on had suddenly worn off and now she was aware of her nakedness.

Saying quietly "Did you tell anybody you saw me? Does my father know?"

"I told Sugarman, but it wasn't a high priority. That's as far as it went."

She stared up into the darkness.

"You thought you had to seduce me to get me to help?"

"You're a man, aren't you?"

She drew a breath, dragged the edge of the bedspread up and drew it over her. He could hear her swallow.

"I know what's going on," she said quietly. Her voice changing, losing the last of its moxie. "I know why he's doing what he's doing. I know what he's planning to do next."

"Who're we talking about?"

"Butler Jack," she said. "The rogue elephant. Who else?"

"How do you know that?"

"It's all written down. I've got the paper."

* * *

He wasn't crazy. He wasn't a psychopath. Not mad. Not nuts or loony or irrational. None of those things. He was sane. He had a damn good logical reason for doing everything he was doing. He had a plan, he had values and codes and beliefs and doctrines. He believed in God. He believed in Jesus Christ. He believed in driving sober, in the value of team sports. He was a good citizen. He supported the poor and underprivileged. He believed in Gandhi and Mother Teresa. The President of the United States. The Constitution, the Gettysburg Address. We hold these truths to be self-evident, and all that.

There had been blood, yes. There had been murder and violence and the ugliness of death. Yes, it was true. These things were true. But that didn't mean he was insane or psychopathic or had lost touch with the difference between right and wrong, good and evil. He knew exactly what he was doing. You could be bad and not be psychopathic. You could be a villain without being nuts. That was hooey. That was bullshit. Result of too many temporary insanity defenses. These days no one could commit a crime without some lawyer calling them insane.

But Butler Roger Jack was not nuts. Not schizo, not a maniac. He knew what he had to do, and he was doing it. Pure and simple. He'd gladly sit down and take whatever tests anybody wanted to throw at him, the cubes, the multiple choice, say a word, tell them the first thing that comes into his mind, the ink spatter. Yeah, he'd do any of those.

Sure, there'd been extreme moments in the last twenty-four hours, losing Monica, his uranium, the pressure in his brain like a crashing jet, when maybe for a few minutes he'd been off in some La-La place. The synapses shorting. But that was over. And name someone who hadn't been insane like that for a few minutes sometime in their life. Losing their faith, cutting loose from the thing that had guided them all their life. Show him someone who hadn't known that. If that was insane, everyone was insane.

But the killing wasn't insane. It was ugly. It was vile. It was evil bubbling up through the ground like toxic waste. No question. But evil wasn't insane. Evil wasn't nuts or crazy. Evil was necessary. It was what kept good from growing too powerful. Saving the world from turning white and pure and sterile. Evil stirred the pot, kept it percolating. Without it there was no change, no movement, no growth, nothing. Pain, violence, blood, those were the twin sisters of change. Hard change, rapid change. Revolution.

Look at Jesus. There was a time when people had called him evil. Throwing the moneychangers out of the temple, hanging with whores, making the lame walk, preaching revolution. They said he was evil and they hung his hide up to dry. In the world he walked through they were right. He committed violence on their safe and happy arrangements. He brought down empires and shook the foundations of business as usual. They fought him, killed him, fed his followers to the lions. They didn't think of themselves as evil.

Now it was the other way. All new arrangements. A different status quo. One century's evil was another century's good. They called themselves Christians, but look at the world. Look at how people lived. Who got thrown to the lions now? One car at the front of the train with velvet wallpaper, stocked with china plates, silver dinnerware, dishwashers, microwaves, the wine flowing, the steaks, the lobster, while the rest of the world rode in the cattle cars. Straw and dung. Lucy, Ben Aram. Look at them.

Butler Jack wasn't insane. That was what they'd like to believe. Like there was a disease at the root of all he'd accomplished. Like he was just some aberration that could be cured with drugs or extensive counseling. As if to say that all his hard work, his years of focus didn't count.

Standing at the bottom of the stairs, Crew Deck, ten feet from the door to the infirmary where they'd put Murphy and Sugarman. Trying to resurrect them.

He stood there a minute thinking. The hallway was still.

He had killed. He had brought on death. He had raised the stakes, more than just money now. He was risking his own death. Wondering about that. He knew a lot, but he didn't know this. How it felt to die. Probably it wasn't special. Like most things. A big buildup, then nothing. Like dropping a stone down a well. You stand there waiting for the plunk, but nothing happens. No noise, nothing. You wait and wait. But there's no water in the well. Because nothing happens. Everybody saying how extraordinary this was, or that was. But it always turned out the same way. All the great secrets and mysteries, they were never anything special. Not love and probably not death. Nothing special. No plunk.

Butler Jack squared his shoulders, drew a long breath and blew it out. He walked down the hallway. His balls hurt, but his blood was glowing.

When he turned into the infirmary door, the first thing he saw was the meat cleaver.

CHAPTER

24

Sugarman knew his brother was coming to kill him. He saw a little movie of it in his head. With sound and everything. The clatter in the waiting room. The grunt, the moan, McDaniels' heavy body falling to the floor. The squeak of rubber soles headed toward the ward. Sugarman lying there, waiting for his killer to arrive. Seeing him enter the room, come over to the bed, the glitter of his knife. The knife flashing down.

Then the quick little movie would replay. No intermission, no coming attractions, just that loop, over and again. Only problem was, Sugarman wasn't sure if the story was set in the future or the past. Either some telepathic message warning him to get ready, or just a dying brain cell screaming out its final image.

The loop repeated. A man coming into his room, standing over his bed, looking down. The knife rising into the air. Sugarman watching him. Looking up at the man, seeing the shine of a knife blade. His heart hammering, Sugarman unable to move. A blip of Thorn in there. Thorn out of sequence, Sugarman's arm slung over Thorn's shoulder. A battlefield scene, fallen comrade helped from the field. Then back to the footsteps squeaking, rubber soles against the high polish of the infirmary floor.

Butler Jack on his way. And the dream told him what to do. Gave him a chance to rehearse. Roll out of bed, slide underneath the bedsprings. The dream warned him. Which was impossible, of course, because dreams were just your own brain doing its little jig of nonsense, a wacky movie that meant nothing half the time and the rest of the time meant something you'd never figure out.

But this dream felt like it was coming from somewhere else, piped into his head from an outside source. A whisper across the dark universe. Though that too was something Sugarman didn't swallow. Whispers from above. Sugarman's universe was too practical for that. What you saw was what you got. No ghosts, no goblins, no guardian angels. Fun to watch in movies, but not real. Not in Sugarworld.

On the other hand, Sugarman had never had a heart attack before. Never paid a call on heaven like he'd done yesterday, so he didn't know what new gifts he might have acquired, the holy winds of Heaven blowing through his soul. The fact was, the dream told him exactly what to do. Showed him without words. Put it into the easy sign language of a movie dream. Coaching him. Giving him an idea he never would have had on his own. Get under the bed, roll onto his back, reach out, grab Butler Jack's ankles, yank. Lever his shins against the bed frame, send him sprawling. The movie showing him the physics of it. Like the universe had chosen sides, decided for reasons of its own to save his ass. Save his worthless, sorry ass.

The clatter in the waiting room. The grunt, the groan, the clumsy sound of McDaniels' body slumping to the floor. The squealing footsteps headed toward the ward where he lay. A whisper across the dark universe.

Butler raised the meat cleaver above his head and chunked it into the corner of the front desk, left it there, stepped over the security guard, and went down the hallway toward the small ward to visit the sick and dying. He had the dagger and he had his zapper. He felt himself straighten as he walked down the short hallway. Feeling confident, secure, carrying his head erect. His balls still ached. They ached every second. They ached in the seconds between the seconds. But Butler Jack was at peace with the pain. He was at peace with his loss of Monica. At peace with his destiny. However bad it might be.

* * *

Dream, reality, dark whisper across the universe. Whatever the hell it was, it was happening. It was happening as clearly as anything ever happened. With all the little gasps and heartbeats and shadows and stutters of a real moment, the right flesh tones, everything. Sugarman lying there in bed, knowing now he should have obeyed the dream, gotten up, crawled under the bed. Wishing he'd done it, but he'd debated it too long, once again letting his brain interfere with his instincts, missing the moment, and now it was happening.

"Hello, brother."

Sugarman didn't stir, staring back into the shadowy eyes.

"That's who you are, isn't it, my brother? Your name is Sugarman. My mother's name before I was born. I know that. I saw it in her things, her papers. I prowled through her desk and I saw the documents. A marriage license. A divorce agreement. Sugarman. That was her first husband, when she was a young girl. A black man like you. Her first husband, Sugarman."

Butler Jack was smiling, a broad empty grin like Sampson's.

"My mother hired you to stop me, didn't she? That's why you're here. To stop your brother. Kill him."

Sugarman looked nothing like Butler Jack. Nothing except the nose, straight and delicate. A little around the mouth. But the rest was different. The eyes were smaller. Butler's lips had a girlish preciseness. Lola's influence. Lovely Lola.

Butler moved closer to the bed, his thighs touching the mattress.

"Covalent bonds," Butler said. "That's what we are. You and I are chemically connected, sharing pairs of electrons. Two things, but one thing. The black fish chasing the white fish. Interdependent. Do you understand me, Sugarman? Do you hear me?"

Butler Jack raised the dagger. He raised the zapper. Both hands sparkling.

"We're the same. We're covalent. The black fish has the tail of the white fish in its mouth. And the white fish has the black fish's tail in its mouth. Round and round they go. Who is going to swallow first?"

* * *

"What's the *Juggernaut*?"

"It's a ship," Monica said. "It was in Baltimore, in dry dock, Bethlehem Shipyards. We flew up there yesterday, early afternoon. I guess it was yesterday. Seems like weeks ago. I stayed in the cab while Butler went to the ship and came back in a half hour. I don't know what he did."

"We can probably guess."

She'd put on the pair of sage chino shorts, a V-neck long-sleeved jersey. White. Thorn watched her dress. The clothes were simple but she did something to them, gave them flair. The shape of Monica's naked body was still radiant in his head. Storing it away in the long-term memory banks, tingling there.

"He sabotaged the *Juggernaut* somehow," Monica said. "That what you mean?"

Thorn nodded. He studied her a moment. The woman was prettier than he'd thought at first. It was a good deal more serious than pretty. Large blue eyes, bone structure impeccably proportioned. But it was not the dull-eyed, skeletal beauty of fashion models or movie queens. Her face was trim but vigorous, clear of makeup, a sharp glitter in the eyes as though there was much in the world that intrigued her, much she had left to say with those generous lips. A little curl in the right corner of the upper lip, a wisecrack mouth. There was also a delicate tension in the muscles around her eyes as if she were constantly steeling herself for a harsh noise or very bad news.

Thorn asked her what kind of ship the *Juggernaut* was.

"A tanker, I think he said. Yeah, ultra-large tanker."

"An oil tanker."

"I suppose so."

"Great," he said. "Fucking great."

She was sitting on the edge of the bed, slapping the blackjack against her palm. Thorn was still lying down. He picked up the sheet of typing paper and read the list again.

"Your name is Thorn. Is that first or last?"

"Both," he said.

"Thorn," she said, vaguely amused. She said it again. His name sounding exotic in her mouth as if she'd discovered a syllable no one else had found.

"Who was that on the phone? Your girlfriend?"

"Ex."

"Just ended?"

"Couple of days ago," he said. "Though I don't feel as bad as I should."

She looked at him, waiting.

He said, "I'm processing it too fast. Like it wasn't rooted as deep as I'd thought."

She nodded, gave him a shy, sympathetic smile that pinged in his bloodstream. Thorn, the sexual simpleton. All dusted off, ready for action.

"So what happened?" he said. "You and Butler were working together, going to pull off this hijack scheme, it starts getting scary and now you want out?"

"I was with him for exactly one day," she said. "He came and got me where I was hiding out, gave me a load of bullshit. I fell for it."

"You were attracted to him?"

She considered it a moment.

"Maybe I was," she said. "But I'm definitely over it now."

"Where was this? Where were you hiding?"

"Where I've been the last few years in the Keys. Sugarloaf Retreat."

"I know that place." Thorn nodded. "Little motel with a dolphin in the lagoon, up the road from Mangrove Mama's."

"Yeah," she said. "Butler showed up a couple of days ago, said he had a plan in mind that was going to hurt my father. That interested me. I went along. But I had no idea."

"You're the 'her.' 'Locate her.' 'Study her.'"

"I'm the her."

"So this is about you? This whole thing, to impress you?"

"It's more than that. But yeah, he had a crush on me when we were kids, never got over it. It grew in his head, became something important. An obsession, I suppose."

Thorn nodded. He could imagine her as a kid. He could imagine not getting over her.

"What kind of security guy are you, no gun?"

"I don't need a gun."

"You're that good?"

He gave her the brightest smile he could muster. "I guess I'll have to be."

"You're going to need more than this, this blackjack."

"Think of it as a truncheon, it's scarier."

"Oh, great. Another word freak."

She crossed her legs, bounced the top one to a fast tune. Thorn looked past her out the window. A distant stab of lightning, gone so quickly it barely registered. A thunderstorm in the chartless dark.

Out on the open water the only landmarks were the squalls. Small islands of weather swirling into view, their violent ceremonies unfolding quickly, then moving past and disappearing into the gray, anonymous distances. It came as a mild shock for Thorn to see that spear of lightning out across the stretch of empty water. He'd forgotten for a while that he was at sea.

For this was like no boat Thorn had ever been on. A giant hotel with its casino and vast nightclub, a half-dozen bars and restaurants, several pools, jogging track and spa and gym and library and assorted boutiques, its marble hallways and brass and neon and chrome. So big he'd lost the scent and taste of the sea locked away inside the laminated, veneered, ceramic-tiled rooms. Forgotten that he was not in some tasteless resort but afloat on the mile-high ocean. Subject to the same inexorable laws as any sailor in any vessel.

When he drew back to the moment, Monica's eyes were fastened to his, a wry smile, as if she'd caught him muttering confessions in his sleep.

He cleared his throat, squeezed the bridge of his nose. "So when you disappeared, all that fuss, the posters, all that, it was no kidnapping after all? You just ran off?"

"I was in college, about to graduate. It all got to be too much. My father, the way he was, so domineering, managing my life, every detail, my boyfriends, everything. Then my mother's suicide. I just wanted to start over. Get away from my father. Wipe out the past, make a fresh start. Do it on my own."

"I know the feeling."

"Look, Thorn, I don't want my father to know I'm here.

He'd just try to pick up where he left off. He was spying on me when I was in college. He found out I was planning to marry this guy I was seeing at the time, David Cruz, so he swooped down, hired him, made him an employee. That's the kind of man he is. He buys people. Finds their weakness, pushes their buttons."

"David Cruz?"

"Yeah," she said. "When this is over, I want to go somewhere, disappear. Get it right this time."

"David Cruz is dead," Thorn said. "He was attacked in his cabin last night. Sliced up very badly."

Monica drew a sharp breath. "Here? On the *Eclipse?* David Cruz?"

"He was security chief, working with Sugarman, trying to catch Butler Jack."

"Last night? This happened last night?"

"Apparently. Though he wasn't found till this afternoon."

She dropped down on the edge of the bed, slumped over, eyes turning muddy. "Jesus God."

Thorn put a hand on her shoulder, massaged her lightly. She pulled away for a moment, then relented. He could feel the strain ease beneath his hands.

"This is my fucking fault. All of it."

"Don't be stupid."

She swung around, glared at him. Held the sap stiffly in her lap as if she meant to test it against his temple. He took his hand away from her shoulder.

"Butler asked me if I'd been faithful to him, if I'd waited for him. Something I scribbled in a note to him when I was twelve years old. He was still holding on to it. And when he realized I hadn't been loyal, he blew up, stalked off in a rage. He blurted out David Cruz's name. But I had no idea David still worked for the cruise lines, that he was on board. It had to be Butler. He walked off full of all that anger. Because of me."

She dropped the sap on the bed, stood up, paced over to the bathroom, went in and slammed the door.

He could hear her in there, quiet at first, then a couple of quiet whimpers escalating gradually until she was sobbing like a desperate child. Great waves of hurt rolling up from the place where they'd been stored long ago. Thorn lay on the bed and listened and felt a grumble resonating inside him, his own matching wail trying to take shape. The howl of one dog setting off the others. But he resisted as he usually did, breathing his way past. Determined not to take any more voyages to the outer banks of gloom and self-pity.

In a few minutes she quieted. The water ran. She blew her nose. A wonderful, healthy honk. A moment or two more passed before she stepped out. Her face glowing, eyes set.

She came over to the side of the bed and looked down at him. She sniffed, backhanded her nose. "I'm sorry about coming on to you like that. My stupid fucking striptease. That's not me. I'm not some slut."

"I can see that," he said. "But I wouldn't have missed it for anything."

"You won't tell him I'm here. My father?"

"I'm not a Morton Sampson fan."

She shook her head, rubbed a hand across her buzz cut. Looked off at another spray of lightning, a cobweb of bright blue.

Thorn said, "It must have been hard for you to stay hidden for so many years. Even in the Keys."

"How do you mean?"

"Well, you're so . . ."

She swung her head around, stared at him.

"I'm so what?" Her face was clenched. "What were you going to say?"

Out the cabin window Thorn caught a glimpse of more lightning, the flashes smothered by a bank of distant clouds.

"You're so noticeable."

She chewed the word for a moment, then her mouth softened, her lips tinged by a smile. He'd passed some test with her, but he wasn't sure what it was.

"Okay," she said. "What do we do now?"

Thorn picked up the list again. He flicked the edge of the page with a finger, lay it aside. "We need to show Sugarman this."

"Then what?"

"Then the captain. We should be able to persuade him to do the right thing."

"Do you know what the right thing is?"

"I'm working on it."

"And then?"

"Then we need to find a dictionary."

She shook her head uncertainly. "What? There's a word on that list you don't know?"

"No, something else. An idea."

Sugarman's howl sounded as if it were coming from the bottom of some moldy pit. Hollow and forlorn. All hope abandoned. Thorn scrambled off the bed. He flung open the connecting door and rushed to Sugar's bed.

Sugarman was sitting up, breathing hard.

"What is it, man? You all right?"

Eyes glazed, Sugarman looked at Thorn for a moment then lunged forward and seized him by the throat and, with startling strength, he slung Thorn sideways against the wall. Before he could roll to his feet, Sugarman was out of the bed, the leather sap rising into the air above him and smashing against Thorn's temple, once, twice. A twisted branch of light filled his head. Thorn yelled, clinging to a thread of consciousness as he raised his arms to ward off Sugar's attack.

Monica must have waked Sugarman from his savage trance. All Thorn knew for sure was that the drubbing stopped. He rolled onto his belly, reached up to feel the damp swelling. The side of his head was numb and aching at once. He heard voices behind him, then felt a cool washrag press against his skull. Felt her turn him over, cradling his head in her lap. Felt her fingertips.

Thorn opened his eyes and the throb was already beginning. His short furlough from pain was finished.

Sugarman sat on the side of his bed, bare chested, his striped pajama bottoms drooping down. The stripes wavering in Thorn's vision. Sugar's skin glimmered, lathered with sweat. He was gasping, wide chest rising and falling, greedy for air.

"I thought it was him," he said. "Butler Jack. Man, I looked at you and I thought you were him. Oh, sweet Jesus."

"Too bad it wasn't him," Thorn said. "You would've killed the fucker and we could've had ourselves a nice boat ride through the Caribbean."

CHAPTER

25

Monica lay on the left half of the queen-size bed, purring in her sleep, barely moving. Thorn watched her for a while, her face lit intermittently by the distant bursts of lightning. The flashes coming as steadily as heartbeats, Monica's face suffused with light as though her flesh were pulsing from within.

Lying on the other side of the bed, he closed his eyes and listened to the soggy rumble of the ship. He fingered the tender lump on his temple and found his mind reconstructing the image of Monica's body. Hearing again their brief conversation.

A woman of the next generation. For years he'd watched her kind frolicking on the beach at Vacation Island, flaunting their iridescent thongs, their taut tans. Pounding across the choppy Atlantic on Jet Skis while they screamed with airy abandon. He'd never managed a successful conversation with one of them before and had not surrendered to the delights one or two had offered.

Thorn had been Monica's age once. About a week ago. Remembering it as a time when fish mattered far more than people. An extended case of cobia phobia. Every night as he fell asleep, planning his fishing stategy, how he would stalk that tarpon, this permit, that grouper. It had been his own version of running away.

Before they'd turned off the lights, Monica described in a

sleepy voice her last three years working as a maid. The hard-scrabble lessons of menial labor. Scouring tubs and showers, cleaning up the cigarette butts, body hair, collecting the abandoned shampoo bottles, unfinished booze and dirty magazines of countless tourists, drifters and deadbeats. Sketching it with modest affection. Her long slow empty days at Sugarloaf. Then drifting to the end of her stay there, describing Butler Jack's arrival, the shock of being recognized.

When she was done, she asked him about himself. Thorn giving the quickest outline he could. Tied fishing flies for a living. Been trying unsuccessfully for the last few years to stay clear of trouble.

"So you're not a security guard."

"Not even close."

"Well, shit," she said. "I guess you'll just have to do."

"You're not the first to say it."

Finally they wished each other good night, switched off the lights, moved to the opposite edges of the big mattress, leaving an empty expanse of sheets. She was asleep almost immediately, which Thorn took to be a measure of her trust in him—a fact that pleased him less than it should have.

He plumped his pillow, resettled his head, and found himself replaying Rochelle's strained voice on the ship-to-shore an hour ago, Rover's bark, her new man's hardass snarl. As Thorn lay awake, he felt the cavity inside his ribs burn like perilous hunger, days without food or drink. A phantom pain. An ache for what was not there and might never be again.

He turned on his side, put his back to Monica. He tried to clear away the clutter of images, the jangling colors and clamor of the last twenty-four hours. He knew he needed sleep, to let his body do its small repairs, wake refreshed.

But he had made the mistake of wandering the ship today trying to get his bearings. And now he was paying for it, as his mind bubbled. Still processing the *Eclipse*'s glittery facades, its cheap golds and silvers, the shiny foils and mirrors, the endless neon, the garish furniture, the noisy shades of carpet and walls. Visual heartburn.

Every corner of the ship seemed to vibrate with false allure, wild geometric shapes, chintzy whirligigs, stained glass, lighted floors, lighted ceilings, lighted walls. Incessant music coming from overhead, always something to jar the eye, the chrome and glass, the clashing reds, oranges, and purples, a great empty razzmatazz. A blaring carnival of bad taste. Not an earth tone to be seen. No fragment of wood, not a single living plant.

It seemed to him that the ship had been designed to rattle the mind. To keep the pace frantic, give you an itch you couldn't satisfy. To jiggle and twitch and startle your heart. A buzz in the walls. A ceaseless flurry rising up through every deck. Fidgety false gaiety that seemed to emanate from the casino, seep through the entire vessel, the raucous bells and whoops and empty electronic celebrations of the slot machines, the whirling fruits, the clatter of quarters filling the metal dishes.

Yes, it was true, Thorn didn't get out much. And this was why.

He twisted his pillow into another awkward shape and saw again the faces of the dead. Dorfman, small and handsome, in his early thirties. His only sin was holding Butler Jack responsible for his foul-up. Dale Jenkins. David Cruz. Their bodies cooling now. Two in the portable morgue. Jenkins stashed in one of the meat lockers in the kitchen. While the *Eclipse* sailed merrily into the Caribbean, the slot machines jingling, the party rolling on.

"You said there'd be no violence."

"I lied."

"It's got to stop." Voice muffled as if afraid of being over-heard by someone sleeping nearby. Or perhaps it was just the bad reception in Butler's headset. A voice full of static.

"I can't guarantee there won't be any more violence," Butler said. "In fact, I expect there will be. I predict at least two more deaths."

He squirmed around for a more comfortable perch. He was nested in the ceiling crawlspace above the chapel. His hideaway. Complete with phone and cushioned mat, pillow, water jug, paper and pen. His duffel full of equipment. He could swivel right and left, squat and waddle ten feet along the ceiling brace, down to the bulkhead, and slide aside the acoustic tiles and jump down behind the pulpit. Be out the door and onto the quarterdeck in two minutes.

A perfect staging spot. Phone cables, two heavy power lines that terminated in the hydraulics room, the controls for the bow thrusters, the stabilizers, the rudder and variable pitch propellers. Best of all, running just overhead was the red bundle of cables that stretched from the signal tower through the bridge to the radio room. Radar, TV dish, ship to shore. Splice into the right cable and you could intercept radio messages, make phone calls to downlinks all across the world. Splice into another one, you could interrupt the steady flow of data going to the bridge. Cut off their contact with the global positioning satellites, the Loran. Force them to get out their sextants, their charts, if they wanted to find out where the hell they were.

It was a cramped space, and Butler's balls ached from being pressed so tight between his legs. But he loved this spot, his command central. His golden place, which had taken almost a year of careful study to locate. For months he had scrutinized the blueprints, overlaid them with the electrical plans and navigational schematics. Narrowing, narrowing, until he'd discovered the one precise location where every cable and wire crucial to his scheme intersected.

Once he'd located his golden spot, it had taken him seven months to colonize it. Finding a few moments on every voyage to steal into the chapel, smuggling several small sheets of plywood for flooring, his rubber mat, then his phone headset, his cables and tools. Little by little, week by week building his camp. And now it was perfect. In the last five months since he'd been using his cubbyhole, not once had he come upon anyone praying in the chapel.

"You've got to promise me, Butler. No more violence."

"I don't have to promise you anything."

"Listen to me. This has to stop."

"Did you know," said Butler, "*cruise* is from the Dutch *kruisen*. Which derives from the Middle Dutch word *cruce,* and farther back from Latin *crux, cruc.*"

"Butler, listen to me, please."

"*Crux* is cross. The place they hung Christ. Interesting, isn't it? Cruise, cross, Christ."

Butler let a moment's silence pass, then severed the connection. It was a perfect telephone. You could call out, but no one could call in. Never a ring, never an interruption.

At five A.M. someone hammered on the door of Thorn's cabin. Three hours of restless tossing. Maybe a half hour's sleep shuffled in there somewhere, five minutes here, five there.

Thorn peered through the peephole, swung the door open. McDaniels looked past him, at Monica sitting up in bed, then at Thorn, a raunchy remark passing through his mind, then he let it go.

"The hell happened to you?"

"Ambushed," McDaniels said. He stepped into the cabin. His right cheek was swollen, eye almost shut. "Fucking creep snuck his hand around the corner of the infirmary door, got me with the zapper. I fell on my face. I guess I'm lucky to be alive."

"And Murphy?"

"He's okay. He's back at work. Doing his shift in the control room. Hatching some new way to catch the guy."

Monica was sitting up in bed, smoothing a palm across her forehead. Thorn walked back over to the bed, taking a look out the balcony window. The sky clear now, a faint rim of purple light at the horizon.

"He could've killed me easy. Me or Murphy. I can't figure it."

"Fucker's toying with us," said Thorn.

McDaniels nodded. "Hell, it wouldn't be as much fun with two less people chasing after him. Guy's got testicles for a brain. Wants to show us what a big bad hombre he is. Put on a show."

"I don't know. I can't figure it."

"How 'bout it, Monica, that how he thinks? A performance?"

"I told you, I was around him exactly twenty-four hours. I'm no specialist on Butler Jack." She hauled herself out of bed. Stood for a moment, blinking, letting the blood find its normal level. "But yeah, all right, I guess he strikes me that way. He's been planning this a long time. It's not just about money."

"It's you he's trying to impress. Show you what he can do."

"Me, his mother. Maybe the captain too. I don't know. He's hungry for love. Starving."

"Aren't we all."

In her chino shorts and V-neck jersey, Monica sat down on a corner of the bed.

"What I want to know," she said. "He's out there walking around. He goes anywhere he wants. Don't you guys know what he looks like?"

"Oh, we know what he looks like."

"It's a big ship," McDaniels said. "Lots of hidey holes." Looking at Monica, a small smile. "So how's Sugarman doing?"

"I'm fine and dandy." Sugarman pushed open the adjoining door open. "Fit as a fiddle and ready to roar."

McDaniels drew his drinking straw out of his shirt pocket, bent it in half, inserted it, began to munch. Taking a second or two to give Monica the full inspection.

Sugarman, wearing only his droopy striped pajama bottoms, moved over to Thorn, touched a gentle finger to the knot on his temple. Thorn winced and swung away.

"Sorry."

"Hey," Thorn said. "Don't worry about it. I'm glad you're back in form."

Moving on by, sitting down heavily beside Monica, Sugarman flexed his fingers, stretched his arms up, yawning. Thorn moved around the cabin turning on lights.

"I was lying there, I couldn't sleep," said Thorn. "I had an idea. A way to go on the offensive. Flush this guy."

"We're listening." Sugarman continued to work his fingers, squishing an invisible tennis ball.

Monica groaned. "Why do I think I'm not going to like this?"

Sitting beside Sugarman, she looked rumpled but rested. Her eyes coming up to meet his.

"You want to use me as bait," she said. "Hook me up, troll me from bow to stern. See who tries to take a bite. That's it, isn't it?"

"You're bait already," Thorn said. "You're number eleven."

Sugarman asked him what the hell he was talking about. And

Thorn got the paper from the bedside table and handed it to him. Sugarman rubbed his eyes and read. A moment later he looked up at Thorn, at Monica. A different look for each. Then he read the list again and handed it to McDaniels.

"What the hell's the *Juggernaut*?"

Thorn said, "An oil tanker. But don't worry, we're not going to let it get that far."

"An oil tanker?"

Monica nodded.

"Oh, shit," Sugar said. "Here we go."

"So what's the plan?" McDaniels said.

"Give me a minute," Thorn said. "I'm thinking."

Sugar stood up, paced the length of the cabin and returned. "Tell me something. Any of you know what a covalent bond is?"

"A what?" Thorn stared at him.

McDaniels shook his head.

"Something from chemistry," Monica said. "I don't remember what though."

"It's when different atoms share the same electrons. The atoms are hooked together."

McDaniels was peering at Sugarman as if he'd spoken in Arabic.

"So?" Thorn said.

"How'd I know that?" Sugarman said. "How'd I know something like that?"

"Maybe you ought to lie down," said Monica.

"Covalent bonds. Two things that are really one thing. I never even took chemistry in high school. I had no way of knowing what the hell that was. But I knew it. It was right there in my head. Now what do you make of that?"

"Sounds to me like you need a stiff drink," Thorn said.

"I knew it because Butler Jack knew it." Sugarman was looking out the window at the distant lightning. "The guy's my brother. We got the same blood circulating. He's my fucking brother. That's what it means."

Paradise. The history of the word was an excellent example of melioration. That is, a word that rose in value over time. Improved. Starting as *pairidaeza,* which meant simply an enclosure in an obscure Iranian dialect. The Greek military leader Xenophon who served in Persia used the Greek word *paradeisos,* taken from that Iranian word, to refer to the parks or pleasure gardens of Iranian kings. When the word migrated back to Greece, it came to mean garden and orchard, and because of its exotic sound was the word used by Greek translators of the Bible to refer to both the Garden of Eden and to Heaven. Later the Romans absorbed the word and passed it down to their conquered lands, where it became eventually *paradis* in Old English. So a simple enclosure, a pen, became paradise. A stable became heavenly. And conversely, buried inside every paradise was a prison, a pen, a confined space. The white fish, the black fish circling. Prison and paradise, opposites intermingled, tails in each other's mouths.

Butler Jack lay on his rubber mat in his private paradise. He rubbed his testicles, trying to restore full blood flow. He was more at home in that cramped space than any place he'd ever been. At home inside the very skin of the ship. It was his ship now, the *Eclipse.* He was the true captain.

Butler Jack had the entire vessel in his head. Every digit, every switch and rotor and toggle and wire. He could roam it in his mind, go anywhere, knew all the specs.

2 × 14 MW CYCLO propulsion drives. 6.6 kV switchboards, four 10.3 MVA and two 6.8 MVA generators, plus six thruster motors, all engineered and supplied by ABB Marine, Helsinki. Electric synchronous motor connected directly to the propeller shafts, providing smooth shaft torque through the entire speed range, thus minimizing vibration. The cycloconverter controlled a standard synchronous motor that was robust and simple and required virtually no maintenance. The CYCLO control system provided flexible control and protection, automatically preventing the generators and prime movers from becoming overloaded at unexpected changes in voltage, load, or frequency in the electrical power system.

Over a thousand miles of electrical cable, five hundred tons of paint to cover the exterior, four thousand fire detectors, twenty-five miles of neon tubes, seventy-two air-conditioning units, five cooling compressors, and over forty miles of ventilation ducts, five hundred tons of marble.

Magnavox I 100 series Maritime Satellite Navigator, incorporating the Global Positioning System, Loran C navigator and Omega navigator, Doppler Log with simultaneous indication of speed forward, aft and sideways and a Voyage Management System.

Propulsion, navigation, air conditioning, water treatment, plumbing, electricity, diesel engines, hydraulics, refrigeration, pumping controls. There was no operation of the ship he hadn't mastered. And now he would show them. And now he would take his rightful place at the helm.

Him, Butler Jack. A boy who had been born with nothing. No father, no money, no education, no class. Watching his mother slave for Fiesta Cruise Lines. Thirty years she'd done their typing, their accounts, taken dictation, imprisoned behind her desk.

He'd watched her humiliate herself, always quick with a secret smile for her boss. Grins and little flicks of the eye, gestures and looks the likes of which, Butler Jack, her own son, never received from her.

Butler studied her. He'd seen her change her stance, an arch coming into her posture when Morton Sampson was around, showing herself, presenting her body. Her tits. A trollop. Sexing her way up the pyramid. Too busy stalking a husband to waste her affections on her own son.

That afternoon twelve years before, the iced turkeys, the Thanksgiving employee picnic, five hundred people eating on the broad front lawn of Sampson's house. Lola had disappeared into the pool house, Morton Sampson slipping in there a few minutes later. Everyone had known it. Smiling, little winks. Everyone murmuring while the money fell from the turkeys, while the food was served, while Morton Sampson's wife, Irene, moved among her husband's employees as though nothing unusual were happening. Monica sitting beside Butler, the golden down on her arm igniting in the sunlight. Butler feeling his blood steam. Feeling the flush rise up his neck, the sun growing dark overhead. Everyone knew. All of them smirking. Lola in the pool house. A whore. His mother fucking her way, little by little, into that big house. Leaving Butler behind.

A boy with nothing. Not mother's love, not father's. Nothing but a brain that absorbed everything that passed before it. A brain and a dream. I will wait for you always, forever, till the end of time. Ice turkeys filled with money. The coins trickling out. He'd waited and he'd waited. He'd watched the money fall, watched it mount up.

He shifted on his rubber mat. And for one final time he consulted the schematic diagrams that were emblazoned in his head, traced the rudder lines from bridge to NFU box, a thousand feet of kinks and twists, moving finally to the rudders themselves, and when he was absolutely certain, absolutely ready, he picked up his black-handled dagger, chose the correct wire, and cut.

CHAPTER

26

Monday morning Thorn and Monica breakfasted outside on the Sun Deck. Seven o'clock and the buffet was steaming. Asian men in lopsided white chef hats stood smiling behind the silver trays. She and Thorn passed by the deep dishes of eggs and bacon and sausage. Pancakes, waffles, omelettes cooked on command. Chipped beef, shrimp, and crabcake. Standing behind a hunk of bloody roast beef at the end of the service line the tall black chef, armed with a carving knife and sharpener, was clearly disappointed at their paltry appetites. Only a muffin apiece and a large mug of coffee.

Just before breakfast Monica and Thorn went back to her cabin and they'd discovered that sometime during the night Butler had come and gone, taken his duffel. Thorn cursed himself for not thinking to stake out the cabin. Monica retrieved her Sugarloaf clothes, the faded denim work shirts, the Bermudas. Changing in the bathroom into a frayed pair of pink shorts, one of the work shirts. Stuffing the rest of her wardrobe, old and new, into a laundry bag, carrying it along.

This morning Thorn had on a pair of white walking shorts and a blue print shirt with marlins and sailfish jumping from a sloppy sea. Stiff creases marked the front of the shirt as if he'd just unpinned it from months on the shelf. The fabric looked as stiff and shiny as tin, and Thorn kept making small wriggles to limber it up.

They chose a table in the lee of the three-story smokestack. Thorn glancing up at it, frowning. Apparently the architects who designed the ship tried to disguise the big exhaust vents with a few tons of brightly painted sheetmetal formed into a windswept design, but the funnels couldn't be completely concealed, what with the air-rippling currents pumping out of them every hour of the day.

Monica munched her bran muffin and watched the TV crew set up the lights, the chairs, the three-step wooden stage where *Lola Live* was to be broadcast back to America in another two hours. They were anchored in a cove about a mile off the coast of Nassau. The water was blue white, shockingly clear. A plump sun rose over the shadowy green hills and to the east cloud slivers piled up like soap shavings. Lining the shore, the white hotels were tinted various shades of pink, their eastern windows harsh golden mirrors. As she and Thorn ate, a breeze washed over them scented with coconut oil, an undercurrent of booze. A black helicopter with red lettering hung in the sky off to the west.

Thorn set down his mug. He opened the paperback dictionary he'd borrowed from the ship's library, paged through it till he found the word he was looking for. He read for a while, a smile playing on his face. Then he closed the book, mouthed a few sentences to himself, opened the book again, studied the passage a little longer, then slid it aside.

"Got what you need?"

"Yeah," he said. "And what I don't have, I can make up. A little song, a little dance, a little seltzer down the pants."

Thorn turned his head, stared across at a long-haired young man in a silk jacket with LOLA LIVE embossed on the back. As the guy watched the stagehands work, he played with the tips of his hair, twirling strands of it between his fingers as if he were rolling a joint.

"A friend of yours?"

"Name is Rafael," Thorn said. "He's the cohost. I like his jacket."

"I know who he is."

Thorn pinched loose a piece of his muffin and dropped it in his mouth. "You've seen this show?"

"Once or twice," she said.

"What the hell's a cohost anyway?"

A smile spread her lips. "You're kidding."

"I'm serious. What's the kid's job?" Thorn continued to stare at Rafael.

"He sits next to Lola, makes fun."

"Makes fun of Lola?"

"Sometimes, yeah. Or the guests. Or whatever the hell zips through his head."

"You watch this show a lot?"

"It comes on at nine. I started cleaning rooms about then. There's not a whole lot else on at nine unless you want to listen to the screamers."

Thorn shook his head, bewildered.

"Screamers," Monica said. "Talk shows where the audience boos the guests. Hoots them down. Bigots, sex maniacs, various losers confessing to all their dirty secrets. Lots of bleeping, dirty words flying around. I can't watch them. Too embarrassing."

"The two of them, Rafael and Lola, it's a weird match," Thorn said. "He can't be more than twenty-five."

"I think that's the idea," she said. "Cover the age spectrum. Lola lures in the middle-agers and the old folks. Rafael is for the rest."

"What? The thirteen-year-olds?"

Monica chuckled. "He used to do a show on MTV. Very hip. Very L.A. Got a cutting edge sense of humor."

"Rafael? He's cutting edge?"

"That's what they say."

"Well, I like his jacket." Thorn watched as a makeup woman ran a brush through Rafael's hair, teased it a little, misted him with hairspray.

"So have you ever been to the Bahamas?" she asked.

Thorn pulled his eyes away from Rafael, gave her his undivided.

"A few times. Last year I sailed over on a friend's boat. Stayed a month on Andros, some little rental shacks my friend knew about. Very nice, very romantic."

"You're a real romantic guy, huh?"

He looked at her for a few seconds, trying to decipher her tone. She didn't know what it was herself. Maybe she was flirting, or maybe she was doing an Irma Slater number. Rough him up a little, get him off-balance. For Irma every affair was a wrestling match. Get on top, work to the pin.

"It was a romantic week," he said. "Living on a beach, cooking fish over the fire, running around naked, watching the sun rise and set, drinking wine. You'd have to be brain dead for it not to be."

Monica finished her coffee, watched one of the TV crew guys roll a big monitor to the edge of the set. Behind the stage a gang of passengers who were squeezed into one of the hot tubs let out a raucous laugh. They'd been out there when she and Thorn had arrived. Pulling an all-nighter.

"Everyone's drunk," she said.

"Free booze will do that."

"Thorn," she said. She drew a breath, let it go. "Look, I've decided something. I hope you're not upset, but I'm going to get off in Nassau. Take my earthly possessions and bail out of this bullshit. The Bahamas shouldn't be such a bad place to start over."

He was looking at her, his face empty.

"I'm sorry if it spoils your plan."

"Don't worry about that. We'll get this asshole one way or the other. You should do what you want."

"What I want," she said. A rueful smile. "What I want."

"Now there's a hard one, huh?"

"Yeah," she said. "But why? A person should damn well know what they want. It should be easy. You should be motivated, yearn for something, work toward a goal. That's how it should be. Right?"

"Maybe you've been on the run too long."

"What's that supposed to mean?"

"You get good at whatever you do a lot of. Maybe you've gotten good at running away."

"Screw you," she said. She pushed her plate away. "You don't know me. You don't know a fucking thing about me."

Thorn took a bite of his blueberry muffin. Brushed a crumb off his lips. He stretched his arms out, flexed his shoulders as if that new shirt were chafing his armpits. "You got any skills, anything you can do beside clean motel rooms?"

"Hey, fuck off, okay. Just fuck off."

"Sure. Whatever you want."

Monica dabbed up a few crumbs of her muffin, sucked them off her fingertip. A tall red-haired guy on the TV crew was doing a sound check. Counting to ten, then singing a few bars of some Jimmy Buffett song. Rafael peered at him through a camera's viewfinder, still twirling the tips of his hair.

"I draw pictures," she said.

"You draw. That's a skill."

"I studied art in college. I was an art major."

"What do you draw?"

"Pen and inks. Small drawings with lots of detail."

"Yeah, but what're your subjects?"

"What, you're an art critic?"

Thorn leaned back in his chair, looked off at the island.

"Things I see," she said. "Objects with odd mixtures of shapes. Tennis rackets leaning in corners. Fishing poles, mangroves. I've done some birds, pelicans, stuff like that. Not exactly art."

"You do faces?"

"People are too hard."

"Yeah," he said. "They are that."

"You know, I don't get it with you guys. You're sitting around, scratching your nuts, thinking up clever ways to catch Butler. Why the hell don't you just go room to room? Bust in, surprise the son of a bitch."

He twisted his head around and stared at her. "There's only three of us. There's eleven hundred rooms on this boat. That's just the passenger cabins. We could spend a hell of a lot of time searching and all he'd have to do is duck out of the way for a second or two, we go by, and the whole thing's been a waste. It's better to draw him out. Set a trap.''

"Doesn't matter,'' she said. "No, I don't give a shit what you guys do anymore. I'm getting off in Nassau, get back to work on my running skills.''

"You feel safe doing that? Knowing Butler's still floating around?''

"Hell no, I don't feel safe. I've never felt safe.''

"Soon as the show's over, we're docking. It's your call. I'm sure as hell not trying to convince you.''

"Oh, sure you aren't.''

He was way too old for her. Had to be in his early forties. With that charter fishing captain look about him. Been soaking up the sun all his life, skin getting leathery. Hair burned to a crunchy blond. A haircut that looked like he might've hacked it off himself with a fillet knife. Blue eyes with some weird distance behind them. A guy who'd spent too much time thinking about the imponderables. Weighted down with what he'd discovered.

"Okay, Thorn, so tell me. How would you propose for somebody to stop running away?''

"It would depend on what they were running from.''

The *Lola Live* theme song began to play from the overhead speakers. Very loud, very upbeat. A few bars into it someone abruptly shut it off. They both looked up at the speakers waiting for Butler Jack to begin yammering. But nothing happened. A young guy in the hot tub whooped and splashed around. Everyone over there laughing at his hijinks.

"I hated being rich,'' she said. "That's one thing.''

"Yeah,'' Thorn said. "I expect rich would be tough.''

She eyed him. Tried to detect any irony in his face. But he was simply squinting across the bay, tracing the flight of a half-dozen gulls. A military jet was moving across the small hills, leaving a contrail like a fresh scar across the flawless blue. The chopper hung a few hundred feet off their starboard side, blurring the water's surface.

"If you're a woman, you're young, wealthy, and you're the least bit attractive, you find out pretty quick you can't trust anyone. You never know what it is that's motivating people. Somebody would get down on their knees, say they loved me, I'd never know why. But I was usually pretty sure it was either the shape of my breasts or the size of my father's bank account."

"No one ever knows why," Thorn said. He brought his eyes back from the distance. "Rich, poor, in between. Ugly, beautiful. It doesn't matter. People say they love each other all the time and you can never be sure what it means. Everyone's guessing, feeling their way in the dark."

"Oh, now there's a great fucking philosophy. Don't trust anybody. No matter what someone says, there's a lie in it somewhere. Everybody's manipulating everybody else. That's cynical as shit."

"Did I say that?"

"Yeah, you did."

"What I thought I said was you can't be sure why people do things. You'll never know what's going on in their heads. So you can turn that either way. Cynical. Not trust anybody. Or you can go the other direction. Take things at face value. Assume everybody is doing the best they can, telling the truth, the best they know it."

"You're a bleeding heart."

"I bleed a little."

"So when you catch Butler, what, you're gonna buy him a drink, sit down and have a friendly chat with the guy?"

"No," Thorn said. "I'm going to pinch his little fucking head off his neck is what I'm going to do."

"But he's doing the best he can."

"Yeah," said Thorn. "But it isn't good enough. Not by a long shot."

CHAPTER

27

At Sugarman's request, the staff chief engineer, Stefano Maranzana, placed a radio call to the U.S. Coast Guard Station in Miami. He got through to Operations, requesting information on the current whereabouts of the S.S. *Juggernaut,* an ultra-large crude carrier that reportedly worked in the northern Caribbean and the Gulf. Its last reported location was dry dock in Baltimore, Maryland.

After a five-minute delay, Miami Coast Guard Lieutenant Bill Ciardi informed Maranzana that their float plan records showed the *Juggernaut* was currently at port in Freeport, Bahamas, taking on a cargo of crude oil. It was scheduled to begin its voyage around the Florida Straits later on that Monday morning, arriving at the Amoco refinery in Galveston by late Wednesday.

Sugarman held out his hand and Maranzana handed him the microphone.

"Lieutenant Ciardi, we have reason to believe," Sugarman said, "that the *Juggernaut* may be the target of either a hijack attempt or some form of terrorist sabotage."

Ciardi was silent for a moment. Static filling the radio room.

"Who am I speaking with?" Ciardi asked.

"Chief of Security Sugarman. Fiesta Cruise Lines."

"What is the basis for your suspicion of this terrorist attack, sir?"

Sugarman told him about the paper they'd discovered.

"A sheet of paper?" Ciardi said.

"It appears to be an outline of his course of action. The paper was discovered in the cabin of a person who is the prime suspect in several crimes committed aboard the M.S. *Eclipse* in recent months."

"What kind of crimes, sir?"

"Casino theft and violence against persons."

"Have these crimes been reported to the Coast Guard? Do we have a case number?"

"They haven't been reported, no."

"And why is that?"

"You'd have to take that up with Morton Sampson."

"Have I heard you correctly, Mr. Sugarman? The *Juggernaut* is merely listed on this paper? Its name alone? No other details concerning this alleged terrorist conspiracy?"

"That's right. Just its name, but—"

Ciardi told him to hold on. There was a click and more static. Sugarman frowning around at the wall of dials and switches. He was gripping the microphone so hard he thought he heard the plastic crack along its seam. He forced himself to back off a notch. When Ciardi returned, the man was brisk.

"Mr. Sugarman, we will radio the *Juggernaut* and request that they perform an immediate internal security check."

"Hey, hold on," Sugarman said. "We need a good deal more than that. You need to keep them in port. Then land some of your engineering people, your explosives team, sweep every corner of the ship. There could be also something wrong with its navigational or electronics equipment. You should be looking for any kind of trouble they've experienced since leaving Baltimore. We're dealing with a man with a thorough knowledge of nautical electronics. He's shrewd and his plan seems to involve the extortion of a large sum of money. And we have a witness who puts him on the *Juggernaut* two days ago in Baltimore."

"Now we're talking about extortion? Not terrorism?"

"Fifty-eight million dollars. We believe that will be his asking price."

"Mr. Sugarman, feel free to fax us whatever relevant information you may have. We'll review it and decide what appropriate action to take. Beyond that, I can't say we are persuaded to take further measures based on the information you've provided so far."

"Look, goddamn it, something very bad's about to go down. Something involving the *Juggernaut*. It would be a grave fucking error if you don't use all deliberate speed to get onto that god-damn ship and check it over with extreme care."

"Negative, Mr. Sugarman."

"Negative? That's all you got to say? Negative?"

"Apparently you're not aware of this, sir, but the United States Coast Guard is straining its resources at this moment. Our mission is primarily search and rescue. We help out with some drug interdiction, but we simply don't have the manpower to inspect a vessel based on a suspicious sheet of paper discovered in a cabin on a commercial cruise ship. Is that understood?"

Maranzana whispered to Sugarman, "It is Cuban rafting season. They are picking up hundreds of refugees every day. This is not a good time to ask favors of the Coast Guard."

"Understood," Sugar growled into the microphone, and clicked it off. "Understood."

Sugarman's plate was stacked high with pancakes, scrambled eggs, strips of bacon, sausage patties, and a cup of baked cinnamon apples. Heart food. He was wearing a pair of khaki slacks, a snug teal shirt with epaulets. Cordovan boat shoes, one of the leather laces flopping loose.

When he set his plate of food at the table and took the seat between Thorn and Monica, Thorn nodded at his shoelace and Sugar bent to retie it.

The TV people had rolled out a couple of cameras on trolleys and passengers were beginning to fill the front rows. Over in the hot tub, the gang of revelers continued to revel. For the last ten minutes they'd been singing a song in unison. So off key and out of sync it was impossible to comprehend.

"Monica wants out," Thorn said.

She glared at him.

Sugarman speared a baked apple and got it as far as his lips then set his fork down on the edge of his plate.

"Okay," Sugar said, giving her a strained smile. "We'll find another way then."

"This isn't my fight," she said. "Butler Jack can have his fifty-eight million for all I care. He'll do better things with it than my father."

Sugarman nodded thoughtfully.

"Probably right," he said. "I'd bail too if I could."

"What're they doing with the bodies? Jenkins and Cruz and Dorfman," Thorn said. "They going to take them ashore here?"

"No," Sugar said. "Sampson wants to keep them on ice till we return to Miami. Soon as it gets out about Dale Jenkins, the shit'll be all over the walls. Sampson wants enough time to invent a good lie. For now the story is, Dale has something contagious. Nobody's allowed in his room. The doc came up with the name of a tropical disease that'll keep him in quarantine."

"What bullshit." Thorn glared at Rafael.

"Next of kin?" Monica said. "Won't someone be looking for him, wondering where the hell he is?"

"The man's got no family. Apparently he's got a habit of lying low. A solitary drinker. All Sampson's worried about is this Brandy Wong woman finding out about the murder. The tropical disease thing is for her."

"Is there a law, reporting a murder in a timely fashion?"

"You got me," Sugarman said. "But the word is, we're going on like nothing's happened. Brandy's running around. She knows something's wrong, big news. But she doesn't know what. I'll give her till sunset before she cracks the shell."

"Oh, she'll know sooner than that," Thorn said. "Soon as *Lola Live* starts."

Monica said, "Forget it, I'm not going to do it."

"Nobody's asking you to do it," Thorn said. "I'm going to do it."

"You?"

"What? You think just because I never watch this shit I can't be a TV star? Hey, stick around."

Sugar gave Monica a small smile.

"He's crazy," Sugar said. "He's clinically out of it."

"Oh, by the way," Thorn said. "What is this shit about you and Jeannie, a divorce?"

"Where the hell'd you hear that?"

Thorn told him about Mrs. Miranda, his neighbor.

"Oh, that woman's got it screwed up as usual. Jeannie went off to California for a few weeks. That's all."

"California."

"Place called Sylvan Farms, near Santa Barbara. Some kind of holistic pregnancy clinic. She sent off for the literature, got all frenzied. Somehow or other these people guaranteed her she'd come home knocked up."

"She take along some of your frozen sperm?"

"I overnighted it out there on dry ice so it would be waiting for her. Can you believe it? I'm letting fly on one coast so she can get pregnant four thousand miles away. Of course, I got my doubts. I think the sperm thing is just a coverup. The place sounds more like a stud farm to me. She goes out there for three weeks, gets boffed by a long line of these surfer boys, comes home with her kettle bubbling."

"But you let her go anyway."

"Yes, I did. If that's what it takes to make her happy."

Monica shook her head.

"You're both crazy," she said.

Thorn raised his eyebrows, twiddled an imaginary cigar. Gave his Groucho imitation a little Mae West inflection. "You think this is crazy? Just wait, honey doll. They haven't even turned on the spotlights yet."

Monica thought they'd argue harder. Force her to go ahead with it. But they shrugged it off, Thorn getting up from breakfast, carrying his dictionary, giving her a wink, and going off with Sugarman. Not even a good-bye and good luck.

She sat at the table watching the TV crew work, the show's

familiar set taking shape. A busboy came by, took the plates, asked her if she wanted anything to drink. She said no, she was just leaving. But she didn't get up.

She listened to the announcements coming over the loud-speakers, descriptions of the various excursions and tours around Nassau, Paradise Island, the marketplace, snorkeling the reef. As soon as *Lola Live* was over, the ship would dock. Around her people were grumbling, wanting to go ashore now. But the TV show needed an audience. How would it look, Lola sitting out on the deck of the *Eclipse,* nobody to clap, nobody to laugh at Rafael's drolleries? Apparently they'd made a tactical decision, anchor up just offshore, show the gorgeous skyline in the background. Keep their audience captive.

Monica got up, headed for the stern stairway. She carried her laundry bag, all her earthly possessions. She'd wander around for another hour, work her way down to the head of the gangway, maybe pick up some toiletries, any other supplies, charge them to her room, be among the first to disembark. Stay with the crowd, she'd be safe. Butler would be distracted by Thorn's little drama.

At the top of the stairs she stopped, turned back, leaned against the rail and gazed out at the island. The Bahamas would be fine. Get off, drift away from the docks, sniff around, find a job in one of the motels. Nobody had to know. Take back Irma Slater. Get another routine going. It would be fine, it would be a new adventure. Go over to Andros. Thorn had mentioned it. She'd heard before it was nice there. Not so touristy. Younger.

Maybe she could work her way down through the islands, St. Martin, Guadeloupe, Grenada, Martinique, Antigua, Nevis. There was no reason she couldn't do that. Explore the blue waters. Take her pad and pen and sharpen her drawing skills. It sounded good. It sounded very good. Romantic, exotic. She was young. She was smart and didn't mind hard work. She could let her hair grow back, maybe choose another name this time, a completely fresh identity. Monique, Manuela. Something with Gypsy charm. There were lots of islands. So many she didn't even know all their names.

All she had to do was walk down that gangplank, step off into a new world. All she had to do was wait till *Lola Live* was over.

Wait till that damn TV show was finished so she could disembark, get back to inventing her life.

She had nothing to say to her father. Thorn was wrong. Confronting him would prove absolutely nothing. She wasn't running away from him anymore. She couldn't care less about him and his new wife. She couldn't care any fucking less if she tried.

CHAPTER

28

It was almost nine. One of the cameras panned across the crowd showing all the chairs taken. More than half the two thousand passengers in attendance. A hubbub as the stage lights cranked up. The image on the screen shifted to the helicopter shot, a wide panorama of the *Eclipse* at anchor, the cameraman panning to the right across the harbor, showing the distant hotels. A camera check.

Another camera took over, showing Lola perched on a tall director's chair, legs crossed, wearing a bright red pant suit, hair drawn back tight, swirled around into a bun. Pearl necklace, pearl earrings. Looking trim and sexy, the top two buttons of the pants suit undone, exposing her sun-freckled cleavage as she leaned forward to chat with some of the lucky folks in the front row. Smiling at them, full of charm. Harlot. Trollop. Slut.

Butler Jack watched the spectacle on his handheld TV, cramped in his nook. Around him were arrayed the portable VCR and the microphone, phone unit and the miniature Magnavox autopilot, each unit spliced into the appropriate wires. All of them switched off for the moment. The ship at rest in the calm bay.

This time tomorrow it would be done. The cataclysm. All the televisions in the world would speak his name. Two-inch headlines. Tuesday his name would be echoing in every corner of the globe.

The man who rose from the bottom of the ocean floor, the rogue wave, the tidal surge, the great wall of water rushing toward shore. He would be more famous than Lola, more famous than Morton. They would know his name, speak it with awe. Butler Jack, who stole millions from one of the richest men in the world only to give it all away to thousands of the poorest.

There he was, on the brink of triumph, and wouldn't you know? His balls had gotten worse. They'd begun to swell, probably from the position he'd been forced to assume for these last twenty-four hours. Lying down, cramped, working out the final details. They were back to tennis balls. Darkening. Tender. Every minor movement sent a wallop through his belly. He was nauseous. A hot twist in his gut as if someone had plunged a dagger there and was thumping the handle.

But even more troubling than his testicles was the woman who'd come into the chapel an hour ago. She was praying out loud. Kneeling at her pew and speaking to God or her dead husband, Butler wasn't sure. She seemed to have the two mixed up. Asking him to help her, explaining she was down to her last three dollars. Lost the rest last night on the slots. Money her husband had left her, sentimental money she'd been using to gamble with all these years and now it had dwindled to just those three dollars. Holding up the hotel envelope for God to see. And she didn't know what the hell to do. Should she wager those precious three dollars, risk losing them, and thus lose all connection to her husband? Should she set it aside, a last remembrance of her spouse? Or perhaps she should donate it to some needy cause, or scatter the dollars overboard? She wept. An old woman with steel-gray hair, a dark blue dress with tiny white flowers. Butler shifted aside a ceiling tile an inch or two to spy on her as she sobbed.

It was always the little things. Butler's Law. The little details fucked you up. Microscopic dust. A fleck of rust that fouled the connection, one small screw working loose. It was an old woman talking to God or her husband. An old woman down to her last three dollars, praying in the chapel for divine help. A woman who would have to be killed, dragged somewhere else. Complicating things. And it was his testicles. Little things becoming big things. Hurdles growing large, threatening to fuck up years of work.

His balls hurt so bad, the thought passed through his mind, maybe he should take the dagger, cut them off. Testicles. The Greek word was *orchis, orchid,* from the shape of the flower's tuber. *Orchidectomy* being the technical term for castration. Cutting away the orchid's roots. Or in the Latin, *castrare,* from *castus,* which meant pure. Castration being used on the eastern slaves to keep the women pure. *Castus,* as in the caste system, to keep the races pure. Cut off their economic balls. Emasculate them. Purify them. Keep them in their place. And there was the other Latin term, *testiculus,* which referred to the ancient practice of swearing an oath by putting a hand on the nuts. Over the centuries the balls evolved into the Holy Bible. Testimony required a hand on the Testament. I hereby swear on my sacred nuts.

Butler had an idea. Smiling to himself as it took form. He squirmed to his right, reached out his hand, and inched aside the ceiling tile. He wormed closer, grinning. He brought his mouth near the slit, pushed his voice deep into his throat, trying to give his tenor some resonance, turn it into a bass, saying "Give your money to the poor."

The woman swung around but there was no one else in the chapel. Butler watched her trembling. Her hand holding the envelope fluttered in the air.

"What?" she said softly. "What did you say?" Staring at the pulpit, the cross behind it.

"The poor," Butler intoned. "Give your money to the poor."

He slid the ceiling tile back in place, rolled onto his back. Had to clap a hand over his mouth to stifle his chortles.

As he lay there, eyes streaming with tears, he turned his head and glanced at the two-inch TV screen. His gaze freezing on the picture. He stopped breathing, bent close. Blinking, wiping his eyes. Not believing what he saw though it was happening right there on the little square of light. Monica in a pair of Bermuda shorts and a work shirt, sitting in the chair next to Lola as the female director counted backward to ten.

"What the fuck does she think she's doing! Get security. Where's fucking security?"

Rafael was doing a little war dance off to the side of the stage set, a jig like his bladder was about to burst. One arm windmilling as he yelled, the woman director shushing him, counting backward, five to four, to three, two. And Thorn tapped Rafael on the shoulder as Monica got comfortable in the slingback chair. Thorn giving her a smile as she settled in.

"You rang?" Thorn said to Rafael.

"You're security?"

"Right-o."

The theme song blared over the speakers. The red applause light blinked rapidly and the passengers responded with faithful good cheer. Rafael hissing through all of it, hissing at Thorn to get that fucking girl off the stage.

Lola had shrunk back from Monica, looked like she might tip over backward in her director's chair.

"Well, then fucking do something. Get her off there now. Do your fucking job. She's not supposed to be up there."

As the applause was dying down, Lola's recorded voice began to narrate a sketch of their voyage so far. All the fun they'd been having. A video clip played on all the monitors. A wide-angled helicopter shot of the beautiful ship, an expanse of blue sea around it, then showing several lush interior views of the Starlight Room, close-ups of plates of gorgeous food, moving on to the Galaxy Nightclub, the tall showgirls strutting, feathers and sequins, Lola describing the first-class entertainment. Quick shots of Brandy Wong, Dale Jenkins, Beverly Mitchell and her backup group.

The woman director, in a pair of blue jean overalls and a black T-shirt, was staring across at Rafael and Thorn, hands spread out in front of her like she was about to catch a basketball. What the fuck?

"Come this way, Rafael," Thorn said.

"Whatta you, crazy? Go get that fucking girl off the stage, man. Do your goddamn job or I'll have your ass up on charges."

"Come on, Rafe. Let's shuffle on back here, talk it over."

Getting a good solid pinch on Rafael's trapezius muscle, twisting it, stealing all his California insouciance, pointing him toward the Ritz Bar, a red leather nook at the rear of the Sun Deck. Shoving him along. Thorn hated to do it. Hated to use intimidating physical force on this guy. Certain he was getting more bad macho karma by resorting to it. But hey. It was probably way too late for this go-round. He'd just have to give it a harder try next incarnation.

"I like that jacket, Rafe. It's very hip."

"Hey, fuck you, man. Get your goddamn hands off me. You're dead, man. You'll never work in this industry again. You're fucking dead."

"Whatever you say, Rafe. You're the man."

"And you're fucked if you don't get your goddamn hands off me right now."

"Not hands, Rafe. One hand, that's all it's taking for you. Just one hand."

Rafael tried to shrug out of Thorn's grip, but it didn't work. A few hundred yards overhead, the shiny black helicopter layered the air, whumping like some giant disembodied heart.

"Hey, fuck you, man. Fuck you."

"You know, you might consider taking a martial arts class when this is over. An important TV hombre like you, you can't afford to let people come up to you, push you around like I'm doing. If you want, I could recommend a class I know. It's a bunch of ladies, but I guarantee it'd toughen you up. Turn you into a stud."

"You motherfucker. You're dead, man. You're one dead shithead."

"Hey, I'm doing this for your own good. Getting you out of the line of fire."

Rafael relaxing at little at that. "What fucking line of fire?"

"You'll thank me later. Really, you will."

Rafael stopped resisting, and Thorn steered him down the center aisle, some folks in the audience staring, but no one rose to help the long-haired cutting-edge cohost. His thirteen-year-old constituency must've been down in the game room zapping electronic gremlins.

"Morton Sampson asked me to speak to you."

Sugarman stood at the edge of the glassed-in makeshift control room that had been set up a few feet behind the last row. The guy riding a swivel chair looked dubiously at Sugar. Boy was half his age, hair in a rigid flattop like Sugarman had worn his thirty years back. The guy's hands were playing the switches and buttons and levers and toggles on his sound board like it was a cathedral organ, fingers moving the whole time Sugar talked. Only took one percent of his brain to deal with grandpa Sugarman.

"You hear me okay?" Sugar said.

"I hear you fine. Morton Sampson asked you to speak to me. So speak."

"We're going to vary from the script today. Things could get a little weird."

"Weird's okay. We like weird."

"So don't pull the plug. Whatever happens, keep the signal going out. Morton Sampson wants that. You understand? Don't go away to commercial until I let you know it's okay."

"I hear you," the kid said. "Only problem is, I don't work for Morton Sampson. Or you either."

The boy had a thin neck and a small goatee. In his white T-shirt he looked like a beatnik, Maynard Krebs, from that TV show thirty years ago. The kid with a severe attitude, like he didn't realize he was discovering the exact same stuff all over again that Sugar and Thorn and his whole generation had already discovered, and the generation before that and on and on backward to the cave men. Figuring he and his buddies had invented cool. And goatees and flattops and smartmouth back talk. The kid still stared at Sugarman with his fingers nudging the slides and toggles.

"So who do you work for?"

"The network, baby. I answer to New York," the kid said. "If they want to fiddle with the show, they'll tell me. So far they haven't. So we're going on as usual."

"Is that New York in your headset?"

"Yeah," the flattop Maynard Krebs said. "New York, New York, a helluva town."

"Let me talk to them."

Sugarman put out his hand. The kid considered his options for a second or two, rubbed his thumb across the bristles of his goatee. Sugarman tightening up his face, drew out his black leather sap, letting the kid get a look at grandpa's attitude.

"Hey, Kyra, I'm handing off for a second. Head of security wants to talk to you. Yeah. Head of security for the stupid boat. Name is . . ." The kid looked up at him.

"Sugarman."

"Sugarman," the kid said into the small black microphone fixed to his headset. "Yeah, right. We're three minutes till air." He pulled the headset off, saying to Sugar "Talk fast. Three minutes."

Sugarman spoke to the woman named Kyra. She sounded older and smarter than Maynard Krebs. Manhattan plutonium in her balls. Didn't give a rat's ass who he was or what he was up to. Telling him they were on a tight schedule.

Sugarman said he understood that. But he wanted to let her know things might get strange on the show today.

"Strange, how?"

"I don't know exactly. Not obscene or anything. But a little different from the planned activities. It's important you keep running the program. We're trying to flush a guy on the ship here. Get him going. If you pull the plug at the wrong time, we might lose him."

"What the hell are you talking about?"

"You'll see," Sugar said. "Just don't unplug us, okay? Hold back on any commercial breaks till I give the okay. We're depending on you, Kyra. We got to make it look real."

"I have to know more than this. I can't just override our standard . . ."

"Nice talking to you." He gave the headset back to the kid.

While the kid spoke to Kyra, Sugarman headed up the center aisle toward the stage. Halfway there, he saw Morton Sampson exiting the side door to the left of the set. The big man halted abruptly, staring at Lola and Monica. It took him a second before it registered, his long-lost daughter sitting up there, knee to knee with his new wife. He put a quick hand behind him, balanced himself against one of the life raft stations. Eyes holding to Monica, as she and Lola sat very still in their chairs, not looking at each other. Not talking. Everybody waiting for the director to point her finger.

* * *

The LOLA LIVE jacket fit a little tight. Thorn's shoulders a couple inches wider than Rafael's. Rafael was having a couple of snorts in the Ritz Bar. A crème de menthe frappé no doubt. Thorn heading toward the stage, the leather sap tucked in his waistband. A beautiful Caribbean morning with just a tingle of subtropical autumn in the breeze. The chopper had lifted up and was directly overhead, rising so high it was almost out of hearing.

The video was finished, the monitors all blank. Commercials must've been playing back in the U.S., floor wax, dishwashing powder, whatever the ad men had figured out Lola's viewers were most susceptible to.

They had no idea which way Butler would come. The stage was backed up against the windows of one of the restaurants. The window glass was covered by a light blue curtain. So they were exposed on three sides. He supposed it was possible he could climb up on the roof of the restaurant, get up next to the radio tower, try to jump down onto the stage. A twenty-foot drop, not likely. It was more probable he'd come from the left or right. There were doors on both sides leading to stairways that went down to the Verandah Deck. From those hatches, it was a ten-foot sprint, two, three seconds from the time he appeared till he could leap onto the stage.

After speaking to the show's young engineer, Sugar had taken a position off to the starboard side of the audience, leaning nonchalantly on the rail. McDaniels sat in the front row. A neon pink Hawaiian shirt with hula girls and speedboats, black shorts, black sandals, and yellow socks. The man's legs were so white they looked like they'd sunburn at midnight. Thorn's eyes ticked across McDaniels as he mounted the stage. McDaniels twiddled his drinking straw in reply. Howdy.

When Thorn drew up one of the other director's chairs, sat on the other side of Lola, she looked at him coolly but her eyes were full of grim recognition. The gaze of an embattled queen standing in her dressing room, her maidservants gathered around her to plump her hair one last time while out in the courtyard of the castle the flaming arrows were landing, and just beyond the moat the catapults were loaded with boulders while the hordes gathered for their final assault. Her kingdom about to collapse, but still holding to her last shreds of power. Dignity, dignity.

"Good morning," Thorn said.

Lola acknowledged him with the slightest of nods, then swept her eyes across her ardent audience.

Hurriedly, a red-haired sound man tucked a wire under Thorn's shirt front and clipped the tiny mike to the heavily starched material and stepped off the stage.

The director moved up to the edge of the stage. Pinpoints of sweat covering her forehead. "We're live in thirty seconds. You okay, Lola? Are we going with this?"

Lola Sampson glanced briefly at Monica, then nodded at the director.

"Fine," she said. "I'm fine. Let's do it."

Clostridium perfringens, Salmonella, Enterococcus faecalis, Escherichia coli, Campylobacter jejuni, Listeria, Shigella, Yersinia. The words so beautiful to his ear. Though, of course, English was not his first language, so David Chan didn't know if anyone else would share his view.

He had studied the diseases, the full range of bacterial infections. He remembered their names though it had been ten years since he'd dropped out of the University of Singapore medical program. Since childhood David Chan wanted to be a doctor, but he had become instead a sailor. Working for his uncle's oil company, forced into this job by bad luck and excessive fornication.

He was the father of six girls and two boys. Two girls arriving before he began medical school, two more coming during his brief stay there. He had no choice but to abandon his dream and go to work. So he left medical school and took his uncle's job and now he sailed with the *Juggernaut* for nine months and for the other three he was daddy to his eight children and husband to his unhappy wife.

For some reason David Chan recalled *Clostridium tetani* with particular clarity. Remembering that it could not survive if exposed to oxygen. So the wily bacterium encased itself in cystlike pustules, small capsules of dark energy hidden inside the rotting carcasses of animals, especially swine.

Pork had been served for lunch on Saturday, which could explain the outbreak of bloody diarrhea aboard the *Juggernaut*. But he wasn't sure. So far, David Chan and Luc Don Way were the only crew members unaffected. David had pulled out one of the medical books he still carried along and consulted it, but had not yet arrived at a diagnosis. Pork was a possibility, but he was not certain.

In an emergency, the ship could be safely operated by three men. Two in the engine room, one on the bridge. Most of the operations were automated. But now they were down to only David and Luc Don. Luc was seven decks below monitoring the big turbines, while David stood alone on the bridge, maneuvering the giant ship away from the docks in Freeport and out into the Caribbean.

The *Juggernaut* had been in dry dock in Baltimore for three days, costing his uncle's company several million dollars in lost revenues. Another delay in their schedule could prove disastrous to ChanCo Enterprises and all involved. So David Chan pressed forward, moving out of the harbor, a ship full of crude oil and very sick men.

Sometimes the cures for bacterial infections were simple. Lots of water for the effects of dehydration. Bed rest. Let the immune system do its work. But the crew members were very weak. They could hold nothing down. Their diarrhea was watery and full of dark blood, and David Chan was sure there were also numerous polymorphonuclear neutrophils in the stool as well, though he had none of the laboratory equipment to make such a diagnosis.

Bad pork or poor sanitation in the galley. Or possibly a failure in the water treatment plant. He would have to check that if there was time. Run a test on the water. He had the equipment for that. Later, when they were beyond the shipping lanes, the way was clear, he would switch on the autopilot, go down, draw a sample of water, use the colored paper slips to see if that was the source of the contamination. This would make some logical sense, for unlike the other crew members, David Chan drank only bottled water. In a few moments, when things were less tense, he would radio down to the engine room, speak to Luc Don and see if perhaps he had been using bottled water as well. That might tell them something.

In the meantime, he had to get the tanker out to deeper water. Then while the autopilot took charge, he would check on the men. Usually so hardy, the straits Chinese crew were never sick. Hardly ever missed a day of work. Like David Chan, all of them had large families. They could not afford to neglect their labors for anything but the most serious reasons.

Shigella, Campylobacter, Yersinia. Such mellifluous words to his ears. But English was not his first language. Maybe the words sounded perfectly normal to an Englishman or American. He wondered.

It was a little after nine in the morning. Today and tomorrow they would sail around the tip of Florida and be in Galveston by late Wednesday. If there was no improvement in the crew by then, he would have to seek medical help. Fax his uncle, describe the dire situation, request permission to use the local hospital emergency room. Red diarrhea should not be taken lightly.

David Chan steered the great ship out of the harbor. He did not want to admit it to himself, but somewhere in a shadowy back corridor of his mind he knew the *Juggernaut* was in serious peril, for he was starting to feel queasy.

CHAPTER

29

From where Thorn sat, it felt like a few thousand cross-haired telescopic sights were trained on him, countless faces in his face, a crowd of strangers pressing close, stealing the air. Never been in front of an audience before. Three, four people maybe, telling a joke in a bar, and even then he usually choked, messed up the timing, couldn't get the punchline right. He was more of a one-liner guy. Stand on the edge of things, insert himself when there was a lull. Nothing like Lola, sitting indifferently with her legs crossed, a thousand people watching her every twitch. Her face flat calm, waiting for the show to begin, so composed it was as if she were severely nearsighted, unable to see beyond the edge of the stage, thought she was sitting there with just these two other people, Thorn and Monica. Not even much aware of them.

It struck Thorn, this must be part of the job description. Stage presence depended on making yourself nearsighted, going into a trance like a boxer, or a high-wire guy. Focused on the two-foot range, keeping it there, not a flick of the eye beyond that or you slip, go down hard. Watching Lola, the way she sucked the focus in, made that little cocoon around herself, it was scary. The rest of the world didn't count, like a kid making the sun disappear, a hand over his eyes. Extinguishing the whole awful world with that little trick.

Thorn wasn't sure which it was. Either the actress part of her spilled over into her personal life and gave her that aloof, impersonal air, or maybe it was the other way, her bland temperament making her the ideal TV star. Either way, Lola was as placid as a wax replica of herself. The buffeting wind from the chopper hadn't even ruffled her hair. Sitting there in front of a thousand people, she didn't seem to give a shit. Not about them, not about anything. Might just as well be zoned out in her living room.

Thorn couldn't manage it. With the all those people staring, he could feel his breath clog his throat, feel the flush rise, a cloud of steam closing in around him. He watched in the monitors as the wide-angle overhead shot from the helicopters slowly zoomed in on them, closer and closer until he could see the freckles on Lola's cleavage. And the director raised her hand high, brought it down, counting for Lola, one, two, three. Go.

Lola Sampson waited for the last of the applause to die and the helicopter to bank away and drag its racket with it. She let a second or two more pass for dramatic effect, then some dormant part of her fired up and she smiled avidly into the cameras, becoming vivacious, almost flirty, bouncing in her chair as she welcomed America along on their seagoing fiesta. They had an absolutely great show planned for today. Bev Mitchell and her gals would be along later to sing a few of their hottest new tunes, Brandy Wong was there to share some clips from her upcoming celebrity interview special on ABC, and later on in this morning's show, she and Morton would narrate video postcards of their first full day at sea.

But before they got to that, Lola wanted to chat with a couple of the intriguing passengers who'd come along for the weeklong fiesta. She swiveled immediately to Thorn, placed a cool hand on his knee, and introduced him as a man who'd always harbored a secret wish to sit in Rafael's chair and today was having his dream fulfilled. Lola focused her unbearable smile on Thorn. One second, two seconds, three, the silence mounting, but Thorn was still trapped in the airless haze of his stage fright.

"Well," Lola said, "I see at the moment our friend is speechless with excitement. So maybe we'll give him a minute or two to catch his breath and get back to him then. How about that?"

Thorn nodded stiffly and a titter ran through the audience.

Lola swung the other way and beamed at Monica, introducing her as another passenger, and asking if she would mind starting things off, describe her impressions so far of the twenty-fifth anniversary cruise. This cruise that was so important to Morton and her, so don't say anything too bad.

"Screw that," Monica said. "I'm not here to promote your business."

As the crowd murmured, Monica scowled across at Thorn, giving a little jerk of the head to prompt him into action. But Thorn was preoccupied with trying to swallow the thick knot of muscle bunched in his throat.

"Come now," Lola said. "Haven't you had any fun at all?"

Monica's mouth was clamped. She stared at Lola for a moment, then swung around to face the camera.

"I'm Monica Sampson," she said. "Morton Sampson's daughter. The girl who disappeared three years ago. Everyone thought I'd been kidnapped, but I wasn't. I ran away. There was a lot of fuss at the time. Maybe you remember."

The crowd took a few seconds to register, then a hoarse babble rose and churned from the front row to the back and to the front again, a rebounding wave of noise. Almost half a minute went by before it was quiet enough on the Sun Deck for Lola to speak again.

"Apparently they do remember," Lola said. Her voice rigid, her vivaciousness evaporating quickly. "So tell us, Monica, where have you been for the last three years? And pray tell, why did you choose today to make your reappearance?"

"I've been hiding," she said. "Hiding out." She glanced sternly at Thorn. "But I'm finished with that. I'm ready, by God, to face him."

"And who would that be, dear?"

"Him. Your husband."

She shot a hand out toward her father who was slouching near the forward life raft station. He drew a hard breath, lifted his head, conjured a sickly smile, and padded toward them, into the view of the cameras, waving gamely at the sprinkling of uncertain applause. The director's arms hung at her sides. She seemed ready to drop her clipboard to the deck.

When Sampson was settled in the chair, the red-haired stage-hand rushed forward, clipped a mike to his dark blue shirt, and ducked away. Sampson studied his daughter for a moment, reached out a hand for her, but she shrank back. He closed his eyes.

And Monica started in. It sounded like something she'd re-hearsed for years, maybe even written down, crossed out words, chosen better ones, memorizing it, perfecting it. An eloquent speech about her father. The man who'd controlled her, tried to break her spirit just as he'd broken her mother's.

Monica's mother, Irene, had taken to her bedroom when Monica was five or six. Woozy or boozy, Monica wasn't sure. But what she was sure of, it was Morton Sampson who'd driven her to it. Morton Sampson who'd slammed her mother's bedroom door, nailed it shut. Allowed her out only for occasional command per-formances as hostess for one of his gatherings.

And she began to recite her father's abuses. His years of hu-miliating treatment. He didn't strike Irene, didn't bruise her, nothing so obvious. But when it was just the three of them alone, he'd spoken to her as you would a stupid pet. A dog that couldn't learn to pee outside. Giving Irene deep slices that didn't show, paper cuts that nicked the bone, day after day, hour by hour, wounding her, bleeding her dry. Emotional abuse. Not as dramatic as the physical kind, not as easy to detect, but just as real, Monica said, and in a way more terrible because her mother wasn't ever sure if she might be imagining it. Insecure, feeling guilty that she might be misreading everything, twisting Morton's innocuous re-marks into something cruel. But Monica had been there, had heard the words, knew it wasn't her mother's imaginings. The man was hateful, destructive, a power monger.

Monica rolling along at a furious clip, letting it all rush out. Directing her speech to the audience but from time to time swing-ing her head around to fire a sentence or two in her father's direc-tion.

A couple of minutes into Monica's speech, Lola's hands jerked to her ears as if she meant to strip off her earrings or bat away a cloud of bugs, then she caught herself and smoothed out the return flight, lowering her arms with graceful nonchalance. It was the first break in her composure Thorn had witnessed, and it set off another murmur in the audience.

Monica continued her list of terrors, incidents, verbatim fragments of conversation, imitating perfectly the hateful sarcasm, the dismissive barbs Morton had used against Monica's mother. As Thorn listened, he saw Murphy bustle out of the starboard hatch, glance around the Sun Deck till he spotted Sugarman at the rear of the audience, then lope back to join him.

"Stop," Sampson barked. "Please, don't, don't do any more of this. Not here, not like this. Please, no more, sweetheart."

Lola seemed to have imploded, shoulders hunched, all the luminescence vanished from her face. Looking nowhere.

No one stirred in the audience. The director had squatted down on her heels and was gazing at the stage with the awe and bewilderment of a soldier looking at a distant mushroom cloud. The end of the world as we knew it.

Without warning, Thorn's nausea passed. The air cleared, the sun brightened, and breath began to stream into him again. The audience became a colorful blur. He heard his own voice call out.

"Butler. Does anyone know the word *Butler?*"

One of the cameras dollied closer to him. The technician pressing his eye hard to the viewfinder. Another wacko about to erupt.

Monica craned forward to peer at Thorn. He could hear the strain in his own voice, knew he hadn't recovered fully, but there was a job to do, goddamn it. A homicidal lunatic to provoke.

"*Butler* is from the French *bouteillier,* which means bottle-bearer. From the Middle English *botel* and the Old French *botele.* I'm probably mispronouncing them, but there it is. The word goes back to medieval Latin *butticula* and late Latin *buttis,* which means cask. So a bottle is a little cask. A *buttis.* A heavy, thick receptacle with a wide flared bottom. Which is the source of a bunch of English words like butt. Or ass. Someone butts in. Or butt as in object of scorn, the butt of a joke, or butt, as in the stub of a cigarette. Or butt as in ass. Posterior. From which we get buttface, buttbreath, buttbrain. Not a pretty word. Butler. He's the ass sent down to the cellar to get the wine, cart it back so the folks at the main table can swill it. Butler. The butt of jokes. A loser. Total loser."

Thorn stared into the shiny lens of the camera, and he could feel him, his eyes staring back. Burning.

"He's concealed in one of three places," Murphy told Sugar. "I laid out all the cross sections, did a comparative analysis of the blueprints. Used the computer, looking for intersections of the media lines, the navigational systems, any other crucial operations, and I narrowed it down to three places. I told Gavini, and he said I should come up here, let you know. Let you decide how to proceed."

Sugarman heard Murphy talking. Heard the words from a long distance away though the young man was standing right next to him. At the moment everything seemed a long way off. The stage up there. Thorn, Monica.

He was listening to Murphy, weighing what the kid said, deciding on the right course of action, his eyes continuing to sweep across the two or three places where Butler might surface, still doing his cop job while he stood there suffocating on the rich tropical air.

"I got it narrowed to those three places. I'm sure that's where he is, hiding in one of them."

"Three places," Sugar said.

Up on the stage they were still talking. Thorn finished with his little word history, sitting back in his chair looking relieved. And now Monica was taking her turn again, forging on with her denunciations of Daddy. Telling the world, the words rushing out of her, tears on her face, something about cleaning the blood out of a boat, her mother's blood. A suicide attempt. A jumbled story. Her father had made her do that, Sampson forcing Monica to get down in her own mother's blood, wipe it up. Sugarman listened to that, listened to Murphy too, all the while his eyes scanning the Sun Deck. Trying to breathe. Trying to swallow down a cup or two of air. That would be nice. Air in his lungs would be nice. Oxygen was important. Everyone said so.

"We could leave McDaniels here. He and Thorn could handle Butler if he shows up. You and me, we go check out the three places. Go down the list. Surprise attack. But if we don't hurry, it could turn out like the Dale Jenkins thing. Butler might've taken a hostage, be using their cabin. Passengers could be in danger. Because two of these places are in the ceilings above passenger cabins on D Deck. So we should go right away. We should move before he has a chance to get away."

She was about seventy-five but spry. *Spry* was the word that came into Sugarman's head. He should look it up sometime, see what its history was. Might learn something. Had to buy himself a better dictionary when this was finished. Seventy-five if she was a day, but marching with the spunk of someone half that. Steel-gray hair, good tight skin, dignified bearing, wearing a blue dress with white flowers on it. White tennis shoes. Something not right about her stride, a little hitch or something, he couldn't say. Coming down the middle aisle toward Sugarman and Murphy, causing a stir in the audience, one of her hands clutching the bodice of her blue dress as if she were chilled. Stopping right in their faces. A white envelope in her other hand. Face wrinkled, lips quivering. Holding up the envelope in Sugarman's face, a few dollar bills showing inside.

"Are you security?" she asked. "They said you were security."

Sugarman told her yes, yes he was. He glanced over at Maynard Krebs. The kid had a juicy grin. He was watching the stage, yammering into his microphone. Eating this up. Watching a family blow apart into bloody chunks on national television. The kid sniggering, talking to Kyra, letting this segment of the show run long, going to blow the cap off the ratings. Yes sir. Big-time mega-businessman and his TV star wife exploding like ripe watermelons before twenty million viewers and he was there. Maynard G. Krebs running the control board. Sugarman watching this. Finally getting a little oxygen down. Only a little, thinking maybe he needed to perform a tracheotomy on himself. Jam a drinking straw through his throat, get a good sip.

The spry grandmother was in his face. Her voice a feeble croak.

"A man in the chapel. I heard him up there. In the ceiling. He dropped down."

"Chapel?" Sugarman hadn't realized there was a chapel. But of course there had to be. This was a floating city. A bobbing metropolis. You never knew when you might want to get married. Have a christening, a funeral. A chapel. Yes.

"In the chapel ceiling."

Murphy bulled in front of the lady.

"That's one of the three," he sputtered. "One of the places I narrowed it to. Two cabins on D Deck and the ceiling above the chapel. It's on A Deck, four doors forward of the infirmary. Five main trunk lines intersect right there. He could control a half dozen of the most critical functions on the ship if he had the right equipment. And knew what the hell he was doing."

Up on the stage Monica was weeping. Morton Sampson laid his arm across her shoulder, trying to comfort her, but Monica squirmed away from him, scooted her chair a foot to the side. Thorn was talking again, seemed to be trying to drive a stake through Sampson's heart, asking him why the hell he would do that, make his daughter get down in her own mother's blood. What kind of fucking monster was he? The audience started to boo. Sugarman not sure who they were mad at.

Maynard Krebs was chuckling. Gobbling it up.

A foot in front of Sugar, the spry old woman in the blue dress wavered like a wisp of smoke. To her left Rafael moved close, gawking.

"Wager this," she said. "Keep it alive. Please?"

The lady waggled the envelope in Sugarman's face.

Her other hand came away from her bodice. A bright red hand. Holding it up, staring at it. She looked embarrassed. Her blue dress falling open, showing her slip with a ragged tear, a heavy bra dangling loose. Blood seeped from her bony white chest.

"He killed me," she said. "The man in the ceiling."

The spry old lady made one last shimmy and began to sink. Sugarman caught her, swept her into his arms, carried her a few feet, and laid her down in the shade of a life raft. Very light lady. Bones felt hollow.

On the speakers, Monica's voice abruptly halted. Sugarman stood up in time to see the TV monitors jitter for a second. Then the sound system squawked and Butler's face appeared, his long blond hair, the precise, girlish lips. At the control panel, Maynard Krebs was no longer grinning. He flicked his switches, tugged his slides up and down, but he could not make Butler Jack go away.

Sugarman jumped up, seized Murphy by the front of his white shirt, dragged him close.

"Get Metzger. Get the fucking doctor up here. Hurry. Do it now. Go! And you, you, Rafael." Sugar snatched the tall man's arm. "You stay with this woman till Metzger comes. Hold her chest together. Apply pressure to the wound. Do you understand me?"

Rafael stared down at the blood fanning out across the impenetrable teak.

"All right," he said. "All right."

"Where you going?"

"To church," Sugar said, and he was off. He was running.

As he passed by the edge of the stage, he stabbed his open palm at Thorn. Stay right there, do what we planned. Then ran through the side hatch door, down the short stairway, while Butler Jack informed the assembly about his first name. Setting the record straight. Correcting what the moron said earlier.

Butler. Telling twenty million viewers that a butler was an officer of the highest rank. Equivalent to captain, to general, to admiral. A leader, a conqueror. And from the old French *bouteillier,* the bearer of the bottle, the rich red wine that was the symbol for the blood of Christ, in other words, the one entrusted to bear the holy sacrament. While at the same time, yes, it was true, butler was a humble manservant, in charge of the lowly wine cellar. Like other notable people he needn't mention, Butler was a man of extreme paradoxes. Born of the lowest ranks, ascending to the highest. Like others whose names he needn't speak aloud.

Sugarman sprinted toward the chapel. His heart flailing.

CHAPTER
30

Sugarman rounded the last stair-
way and caught sight of Butler Jack as he was coming out of the
chapel, shutting the door behind him. Fifteen feet away, Sugar
slowed to a stroll as Butler turned and faced him. Shock flickered
briefly on his face, then Butler spread his lips into a smile. The feral
eagerness of a cornered wolf.

Behind him the hallway was empty. The lap of Butler's blue
overalls was blotched with the spry old lady's blood.

"You found me. You're good."

Sugarman came forward two more steps, leaving only ten feet
between them. There was no way Butler could turn and outrun
him. Not unless the kid was a world-class sprinter, and even then,
the mood Sugarman was in, the amount of adrenaline flooding his
veins, he wasn't worried. He'd go against a cheetah at the moment, take any odds.

"If I'm good," Sugarman said, "I got it from my father's
genes. The ones we don't share."

Sugar held his ground as Butler approached a single step.
There wasn't going to be any footrace.

"Don't be so sure." Hair loose down his back, an easy grin
that showed no teeth. "Lola's in both of us. Her cold conniving

mind. That's where we get it, you and me. That's why we're here now but no one else is."

Sugar cut his eyes to Butler's hands. Both hanging easily at his sides as he narrowed the gap between them by another half step. Knife in his left, the silver prongs on the fingertips of the right. His arms went taut and he could feel the numbness creeping into his blood, the same dark paralysis he had suffered before when he'd faced off with Butler Jack.

"Covalent bonds," Sugarman said quietly. "That's what we are. We're atoms with shared electrons."

Butler lost his smile briefly, wowed by Sugar's command of the language.

"That's right," Butler said. "Exactly. Covalent."

"That's why you can't kill me," Sugarman said, still quiet. "You tried on the docks in the Everglades, you tried again when I caught you in the media room. And last night you went to the infirmary to do it again. But I wasn't there. I wasn't there because we have shared electrons. You can't kill me. We're partners. You move, I move. We anticipate each other. We're hooked together. You swing, I duck. I swing, you duck. We're the white fish and the black fish, each of them with the other's tail in his mouth. Neither of us can swallow. We depend on each other. We circle and we circle. We're the same fish, and a single fish can't swallow itself."

Butler closed the gap between them to two yards and stopped. His smile had emptied of meaning but was hanging on by the sheerest willpower. And Sugarman saw it then. Saw it and realized he'd known it for days, maybe known it from the first time he'd seen Butler Jack on the videotape. Hadn't let it surface. Too weird. Too many tangled implications to consider. But the smile on Butler's lips, that empty grin was a perfect echo of Morton Sampson's.

"I'd like to stay and gab, Sugarman, sort out all this compelling philosophical bullshit, but I have more important matters to take care of. A ship to pilot."

"And hungry kids to feed?"

"That's right."

"Kids like you used to be? Poor, underprivileged."

"I was poor, yeah. Damn poor."

Sugarman saw the knife hand begin to move. A nervous tic, Butler rolling the black grip lightly with the fingertips of his left hand like a pitcher fondling his baseball as he shakes off sign after sign.

"You believed you were poor and you hated it."

"What're you talking about? Everybody hates being poor."

"I didn't. I was happy."

"Bullshit."

"The two sisters who raised me didn't make in a year what Lola Jack made in a week when you were growing up. You weren't poor. You weren't starving. Not for money anyway."

"What do you know about me?"

"We're covalent bonds, remember? I know everything about you. I know when you're going to rush me, which way you're going to feint, and I know which of those weapons you're going to try to use first. And I also know exactly which way you're going to fall when I'm done with you."

The grin returned, more sneer than smile.

"You're scared of me, aren't you, Sugarman? I'm your little brother and you don't want to hurt me. You're too compassionate for your own fucking good. I saw it in your face the other two times, I see it now. You're scared of me, and scared of yourself, scared you'll roll up into a ball again."

"Try me," Sugar said.

Butler stood there measuring angles, eyes roaming Sugar's body. A cool, disinterested appraisal. Sugar's arms hung heavy at his sides as if the molten steel in his veins was threatening to cool and harden, turn Sugarman into a park statue, pigeons roosting on his immobilized shoulders.

But his mouth still worked, his lips limber.

"Poor powerless Butler, his mother working for a rich and famous man. It must have infuriated you. Seeing such wealth, not having any of it. It must've twisted you up inside. All that money so close, your mother so impressed by it, sucking up to it, doing anything she could to wheedle her way inside that mansion, and there you were, so poor, so sad and fucked over."

"You're wrong. I didn't care about money. I still don't."

"Yeah, then why do you steal it? Why go to all the trouble to show how smart you are, how clever? The smoothed-off quarters in the slot machines. Stealing the chips. No, you don't care about money. Not much you don't. You're fucking obsessed with money, Butler Jack. If you'd just had enough of it when you were growing up, maybe your mother would've loved you better. Maybe she would've stayed at home, given you what mothers are supposed to give. Maybe if you had enough of it right now, she'd take an interest in you. Give you a little of her sunshine."

"Bullshit. That's your story, not mine. You're the one she ran away from."

"Mine and yours, Butler. Both our stories. Same mother, same story. Lola is incapable of giving what either of us needed. But I was the lucky one. She ran away from me. If she'd stayed, hell, I might've turned out like you."

"Bullshit. You don't know what the hell you're talking about." His eyes fastened to Sugar's like the dark barrels of cocked pistols. A tremor had begun to show in his right cheek as if the nerves in his flesh were reawakening from a long slumber.

"I know another thing too, Butler. And it's going to drive you fucking nuts. I know who your real father is."

"You don't know shit. Not about me, not about anything."

Butler narrowed the gap between them by another half step. He made a fist of his right hand and the blue spark crackled between his fingertips.

"Morton and Lola," Sugar said. "They must've been going at it, banging away like goats for twenty years, sneaking around, doing it behind Irene's back. Took Lola that long to finally hook him, reel him in, get him to the boat. Oh, maybe he would've married her sooner, but he probably got nervous when he saw Lola's baby boy, how fucked up he was. Little Butler Jack. Shit, that probably set Lola's timetable back another ten years. It must have cooled old Morton's horniness considerably when he found out what a goddamn freak he'd fathered."

"He's not my father."

"Sure he is. He's Monica's father, and he's your father. Hey, we're all related. A half here, a half there. One big extended fucked-up family. And you're our pride and joy, Butler. Our mascot. The biggest fuckup of them all. Your own shrink tries to drown you. So dumb you can't even tell the difference between a water valve and a hydraulics valve. Can't even hold a job in a company your own father owns.

"Only reason you aren't in jail right now is because Morton knew it was you stealing from him, and he took pity on you. He wanted me to catch you, be all nice and tender with you. Not bruise your ass. Morton and Lola think you're so pathetic and fucked up you couldn't hold a regular job, they just have to subsidize your little hobby. Let you keep on stealing from the cruise lines. But now even your own parents have had enough. They're cutting you off. And I'm the one doing the cutting."

Butler's smile crumpled and a noise whuffed out of his mouth. He lowered a shoulder and rushed forward. And it was like the old days for Sugarman. The football days. Baiting the guy in the line across from him. Some guy who'd jabbed his finger in Sugarman's eye once too often down at the bottom of a pileup. Sugarman forced to tamper with the guy's head. Hup one, your mother's pussy is so big, hup two, it took six of us, hup three, before she knew she was getting fucked, hike. And the guy lowered his shoulder, doing what his blood told him, not what his coaches had been drilling into him for five hot months. Driving forward, completely off-balance, and all it took was a hand on his ribs, a simple push and Sugar was around him and gone. Catching his touchdown pass.

Butler came like that, the knife waving, the voltage sputtering at his fingers, and Sugar kept himself planted, calm and focused, until he could taste Butler's breath, smell his angry sweat, and he sidestepped right, dragged a foot behind, tripped him, slapped a hand on his back and shoved him on his way. Butler pitched forward, head banging the metal door of a storage closet.

Sugar gave him a moment to turn his face around. And there it was, that frozen second of time, hanging, waiting for Sugarman to act. All he needed.

Sugar drew back his arm. Looking into his little brother's lifeless eyes. The moment inflating, the headlights shining bright, making him squint, a half second that lingered for minutes, long enough to mire himself in the pluses and minuses, the moral complexities and psychological fucking ambiguities of his action. But he didn't let it happen this time. Didn't think. Just hesitated that half second then let his body do what it had been trained to do when attacked by felons and crooks, robbers and bandits, muggers and killers.

Sugarman let it fly, cracked a forearm across his brother's face, and instantly a dark jelly began to well from Butler's mouth and nostrils. Sugar clamped a hand on each of his brother's wrists and spread them wide, pinned them to the wall.

Growling, Butler squirmed hard, ducked his head, lunged and tried to take a bite from Sugar's face. Teeth clacking an inch from the tip of Sugar's nose. And reflexively, Sugarman kneed him in the crotch.

Butler's face went slack. The nerve pathways overloaded for that moment, the circuitous trail from nuts to brain jammed with bad news. A second passed, two, then Butler howled. Bellowed totally out of proportion to the force of the blow. So Sugarman tried it again, purely as an experiment, to find out if he'd heard right. Slammed his knee a second time and then a third, Butler shrieking now, sobbing. The dagger dropped away.

Sugar released the left wrist, yanked the right one down with both hands, forcing Butler into an awkward stoop. Holding him there, Sugarman tore lose the zapper contraption, ripped the wires from Butler Jack's sleeve, pulled loose the battery pack from his belt. With his hip, he mashed Butler against the metal door. Butler was panting hard, sobbing between gasps.

Sugarman ripped the last of the small wires loose, then got hold of his wrists again, spread him wide and pressed him flat against the door, and drew his right leg back to let Butler see what he was going to do, the kid closing his eyes, wincing, saying, no-o-o-o, a ghostly plea.

And Sugarman let his knee go, gave him another thud. This time got his kneecap so deep into his brother's groin it probably made acquaintance with his larynx.

Not something he should have done. A violation of his own strict rules. Crossing the line from self-defense into the realm of torture, punishment. But doing it anyway. Doing it for Emilio Sanchez and Dale Jenkins and for Dorfman and David Cruz and spry old women everywhere, and for any others he hadn't found out about yet. Doing it to free himself finally and forever from the plaster cast he'd been trapped in for these last weeks.

Totally wrong. Something he knew he would deeply regret tomorrow, the next day, the rest of his life. He would have to live with the shame. Torture, revenge.

But at that precise moment he felt fine. At that moment, slamming his knee into his brother's crotch, he felt fucking wonderful.

Thorn had to drag Sugarman away. He was going about his business in a passionless, mechanical way, kneeing Butler Jack. Kneeing him again. Butler apparently unconscious, pinned to a storeroom door, while Sugar exacted his retribution.

Thorn had to use all his strength to muscle him off, and even then it was only because Sugar decided to yield that he was able to do it. Thorn left him standing there over Butler's body while he stepped away and scooped up the dagger.

Butler lay bleeding from the mouth and nose, his body sprawled across the hallway, head cocked up against the wall. Nose starting to swell.

"Berserk," Sugarman said. "I went berserk. He came at me and I slammed him into the wall and held him there while I kneed him in the nuts. I lost it. I lost control. Berserk."

His eyes were glassy and he looked off into a pocket of air above Thorn's head and asked Thorn if he remembered the word berserk. Thorn said yes, yes, he did.

Sugar said, "Running without their bear shirts into enemy lines. The Vikings. That's where it's from. The fucking Vikings. Warriors of the first order. That's how I felt."

"Thank God for the Vikings."

Sugar slumped against the wall. His face seemed shrunken and his flesh had lightened to a ghastly yellow as if his blood had retreated to those secret places where blood goes when the brain has had enough of the world's pain, enough of sight and smell and self-analysis, the blood stealing away with its bright treasure of oxygen, leaving the pulsing tangle of gray matter to gasp and sputter and fend for itself, leaving Sugarman to wither to the deck in a breathless heap beside the creep who did not deserve to be called even half his brother.

CHAPTER
31

His Day-Glo pink shirt darkened with perspiration, McDaniels came huffing down the corridor of the Crew Deck as Sugar was swinging open the door to the ship's single jail cell. Thorn held on to Butler Jack, a rigid armlock, probably shoving it harder than he needed to, forcing the cartilage to pop, maybe tearing a tendon or two. About half a pound of pressure away from wrenching the fuckhead's arm out of the shoulder socket.

Thorn stepped up alongside Sugar and McDaniels, lurching Butler forward, and the four of them peered into the cell.

"Looks like my cabin," said McDaniels. "Only bigger."

The brig was a ten-by-ten steel box with welded seams and a single recessed light in the ceiling, the bulb covered by a steel cowling. No furniture, no cot, not even a mattress. Hard time at sea. Positioned at eye level in the thick steel door there was a foggy square of viewing glass with embedded silver reinforcing wire.

"Whatta you think, buttface?" said Thorn. "Comfy enough for you?"

Butler Jack rolled his head up off his chest, gave Thorn a bloody stare.

Thorn handed Butler off to McDaniels, then he and Sugar stepped inside the cell and began to bang on the walls with their saps, testing the floor, the ceiling. When they were satisfied it was secure, Sugar shut and locked the door on Thorn to see if he could rattle the hinges from inside. No way.

"Must've been expecting Jack the Ripper," Sugarman said as he set Thorn free.

"Well, now they got him."

McDaniels shoved Butler inside the vault, and he stumbled across the room and collapsed in the far corner. He lifted his head and broke into a gloomy grin. When he spoke, his voice had the parched and raspy sound of a man gagging on sand.

"*Regere*," he said. "Latin. Where regal comes from, regency. Ruler. Rex and rector and reign. And surge, which combines *sub* with *regere* and means to come up from below. Which is what great men do. Kings and emperors surge to the top. Also *rectus*, which means straight, which is the source of rector, rectitude, and rectum, 'where the intestines become straight.' Surge and straight. The leader who will reign over you shall rise from below, surge straight upward from a low position and one day shit on your heads. That's who I am. That's who you're dealing with. Rex, the king. The monarch. You can push me down, but I'll be back where I belong very soon."

"King of the assholes," Thorn said.

"Fuck you," Butler Jack hissed. "You can't keep me locked up. I'm the blue haze that seeps under your door at night. Go on, try it. You'll see. I'll be there beside your bed when you wake. You'll see. You can't lock me away. I'm Rex. I'm surging up from below."

"Well, you got a long fucking way to surge," Sugarman said, "before you get up here with us human beings."

Sugar slammed the door and locked the three deadbolts, peered into the cell briefly then stepped away. He was angrier than Thorn had ever seen him. His pulse throbbed in the dark blue veins and tributaries that mapped his temple. His eyes were bloodshot and seemed to be skating aimlessly.

McDaniels located a chair in a storeroom down the corridor and dragged it back. He sat down, holding his leather blackjack in his lap. In his wild hula girl shirt, yellow socks, and black sandals he looked like a bouncer at a nightclub for utter nincompoops. He smiled up at Sugarman and told him not to worry, they should go do what they had to do.

"Don't open that goddamn door till we're back and ready to take the fucker ashore. Not for anybody. Not Sampson, not Gavini, nobody goes in there."

"Don't worry. The monarch of the assholes himself could come marching up in his shit-brown robe, I wouldn't let him in." He threw Thorn a giddy smile.

"And watch out for the blue haze too," Thorn said.

Sugar drew the knife from his belt and extended it to the old soldier. McDaniels took it, pressed his thumb to the blade.

"You think it's wise, getting our fingerprints all over a murder weapon?"

"I think we're a long way past that." Sugar patted McDaniels on the shoulder and left the man chewing attentively on his straw.

Thorn and Sugar went back to the chapel. After a quick debate on who should do the honors, Thorn hauled himself up into Butler's nest, had a peek at the tight quarters. An odd clash of high tech and primitive that reminded Thorn of the cockpit of one of the early space modules.

An array of very sophisticated looking electronic gadgets and circuitry was wired into the bundle of cables overhead, while all around the small work area were exposed plumbing pipes and the aluminum ductwork of the air-conditioning system. Butler had fashioned a plywood floor and covered it with a thin rubber mat and pillow. Beside the pillow was a fancy telephone. The operating space itself was so cramped it was hard to imagine a man Butler Jack's size squirming into it. But he had. Mr. Blue Haze.

When he dropped back down to the floor, Murphy was standing beside Sugarman. He gave a little bounce of excitement.

"I'm next," he said, flashing his eager smile.

"What's going on upstairs?" Thorn asked him.

"Nothing much. TV show is still going on. Bev Mitchell and her three whores."

"Ho's," Sugarman said.

"That's what I said, whores."

"Going on like nothing ever happened," Thorn said. "Wow."

"It's television," said Sugarman. "No attention span."

Thorn boosted Murphy to the ceiling and he chinned himself the rest of the way into the crawlspace. A minute later he poked his head out.

"Holy moley," he said. "I gotta hand it to him. The guy had it all figured out. He's got a circuit board spliced into the main rudder control line, looks like it's the brains of an autopilot control panel. If he's got it programmed right, it could steer the ship right to a piece of ocean the size of a postage stamp a thousand miles from here. Once it was switched on, there was nothing anybody could do to shut it off, override it or anything except track it down, cut it out. He's got a VCR, a twelve-channel telephone, enough food and water for a week."

"His little Ritz-Carlton," Thorn said.

"VCR? Why the hell would he want a VCR?" Sugarman helped Murphy lower himself back to the chapel floor. The effort left Sugar breathless and he had to sit on the front-row pew.

"Maybe he wanted to watch some old Disney films," Murphy said. "I read that somewhere. There's a high correlation between serial killers and early exposure to Disney cartoons."

Thorn stared at the kid. "Get outta here."

"No, I read it somewhere. Ted Bundy, Dahmer, all those guys had four things in common when they were kids. Bedwetting, torturing animals, setting fires, and Disney movies. That's the profile."

"He read it somewhere," Sugarman said. "It's got to be true."

"Maybe you ought to offer Murph a job. Guy's got an impressive command of criminal justice trivia."

Sugarman was peering down at a stain on the tan carpet just in front of the pulpit. A spray of blood that was shaped like a small stingray. Another bloody spritz marked the front of the oak pulpit as if someone had snapped a wet paintbrush from an inch away.

"What about that telephone?" Sugarman said. He continued to study the shadow of blood, his voice at half power.

"What about it?"

"Why the hell would he want a phone? Who would he call?"

"Order a pizza?" Murphy offered, grinning.

Thorn said, "Maybe he was going to ring up the networks

back in the U.S., the TV people, get some publicity going for his fucked up cause. Get his name on the airwaves."

"Maybe so," Sugar said, staring at the polished brass crucifix on the wall behind the pulpit. "Yeah, maybe so."

Thorn took his time wandering back to his cabin. Eavesdropping on snippets of nervous conversations, passengers getting very antsy to go ashore, not sure exactly what was going on. The printed schedule said they should've been on land an hour ago. But so far the ship was still at anchor.

He knew these people now, had met their kind before when they'd wandered mistakenly into the unpredictable Keys. They were infected with the theme park virus, its major symptoms being an impatience for anything not on the prepackaged itinerary. For them the cruise ship was locked onto rails, riding its reliable route, skimming above a five-inch simulated sea. They wanted safety and predictability. They wanted to be assured in advance exactly what kind of fun they could expect, what clothes they'd need, who to tip and how much. They came in herds to Miami International, followed a smiling hostess in the cruise ship uniform with her upraised sign. Their luggage was transferred automatically. They rode a bulletproof bus across the city, wound through the cattle guards and boarded the ship exactly on schedule. They were old and wanted a neatly organized program. They were young and wanted to get exactly their money's worth.

When they disembarked in Jamaica or Nassau or Cozumel, they moved in herds along preprogrammed routes. If any of them chanced to wander off, encounter some unseemly reality, a grubby unwashed child playing in the ordinary dust, some tavern filled with genuine roughnecks, they would no doubt scurry back to the group with wild tales of poverty and danger. That's another thing the theme park disease did. It trivialized everything evenly. The pleasure, the awe, the terror. Made the authentic into just one more carnival ride.

After their cruise they would flow upstate to one of the plastic theme parks where the great white shark would lunge predictably, the rocket ship would plummet right on schedule, the ferocious beasts would charge their car on the hour every hour, and the black-hearted pirates would carry away shrieking damsels, all of it on steel tracks, a conveyor belt dragging them forward smoothly and dependably and safely above the shallow sea. This was Florida. This was his home, what it had become. Where the false and the true had become so interchangeable that hardly anyone could tell the difference. And those who still could were so worn down they barely cared.

He stopped at an empty span of railing on the Sports Deck, his gaze drifting out beyond the crystal water of the harbor, looking at the distant Caribbean. Out there the sky was scoured clean, its blue had the hard glossy shine of wet enamel. Coasting a few hundred feet up was a lone gull. A warm aroma wafted on the breeze, the scent of smooth black river rocks heated by the sun.

Two men and a boy in a rough-hewn outboard fishing craft were heading straight for the *Eclipse,* then twenty yards shy, the skiff veered west and peeled open a frothy seam on the flat green water. The midmorning sun plated the boat and its passengers with silver glaze. Their tackle was ready, their bait rigged. Full of the same reliable hunger and hope of all fishermen heading out, a yearning he realized with a wicked jolt that he had not experienced himself for many many months.

Somewhere along the way of courting Rochelle and mass-producing his flies and performing the never-ending upkeep on his house and boat and equipment, he'd lost the habit of going out on the water. Only that one trip into the Everglades with Sugarman, one trip in many months. He couldn't even remember the time before that one. And that, of course, was the answer. The reason his flies had lost their allure.

He had always tied them for himself. Sold his extras. The compulsion behind each one was the simple desire to snag his own bonefish. To concoct a bait so appetizing it would guarantee the thudding strikes and wrenching excitement he had relied on for over thirty years. But he'd lost something, tying them exclusively for others. His fingers committing the same act, tweezers and scissors and vise, Mylar and feathers, hackle and ribbing. Everything exactly the same. Identical to the eye. But now they were duds. Failures on some level so subtle, so subatomic that only the fish could see it.

Over the last half year, his craving to go out on the water had dwindled to little more than a glimmer. He had fallen into the tedious and consuming rituals of the land animal, lost his hunger to hunt for those bright, wild creatures.

Now, standing at the railing of that boat that was not truly a boat, looking out at that primitive fishing skiff as it swung around a palm-lined point, with the yeasty, sun-baked scent of the sea in his lungs, the screams of the gulls overhead, the relentless magnetism of the blue distances, it was as though a layer of calluses and epidermis had been flayed back, and the bright tender nerve endings were suddenly exposed to the shock of the familiar. A fresh discovery of what he had always known.

To him a house had always been merely a place to clean fish and reels and plot the next voyage. From the earliest time in his life, his incompetence at social discourse and his craving for isolation had fueled his calling. He'd spent the majority of his waking hours for the last thirty years wandering across the markerless flats of the Keys, rod at the ready, tracking the fleeting shadows that he'd trained his eyes to see. He had never felt at home with the rules of land. Had never known more than a marginal happiness traveling its well-worn thoroughfares.

Now after only two days at sea, even in such a ship as the *Eclipse*, he felt again the tingle in his blood. Some stagnant cluster of molecules rousing. He watched as that skiff headed out to the wrecks and reefs and deep underwater trenches where the big bottom fish lurked, or farther out where the weedlines or circling, diving gulls would steer the fishermen to schools of migrating dolphins. Or perhaps those men were headed to the flats where the jittery permit and tarpon registered every tremor in the tide and were spooked by clouds tickling across the sun or a single human utterance a mile away.

As they disappeared around the point, their boat lifting up onto a sluggish plane, Thorn knew exactly what was alive in their nerves. The weight of every fish they'd ever lifted from the water. The thousand sharp colors, the wavering silhouettes, the blinding speed of barracuda and hammerheads and bone, the snapper's cautious nibble before the tug, the yellowtail's bump, the trout's nervous plucking. All of it was there, stored for all time, the jig of the line, the slow, deliberate reel, the long false casts and the release, the jarring strike and steel-melting power of marlin and tuna. All still there, even if it had been dozing in some desiccated twist of cortex for far too long.

Thorn held up his hand, wriggled his fingers against that polished sky. It might take a week or two of steady fishing, some hard sweaty hours of fruitless labor, but now he was fairly sure he knew how to restore the suppleness to his fingers, how to regain that simple, baffling sorcery that once came so easily.

Monica showered. She burned her skin with the hottest water she could stand, piped up straight from the boiler. Poaching herself. Then she backed it off, lathered with the ship's lavender soap. Scrubbed away a layer and another.

With her flesh bright and quivering, she put on one of the terry-cloth robes from the locker, drew the curtains against the brightest day she'd seen in years, and lay down. Her eyeballs burned as if they'd been packed in salt, throat so scalded it felt as though she'd been vomiting for days.

An hour ago when she'd walked off the stage, her father calling after her, she had not turned to face him, hadn't answered his cries. She'd marched away, the hard, tangible core of her anger vaporized, leaving an acrid residue that made her breath burn and her mouth taste like dirty copper. There was a sickly ache in her belly as if she'd been punched repeatedly.

Maybe she slept. Maybe she only imagined sleeping. Maybe she dreamed or maybe she only dreamed she dreamed. Confused and feverish, every breath a struggle, every heartbeat sending a pulse of grief through her gut.

With her eyes shut, she heard the cabin's lock come open, heard him come in, pad across the floor. Felt the mattress give as he sat across the bed from her. He looked at her a long time. He must have seen her eyes wide awake behind her lids. When he spoke, Thorn's voice was as quiet as the first shadows of the evening.

"You feeling any better?"

She opened her eyes, stared up at the ceiling.

"Of course," she said. "I purged, didn't I? I purged big time, in front of twenty million people. I bashed my daddy, I spilled it all out. I drew major quantities of blood. Wrecked his reputation. Did you see? He wasn't smiling anymore at the end of it. I took away his fucking smile."

"You disemboweled the bastard."

"Yeah, I cut his heart out and held it up, and let everyone watch it pump."

"And now you feel shitty."

"Ten times worse than shitty."

"But you did it. You needed to do it, and you did. It's over now."

"It's that simple?"

"Isn't it?"

"Fuck no, it's not."

Thorn eased onto his back, settled his head on the pillow, and looked up at the spot on the ceiling she had been studying earlier. "Butler is in the brig. Locked up. That part's over anyway."

She blew out a breath. "Thank God."

"Now you're free."

"Yeah, sure," she said. "I could go back to Sugarloaf, or I could go somewhere else. But how's it going to be any different than it was? That's all horseshit. I've unburdened myself, but it's all still there. There's no magic in saying the words. I still gotta do something. I still have to start over, hack out something for myself. I'm still me. Same curse as before."

"Not such a bad curse."

"No?"

"Your father will disinherit you. So that solves the money problem. Then all you have to do is wait a few years, you won't be beautiful anymore. It happens all by itself. The wrinkles, the sag."

"You're great, Thorn. A real help."

"Maybe you should be thankful you have such a challenging problem. You might've been one of those people who just skimmed through without a concern."

She rolled up on her elbow and stared at him.

Thorn said, "This way you have an edginess. You're always alert, dealing with it. You know what they say. A person can get too comfortable, stop questioning. Lazy faith is no faith at all."

She shook her head. "They say that, do they?"

"I don't know if *they* do, but I heard one guy say it."

She came down off her elbow and let her head rest on the middle pillow. She tightened the belt on the terry-cloth robe.

"Words," she said. "Fucking words."

"Maybe you feel better than you know," Thorn said. "You're still churning inside. Could be, it's too soon to know how it's going to be. A couple of days from now, the storm is a few miles up the coast, the sun comes out, maybe you'll be able to take a deep breath, have a good chuckle about it all."

"You're not very smart, are you, Thorn?"

He smiled. "I've met a couple of people who were dumber. Not many."

"My father is still my father. My past is still my past." Monica touched a finger to the bristle on her scalp. Hair longer than it had been in a while. She drew a line from front to back along the path where she'd once parted her hair.

"The past," Thorn said. "It's just a bunch of stories you've decided to tell yourself. You can always tell different ones if you want. It takes some work, but it's possible."

"You can, huh? Just lie to yourself?"

"Not lie. But go back, find some stories you've forgotten. Things just as true as the ones you've been holding on to. Tell the new ones to yourself for a while. Slant it a different way. Everybody's got a shitload of stories, a shitload of different pasts. No reason to get stuck with just one set."

"Is that what you do? Make up new pasts?"

"I try."

"And does it work?"

"Not very often," he said. "But I keep hoping."

She rolled onto her stomach, craned her head his way. He was still looking up at the ceiling, but his eyes were flickering as if he knew exactly how far away her lips were and it distressed him a little. She leaned forward and kissed him on the temple, the hard lump his friend Sugarman had left.

He made a noise in his throat. An I-don't-know-about-this hum. Kept his eyes focused upward.

"I'm too young for you," she whispered.

"Absolutely."

"You're an old man. You could be my father. Your arteries are halfway clogged. You've got a twisted sense of humor. We have nothing in common at all."

"I'm pretty," he said. "We have that. I've been told I'm gorgeous."

"Fuck you, Thorn."

"Although the truth is, no one's said it lately. Actually, no one's said it in years."

Monica kissed the knot again and he made another noise in his throat, another hum, this one not quite as pessimistic. It took two more kisses before the hum had some pleasure in it and two more after that before Thorn turned his head and met her lips with his.

Nuts. Crazy, or passionate. A devotee, a fan, as in "sports nut." And the coarse slang for testicles, of course. All the words growing out of the Dutch *noot* or the German *noos* meaning the kernel of a hard-shelled fruit. All the slang spinning out of that, the testicles' resemblance to acorns or walnuts, only soft and vulnerable. Having in common with acorns, beyond the size and shape, that they were also full of life, the seeds of the new tree. The storage place for new existence. Eggs and nuts. The association with passion sprang from the copulatory connection with seeds and sperm. Crazy following from that passion. Extreme passion, copulatory madness. Nuts.

Butler's nuts were bowling balls. Black and hard and huge. They were dead. They had moved beyond pain into the realm of absolute horror. The nerves had suffered more than nerves can suffer. He could not move. Lying in the corner of the metal cell, glancing up from time to time to meet the old man's eyes in the window, the man with the straw in his mouth peeking in to see Butler.

His nuts were nuts. Crazy and hard.

He was dead and paralyzed and full of anguish that was so far beyond any misery the body could absorb or the brain could categorize that it was as though he had no pain at all. He hurt so bad he didn't hurt.

His nose was broken probably, numb, no air passing through. It felt skewed to the side, loose on his face. He knew he could not stand. He knew he could not walk and probably couldn't speak. There was nothing his body could do to release him from this box of iron. He was as helpless as a newborn. Crying. Wordless. Staring out at the cold fog, the bright silver room.

Butler Jack was nuts.

Nuts to believe he would ever escape, finish his plan. Nuts to believe that all was not lost.

But he did believe that. As nuts as it was. He believed it. Knew it to be true. Knew that his plan was still unfolding even though he was here in an iron room. Caught by the black man with the white name who shared his atoms. A common egg, different nuts.

He knew he would be free soon. Then he would have to stand. He would have to walk and speak. He would have to complete the last few steps on his list. And he would do all of that. For the swelling would subside as swelling always did. Things would shrink again to the normal. Pain would slacken until it became only the low-frequency noise that was tolerable. He would rise. He would walk. He would kill anyone who tried to interfere.

The eyes were at the window again. Butler Jack giving them back everything they gave him and more. Sending out all the anger and hate and disgust and horror that was brimming in him now. A lifetime of it. Focusing it through the double magnifiers of his corneas, a laser look. Firing that at the man's eyes in the window.

And to Butler's amazement, the man in the window flinched, his eyes filling with terrible pain and revelation. And he threw his head to the side and sank out of view. A few seconds passed. Butler's heart was howling. And then those old man's eyes were replaced by other eyes.

And Butler Jack was saved.

CHAPTER

32

The sun was setting in the east.

Or else his compass was upside down, the N and S reversed. Then again, perhaps David Chan was about to die from diarrhea and dehydration and this was simply a final hallucination before the sky swallowed him. North becoming South. Heaven becoming Hell. It was possible and entirely harmonious when you considered it. The universe playing fair. David Chan had had an exceptionally prosperous life and now the pendulum was cocking in the other direction and he was going to be sent on a hellish journey.

He believed in the prophecies of the *Tibetan Book of the Dead* in which the soul when set loose from the body begins to roam the dark plains of afterlife searching for some speck of light. Finally seeing it, moving toward it, then entering it as the sperm enters the vagina and battles its way up the hostile twists of tube to reach the great mother egg. A dead man wanders until he sees his new parents, then reenters the world through their moment of great pleasure. Becoming a child again, a disembodied scream. All of it starting over and over and over.

David Chan stood on the bridge of the *Juggernaut*. It was five o'clock. Five in the afternoon he believed, though a little while ago the sun had disappeared behind a bank of clouds and now it was dark and rainy, as sunless as midnight. A storm without benefit of lightning. The *Juggernaut* gliding easily through the swells. The great ship with her burden of oil had no trouble whatsoever except that he was not sure if the compass had failed or his mind had failed. Five o'clock, that much he knew, unless, of course, the timepiece was malfunctioning like all the other instruments.

He had found the old man, Su Long Doc, in the auxiliary water storage tank. His body had been decomposing for several days, a great swollen mass, rubbery and cold like the inflatable doll a Chinese crew member had brought along several trips ago. Its mouth puckered open, its face a plastic cartoon. An inflatable doll overfilled, cold to the touch, ready to burst.

The dead man, Su Long Doc, had served as security guard while the ship was in dry dock in Baltimore. In his late sixties, with no family, Su Long was the ship's machinist. He had been missed when the repairs were finished in Baltimore, some frantic efforts were made to locate him, but finally David Chan was unable to wait any longer for him, so they had left port one man short.

Apparently Su Long Doc had been killed, his body stuffed into the water reservoir, and it was the bacteria from his offal and his rotting flesh that had caused the spread of disease on the ship. Two men were near death and three others would be heading that way.

Some time ago David Chan had radioed a distress signal to the U.S. Coast Guard and they had agreed to dispatch a helicopter from Miami. But now he was not sure he had provided the Americans with the correct coordinates. His Loran was giving him one location and his GPS was giving him a reading almost a thousand miles away. The compass showed their course to be almost due west when David Chan knew the autopilot was programmed to take them south by southwest as they approached the Gulf Stream, which was where he thought they were.

Of course, the storm might have interfered somehow with his instrumentation. Or it was possible, entirely possible, as he had remarked to himself earlier, that he was hallucinating. But how could you be certain you were hallucinating? Did that not require a second viewpoint, someone who was fairly certain he was not hallucinating who could compare observations? But there was no such person aboard the *Juggernaut*. There was no one on this very large ship, one of the largest ships ever constructed on the planet, no human being who could confirm or deny that David Chan was hallucinating.

For all he could tell, a monumental holocaust had befallen the earth. A meteorite had passed close by and the magnetic poles had swung around. North and South had been reversed. Heaven and Hell. And now the world was toppling out of control through the galaxy.

The joystick was dead in his hand and the throttle had no effect. The *Juggernaut* was guiding itself to a destination it seemed to have decided upon on its own. Plowing ahead through a vicious following sea, going much slower than usual, five knots, four, David Chan had no earthly idea where he was, no idea where he was headed. And he had begun to feel that it would not make much difference if he did.

Thorn and Monica showered together and Thorn was instantly ready again. Something to be said for the age spread, something on both sides. Monica shaking her head at his erection, taking it in her hand and pushing it down as if it were a catapult. Letting it spring back up. Set a boulder there and fire, by God. Send it over the wall.

"How old are you again?" she said.

"I forget," said Thorn. "I'm at the age where I can't subtract the year of my birth from the current year anymore. I stopped being able to do that the last couple of years. In any case, I know I'm younger now than I was an hour ago."

She soaped him between the legs. Ducking down, she slid her hand between his cheeks, came up on the other side. Thorn going "Wheee." But not completely sure it was out loud.

That's how it had been for the last hour. The separation between inside and out had dissolved. He wasn't certain if she was in his head or he in hers or neither of the above. Something he remembered from his dope-smoking days. Impossible to tell which words were spoken, which were merely thoughts.

The soap was down to a double-thick credit card, just enough to lather Monica's abundant blond patch. Big triangular foam, working his fingers in, getting her folds clean, the folds inside those folds. Another "wheee," but he wasn't sure if that was her or him or just a random creak of the ship.

They'd probably docked already. The passengers had probably bought every geegaw in Nassau, every straw hat, every voodoo doll, and reboarded, and they'd crossed the thousand miles of sea to Jamaica and on to Mexico by now. Gone through the Panama Canal, come out the other side, into the Pacific. That's how he felt, that bar of soap gliding over her and gliding over him. A slippery finger, a tight velvety place, the nubs and pleats of her flesh. The Panama Canal, easing through the locks. Moving from one body to another, that isthmus, that narrow neck of land. A ship slipping in one side, slipping out the other. Entering a new place. As if the two of them were pouring warm milk from one pitcher to another and back again. He was one vessel, she the other. Back and forth they poured the milk.

The shower was warm and her body was fitting better than it should for someone so different from anyone he knew. For the moment she wasn't twenty-five and he wasn't twenty years older. They were meeting somewhere without numbers and almost without words. Tasting the bitter soap on her lips, committing rubbery kisses, while she got him very clean and he got her just as clean in return. The cleanest he remembered being. Cleaner than that. So clean he might squeak the rest of his life. "Wheee," one of them said as the soap shot out of someone's hand. Or was it soap or was it a ship through a canal going to the other side, the Pacific Ocean, that wide body of peaceful water. Milk flowing back and forth, warming one pitcher, then the other.

"You make noises," she said.

"Was that me?"

"You're very loud," she said. "You're embarrassing."

"Maybe I'm celebrating," he said. "Maybe this is a national holiday. A day to cheer. The king of the assholes is in jail."

"Okay, then, fine. As loud as you want. A holiday."

There was toweling off. There was movement into the cool twilight of the cabin and a moment of straightening the sheets and then they were there again. Passing the milk back and forth. His jar, hers. Warming each of them, finding the right rhythm so none of the fluid splashed.

The gentle rocking of a ship at anchor. The bright daylight knocked down to dusk by curtains. The smell of her soapy clean flesh. He made observations about her body and promptly forgot them. The specifics of her flesh didn't matter. Although the specifics were very good. He noted them but could not hold them in his mind. Nipples, breasts, hips and waist, the fit of their parts, her lips. Her natural aroma. It wasn't something he wanted to trap with words. So he let it all go. He would think about it later. This was one of those moments that was more than he had prepared himself for. Better than his vocabulary.

Afterward they lay still and listened to each other breathe.

"You're not so quiet yourself," he said.

She nuzzled in. Thorn counted her ribs, made sure she was human.

"I'm a lady. I don't scream."

"That must have been our neighbors then."

The wrong words. The game was suddenly over. He had invoked the world a few feet beyond their walls and destroyed their isolation. Their fingers lost the grip on the cliff they'd climbed. He felt them dropping side by side back into the moment.

"Where are we?"

"In what sense?" he said.

"Physical," she said. "The physical sense."

"I'd say we're in a good place."

"I mean, have we docked?"

"Oh."

"I feel like we've docked."

"Then we must have. Then we must be there. We should get up, get dressed, go out, do whatever you do when you go to Nassau. Dance the local dances, drink the local brews."

She drew away, took a deep breath, which seemed to bring an instant chill to her flesh.

"I should go find my father," she said. "I should apologize for what I did. It wasn't fair. I ambushed him. He's a bad man. He did everything I said he did, treated my mother horribly, but what I did this morning, that wasn't right."

Thorn didn't join the conversation. She seemed to be handling it just fine. He lay still and listened to her voice mingling with voices passing in the hallway, and that blending with a breezy tune from the PA, its volume set just loud enough so it insinuated itself through the cabin walls, floated there on the margins of hearing.

"Those posters my father made, the ones you saw with my photograph, I always hated him for that. Making our problems public. Putting my face out there, on TV, plastered on bulletin boards. Exposing our family. I always thought he was doing it for self-promotion. He'd found a way to get a whole lot of free advertising, get his name and face in front of the cameras. That's what I thought.

"But now I don't know. I heard something in his voice this morning. It was there in his face too. Not what I expected. Shock, yeah. Anger, hurt. Sure. But there was something else I'd never seen in him. Even when I was slamming him, even when I was putting it all out there, all the brutal details, hurting him as much as I could, there was something in his eyes. Staring at me like he was pleased. I'm cutting him open, tearing out his goddamn liver, and he's looking at his little girl, full of fucking pride and respect."

"The bastard," said Thorn. "How dare he love his daughter."

She turned her head, cheek against the pillow, squinting at him with perplexity as if he had just parachuted into the room, landed in the bed beside her. "Now all of a sudden you're on Morton's side?"

"He's your father," Thorn said. "He probably can't help how he feels about you."

"He made me wipe up my mother's blood."

"That was a terrible thing to do to a child. To anybody."

"But I'm supposed to forgive him? That's what you're saying?"

"Either that or you could go on finding new and creative ways to punish him."

"Is this what you do? You go to bed with someone, then you stick them on the rotisserie and have some fun?"

"Not usually."

"I hate that man," she said, and rolled her head away. "I do. I hate him."

"I believe you."

"I'm supposed to forgive what he did to my mother? Just

sweep all that away? It drove her to suicide, for christ sakes. He killed her. Belittling her, humiliating her, freezing her out."

"Are you sure?"

"I saw it. I was there."

"Okay."

"Jesus Christ, Thorn. Quit fucking with me."

"I said okay. You were there. You saw what you saw. You heard what you heard. Okay. Fine."

"But you're implying I could be wrong. I was a child. I might have misunderstood. There might've been more going on between them than what I saw. Two people collaborating on their mutual unhappiness. That's what you're trying to say?"

Thorn saw a seam of blue at the curtain. The beckoning sky.

He took a second to savor the sensation again, the warm delight of his morning revelation on the Sun Deck. He knew what he had to do. He knew what had been missing for months. And even though it was still missing and would be for a while, everything was okay now. Everything was fine. He knew how to get there. He knew how to return.

"This year I've been rereading books I read when I was a kid. A project, an experiment. Books I liked. Books that scared me. Some that filled me up with what I used to think of as white light. Inspirational books. I have a whole stack of them that have been on my shelf for thirty years. All that time dusting them, rearranging them, looking at their covers. Books I saved because they'd meant a lot to me once, helped shape my values, gave me ideas I would've never had otherwise. I've read maybe ten of them so far. Just scratched the surface. And it's been pretty disappointing. They aren't much good.

"It's sad. I don't want to be wrong about those books. I want them to still matter. I've got a lot invested in my memory of them, how it felt when I was reading them the first time, the sea stories, the adventures. I can even remember specific afternoons, raining outside, thunder, lightning, and I'm curled up in bed reading Frank Buck, *Bring 'Em Back Alive*, stalking rhinos in Asia. And when I go back to that time in my head, when I think about who I was, how the things I believe are anchored in those books, it bothers me.

"I wanted them to be as true and profound as they were back then. I don't want to tear it all apart, start to doubt my own history. But now what I see is, the only way they're going to stay as wonderful as they were when I read them the first time, as poignant and thrilling, is to leave them sitting on my shelf. That way I can play with all those pleasant memories as much as I want, not risk losing them. But if I go back and take what I know now, who I am now, get right up in the face of that kid curled up in bed, I'll see it all different than he did. Those books turned me into somebody who doesn't need those books. I'm past that. I'm over it."

"So throw them away," she said. "So burn them."

"No need for that. I don't hate them. Just because they aren't what I thought they were, it doesn't make them bad."

"So that's what you think? I'm stunted? I'm still reading the same book I read as a kid. Reading it over and over, stuck right there?"

He watched a breeze belly out the curtains, the crack of blue becoming a bright wedge. Something out there firing a shaft of excruciating light through the opening, etching itself onto his cornea. Thorn shifted his gaze to Monica, her right breast lit with the fierce daylight, her left in shadow.

"I don't know you, Monica. I'm just talking about myself."

"What bullshit."

She shook her head, pointed her finger at him and was midword when the PA crackled out in the corridor.

Butler Jack's voice was a hoarse echo of itself. As if the pain had hollowed him out, taken the resonance from his words. He was brisk. No time for bogus eloquence. He wanted fifty-eight million dollars in hundred-dollar bills delivered to the Sun Deck by helicopter. It should be placed in a footlocker and lowered by the chopper. Either the fifty-eight arrived by midnight tonight or the *Eclipse* would be destroyed.

CHAPTER

33

The burnished point of the dagger poked from the right side of McDaniels' neck cocking his head awkwardly toward his chest as if he were trying to hear his own last heartbeats. The chrome hilt was jammed hard against the left side of his throat, six inches of flat steel dissecting his windpipe.

A deep gash curved from his temple to the back of his neck, cutting his ear almost in half, and another more shallow cut ran horizontally between the shoulder blades of his pink hula girl shirt. Apparently someone had surprised him from behind, taken a couple of quick slashes, put him on the ground, then he'd been finished off with the blade hammered through his throat.

The cell door was ajar. McDaniels lay on his back, his body blocking the corridor, his eyes open, fixed on a spot an incalculable distance beyond the ceiling. His red-striped drinking straw was clamped in his lips as though he had sucked one last lungful of air from this world before he sank below the surface of the rice paddy.

Sugarman was staring down at the body when Thorn arrived. Thorn halted abruptly, almost stumbled across the body, then swiveled away to lean against the wall, breathing hard from his run.

"Shit, shit, shit."

"Add mine to the pile," Sugarman said.

"How'd the fucker do it? McDaniels wouldn't open the door for him. How, goddamn it?"

Sugarman stared into McDaniels' eyes with some slender, half-assed hope that he might get a refracted glimpse of the last clip of film still playing in there behind the foggy hazel irises. But whatever flitter of light he imagined seeing in the dead man's eyes vanished when Gavini's voice sounded overhead.

In a tightly measured tone, the captain recited the words he must have memorized for just such a dreaded occasion as this. He instructed passengers and crew to proceed to their assigned life raft stations. Disembarking procedures would begin forthwith. While there was no fire, no immediate danger, and absolutely no reason to panic, all passengers should gather their family members at once and proceed without luggage or other encumbrances as efficiently and quickly as possible to their designated evacuation zones. Patrol boats and other harbor craft had been summoned from Nassau to meet the lifeboats, so Gavini could assure the passengers they would not have a long duration in the water.

"The instruments are dead again," Sugar murmured. "They've been up there tearing the bridge apart. Gauges, screens, everything's blank, just like Sunday afternoon. Ship-to-shore still works, telephone and PA, all the communications, but everything else is down. Sampson and Gavini wrangled about making that announcement. But after Butler Jack came on the PA, the captain must've won."

Thorn turned away from the body, stared up at the round perforated lid of the PA speaker. Gavini was repeating his announcement, assuring the passengers that there was no danger. No danger whatsoever. "Well, it's over now," Thorn said. "We can turn in our truncheons. Every law enforcement officer within a thousand miles is going to be crawling on the *Eclipse* within an hour."

Sugar lifted his head, gave Thorn a weary look. "Sampson won't give them access. Still in full denial." Sugarman bent down, drew the straw from McDaniels' teeth.

Gavini continued to speak, soothing Uncle Gavini, though Sugar could hear the quaver growing in his words.

When all passengers had completed disembarkation, then and

only then were crew members to follow. Engineering staff, kitchen workers, cabin stewards, engine room mechanics, everyone in the entire ship. Please proceed quickly to assigned assembly points. There were plenty of boats for everyone. No need to rush. Above all an orderly evacuation was crucial for everyone's safety.

"Where is she?" Sugarman said. He stood up again, tucked the straw in his shirt pocket. "Monica. Where is she?"

"Getting dressed."

"What, in your room? She's there alone?"

"Christ, Sugar. She's all right."

"She's number eleven, Thorn. She's on his fucking list. What the hell were you thinking?"

He shook his head. "The cabin door's locked. She's fine."

Sugar dragged in a breath, squeezed his mouth into a sour smile. "The door's locked? The fucking door, Thorn?"

Thorn rocked forward and back. His face tensed, he stared down at McDaniels' body. Then with a growl he spun around and ran.

Thorn sprinted to the Crew Deck foyer, but all the elevators were in use, and moving slow, so he took the stairs. Panicked passengers were flooding in both directions. Thorn fought the flow for nine floors, legs weak, breath burning.

When he arrived on the Verandah Deck, the doors to all the cabins on the hall were standing open. Including his. Monica gone. No note, no sign of struggle. He studied the lock, the doorknob. No scrapes on the metal. He looked in the closet, the shower, ran back out into the hall, called her name. His voice joining the chorus. Bill and Dorothy, Hector and Jean. Bill, Bill, Bill, where are you?

He worked his way to the outside deck, began to circle the railing. He peered down at the lifeboats, all those shocked vacationers in their orange vests already beginning to lower to the harbor. He searched for her golden buzz cut. Twice he thought he saw her but both times it turned out to be teenage boys.

He found a position near the stern rail where he could watch the lifeboats from the starboard side coming round the stern and still catch the port ones going down. Ten stories away it was nearly impossible to be sure, but he thought he spotted her blond burr head, her faded blue work shirt beneath the puffy orange vest. A group of teenage girls were packed in on either side of her. He made a megaphone of his hands and called her name but his voice was lost in the welter, dozens of people still singing out for their loved ones.

While he scanned the other boats, one of Gavini's first officers jogged up, halted a foot from Thorn, and ordered him to proceed immediately to his fire drill station. Thorn looked at the young man and shook his head.

"I'm staying," he said. "I'm with security."

"It's a full evacuation. No one's allowed to remain."

The officer was an inch taller than Thorn, about his weight. He had what looked like gym-swollen arms and the inflexible voice of command. Thorn said no, he wasn't leaving.

The man reached out for him and Thorn fanned away his hand. And he swept off his next grasp as well, coming around to face the man, letting his legs go limber, assuming the position. It took two more swats before the officer saw it was useless.

"If you persist, sir, the management of Fiesta Cruise Lines cannot guarantee your safety."

"They haven't been doing such a great fucking job so far." Thorn turned his eyes back to the exodus.

He watched the boat he thought was hers work its way slowly across the harbor. For the next hour he kept his vigil at the railing, continued to scrutinize every life raft, until the last ones were lowered. The white uniforms, the gold braid, Gavini riding down with his men. He saw the officer he had brushed aside staring up at him from two hundred feet away, and Thorn could feel the smolder of his gaze.

The last lifeboat was a hundred yards from the *Eclipse* when a grating noise began to resonate from somewhere in the distance. Warily Thorn eased forward along the rail toward the ratcheting grind. Not till he was at the foremost rail, leaning precariously over the bow tip, was he sure what he was hearing.

The anchor motor had engaged and the two-ton galvanized steel hook was rising from the harbor floor. Around the chain the clear green water boiled and a plume of gray foam swirled. All the marl, the loam, the ancient tombs of clams and oysters and nameless crustaceans were being violently exhumed, dragged to the surface for one final look around.

Blaine Murphy was going to be a hero. It was printed in the heavens the day he was born. That's what he believed. That's what his mother believed too. It was possible even his father believed it as well, though he'd never said the words aloud. Blaine was their only son and he was going to be their hero. He had all the prerequisites. He was a loner. He had a very high tolerance for pain, an unquestioning faith in God, and no taste for alcohol. He was smart and focused and every molecule in his body was ambitious. His goal in life, his dominant aspiration, even more than becoming chief engineer, was to return home from a tour of duty, sit down at the breakfast nook with his mother and father, and for his father to lower his newspaper and lock eyes with Blaine for the first time in his life and say, "Son, I'm proud of you. And I love you dearly."

That was all. Didn't sound like much really. He could probably go home now and spell it out for his dad and the words would get spoken. But that wasn't the point. It wasn't the words so much, it was the unsolicited nature of the event. He simply wanted one single time for his father to give him what his mother gave him every second. Uncritical, outspoken approval.

He had always believed it *would* happen, and now he knew exactly *how*. His moment of heroism was at hand. The incident growing larger with every passing hour. People dying, the ship foundering, the captain giving up, abandoning the *Eclipse,* taking the crew and first officers with him. At every juncture, Blaine's role was growing larger. Until now, four o'clock in the afternoon on Monday, with all the passengers gone, all the crew and officers fled, it had fallen squarely to Blaine Murphy to face off against Butler Roger Jack and rescue the *Eclipse,* perhaps even save Fiesta Cruise Lines from financial disaster.

This time his father would have to lower the paper. He would have to look him square on. "You are a grind, son. Your best feature is that you're too stupid to see how stupid you are."

That's what he'd said a year ago. Blaine standing at attention in front of his father's desk. His father puffing on one of his many pipes, looking up from his stock portfolio, replying to Blaine's announcement that he'd been promoted once again.

But this would change everything. This would lower his paper, keep it lowered. Blaine saving a four-hundred-million-dollar ship, coming to the rescue of a company worth several billion dollars. Those were numbers he would appreciate. Morton Sampson, one of the world's richest men, everlastingly indebted to Blaine Murphy. His father would see what he'd accomplished printed in unforgettable headlines.

"How long will it take?" Sugarman said.

They were in the control room. Morton Sampson standing stiffly near the door. Sugarman, Lola. Half an hour earlier, after the anchor drive had come alive, the big motor hauling up the two-ton hook, the ship had begun to idle out of the harbor. The last of the crew had escaped just moments before the ship started churning toward open ocean. Moving like magic, no one at the helm.

Murphy looked up from page ten of section 2 in the ship's engineering schematics. His gaze flicked from Lola's red and swollen eyes to Sugarman's scowl, which seemed to be set in cold marble.

"Well, what I have to do, I have to trace the steering gear remote control system from the bridge all the way to the rudder room. There's gotta be a device along that line that's intercepting the bridge controls, overriding them. Probably another autopilot unit like the one I tore out of the chapel ceiling."

"How much of a job is that, tracing the steering gear system?"

"Can't be sure. Far as I know no one's ever done anything like that."

"An estimate," said Sugarman.

"I've got to crawl through spaces like that one above the chapel, some even smaller. I might have to go all the way from bow to stern. Close to a quarter of a mile. I can't risk missing a single inch. So, it could take a while. Hours."

"How can we help?"

"You?"

Sugarman nodded. "Yeah, me. Thorn, the rest of us."

"First off, you're all too big. You'd never fit in the spaces that need checking. And second, you wouldn't know what you were looking for. It's mine to do. I'm the only one the right size. I'm the only one who knows the ship well enough."

"Anything we can do to speed this up?"

"You could locate Butler Jack, beat it out of him."

Sampson winced, shook his head in disgust, and stalked over to glare at the wall of circuit breakers. Lola continued to study the gunmetal gray door of the control room.

Sampson said, "What about the goddamn engines?"

"What about them, sir?"

Sampson swung around and glowered at Murphy. His perpetual smile seemed to have gone into remission. "Just shut them down, goddamn it. Why can't we do that? Go down in the engine room, pull the plug wires off, switch off the fuel lines."

"Nobody told you, sir?"

"Told me?"

"We can't do that, sir. Can't get in there."

Sampson glared at him as though he'd spoken gibberish.

Blaine said, "As the ship was pulling anchor and getting under way, the engine room fire alarm went off. The room's filled with CO_2 gas."

"Jesus Christ." Sampson stabbed a look at Lola, but she was still watching the door. He turned back to Murphy, his face tight and red. "It's got to be cleared by now."

"No, sir. It could take several hours to clear."

"Hours! What about the air pumps?"

"Dead," Blaine said. "We couldn't get in there without oxygen tanks. And we don't have any onboard as far as I know. So the engine room is off-limits until tonight, maybe tomorrow."

"Holy God." Sampson made a fist, glanced around as if searching for something to punch. Then he snarled and flattened his palms together, pressed them to his chest like a kid kneeling by his bed to pray. Dark veins rising in his throat.

"How the hell did he accomplish this? How the hell did that idiot manage to tamper with so many fucking operations of this ship? Tell me that."

"I was thinking about that, sir," Blaine said.

Sugarman made a small underhand wave. Hurry up with it.

"The *Eclipse* was in dry dock in Baltimore nine months ago, sir. You may remember we were installing the variable pitch propeller system and the manual rudder wheel you wanted. The ship was up on dry dock for two and a half weeks. He may have managed to get aboard during that interval, sneak around, tamper with things. Security can be a little lax at dry dock. That's been my observation, sir."

Sampson eyed Murphy while the flesh around his throat jumped and quivered like the lid of a boiling pot.

"That would square with our information," Sugarman said. "We think Butler sabotaged another ship when it was in dry dock last week in Baltimore."

"What!" Sampson swung his stare to Sugarman. "How do you know that?"

Lola slapped her hand hard against the wall beside her. She steered a furious look toward her husband. "What difference does it make, Morton? If Sugarman said he sabotaged another ship, then he did it." She drew a breath and took a moment to master her anger. She turned on Sugarman. "Let's just get on with it. Send this young man on his way, find the units, whatever they are, and be done with this."

Sugarman took a step in her direction. He drew a plastic drinking straw from his shirt pocket. With his right hand, he kinked the straw into segments, folded them over. He and Lola in an eye duel.

"You should've gone ashore, Mrs. Sampson," he said quietly. "Back in Nassau. There was no reason for you to stay. We can still put out a distress call, have you evacuated. We're close enough, they could send your chopper for you."

She watched him give the straw a workout for another second, then shook her head. "Is that what you think? I'm supposed to sneak away, let the men handle things? Is that your take on me? Hustle the old broad off to the back lines, keep her safe, our little China doll. Is this how you've turned out, how you see women?"

Sugarman held her angry eyes. Something passing between

the two of them that Blaine Murphy didn't understand. But the heat of it, the invisible steam rising between them, that he recognized.

"How I've turned out, Lola, doesn't have anything to do with you. Not a damn thing."

The color drained from Mrs. Sampson's face, and she looked for a second like she would rush across the room and fall on Sugarman in a flurry of fingernails and teeth. Sugarman held her gaze for a few seconds more then seemed to grow bored with the exercise and swung around to face Murphy.

"Which end will you start with?"

"Well, now, that's the big question, isn't it? Butler could have planted the unit dead in the middle of the ship or toward the bow or stern. It could be right in the rudder room itself. If I choose wrong, it could take ten, twelve hours. Choose right, I could find it in a few minutes."

"What about help?" Sugarman turned to Sampson. "What about flying in some of the engineering staff from other ships, give Murphy a hand, speed this up?"

"No," Sampson said.

"Why not?"

"I told you already. I don't want anyone else involved in this. As of this moment, I believe we've contained our problems. I spoke to Brandy Wong before she went ashore. I convinced her to sit on the story at least for a while. Promised her an exclusive interview when this whole thing is over.

"We've found hotel space on Paradise Island, two-night stay for the passengers. We're sending in another ship to take them for the rest of their cruise. I think we can get out of this without having a major public relations embarrassment. Maybe even find a way to turn it to our credit."

"You stupid, stupid, stupid, son of a bitch," Sugarman said. "We've got five people dead. We're a floating morgue out here, and you think this isn't going public? Christ, your own TV show exploded in your face. You got three thousand people swarming over Nassau who heard an extortion demand over the intercom. Everyone knows something's gone haywire."

"Look, let's just get going, how about it?" Sampson said. "Let's hop to. Yank Butler's little toys. You let me worry about managing the public relations."

"There could be explosives," Sugarman said. "There could be a timer for all we know."

Blaine blinked, swung his eyes to Sugar. "A bomb?"

"We have no idea what we're dealing with. He said in his message he'd destroy the ship. Explosives come to mind."

"Pay the money, Morton," Lola said. "Just make the phone calls. Pay the damn money."

"I wouldn't do it even if I could," said Sampson. "How the hell would I get fifty-eight million dollars together in less than twelve hours? How the hell would I do that, Lola? Do you have any idea? Tell me. You know the books better than I do. You know our friends at Suisse Credite, Citicorp. You have that kind of money tucked away in one of your jewelry boxes, do you?"

"There's Wally Bergson."

Sampson scowled. He worked his tongue against the inside of his front teeth like he was trying to dislodge a kernel of corn.

"Bergson," he said finally. "Fuck Bergson. I can manage this."

Sugarman patted Murphy on the shoulder. "Go on, Murph. Get started. Rub whatever good luck charms you got, rub them twice, and move your ass."

In the two hours since the ship had gotten under way, Thorn had used the passkey on every cabin. He'd discovered seven people still aboard. His tablemate, the TV lawyer, had left his kids behind in the game room. Each of them was hard at work with the joystick of a fighter jet simulator. Thorn watched the boy destroy a half-dozen villages and several vicious-looking tanks. His sister was even more deadly. Stacked on the lids of each of their machines were a dozen rolls of quarters. There were candy wrappers and potato chip bags at their feet. Thorn decided not to try to wake them from their reverie.

There were two maids asleep in the crew quarters. They were curled up together in a narrow bed inside a darkened cabin just across from the ship's laundry. They spoke no English and seemed indifferent to his presence in their doorway.

In the large hot tub on the Sun Deck, two British men and a Scandinavian woman were giddily singing what sounded like soccer fight songs. As Thorn passed by, one of them hailed him and ordered another round of Mai Tais. He stopped and met their grins, and whatever was showing on his face extinguished their hilarity in an instant.

"We stayed on," one of them called out with boozy affability. "We bought our tickets, we're taking our bloody ride. To the bitter fucking end."

Thorn searched the kitchen, threw open all the oven doors, every food locker and storage bin, the giant refrigerators and freezers. Using a huge soup spoon for a crowbar, he jimmied the door to the chef's quarters, for it would not yield to his master key. The room was a shambles. A stack of color photos of naked Asian boys lay on his bedside table. No one home.

He worked systematically through the rest of the Crew Deck. Every bathroom, every closet. He toppled Coke machines to see behind them, he shouldered open the locked fiberboard door in the recreation room and started an avalanche of Ping Pong balls and paddles, boxes of Monopoly and Parcheesi. He stood there and watched the balls scatter across the linoleum.

He worked through the afternoon, going forward toward the seven-story atrium, entering each of the boutiques, the drugstore, the cigar shop and library and casino. He pulled back curtains, pried open storage lockers, he bloodied his fingers on the metal edges of mirrored doors. He was systematic, methodical, and crazed, working room by room, deck by deck, till he had tossed every cabin, peeked under every table, and plundered every storage bin on the ship.

She was not there. Monica was gone.

Thorn found it difficult to believe she would have joined the lifeboat exodus without at least dashing off a note. But he wasn't positive of that. He had spent an hour with her tangled in the sheets. They'd had an intimate conversation or two. He knew about as much about her as one can know from such time together, but not enough to know if Monica would leave behind a bread-crumb trail.

He circled back, retraced his steps, kicked open doors he hadn't noticed before. Found a couple of nooks, a few crannies he'd missed. He stood on chairs and dressers and tore down random ceiling tiles. He took another hour, another after that. Through the broad tinted windows he caught glimpses of the sun setting, a vast and gaudy display directly ahead of them. With his heart thrashing aimlessly in his chest, Thorn continued to search for her as the *Eclipse* sailed west into the darkening Atlantic, a ghost ship sailing through a ghostly sea.

CHAPTER

34

"**M**onica's not on board," Thorn said.

"That your intuition talking? Jizz?"

"I searched. I couldn't find her. But, yeah, intuition's part of it. She's gone."

"And Butler? What's your Ouija board say about him?"

"I assume he's slithered into some other nook. He'll pop out when he's ready."

"I hope you're right."

Thorn peered into the empty dark. The sky was untroubled by stars. No moon. No ambient light haloing from the *Eclipse* as she barged across the flat sea. Sugarman had gone down to the kitchen, made a plate of turkey sandwiches. Flat slabs of breast meat, lettuce, mustard, hamburger dills. He'd plundered the Ritz Bar, filled a champagne bucket with Pilsner Urguell and several handfuls of crushed ice.

They'd pushed their deck chairs over to the rear edge of the jogging track so they were overlooking the Sun Deck. Below them the British guys and the Swedish lady were still yodeling with laughter in the hot tub. Thorn caught a whisper of marijuana floating up from their direction.

He'd finished one sandwich, was moving nicely through number two. It was seven, seven-thirty. He'd eaten nothing since that muffin at breakfast and was famished. A day of furious running from deck to deck and back again. Making love till he was light-headed. Hauling bodies to the morgue, scouring a cruise ship for a woman who'd vanished. Another routine day for Thorn.

"Sampson made the call to Wally Bergson."

Thorn chewed the turkey, closed his eyes, savored the warm twenty-knot breeze.

"He had to, I suppose," Sugarman said. "If he wanted to save a half-billion-dollar ship, what choice did he have? At least with the *Eclipse* in service, he'll make back his fifty-eight million in a month or two. They'd been negotiating for some time, so apparently the paperwork was just sitting there, lawyers all ready to jump."

"Who's Wally Bergson?"

Sugarman chuckled. "I love you, Thorn. You don't have any idea who's in the White House either, do you? Attorney General, Secretary of State, none of it. You don't know what wars are being fought. Never heard of *Love Boat;* Christ, and you don't know Wally Bergson."

"Wally Bergson's Secretary of State?"

Sugarman chuckled again. He had a sip of the Urguell then set the bottle on the deck beside his chair. "He could be if he wanted the job. But Wally wouldn't waste his time on some pissant appointment like that. He'd rather run the shit that counts, sports teams and TV stations, grocery chains, trucking companies, liquor distributorships. Where the real money is. The real power."

"Richer than Sampson?"

"I'd say so. Twice, three times. And meaner."

"Sampson gets a new partner then."

"Like having a brain tumor for a partner. You don't get rid of Wally. And he doesn't leave much behind when he's finished with you."

"That's exactly why I don't read the newspaper. It's full of Wally Bergson."

"I was there when Sampson talked to him," Sugar said. "I couldn't follow how they structured the arrangement, but Sampson was holding the phone with one hand and his nuts with the other."

"Bad sign."

"These people are amazing. The numbers they talk in. Fifty-eight million dollars. Call up a guy, make a deal on the phone. What's he do, run down to the ATM machine, draw out the fifty-eight? Or is it sitting around in a cookie jar? I mean, I'm waiting till Busch beer is on sale at the Winn-Dixie, it's still hard to make the mortgage payment, and there's Wally Bergson and Morton Sampson and all his pals, they can put their hands on money like that in a few hours."

"You wouldn't want that kind of money."

"I wouldn't kick it out of bed."

"Any of these people strike you as particularly happy?"

"Yeah, yeah, sure. But I'd do a better job spending it than they do." Sugar leaned forward, massaged his temples.

"By the way," Thorn said. "Have I thanked you lately for that Orvis fly reel you gave me?"

Sugarman turned his head, looked at him. "Christ, that was a century ago."

"I was cleaning it the other day. It's a beauty, Sugar. The best thing I own. Thank you."

Sugar patted him on the knee.

They ate in silence for a while. Thorn finished his third beer. No buzz. Just a dreary melancholy growing drearier with each sip. Pouring the numbing fluid on an already numb brain.

"Butler Jack has it rigged so we're supposed to ram this other ship, the *Juggernaut*. That's what you think?"

Sugarman blew out a breath. "Appears that way. Which would explain his little demonstration Sunday, showing us what he could do."

"But our man Murphy's on the job," Thorn said. "And even if he doesn't find the autopilot in time, Sampson's going to pay the money, so I guess we should just relax, enjoy the rest of our god-damn cruise."

Thorn brought the beer to his lips but couldn't drink. He set the bottle down beside Sugar's. Sugarman looked over at him, patted his arm.

"It's okay, man. Don't worry. She's safe. She's probably in her hotel ordering shrimp cocktail from room service, charging it to Daddy."

"Yeah," Thorn said. "Let's imagine that."

"You and Monica, I take it you got to know each other?"

Thorn sighed. Couldn't hide a fucking thing from Sugarman.

"I mean, come on. It's pretty obvious, Thorn. I can see that thing you get in your eye. A little twitch of light."

"Twitch of light!"

"You didn't have it with Rochelle."

"Oh, Christ. Here we go."

"I like Monica. She's your basic woman."

"Basic. You like her because she's basic."

"Basic is good. It's simple, earthy. No bullshit."

"Your vote is tabulated."

Sugar let go of a long breath. "What if you're wrong, Thorn, and the fuckhead's not on board? What if Butler left in the lifeboats with the others?"

"He's not here, why the hell does he want the money delivered to the Sun Deck?"

"I been thinking about that."

Thorn swiveled around to see Sugarman's shadowy silhouette.

"I think it's Lola."

"What?"

"I think Lola's in on it. In cahoots with him. Or maybe even running the whole show."

Thorn's heart added a couple of extra beats. "Lola and Butler? No way. Can't see it."

"We know there's somebody else. There has to be."

"But Lola? That's your anger talking, old buddy."

Sugar turned and gave Thorn a steady look, then shook his head. "McDaniels would've been on his guard with Sampson, anybody else. But he had a soft spot for Lola. Everybody does. So what if she distracted him, maybe came on to him or something, batted her eyelids at him, then yanked his knife away, took a couple of swipes, and while he was down, she let Butler out of his cell and he finished McDaniels off? That could explain it, the wounds, all of it."

"Jesus, Sugar. I mean, yeah, she's an ice queen. But stabbing McDaniels? No, I'd vote for Sampson."

"Sampson has no motivation. Nobody goes into business with Wally Bergson willingly."

"And what's her motive?"

"Same as always. Money and power. She gets a big chunk of change, then a year from now she divorces Sampson, gets herself a nice alimony settlement to boot, or maybe once she has the money she just disappears."

"She's got all the fucking money she could ever want right now. TV star, wife of a millionaire. I don't see it."

"But she has to work for that money. She has to be on call. She has to smile, make small talk, chat with Rafael every morning at nine."

"Yeah, well, that would do it for me. I don't think I could manage chatting with Rafael more than once a year."

"Lola's spent more than half her life working for Morton Sampson. And here she is, she's still working for him. Sure, she's well paid, but she's an employee."

The hot tub woman gave a giddy shriek and water splashed. Goosey, goosey.

"She's got the money," Sugar said. "But not the power. She may have personal power over Sampson. You can see that, the way he knuckles under to her. But he's still the one who writes the checks. She's on his payroll. On a higher level than before, but still punching the clock. Everything she has is because of him. And I don't think that sits well. I think she wants to be lying on an island somewhere, Bali, Tahiti, look out at the ocean, sip rum drinks. Be waited on. I think she's always wanted that. Thought her good looks entitled her to it."

"You've thought about this. You've given it some serious study. Lola, how she thinks."

"Okay, yeah, I have. And I think when Lola Jack went after Sampson, she must have known how hard the man worked. But what she didn't realize was how hard she was going to have to work too. She got a promotion, that's all. A guy like Sampson doesn't vacation in Bali. He doesn't lounge around, sip drinks. He works and then he works some more. He slaves his butt off every hour of the day. And I think what happened, when Lola finally got inside that world, it turned out to be a lot less fun than she thought. Found out she had to sing for her supper. And I don't think that's what she had in mind when she set her sights on Morton Sampson."

"This is your mother you're talking about."

Sugarman tore off a hunk of his sandwich, chewed it defiantly. Set his plate aside and held his Pilsner Urguell to his lips and slugged down half the bottle. When he was done, he backhanded his lips and turned his face to Thorn.

"I don't have a mother. I didn't have one for the last forty years, and I still don't. She's just another hustler working her con as far as I'm concerned. I used up my year's supply of compassion and understanding on Butler Jack. And that just about killed me."

"So Butler's escaped, he's in Nassau, that's going to be our operating theory?"

Sugarman leaned forward in his chair, forearms against his knees. His shoulders sagged as though the freight he'd carried for years was finally showing its crippling effects. Thorn had never considered it till now. That photograph Sugarman kept on his desk. Lola at nineteen, cigarette smoke curling past her eyes, a can of Schlitz in her hand, sitting on that ratty couch while she laughed at someone's joke. Probably Sugarman's father. But those eyes were somewhere else. Thorn had always thought she was haunted by dreadful memories, but maybe that wasn't it at all. Maybe her eyes were straying beyond the borders of the frame, longing for Morton Sampson or one of his kind, to rescue her, take her off to his mansion, the glossy life she'd only glimpsed on magazine pages or Sunday drives through the glamorous neighborhoods of Miami. The sad and vacuous American Dream. Rising up beyond her class, beyond her birthright. There had to be a way. Some way to get off that ratty couch. That was in her eyes then and it was still there, a harder, colder version. Desperation. Her time ticking down.

Sugar said, "We have to watch our backs. We don't know for sure, Butler might still be aboard. But we have to keep one eye on Lola too. The money comes, Wally Bergson's money, it sits out there in plain view, and you watch, Lola's going to make something happen. Some kind of distraction, and we're going to take our eyes off of it for a half second, and that money's going to be gone."

"But it'll still be on the ship. Where's it going to go?"

Sugarman picked up his beer and bubbled the last of it down. "Hell, I don't know. She drops it overboard. It's got a radio transmitter on it. Some other high-tech James Bond bullshit. Then Butler comes in a boat, plucks it out of the ocean. Something like that."

"But we won't be distracted. We won't fall for it. We'll sit up here on the balcony, she goes for the money, we nab her."

"Yeah," Sugarman said. "We're too smart for her. We'll nail her."

"So what's wrong? What's eating you?"

He cleared his throat, sat up straight, slicked his hands across his close-cropped hair. Then he gave his forehead a couple of thumps with the heel of his hand as if trying to jar the water from his ear. "I don't know. I feel like I'm missing something. Like there's another aspect to this, something obvious, and I'm missing it."

"Shit, I feel like that all the time."

Sugarman sighed. "You would, Thorn. You would."

Booby. From the Spanish *bobo*, for idiot or moron. With some help from the Latin *balbus*, meaning stammering or stuttering. Also one of various sea birds related to the gannet. Booby hatch being the nautical term for a small companion or hatch cover. Something so small a bird could use it. Or booby prize, a reward given to the last-place finisher, something to mock the stupid loser. Or booby trap. A practical joke to catch the unwary. An apparently harmless, innocent device masking something quite dangerous. A trap that only a stupid person would fall for. Only a stuttering, stammering, bird brain of a person. Or boob, as in breast, that soft and succulent glob of fat that made men gurgle and stammer from the time they were babies till adulthood. Women. Booby prize. Pap, sap, booby trap.

Butler Jack sat in the lobby of the Hotel Sofitel on Paradise Island. He'd tucked his blond hair inside a wide-brimmed Panama.

He had on narrow wraparounds, so dark he could barely see in the poor lighting of the lobby. He had changed into a pair of faded blue jeans and a black tennis shirt. About as nondescript as he could make himself.

He was off in a back corner of the lobby. The fronds of parlor palm shading him. Across the coffee table from him sat two Germans wearing *Eclipse* T-shirts. Man and woman in their fifties. They were badly sunburned and for the last half hour they'd been ordering rounds of drinks, charging it to their hotel room. They were smoking heavily and speaking German and seemed to be oblivious to him. Fine. That was fine, everything was fine. He was ashore. And he hadn't even had to make the evacuation call himself. Gavini had beat him to it. Fine. Good. It didn't matter who sent them scurrying, just so they did.

He was here now, nursing a Perrier, watching the passengers from the *Eclipse* trickling down from their rooms. Checked in, showered, maybe had a quick room service meal, now some of them were headed out to walk around the gardens, drink at the outdoor bar, watch the turtle races, join the limbo contest, exercise their luck in the casino. Fine. That was okay. Let them wander.

Butler closed his hand, looked down at his zapper. One of his replacement units. Holding his fingers out, he stared at the steel prongs inside the rubber tips. He could feel the tingle of power asleep in the batteries at his belt. A single touch. Four hundred thousand volts. A single devastating touch.

He was sitting on the leather couch with his sparkling water, feeling his balls throb and his nose too. Nose swollen, eyes growing dark circles. But even that was fine. Even that was no longer a problem. Everything was still on schedule, moving down the list. A little creative twist thrown in. His new number eleven. Sacrifice her. Yes, that was fine. Creative twists were fine. You couldn't expect to follow your schedule in lockstep. You had to remain flexible, be ready to adapt. And Butler had. Yes, indeed he had adapted. He was flexible. He should probably go out now, try the limbo contest. Flexible Butler, double-jointed Butler.

That's where he was now. Limbo. An intermediate state. The place where innocent souls waited their turn. From the Latin *lim-*

bus, which was an ornamental border or fringe. That's where Butler was, on the fringe of the lobby, on the fringe of humankind,
just on the border of heaven. That's where he was. Flexible Butler,
in limboville.

Waiting for her to come down. Waiting for Monica to join her
shipmates, wander the grounds, work off her nervous energy. Sitting in the lobby of the Hotel Sofitel. Thinking about booby traps,
thinking about limbo, about number eleven. Sacrificing her. This
woman who had betrayed him.

He would wait a little longer. He had time before his other
appointments. It was nine o'clock. He had till ten-thirty to get out
to the airport, then things would begin happening fast. Until then
he would sit on the couch and feel his heart pound in his testicles,
watch the Germans drink and smoke, watch them in their short
pants and their heavy sandals with their bulging bellies. He would
watch them until he could stand it no longer, then he would go up
to room 416. Her room. Monica's. And be done with her. Sacrifice. A holy killing. An offering. As all of them had been.
Sacrificium. A propitiation of sin. Cleansing her of David Cruz,
returning her to innocence.

The Germans were staring at him oddly. Butler didn't know
why but a lot of people did that. Always had. He looked back at
them, but that didn't stop them. They just kept staring like he'd
said out loud all the things racing through his brain.

He craned his head forward, gave them an even uglier look,
but they kept staring. So he held his fingers up, V for victory.
Something those bucketheads ought to understand. And he let the
voltage crackle.

Was Monica running away again? She wasn't sure. Was she
going to be a poster girl one more time? Definitely not that. This
time she was damn certain Morton Sampson wouldn't have any
posters printed. Wouldn't be offering any reward.

She showered again. She put on one of the new outfits she'd
bought Saturday night. She didn't even remember picking it out.
A red lightweight rayon crepe with button front and fitted bodice,
thin shoulder straps. White stars printed in the red. Something

bright, noticeable. A dress that could be spotted a few hundred yards away. In case Thorn was around, in case he'd come ashore in the last wave. In case he was looking for her.

She'd called down to the desk three times now, asked if a Mr. Thorn had registered yet. By the final time the operator recognized her voice, told her sadly, in an island patois, no, he was not yet arriving. I ring you the moment when he appears.

But the phone sat dead.

Like Monica. Only thing moving in the room was the floor. The rock of the ship buried in her muscles, her inner ear gyroscopes had been knocked cockeyed. She was getting seasick from being ashore. Sitting on the edge of the bed in front of the mirror watching herself sway, glancing over at the dead phone. She was feeling queasy.

Studying herself in the mirror to see if she could spot any changes. The assault she'd delivered to her father still echoed in her ears. The great disgorging of all that hurt. But now all she felt was vacant and ashamed. Frightened as well. Afraid that now she had nothing left inside her. A complete blank.

Perhaps Thorn was right. She'd made a religion of her discontent. She'd worshiped at the daily altar of her hate, made her tormenting memories into a mantra. She'd addicted herself to vexation and now there was not going to be an easy cure. A habit she had practiced and refined for twenty years was not going to be purged by a single morning's gushing. Even if it was in front of twenty million people.

Monica got up, made herself a vodka and tonic from the minibar. She went out on the balcony and drank the vodka solemnly and looked out at the blaze of red, green, and blue festival lights that were strung through the palms below. A group of people were cheering by the enormous swimming pool. There was reggae coming from a thatched bar down by the beach.

She should have left Thorn a note.

She should have said something cheerful and flirtatious. He was someone she could imagine spending another hour or two with. Hadn't even been tempted to spring the trapdoor beneath his feet. But she hadn't left him a note because when she left the ship she hadn't known if she was running away again or not. She still didn't. Maybe she never would. Maybe the difference between running away and staying put wasn't as great as it had always seemed. You could be running away even when you were staying in one place. Or you could keep running and running and never get a single step away from what you were fleeing. She would have to play with that, consider it. Talk to Irma Slater about it.

The vodka was giving the palm trees a hazy shimmer. It was making her thoughts fly too quickly to be trapped in words. She should go downstairs, join the party. Give herself to the celebration. After all, she was wearing a red dress. She could easily be mistaken for a woman looking for fun. The way she felt right now, she might just turn into whoever she was mistaken for.

She took the elevator to the lobby, headed out a side door toward the grounds, the reggae, the festival lights. The vodka on an empty stomach was putting a fine mist on things, the sidewalk shifting slightly beneath her, sea legs becoming land legs. She recognized some of the other passengers at a long picnic table drinking frothy pink concoctions. She nodded their way and a couple of them smiled back at her. She saw something in their eyes. A little click of recognition and then saw their gazes shift in unison to something a few yards behind her.

Monica Sampson hesitated briefly, didn't turn. She considered running, screaming, but her lungs wouldn't fill. Her legs were woozy beneath her. She increased her pace, a whir of impressions, the manicured gardens, the festival lights, the reggae, the laughter, some whoops of gaiety down on the beach. Not looking back, not having to because now she'd heard it, that unearthly noise she'd come to recognize, the sputter of current arcing like a terrible blue wire between his fingers.

CHAPTER
35

Murphy had been finding notes.
All of them on index cards, printed in ink. He was wedged into a
cubbyhole above the massage rooms, shining his flashlight on the
white rectangle, his third note.

"Beware of booby traps."

The first one had said, "Congratulations. You're headed the
right way." The second one was taped to a bundle of wires ten feet
downship of the bridge. "You sure you want to do this?"

Murphy was sweating hard. Working the flashlight in one
hand, squirming into places that weren't meant to be squirmed
into. Very hot, pissed off. Having second thoughts about being a
hero, pleasing his dad, all that. Chewing on the possibility that
maybe it wasn't worth it. All this just to get him to lower the
newspaper, say how proud he was. What difference did it really
make if the old man said anything or not? He was one cold bastard
anyway. He'd just go back to being the way he was. Nothing
would change, not really. Nothing ever did.

Murphy considered starting over at the rudder room, work
from stern to bow instead of vice versa. Or maybe begin somewhere around midship, flip a coin, choose one direction or the
other. Thinking Butler's notes might be reverse psychology, or
reverse reverse psychology. No way to know. Anyway he couldn't

start over. He'd begun at the bow and by God he'd just keep working his way back to the stern. That's who he was. Systematic or, like his father said, a grind. Once he started something, he always finished. He was dogged. Yeah, one of those pitbull brains, doesn't know how to back up, start over from a different angle. Yeah, he knew it was his weakness. But hell, it was his strength too.

He was crawling along a fairly open section next to the air-conditioning duct above the spa. A place he hadn't known existed before. Thinking maybe he'd come back here later when the ship was full of passengers again. From up there he could spy on the naked ladies. Make himself a peephole, watch the locker room, see into the massage cubicles. Spend his free time voyeuring. Or maybe just set up a videocam. But no, no. Blaine wasn't going to risk his career with Fiesta for a few naked bodies. No, he could keep getting by with *Playboy*.

With his hands running along the rudder line, eyes focused a foot or so ahead the whole time, Blaine kept moving. Somewhere there was a circuit board, an autopilot unit spliced into that line. There had to be. It was steering the ship to some location Butler had programmed into it. It was just sitting there, the brains of the ship, taking control.

For most of Murphy's teenage years *Kon Tiki* had been his favorite book. Until he was eighteen and stumbled on Clancy, he'd been fascinated with the Polynesians, how they navigated their pontoons and big canoes across thousands of miles of unexplored ocean, absolutely certain there was land out there. Little dots of earth, atolls, coral islands. Because a thousand miles away a Polynesian could read the wave shapes, the anatomy of the water. Ripples, flutters, rollers, swells, eddies. They could tell which waves had sliced across a strip of land two weeks ago, the messages still printed in the structure of the water. Like weathermen read the anatomy of clouds. Tatters in the water, rips, small seams, like arrows pointing toward the distant safety of land.

Not like today. Everything numbered now. You hold up your portable GPS and see where you are, punch in your destination and an LED pointer steers you there, giving you corrections every step of the way. Each inch of earth had its own number. Every tiny quadrant of the globe was mapped and entered into the program, beamed down from satellites. No one needed to read waves any-more. Which was fine by Murphy. He'd graduated to the gadgets of Clancy. Became a techno-nerd like everybody else in this busi-ness. Blaine left the Polynesians behind in his boyhood. Another of those skills that was no longer necessary. You could buy a device, see your location on a screen. Simple, anyone could do it. You didn't need ancestors to pass on centuries of knowledge. You didn't need fathers teaching their sons about waves.

A good thing too. Because what the hell had his father ever taught him? Not shit. Everything Murphy knew about the sea, about finding his way, he'd learned from books, from manuals, or from listening to the captain and his officers talk. It was a damn good thing you could buy a machine to tell you where you were. Damn good thing.

Blaine figured he was somewhere above the balcony that cir-cled the seven-story atrium because he could see the passage up ahead begin a small curve to the right. He was moving fairly rap-idly now, the spaces opening up a little. Several different systems coming together. Plumbing, electrical, hydraulic. At his current rate of movement, he could be at the rudder room in a couple of hours.

He was scooting along, paying attention, shining his light ahead of him. Looking for the next note, the autopilot. Or maybe just a single narrow wire leading away from the rudder line off to some less obvious location. He knew Butler was smart. But this was one of those areas with only a few possibilities. Like chess. The board was a fixed space. The moves and countermoves were lim-ited. The number was very high but it was finite. Butler could only do so many things to keep the ship operating like it was. He was limited to a set range of physical alternatives. And Murphy, the pitbull brain, was on his ass. A pawn move, another one. Inching ahead toward victory.

He followed the circle to the right. Fingers tracing the rudder line, scooting on his knees. Not much worse than working across a cramped attic or the crawlspace beneath a house. He was thinking about those notes. The way the asshole was toying with him. Screwing with his head. His pulse shot up when he'd seen that booby-trap warning. But now he was calm again. Butler was just trying to yank his chain, keep him from thinking straight. Trying to make the pitbull stop, come down from the ceiling, the one guy Butler Jack knew could beat him.

He was somewhere over the balcony outside the casino when he saw the headset hanging from a bundle of overhead wires. The headset had a small microphone on a stem and two fixed earplugs on the horseshoe clamp headpiece. Another index card was Scotch-taped to it. "Do you dare speak with me?"

Murphy reached out, yanked it down, and slipped the headset on. Pressed the earplugs into place. He was crouched on all fours, sweating heavily now, knees scuffed up, head scraped in a couple of places. He was looking out at his flashlight beam cutting through the darkness. He swung the tiny microphone down so it was an inch in front of his lips.

"Okay, asshole," Murphy said. "I'm here."

Murphy heard only the buzz of empty audio line. Nobody out there. Thinking hey, this was something to relay to the others. Something worth opening up the ceiling for, climbing down, going to find Sugarman and Thorn and let them know. About the notes, and now a headset that wasn't working. Which indicated that Butler had abandoned his plan and fled. Must've known Murphy was on his tail.

Murphy was reaching for the headset to tear it off so he could go alert Sugarman when something sputtered in his ears and he felt a sudden burn against both eardrums. Booby trap, he thought. Checkmate. A few more words sped through his head as two spikes of electricity hissed then jabbed through his inner ears and sought each other, jumping across his brain to do it. Positive seeking negative, two poles trying to join, make a continuous pathway.

Murphy's body stiffened, flat on his belly, then he felt himself bucking inside the confines of the ceiling crawlspace. A wild convulsion that sent his feet kicking through the ceiling tiles, broke the flooring that supported him. Brain sizzling with pain. He sprawled through the opening, dropped awkwardly, ribs crashing against the atrium balcony rail, body hanging there, the breath knocked from him.

He wasn't dead. It hurt too much to be dead. At least he'd torn loose from the connection with the earphones. Electrocuted but not dead. If he could just get some feeling in his body again, move his legs, slide down from his perch on the rail. He thought for a second that he was doing just that, but then he felt his head tip forward, leaning precariously over the atrium, his waist a fulcrum. He tried to edge the other way but Murphy was unable to halt the tilt. Gravity had him.

Blaine Murphy somersaulted forward, felt sudden wind, his body sailing. He opened his eyes and saw through the blur, the lobby floor coming fast, cold white marble, seven stories shrinking to one.

In open space Blaine did a sit-up, thinking in that half second that somehow all those sit-ups he'd done for years might save him. That's what he had on his side, those sit-ups, thousands and thousands, his abdomen like iron. Maybe that would be enough. Then he had no more time for thinking. No time for anything but a quick yip at the end.

It was almost midnight when Thorn saw the chopper's spotlight sweeping left and right across the dense black sea. It was cruising in their direction a few hundred feet above the water, and when the beam rolled toward the front of the craft, Thorn held his binoculars to his eyes and saw the glossy black body and the red lettering on the chopper's side. *Lola Live.*

Thirty yards away, down on the dark Sun Deck, Sugarman was stationed in the hot tub with the rollicking trio. The tub was only a few dozen feet from the elevated platform where Sugar had set half a dozen battery-powered lanterns in a circle to indicate the drop zone for the footlocker. A couple of light-years ago as the *Eclipse* left Miami, that platform had served as a stage for the reggae band.

From Sugar's position it was only a two-second sprint to the little stage. Thorn was maybe thirty seconds away. Their strategy was simple. When the inevitable diversion came, a scream, a gunshot, a small fire, whatever it was that Lola had arranged, Thorn would make a show of running off in that direction while Sugar kept his place. Not much of a plan. But that's where they were, down to the basics. Thorn pretends to go one way, Sugar stays put. Then Thorn circles back, a pincer movement.

What he wanted to know at that moment was how the hell the helicopter had located them so far out at sea. Under way since early afternoon, traveling at fifteen knots, they must have been across the Gulf Stream already. Maybe Murphy could explain that when he got back. Who was guiding the chopper to their small lightless part of the ocean and how the hell did they manage it when all the navigational equipment was malfunctioning? No one could relay Loran coordinates or GPS reading because there were none.

Thorn set the binoculars on the deck. Now the chopper hovered a hundred feet above the deck, its spotlight scanning back and forth, washing over Thorn, holding a moment, then moving on to the hot tub, the gang waving up at the savage noise. Four giddy drunks. Then the powerful beam found the lighted circle and held. Sampson stood at the rim of light, shielding his eyes, staggering a little in the violent wind.

A few moments later the footlocker, green and shiny, came down inside a rescue net. It wavered in the air about ten feet above the circle, then settled onto the deck. A smooth, easy, direct hit as if this were part of the chopper pilot's normal training, delivering extortion money.

Sampson dragged the locker free of the net, stepped to the side, gave a wide wave, and the helicopter banked away, whupped off into the blackness. Sampson opened the lid of the trunk, looked inside for several seconds, then closed it up, snapped the clamps.

"Okay," Sampson called out into the dark. "It's here."

"Well, let's fucking well spend some of it," one of the Brits called out. "Let's divvy it up."

Carrying a drink, Sampson walked past the hot tub, came up the short stairway, and sat down next to Thorn. "Now what?"

"Now we wait," Thorn said. "Enjoy the beautiful night."

"You think that boy's just going to come waltzing up, hoist up that footlocker, and carry it away? You think he doesn't know we're sitting here waiting for him?"

"I don't know what the fuckhead thinks, but from what I've seen so far, that sounds exactly like the kind of game he'd enjoy. How to get the money out from under our noses."

Sampson had a pull on his drink, then settled it into his lap. They watched the helicopter's lights shrink in the south.

"A trunk full of hundred-dollar bills," Thorn said. "What fun."

Sampson grunted. "That's my life sitting out there. That's everything I am."

"Now there's a pitiful thought."

"I've had some bad days," Sampson said. "I lost a wife, lost my only child, lost a ton of money. But never a day this miserable."

"You're not alone."

Thorn was focused on the footlocker glittering in the circle of lights. "Where's the wife?"

"Lola? She's in her cabin. This has been very hard on her as well."

"Yeah, sure it has."

Sampson swung around to Thorn. "Watch yourself, young man."

Thorn kept his eyes on the footlocker.

Sampson filled his lungs. The ice in his drink rattled. "You don't think Lola has feelings? You don't think she's agonized these last few days? Is that what you believe, just because she's outwardly composed?"

"Hey," Thorn said. "A half-dozen decent people got massacred because of Lola and you. Your fucking games. If the two of you had any feelings, you would've held hands and jumped overboard by now, fed yourself to the minnows. But no, you had to keep the illusion going. You're both week-old dogshit as far as I'm concerned. And as soon as we dock, if nobody else wants the honors, I'm on the phone to Brandy Wong and her buddies. This isn't going to get swept away. The fiesta's over, Morty. I have a strong feeling this is your last fucking cruise for a while."

Thorn lifted the binoculars and focused on the footlocker as Sampson got to his feet, stood for a moment beside Thorn's chair. Then he turned and marched away into the flawless dark, the ice in his drink tinkling loudly like a skeleton that has suddenly come unglued and collapsed to the floor in a pile.

David Chan stood before the *Juggernaut's* impotent control panel and watched the city lights approaching. Maybe if his head weren't whirling he would be able to recognize what city it was. It was the shoreline of America, of that he was fairly certain, for the lights stretched endlessly to the north. One enormous city that ran from the tip of Florida to Maine, populated by a limitless string of millionaires.

The *Juggernaut* was sliding forward toward the lights. It was three in the morning according to his wristwatch. Amazing that so many lights would still be burning at this outlandish hour. All that electricity being consumed, the power plants working through the night to light the way for the few who were still seeking amusement.

Ahead David could make out the white foam of the surf. The phosphorescent glow of the sandy beach. The *Juggernaut* was going to run aground. That was clear. There was no turning her now, even if the controls were suddenly relinquished to him. They were less than a mile from the lights. So close it would be only a minute or two before the keel scraped bottom.

The *Juggernaut* weighed five hundred ninety thousand deadweight tons. State-of-the-art safety engineering, segregated ballast tanks, crude-oil washing facilities, inert gas systems, dedicated clean ballast tanks. One of the three largest ships ever built. Carrying enough crude oil at the moment to supply an entire Caribbean country for a year.

Inside his dizzy fog, David Chan felt no dread of the approaching crash. At the current speed, he doubted any of the tanks would be ruptured. Of course, fire was always a threat, but this close to shore, even in his weakened condition, David felt sure he could go over the side and survive the short swim to the beach. At the very least, now his crew could get the medical attention they required.

In anticipation of the crash, he stepped out of the bridge and stood for a moment at the railing, trying to select the spot where he would plant himself for the fateful moment. The lights were growing steadily brighter and he noticed that the hotel buildings were far more slight than was typical of a Florida coastline. Four stories, five. Not the usual monstrosities of glass and cement. And he saw neon, garish reds and blues and greens and yellows. The bright tubes coiled into letters and abstract shapes.

Beneath his feet, David Chan felt the deck shudder. The *Juggernaut* must have brushed across brain coral or perhaps a limestone boulder, already leaving its terrible gash in the sand or reefs. There was not even enough time left to select the best place to weather the collision. In seconds the ship would embed itself impossibly deep in the sand.

From the shore came a panicked scream. A woman must have glanced up and seen the enormous ship's sudden emergence from the dark. David Chan gripped the railing, pressed his back hard against the bulkhead, and stared out at the neon. Automobiles cruised the street in front of the hotels. A traffic jam. The people of the night were wandering aimlessly, searching no doubt for what all young people seek, someone with whom they could perform a sexual act.

David Chan could warn them about that. For David knew all too well the consequences of excessive fornication. Oh yes, he knew. It was the reason his dream to become a doctor was never realized. And it was that same lack of self-control which led him inextricably to where he was tonight, responsible for one of the world's largest ships running aground onto one of the earth's most expensive beaches.

CHAPTER

36

"Murphy's dead." Sampson was panting hard. He hulked beside Thorn's deck chair, a hand pressed to his heaving belly. "His body's in the center of the lobby. A fall."

Thorn blew out a bitter breath. He looked out at the rising light. It was close to dawn and an electric blue slash showed at the eastern horizon and the dark air was filled with a thickening luminous mist, the first faint traces of daylight. Tuesday, two days before Thanksgiving.

With a sigh, Sampson dropped into the chair beside him. "Aren't you going to do anything?"

"About what?"

"Murphy. You heard me. He's dead."

"What, clean up the mess?"

"Don't you see what that means? Butler must still be on board. He's here on the ship somewhere."

"Good," Thorn said. "When you find him, tell him I'd like a word with him."

The two British men had passed out on the lounge chairs near the hot tub. Sugarman and the Swedish lady were having coffee at a table nearby. She'd brought Thorn a mug a while ago. She said her name was Marie. With a giggle, she showed Thorn her fingertips, deeply wrinkled from being in the water so long. She tried her English on him, but he wasn't feeling chatty.

"I'm Swedish," she said. "And those two are my meatballs."

It must've been one of the jokes her British boyfriends had roared at earlier, but Thorn gave her no response and the young lady humphed her disapproval and stalked away.

The night had passed without diversions of any kind. And now the ship had been steaming forward for over sixteen hours, guided by electronic impulses programmed by a madman. Thorn's sense of humor was gone. His inner landscape was as harsh and arid as the deserts of the moon. His skin prickled, his eyes burned. A jangle had begun to grow in his chest as if he'd been cruising above the stratosphere for weeks and now was plunging back to thicker air and heavier gravity.

He lifted his binoculars, swiveled around, turning his back to the footlocker for a moment, and sighted forward over the bow. Fighting off the angry jitter in his hands, he made out some vague sporadic lights miles away. Land ahoy. He lowered the glasses, swung back to the Sun Deck, and looked again at the footlocker still sitting inside its ring of lights.

He'd been staring at that goddamn box so long its image was probably etched onto his retina. This time next year he'd be able to shut his eyes, still see the damn thing.

"Where's he taking us?" Sampson said.

Thorn glanced at him. The man's voice was no longer coming from his diaphragm, full of bombast and overblown confidence. It was bleak now, and had an uncertain tremble, the sound of an anxious teenager's straining vocal cords.

"We're headed west. He's taking us back to Florida."

"You've got a compass?"

"Unless the asshole's tampered with the earth's orbit, I don't need one."

Thorn looked over at Sugarman. He was settled deep in his chair, sitting very still, hands folded in his laps, eyes half closed as if he might be lost in the depths of contemplation. But somehow Sugar registered the brush of Thorn's gaze and raised a hand and trilled his fingers, a toodle-doo.

"You know," Sampson said. "It was never about money for me. My motivation, it's always been more than that."

"Save it," Thorn said. "I'm no priest."

"The ships, that's what keeps me going. I love the boats, the ocean, all of it. I loved them as a boy, the great sailing vessels, and I still love them. All I ever wanted was to be around ships, sailing, the ocean. That's what it's all been about. The money, the business, that's just a way to be near what I love. To design the ships, build them. You didn't know that about me. You think I'm just a businessman, everything is about cash. But that's not me. I could be selling stocks and bonds and make more money than I do. It's about the ships."

"Fine," Thorn said. "It's about the ships. Fine."

"I watched my father sail away on a tramp steamer. I was five years old. He never came back, and I always thought it was because of me."

"It probably was," Thorn said.

"Jesus Christ," Sampson moaned. "Don't you ever forgive anyone?"

Thorn came around slowly and leaned close to the man.

"You realize," Thorn said, "with Murphy dead, we have no fucking choice but to hope Butler will keep his word. I don't know about you, but I'm not overflowing with faith that he'll shut down the engines once he has his money."

"What do you propose?"

"Shut them off ourselves. The engines."

"The engine room's filled with CO_2 gas. I was down there ten minutes ago. There's no way we can get inside."

Thorn stared into the man's shallow eyes.

"Even if you held your breath, somehow managed to switch off the fuel valves, the turbines would continue to run," Sampson said. "Half an hour maybe. Slightly longer. They'll have to burn up whatever's left in the fuel lines."

"It's all we have now," Thorn said.

"Butler will shut them off," Sampson said. "He won't run us aground. He wouldn't do that."

"And why wouldn't he? You think his conscience will switch

on suddenly? Bullshit. He's probably out there on the beach right now waiting, working on a big giggle."

Thorn slugged down the last of the cold coffee, got to his feet, and looked out across the water. The sky had almost finished refilling with light, a patch of faded denim blue to the east. He stretched his arms inside the shirt. When he'd put it on twenty hours ago it had felt like armor. Now it was as limp as a damp wash cloth.

"You going to show me the fuel valves, or do I have to fumble around for myself?"

Sampson conferred with the remains of his drink, then snapped a look up at Thorn. "I spent the last forty years creating this company. I'm not going to let it be destroyed in one night."

"All right then, come on."

Sampson was just struggling to his feet when the PA squealed and Butler cleared his throat and once again said hello.

Sampson dropped back in his seat and slumped forward as if he'd taken a blow to the back of his neck. On the deck below, Sugarman stood staring at one of the TV sets mounted above the outdoor bar.

"And now for one last vocabulary lesson," he said. "Tonight our word is one I'm sure we're all familiar with by now. *Murder.* Yes, yes, murder, coming to us from the Middle English *murther,* which in turn is from Old English *morthor.* Which I must say parenthetically sounds a great deal like mother, now doesn't it?"

One of the British men woke with a start. "Fuck me, if he isn't having another go at it."

The man held his head up a moment more then slumped back into unconsciousness.

Thorn hustled down the stairs and over to Sugar. On the TV screen Butler was standing against a harshly lit yellow backdrop. He wore a blue jumpsuit and his hair was loose across his shoulders. He smiled at the camera, pausing for a moment apparently to give his startled audience time to assemble. Then he brushed his hair from his face and went on.

"These English words are derived from much older words in the Latin, *mort* and *mord.* Is that perhaps where Morton comes from? The man of death. Anyway, the Latin derivatives meant simply death. Not unlawful or violent death as we use their ancestors today. But simply death. The reason is, back then deaths were almost always violent, so there was no reason for a separate distinction for murder. The idea that killing should be considered a crime, and need a word all its own, is a modern creation that's more a function of the English concern for lawful transference of property and inheritance laws than because of any high value placed on human life."

Cutting a quick look at the footlocker, Sugarman said, "You recognize that place where he's standing?"

Thorn said no. He stared at Butler smiling on the screen.

"Looks like the media room to me," Sugar said. "Though I might be wrong."

"Like so many things these days," Butler said, "the word *murder* is making a cyclical return to its former meaning. The reason is simple. When most people in a given society die violently or by the hands of others, then murder as a separate description of death is redundant. As in the American black ghetto, for instance, or in most of the impoverished third world where violent deaths are the norm. Interesting, isn't it? How murder can simply slip back to being the more generic *mort* and *mord* in cultures where violence is the norm. And as a result it frees up the word murder and kill for use in new contexts. As in 'that was a killer concert.' A designation of extreme, but no longer a pejorative term. Interesting, isn't it? 'This weather we've been having is real murder.'"

Thorn glanced over at the footlocker. Still there.

"So here's a killer of an idea," Butler said. "Why don't all of you clear the fuck off the Sun Deck right now. Because if you don't I'm going to *mort* my sweet mother, Lola. I'll give you exactly three minutes to get down to the control room and close the door behind you. Not a second more. If all of you aren't inside that control room by then, Lola Sampson is *mord*. Isn't that right, Mommy dearest?"

Butler Jack stepped out of view and the picture jostled briefly, dipped and rose. Then the camera focused on Lola Sampson in her bra and panties tied up in a wooden chair. The quick shot of the room gave Thorn no hint of where it might be. Lola was gagged with a red handkerchief, her face swollen with terror or rage. She twisted back and forth against the pressure of her bondage.

"Your three minutes starts now," Butler said. "So go on, get moving. And don't try to leave anybody behind to catch me because I'll be watching."

"Do it!" Sampson screamed. "Wake those morons up and haul them with you. Now! Do it! Let's go, hurry up."

"We gonna let this happen?" Thorn said.

Sugarman kept watching the television screen after it had turned dark. "I don't see the alternative."

"You Americans," the Swedish woman said. "You really know how to put on a show."

"Let the fucker have his way? Walk off with fifty-eight million dollars?"

"You got a better idea, let's hear it quick."

"Just stay here, call his bluff."

"We can't risk Lola," Sugarman said.

"But she's in on it. She's a willing participant. It's a trick."

"That's just speculation, Thorn. We can't gamble her life on a guess. I want to catch the asshole too. But he's got us this time."

"What're you waiting for!" Sampson cried from the hatchway. "Come on, come on."

Sugarman helped Marie lug her buddies to their feet, and under their drunken weight Sugar and Marie trudged toward the hatchway door.

Thorn lingered at the bar a moment more, staring into the empty TV. He'd seen something. He wasn't sure what. But something wasn't right about that image on the screen. He turned and was heading for the stairwell when it struck him. It wasn't something he'd seen. It was something he hadn't.

Thorn rushed to the stairs, called out for Sugar, but he and the others were already a deck or two farther down. Thorn swung around and looked at the footlocker. He'd had his eyes off of it no more than a second or two. It was still in its place inside the ring of lights.

What was wrong was Butler Jack's nose. Yesterday Sugar had

cracked it hard, bent it several degrees to the left. At the very least his nose would be badly swollen this morning, and more than likely he would have two black eyes surfacing into view. But the Butler Jack on the TV screen was smiling and unblemished. The video was clearly made days before and now was probably playing on a VCR like the one they'd found in the chapel ceiling.

Thorn ducked behind the hatchway and waited. A moment or two passed before he chanced a look out on the deck, glimpsed the footlocker, and dodged his head back. He gripped the edge of the hatchway and began to count the seconds. He got to sixty, started again, got to sixty twice and then once more. Plenty enough time for their three-minute deadline to have elapsed.

But no one had shown. For good measure he counted to a hundred, taking regular peeks around the edge of the door. The Fiesta Cruise Lines flag snapped in the breeze just forward of the smokestacks. One of the electric lanterns lighting the footlocker blinked and gave out.

Thorn waited another minute, then he stepped out from behind the doorway. No one had shown and, if Thorn's suspicions were right, no one was going to show. No one had to.

He was pretty sure he understood why. He didn't know all the particulars yet, but he believed he'd divined the outline of the scheme. The revelation coming to him as such revelations always had. Staring at the camouflage so long, his eyes had grown weary, gone out of focus, then there it was, the shape that had been hidden so artfully was now standing out in full relief. It was the way he spotted bonefish through the bright sheen of sunlight on the surface of the water. His eyes becoming relaxed, easing past the glare.

He sucked down a breath and jogged over to the footlocker. He swung around and took a look from there. As he had known it would be, the deck was clear forward and aft. The hot tub bubbling mindlessly. In the sunlight beyond the rail the calm Atlantic was regaining its deepest shade of blue.

Thorn flipped open the clasps on the footlocker and swung back the lid. He squatted down and peered at the small green flowers printed on the inside walls. He breathed in the aroma of brass and rubber cement. The footlocker appeared to be brand new. And it was empty, as bare as the day it rolled off the assembly line in some Chinese prison factory.

He stood up, squinted out toward the west. He walked down the rail to the bow. Just above the distant horizon, he could make out several objects hovering in the sky. Ten miles ahead, maybe slightly more, the sea was thick with boats. He raised the binoculars, pressed them to his eyes and focused.

Through the glasses he could make out South Beach. The low hotels, the pastel shapes. A row of coconut palms. He counted four choppers hanging near the shore. A half-dozen boats with the oblique orange stripe of the Coast Guard. And in the center of the frenzy was an enormous black ship. The tanker was still too far away for Thorn to decipher the letters printed on her side, but it didn't matter because he knew her name. Butler was one step ahead of them. He'd scratched off number ten and, Thorn realized with a painful groan, Butler might already be moving on to number eleven.

He drew the binoculars away, glanced around and began to take his bearings. He felt the speed of the ship under his feet, watched the shoreline inflating into view. He conjured up an image of the coastline's shape, recollected from maps he'd studied over the years and from his observation Sunday afternoon as they'd passed out of the mouth of Government Cut.

As near as he could reconstruct it, the tip of Miami Beach angled slightly southeast like a little outturned goatee off the chin of the beach, then came a small gap of water, and then Fisher Island, Virginia Key, Key Biscayne, trickling away to the south and west. He held that map in his mind, stared out at the coastline, did a quick triangulation off the giant condo tower on the point of South Beach and made his second locus the high-rises that he knew were some thirty blocks north. He put the *Eclipse* in her place on the map, then swung around and stared out at the quartering sea, tried to calculate the steering effects of the tide. Drinking this in, as much as he could absorb, its jizz, the interaction of its diverse parts. He approximated the distance to the shore one final time then turned and rushed down the stairs.

The *Eclipse* was certainly no canoe, and this was not the shallow bays of the Everglades, but big as the ship was, she was still merely a boat and had no choice but to obey the same inexorable laws as any craft at sea.

Thorn located the others in the media room. Lola was wearing only her bra and panties and a string of pearls and had been lashed to a chair in the media room. All the pieces looking very realistic, the deep rope burns on her wrists, the buzzing video camera stationed next to her. Sampson had grabbed a terry-cloth robe from a nearby cabin and was slipping it over Lola Sampson's shoulders. She was teary-eyed and out of breath.

Thorn took hold of Sampson's shoulder and swung the big man around.

"Where the hell have you been, Mr. Thorn!"

"Did you switch off the fuel valves?"

"Of course not. There wasn't time."

"Well, do it now. We've got about twenty minutes," Thorn said. "Seven miles, maybe less, and we're going to plow into the *Juggernaut*. An oil tanker."

"What!"

"It's already run aground on South Beach. That's where we're headed."

"He was supposed to shut the engines off. We gave him the money." Sampson shot a look at Lola. "He lied. The bastard lied to us."

"Surprise, surprise," Sugarman said.

"We don't have time for this shit. Come on, Sugar."

Sugarman caught up to him at the head of the stairs.

"Rudder room," Thorn said as they ran down the narrow stairwell. "That wheel Sampson had installed. Let's hope it's more than ornamental."

"Twenty minutes, that's all we have?"

"Twenty may be optimistic."

They burst through the hatch door, sprinted down the corridor to the last doorway. Thorn threw open the steel hatch and they entered the tiny sky-blue room.

"You sure about this, man?" Sugar said. "You sure you want to be down here when this goddamn monster crashes?"

"It's not going to crash, we're going to turn it."

Thorn was hunting the wall for an indicator gauge, something that could tell them their angle of turn. Sugar stood beside him heaving for breath. He sat back on a valve wheel and pressed the heel of his hand to his chest. "Heart, don't fail me now."

Thorn was staring at the starboard wall. Someone had hung a simple boy scout compass on a peg. Thorn grabbed it down, held it in the palm of his hand, watched the needle quiver briefly then swing around and settle into place.

"Jesus, a compass," Sugarman said.

"No," Thorn said. "It's a trick."

"What the hell?"

"That's not north." Thorn pointed toward the door they'd entered. "It's that way." He shifted his hand a few degrees to the left.

"You're sure?"

"I'm sure."

"Let's go," Sugar said. "Let's turn this mother."

Butler Jack had to park the Winnebago three blocks off the beach. All the excitement down by water's edge had brought out the gawkers and oglers, the rubberneckers and blood lusters, same goddamn people who caused the miles-long traffic jams around Miami while they slowed to gape at some poor soul changing a flat tire.

The professional gawkers were there too, the newspaper geeks and the TV charmers, the evening tabloid shows, those fucking ghouls, the entire national community of rapacious assholes had assembled on the beach. *Good Morning America* was there. *The Today Show*. CNN had been going out with it for hours. He'd been watching it on his TV in the Winnebago as he drove over from Bayside Marketplace to the beach, flicking between channels, his heart zinging.

Along Ocean Drive satellite trucks were parked four deep. No traffic moving. Butler Jack found a table on the porch of the Delano Hotel. Surrounded by muscle jocks and rollerbladers in bikinis. Lots of binoculars. He ordered coffee, a Danish, and watched the crowds milling around.

The *Eclipse* was out there, ten miles maybe, a small white dot on the horizon at the moment. Nobody had noticed it yet. Nobody had any idea.

Thorn and Sugar worked on opposite sides of the wheel. Thorn crouched beneath the starboard side, pushing up, Sugar on the other side thrusting down, hanging, kicking his legs for more pull. The giant bicycle chain inched around, movement so fractional Sugar thought he might be imagining it. Wishful thinking. They had been unable to locate the shutoff valve for the hydraulics, so they were not only forcing the rudder by hand against the resisting pressure of the water, but also against the electronic messages being sent down from the autopilot, which pressurized the oil lines and rotated the gears, nudging the vast ship in the direction it had chosen.

Sugar found himself wishing he had eaten more fatty foods in the last few weeks. He wished he'd bulked up, had more weight to throw against this frozen wheel. But it did seem to be yielding slightly, at least he thought so. Common brutish strength working against the force of science, against a hundred small devices and motors and gizmos and oil-filled lines. And the brutes were getting it around.

Thorn groaned. His muscles trembling as if he were trying to lift the weight of the earth above his head. Sweat poured down Sugar's face, his heart was wild inside his shirt. They reset their feet, found better handholds, budged the chain around on its track, turned the sprocket, angled the rudder, feeling the ship resist. Inch by inch, moving it round.

They were blind. No way to know their angle of turn. No way to know when they'd cleared land. No way to know when they should stop turning and head on out to sea, run out their fuel, wait for help. If they turned too short they'd crash ashore on one of the islands farther south; if they turned too far, they'd circle back and could easily run aground farther north. If they turned too hard, they'd tip the behemoth onto her side, sink her in a minute.

There was a fairly good degree of error, a wide sea to steer back into, but down there in that small room, every link of chain a major victory, there was no way to tell, no way to count.

Sugarman had lost touch with their relative position. Lost all touch with anything beyond the strain in his arms, the wriggling weight as he hauled down on the wheel. Hauled down and around. Thorn's eyes were unfocused as if he were conferring with his God.

Sugarman put his mind somewhere else. He thought of Jeannie. He wondered where she was, what she was doing. It had been days since he'd thought of her, but now, as he strained every sinew against the pressure of the wheel, he imagined her white sleek body. He roamed it in his mind. The woman he had once loved so much. The woman who was trying to bear his child. Starting at her toes, running his finger in the damp seams between each one. They were small toes, curled downward. They fit together in the perfect mesh that toes often had. As if the foot had been molded from one piece of clay and the toes slit apart carefully by a paper-thin blade. He moved up her arch to her narrow ankles. He was massaging the ankle bones with his imagination when Thorn barked for him to stop.

"What?"

"Let go. Let go now."

Sugar's heart was leaping. "You're sure?"

Thorn looked him in the eye. Sugar uncurled his fingers from the wheel. They stood for a moment and listened to what sounded like the crunch of seabed beneath them. Then the jarring lurch that knocked them sideways into one another as the keel must have cut deeply through sand and shoal. And then sudden free movement across the surface of the water. Steaming clear.

"How the hell did you do that?"

"You got me," Thorn said. "But let's don't think about it. It might go away."

"Man, I'm dead."

"This is just the rest period," Thorn said.

"What?"

"The autopilot is going to swing us around, take us right back to where it wants us to go."

"No. Tell me it isn't true."

Thorn nodded.

"We have to keep doing this?"

Thorn nodded again.

"Man, I'm out of gas already. I don't think I can heave this sucker around again."

"We need to get Sampson to shut down the fuel lines," Thorn said. "It's either that, or wait till help comes. And who knows how long that might take."

The *Eclipse* headed three miles out to sea before it began to circle back to shore. Twice more Thorn ran five flights up to take a sighting on the beach, then ran back. Twice more they wrestled the rudder, steering the ship away from the beach. While the two of them struggled with the wheel, Sampson shut off the fuel lines, bled them dry. It was ten-thirty on Tuesday morning before the big engines sputtered and died and the *Eclipse* fell silent, coming to rest just two miles off Miami Beach.

Butler watched it with growing horror. Those bastards. They'd sailed right up to the beach, two hundred, three hundred yards, sending the onlookers running, the Coast Guard ships blowing their horns, blowing them and blowing. Then roaring off, out of the path of the enormous ship.

The *Eclipse* curved in toward the beach and did a slow turn back out. It made two more passes before its engines gave out.

Butler trudged back to the Winnebago. He pushed by a woman on the sidewalk and she snarled at him, and he pressed the stunning voltage to her neck. Put her to sleep for an hour or so.

He walked back to the Winnebago in a gray haze. He might have zapped a few more people. He wasn't sure. He wasn't sure of much of anything at the moment. He didn't know when he would ever be sure again.

CHAPTER
37

The lawyers' twelve-year-old son warned Thorn if he touched either him or his sister, both of them would damn well litigate his ass off. The girl said she was one quarter away from the all-time record score on her machine and her brother was maybe three quarters away. Thorn watched them work their joysticks for a half minute then he stooped down and yanked the plugs on both machines. They all watched the numbers fade from the scoreboard like stars against a dawn sky.

He hooked each of them under an arm, scooped them up, and carried them, squirming and cursing, down the gangplank onto the Port of Miami docks. Handling the kids with that miraculous restraint he'd acquired in his months of passive arts training.

Sugar and Thorn spent most of Tuesday afternoon in an interrogation room in the Coast Guard's central office along the Miami River. Thorn giving the young lady who questioned them Butler's name, which she already knew from the reports of dozens of passengers who'd disembarked in Nassau. Beyond that he played dumb. Sugar did as well. The Coast Guard woman was replaced by an FBI woman in a dark suit. She went through the same list of questions but didn't seem terribly interested in prying more from them. Her eyes kept straying to the door as if the good stuff was happening in the next room and she was irritated to be stuck with these minor players.

Afterward Sugar drove them to a limousine rental service on Biscayne Boulevard where they secured a 1969 Rolls Silver Cloud with deeply tinted windows for twelve hundred a week. Sugar took a deep breath and wrote a check, and while they stood in the limo office waiting for the car to be brought around, Sugar flipped a quarter to see who got to wear the chauffeur's uniform. Thorn won.

"You sure we need this thing?"

"You ever been to Star Island?"

Thorn said no, he hadn't.

"Well, people out there, their gardeners wear tuxedos."

Sugar sat in back and directed Thorn across the causeway to one of the luxury islands on the way over to Miami Beach. He called Thorn Jeeves and said "Home, James," several times, but it wasn't funny. Nothing was.

Thorn drew up to the guard house and Sugarman climbed out and spoke for a while to the young security man. For the last forty-eight hours Sugar had been wearing the same pair of khaki slacks and teal shirt and he smelled like he'd been marinating in ammonia. Even in the freshly laundered chauffeur's uniform Thorn wasn't much better, although after one experimental whiff of his shoulder, he seemed to have deadened his olfactory nerves sufficiently to survive. Sugar's odor didn't seem to offend the uniformed guard. All smiles, the young man accompanied Sugarman back to the car, opened the door for him, and gave him a salute as they drove onto the island.

"What the hell did you tell him?"

"We're government agents. NOSA. Guarding Sampson's property till this Middle East terrorist scare blows over. Nobody's supposed to know we're out here, not even Sampson. National security."

"NOSA?"

"It just popped out."

"He didn't want to see some ID?"

"Hey, Thorn. Not everybody is as untrusting as you."

There were two red Jaguar XJ-6s parked out front in the Sampsons' circular drive, both convertibles. Their estate was a Mediterranean affair, fountains and walkways, red tile and thick stucco. An acre of tightly pruned fruit trees. The Sampsons had two or three hundred feet on the bay and a view east toward Miami Beach. There was a dock out back but no yacht.

They found a small playground a block away. From the northern edge of the park, Thorn could see the front gates of the Sampson estate, and he could also monitor the one road leading past the guard house off the island to the causeway.

The playground had two teeter-totters and a curved slide and a swing set. No one seemed to use the park except a couple of black poodles whose owner, a white-haired woman in a Madras golf skirt and a garish red top, came around suppertime and steered her dogs to the deep sand beneath the swing set where they deposited their delicacies. Normally Thorn might've made a joke about the lady, her dogs, the size of their turds, something to force a chuckle out of Sugarman. But he didn't feel much like conversation. Breathing was labor enough.

On the Rolls' TV, they watched the evening news. Brandy Wong's interview with Morton Sampson, her worldwide exclusive. Morton giving his own sanitized version of the frightful events on the *Eclipse*. He reduced the body count by five and Brandy didn't contradict him. Morton said he considered Dale Jenkins' untimely death a national tragedy. Under Brandy's rapid-fire questions, Morton was brave and appropriately angry and humble. He swore he would do whatever he could to assist the FBI in their investigation. This was an appalling act, a terrorist attack on one of America's finest family-owned companies, and it only went to show that no one was safe anywhere these days. If you couldn't go away on a cruise ship vacation and expect absolute safety, then where could you go?

"When I die," Sugarman said, "I damn well want my death to be timely."

Sugarman used the car phone to call the Coast Guard office downtown. It was after hours, but everyone was still working. He asked to speak to the lead investigator on the *Eclipse* case. When the person came on the line, Sugarman deepened his voice, sped up his delivery, and gave his name as one of their fishing friends from Key Largo, saying he was a field agent with the FBI and was doing an ancillary background check on this Mr. Butler Jack. Did they perhaps have Mr. Jack's Coast Guard service record available?

Sugarman covered the receiver.

"She's going to check," he said.

"Ancillary?" Thorn said.

Sugarman shrugged. "A good vocabulary opens doors."

"So they say."

Sugarman ducked his head and focused on the voice in his ear.

"Yes, good," he said. "What I need to know, Lizzie, did Mr. Jack receive any kind of flight training while he served with the Coast Guard?"

Sugarman made some noises in his throat, nodded, and told Lizzie she'd been a great help and he hoped she had a wonderful turkey day. He hung up the phone and crossed his arms over his chest and sat back in the seat.

"Well? Did he?"

"No, he didn't," Sugar said. "He didn't need the Coast Guard's help. He entered the service with a goddamn pilot's license already. For most of the two years he was with them, he flew a Bell Jet Ranger chopper, plucking refugees out of the Gulf Stream."

"Good."

"Good but insufficient," Sugarman said.

Sugar went through long-distance information, tracked down the number to the New York office of *Lola Live*. He asked to speak to a woman called Kyra, had to bullshit a couple of people on the way, using his FBI alias again, but finally he got her home number.

He spoke to Kyra like they were old pals. Been through the wars. Apparently she was thrilled with the surge in the program's ratings. Even though they'd had to cancel the rest of the week's shows, they expected next Monday, when Lola returned to the air, to be their all-time best day. Sugarman repeating it for Thorn's benefit.

"So, Kyra. Reason I called was to ask you about the chopper pilot for the show. Yeah, yeah, the helicopter pilot. Danny Bond, yeah, that's right. You heard anything from old Danny?"

Thorn could hear Kyra's voice peeping from the headpiece. Sugar registered it all impassively, thanked her immensely for her help and hoped he'd see her next time he ventured up to the Shiny Red Apple. Sugar cradled the phone, turned to Thorn, smiled seriously, and said, "Voilà."

"The *Lola Live* chopper pilot is nowhere to be found," Thorn said.

"Exactly. The last anybody saw him, Danny was racing off to the airport to fly the money out to the *Eclipse*."

"And the chopper?"

"Landed late last night in Miami, down the road from here at Chalk's Field. So they think Danny flew his mission, landed in Miami, went off on a bender or something."

"Bet me. A week or two from now, old Danny boy will come washing up onto the beach in Nassau. Spine here, jawbone there."

Sugar nodded. He stared out at the teeter-totters.

They slept in shifts; the front seat of the Rolls was every bit as comfortable as Thorn's bed at home. When he woke in the half-light Wednesday morning, the poodle lady was back. In her housecoat this time, once more guiding her dogs to the sandy pit below the swings.

Thorn had been Sugarman's friend for almost four decades, but in all those years, he'd never known what a great tolerance Sugar had for radio. He could listen to it all day. News and talk shows. By nine that morning he'd settled on a station with a hate-mongering host who insulted his callers, most of whom seemed to have no idea they were being mocked. All morning they listened to endless dissections of the Dolphins' upcoming game and hours of blather about the never-ending invasion of Cubans and Canadians and Haitians and all the other English-deficient idiots. The irritating guy was interrupted only by news, weather, and sports every fifteen minutes. By noon Thorn was so caught up on national events, politics and wars, the NFL, the Hollywood scene, the most recent twists in the latest national murder trial, he wouldn't need to check in again for another five years.

From the security guard, they got the name of an Italian restaurant that delivered. Ate subs with big kosher dills. When it grew dark, Thorn drove past the estate, and they saw lights on throughout the house. On another pass they caught Morton standing on a balcony holding a phone to his ear, staring out at the glittering water. Later they saw Lola walk out to the front gate to retrieve yesterday's newspaper.

"They're hunkered down in there."

"Their own little five-million-dollar bunker."

At eight they had a pizza delivered to their car, extra Cokes, extra ice. Thorn started to feel the chauffeur's suit pinching at his waist. They took turns using the meticulously clean men's room on the north perimeter of the playground. That night they stayed awake in shifts. Though Thorn had little interest in sleep. Sugarman turned the radio low, tuned to the syndicated preachers and the political philosophers who spewed their gibberish to insomniacs nationwide.

Thursday was the same. Thorn doing some stretches and leg lifts and sit-ups in the grass beside the car. Lying out in the sun, as stiff and empty as a month-old corpse. Both of them took sponge baths in the men's room using the rough brown paper towels and pink squirt soap. The weather was in the sixties, the sky clear. A steady breeze rattled the royal palms that lined the main thoroughfare. People in the neighborhood came and went, scrupulously ignoring the Rolls parked beside the playground. The Sampsons stayed at home.

On the radio news there was no further mention of the *Eclipse* and her troubles. Dale Jenkins was laid to rest in Evansville, Indiana. Most of the stars of the American media made the ceremony. Notably absent were Lola and Morton Sampson. But the really big story was the upcoming game. The local university football team was to play its upstate rival on Saturday afternoon. Fans calling in on both sides to say loathsome things about the other team, the other city.

The poodles came and went.

Early on Friday morning, a convoy of catering trucks passed by and were admitted to the Sampson estate. A while later Thorn took a stroll down that way and watched the crews erecting long tables and a canopied field kitchen. Just after noon, cars began to arrive by the dozen. Old Fords and Chevies and pickups and vans parked up and down the street outside the Sampson estate. Thorn walked down to the guard house and asked the young man what was going on.

It was Fiesta's annual employee picnic. A last-minute switch, according to the cop. The company vice president had been scheduled to host the event because the *Eclipse* was supposed to be at sea, but Morton apparently thought it important to put on his best public face. Run the show himself. In fact, the guard said, even Wally Bergson was attending. Did he know Wally Bergson?

"What? Do I look like I live on the moon?" Thorn said.

Later on that Saturday afternoon, Thorn drove the Rolls by Sampson's front gates. Out on the wide lawn the dozen long tables were covered with food. Frisbees were flying, a couple of kites fluttered high over the bay. Kids and parents lounging around in the sun. On the center of every table were large ice sculptures melting on silver trays.

"This isn't getting us anywhere," Thorn said. "Maybe we should just crash the party, take Morton and Lola for a ride somewhere, have a serious talk."

"Relax, this is a stakeout. This is what happens. Nothing."

"Maybe we got this all wrong. You ever think about that?"

"Every minute for the last three days."

"They aren't that stupid. They aren't going to get in their red Jaguars, drive off and meet him somewhere. It won't happen like that. This is a waste."

Thorn drove back to the park and found some shade under a black olive tree. Sugarman let his seat back, closed his eyes. He heaved out a major groan.

"Now what's wrong?"

"I'm just disappointed. I guess I was hoping Lola was the bad guy."

"She is."

"Yeah, but I wanted it to be her alone. It would feel better."

"You mean you could hate her better."

Sugarman was silent.

"But we know Sampson's in on it," Thorn said. "We saw him look in the footlocker, pretend there was money in there. By then the money's already flying back to the U.S., but he's acting like it's sitting out on the Sun Deck. Acting for our benefit, I might add.

And all that bullshit about not wanting outside help, that was part of the blueprint. If we'd had a couple of electronics wizards on board, somebody smarter than Murphy, they would've found the autopilot, ripped it out, the whole thing's over in a second. Even the way he dealt with Gavini. His little compromise to stop in Nassau. He knew that was where everything would begin. It wasn't any compromise."

"I don't know, Thorn. I'm beginning to get doubts."

"You see something I don't?"

"We know Fiesta's in trouble. Sampson told me that much. Cash flow problems. But if he wanted fifty million dollars, why the hell wouldn't he just sell the damn company, cash out, walk away? You heard that radio report, Wally was offering him somewhere around fifty as it was. Papers all drawn up, ready to go. Sampson could've taken that money and gone. He didn't need to pull a stunt like that. All those risks, people getting killed, all that."

"Maybe he wanted fifty-eight times two."

"Times two? How's that work?"

"Insurance," Thorn said.

"What? You think he took out extortion insurance?"

"There's umbrella policies."

Sugarman sat up, turned down the radio. This morning Thorn had finally talked him into a jazz station. He'd heard so much radio chatter and recycled news it'd probably cut his IQ in half.

"He steals the fifty-eight from himself," Sugar said. "Then gets reimbursed?"

Thorn rolled down his window. The breeze off the bay was scented with roast turkey. The happy cries of children at play came floating down from Sampson's.

"He doubles his money. Gets the fifty-eight from Wally. Right away, it's stolen in a big-time terrorist assault. Lola is hurt. Dale Jenkins is murdered. The ship is hijacked by some kind of remote-control autopilot bullshit. All very high profile, makes the number-one slot on the evening news, all that.

"The insurance people don't even need to send an investigator out to look things over. Everything's been on TV already. Everybody in America knows all the details. The insurance people fork out the fifty-eight. They want to keep Fiesta's business. Hell, they're going to get to raise premiums big time now with all this mess. So now he's got a hundred and sixteen million. That ought to be enough to retire on, or start a new company if that's what he wants. A year from now he turns to Wally and sells him the rest of his shares. That should cushion his old age."

"Then why the *Juggernaut*? What's that all about?"

"It could be for the exposure," Thorn said, "make sure the TV people had it all. If there's a big splash, Sampson's and Lola's lives at risk, nobody's going to be suspicious of them."

"I don't buy it. They could've died out there. All of us could have."

Thorn watched a small snowy egret pecking in the sand below the swings.

"Gotta be a double-cross," Sugar said. "Butler takes the money and runs. Leaves them behind to die. They think the auto-pilot's going to shut down, but he's programmed it to keep going."

"Then all this is a waste, sitting out here. There isn't going to be any meeting. Butler disappears with his cash. Story's over."

Sugar leaned forward, thrust his head through the sliding partition. "Unless Butler still wants them dead. And that's why they're hunkered down in there, because they're afraid."

"We thwarted his plan," said Thorn, "turning the *Eclipse* like that. Gave him some unfinished business."

"We should lay all this out for the cops," Sugar said. "This lone-wolf bullshit, I don't like it. We can't protect them."

"Look, it's still the same thing. If there's a chance in hell of finding Monica, then Sampson has to be walking around, free to move, contact Butler, get his money. Even if it's the other way, and Sampson's a target, then we have to stay put, keep him in sight. We find Butler, we find Monica."

"I got a bad feeling. I never liked lying to the police. They could've handled this better than we could."

"Oh, come on, man. You think our FBI lady friend would've sat there and listened to a couple of citizens? A story so weird, complicated, so goddamn extreme. Hell, Sugar. Cops're like everybody else. They like Sampson, they're in love with Lola, lining up to get their autographs. They want to believe in those two. Worst case, they would've brought Sampson in, had us face to face. Then where would we be? You think we'd ever have a chance of seeing Monica again?"

Sugar's face was empty. Eyes fixed on the flight path of an incoming passenger jet.

Thorn turned up the radio, a slow saxophone full of cheap booze and sexual heat. Sugarman leaned over and turned it down.

"You're Morton Sampson, Thorn, you're a smart guy, well known, well liked, richer than the Pope and all twelve apostles together. Are you going into business with a wacko like Butler Jack? You going to attempt a big-time out-in-the-open scheme like what we just went through with a fucking loose cannon like him? I don't think so."

"It's what happened."

"It's too weird."

"It's simple," Thorn said. "One, two, three. Butler delivers the empty footlocker, flies off with the money. And with Monica."

"We hope with Monica."

"He flew off with Monica. That's how it went."

"Okay, okay. He's decided to stall on number eleven. For reasons completely unknown, and unverifiable, he's not going to do the last thing on his fucking list. He's done everything else right on schedule, but he's not going to do that."

"Screw you, Sugar."

"I'm just trying to prepare you, Thorn. I'm just stating the obvious."

The big game started at one o'clock. Thorn tried to interest himself in it, but to do that he had to choose sides, and after listening to the fans for each team ranting for the last couple of days, he couldn't work up any affection for either of them.

Sugarman went to the bathroom to wash, Thorn had his seat reclined a couple of notches. Listening to the war chants of the opposing football fans. His eyes were drifting closed, the first gray shreds of a nap when something tweaked his peripheral vision. He lifted his head, then cocked the seat straight up and watched a white Winnebago roll past the guard gate and head down the lane to Sampson's estate.

Breathless, Sugar threw open the rear door and slid inside. He thumped Thorn on the arm. "What're you smiling at, Jeeves? Go, go."

"Maybe we should just sit here, let them settle things. Nab whoever is left standing."

"Go on, Thorn. Go on."

Thorn started the big beautiful car, slid it into drive.

And it was true what they said about Rolls-Royces. Even when you raced the engine to redline, all you could hear was the tick of your own heart.

CHAPTER

38

*C*limax. The Romans took it from the Greek *klimax,* meaning ladder. A series of steps of increasing forcefulness, one above the next, leading upward to a peak or culmination. Taking one to a high point above the earth, a place from which a greater vista could be seen. Also referring to a moment of ecstatic sexual excitement in which one reaches the peak of erotic agitation, the top rung of the carnal ladder, a place and time when one can go no farther and must let go, drop off and fall back to earth. A ladder. Step one, step two, step three, four and five, six, seven, eight, nine, ten, and then finally eleven. Ever upward toward the zenith.

Or in a narrative, that moment when, as Aristotle and his buddies said, the moment of revelation is at hand, all prior moments leading inevitably to this. Romance, foreplay, copulation, climax, afterglow. Sex and story, climbing ever higher.

Butler Jack knew it now. He had climbed to the top of the ladder he'd erected. He had seen what could be seen from there. But the ladder was wobbly and he had not poked his head through the veil of clouds, looked on the face of God. The view from the final rung was not much better than it had been from the ground.

He had climbed on top of Monica's body and reached the climax of his story, but his revelation was not at hand. She lay there like a dead woman. She lay there like number eleven. His penis had remained flaccid; no matter how much he ground his naked hips against her thighs, he'd been unable to grow hard. Unable to achieve the climax he had climbed the ladder to reach.

Of course, it was partly due to his nuts. They were damaged, maybe permanently. Recoiling, shrinking into the protective cavity of his body, cringing out of sight to avoid the mission that was assigned to them. Mission, emission, omission. Ladder to a sky that wasn't there.

Butler parked outside Morton Sampson's gates.

The ice turkeys sparkled in the sun. Coins fell onto the silver trays and the children squealed with avarice and greed. A large man in a gray uniform stopped him at the gate, asked for his invitation. Butler touched him with the power in his hands and the man fell silent.

Butler marched on, down the rows of tables. Both his hands were wired today, sparks on the left and right. Two battery packs on his belt. He stalked toward the pool house where Morton and Lola sat in the shade, enthroned in straw chairs, their faithful employees lined up to genuflect, kiss their rings. The same pool house where the two of them had disappeared in that other story so many years ago. Some of these same people had been there twelve years ago and had seen Lola and Morton sneak away into that den of debauchery. And they had snickered.

Time was a lie. Twelve years ago was today. It lived out there under the same sun. Butler was twelve years old. His mother was as young and beautiful as a fairy-tale princess. She deserved to live in the castle. Everyone said so. But Butler was the problem. Butler was her embarrassment, her shame. The odd boy who weighed her down, complicated things, diminished her market value.

Butler walked toward them. The pool house.

The coins fell into the silver trays and small hands shot out, the strong grabbing money from the weak. One side or the other. It's a war. She'd said that. Monica, the girl. The beautiful girl with the golden hair sprinkled on her arms. She'd said that. I will wait for you always, forever, till the end of time. Those were the words. Now this was the end of time. This was the climax. The ladder. Moving to the top, the sky only inches away.

Morton's eyes were on him now, watching him approach. Lola looked up too. She came to her feet, she raised her hand, she opened her mouth. His mother. The one whose body had formed him. The one whose body had nurtured and then expelled him into the harsh empty air of the world. They had cut him loose from her. Slapped him on the back and sent him on his way.

The crowd parted. They weren't snickering anymore. They looked at him with awe. Lola and Morton backing away from him. Nowhere to hide.

He was here again. Both hands buzzing. Ready for climax.

Thorn and Sugar separated. Sugarman ran through the gates, bent down to check the pulse of a man lying in the grass. Then he rose and headed at a run down the rows of tables.

Thorn watched him go. Then he walked over to the Winnebago, and halted for a moment, listening. Sensing something, he wasn't sure what. Feeling his heart tighten, the blood singing in his ears.

He stared at the door. He'd seen what had happened to Murphy, some booby trap Butler had laid out for him. A succulent square of cheese on an electrified silver platter. Murphy's body was sprawled in a sickening tangle on the lobby floor, his cheeks blackened, his hair singed. Eyes locked open, an appalling grin.

With that image in his head, Thorn drew his hand back, refused the lure of the doorknob. Instead, he moved around to the side of the van, took hold of the lower lip of the single window, and chinned himself a foot off the ground. Through the gauzy curtains he saw her sitting upright on the edge of the lower bunk. Her hands seemed to be secured behind her. She was wearing a silky negligee with a ragged tear at the neckline.

Monica had her right foot extended straight before her like a dancer doing a warm-up stretch. With her toes she seemed to be trying to pluck a tissue from a Kleenex box that sat on the workbench across from her. Thorn raised his fist to rap on the glass, then jerked it away. He'd noticed the contraption on her head, the same headset Murphy had been wearing when they'd found his body, the two small earplugs melted inside Murphy's ears.

Through the filmy curtains Thorn could see the microphone

stem on Monica's headset was cocked down so there was only an inch of clearance between it and her wide arresting lips.

A word would kill her. Any word. The sharp sound of it. Its scrape, its resonance, its bumbling buzz.

She'd never liked words anyway. What tiny freight a few syllables could convey was nothing compared to an artful slash of ink across an empty page. The eye was a thousand times more discriminating than the ear. What could be said, after all? The world was sight. Color and light and the fine etchings of even the smallest organisms, the most ordinary textures were more beautiful than the greatest music. Well, that might be pushing it. But still.

Take that single Kleenex poking out of its box, inches out of reach of her big toe. The way it hung like a membrane of smoke above its container. Like a sheet of parchment made of gas. She could draw that. She could show it, its fragility, its impermanence, its motionless movement. She knew she could do it, even though she'd never tackled a subject such as that before. All its surfaces, as soft and flowing as fog, an airy Möbius strip, even more complex than that. She would make it her next project. Yes. She would focus on the simple things. The easy objects of the world, those trashy, always present articles, underappreciated for their beauty, though they populated every corner of our lives, gave texture to our simplest moments.

She stretched her leg, straightened and softened her muscles, and with that prehensile ability that women sometimes have in their feet and toes, some wonderful vestige of the tree life, she snatched loose a tissue.

Then bent her leg toward her, a weird yoga, stooped forward carefully, inched her toes and the tissue close to the tiny microphone. Perhaps even the scratch of something as soft as Kleenex would set off the voltage. Perhaps she was about to kill herself with an object as flimsy as air.

But it didn't matter now. Better that, to go down struggling, take a shot at wrapping the microphone, knot it tight with Kleenex, muffling it so she could scream, better that than have Butler Jack climb onto her again, attempt another rape. Better to die now in the street outside her childhood home, die in her own way than by whatever method he had planned.

She lipped the tissue from her toes, creased it, puckered her mouth and, with her eyes crossing as she marked her progress, she settled the Kleenex across the black stem. When it was done, hanging there, she allowed herself a deep breath. With horror she heard it whistle through her clogged nasal passages, almost a shriek. She braced herself, tensing her arms against the numbing bite of the handcuffs. But the violent shock didn't come.

After the moment passed, she opened her eyes, looked across at the next sheet. Only an inch of it had peeked through. A harder job, this time. She raised her foot, stretched it out, opened the clamp of her toes.

And at the edge of her vision, she saw him.

She didn't look right away. Didn't want to see his pasty skin, his empty eyes. She lowered her foot as he came forward. It wasn't Butler Jack. He didn't speak, didn't have to. She recognized the way he displaced the air. She turned to him.

Thorn stood in a stream of brightness from the skylight door swung open above him. He wore a gray suit with gold buttons and red piping on the sleeves like a Confederate band leader.

There was a moment of airless silence as he smiled then opened his mouth to speak. Monica jerked forward, panicked, clenched her lips into a shushing pantomime. He nodded that he understood, quickly raised both palms in a calming gesture, and mouthed the words very slowly, just a whisper of breath behind them. I know. I know. I know.

"The money's all gone," he said. "I wrote the checks, sent them off already."

Butler grinned at them.

Lola and Morton were standing in the shadowy cool interior of the pool house. Wood louvers on the door and windows. White canvas covered the overstuffed pillows on the couch and chair. A vase of daisies on the leather-padded bar. Overhead a ceiling fan turned idly.

"Fifty-eight million dollars, minus some expense money for

me. I sent it to Lucy and Tawana and Sutu, wrote the checks yesterday. My two thousand children."

Smiling at them. His parents cowering. Lola in a yellow sun dress, Morton in white pants, a French blue shirt with a dark pattern of sweat outlining his little belly.

"That's fine, Butler," Lola said. "You're a good boy. You're generous, you're kind."

"No, I'm not. You must be thinking of your other son."

He extended his left hand and sparked it at her. "And anyway, I don't need your approval, Lola. Not anymore. I do what I do for my own reasons. I took the money and I gave it away. It's all gone."

Smiling. Feeling the smile widen as he raised his right hand and sparked it at Morton. The big man flinched. Two steps away. He'd backed them against the bar.

"So, tell me. Is that where you did it? That couch over there?"

Lola glanced toward the white rattan sofa. Morton continued to stare at Butler's hands. His mouth had fallen open like a dreamer about to snore.

"Or did you do it on the floor, right here on this straw mat. Like dogs. Tell me, Lola. Where did you perform your act? What exactly did you do to hook him anyway? Oral? Was that what he liked? Is that it? Did you let him hurt you, take unnatural advantage? Tell me. I'm a big boy. I understand these things. Matters of fornication. I want to know what happened here. Everything. Did he pay you afterward?"

"Stop it, Butler. You've made your point."

"They were snickering," he said. "Did you know that? Did you know that all your employees saw you sneak into the pool house? They all knew what you were doing, Lola? Everyone saw it. Even Irene. Monica's mother. She knew."

"What do you want?" Lola said. "You have the money."

"Is that why Irene killed herself? Because you were unfaithful, Morton? You were screwing Lola right out in the open, flaunting it. Is that why she took her own life?"

"Stop it, Butler, please."

Butler sparked one hand, then the other. Flicking his wrists toward each of them as if he were throwing darts at their chests.

"You lied to the police and to the reporters. You lied to every-one. You didn't tell them my name. I listened to the news stories, I read the paper. My name wasn't mentioned anywhere."

"We told them your name," Morton said. He was easing to his right, putting some distance between him and Lola. As if Butler weren't paying attention. As if Butler were stupid.

"The authorities are looking for you," Lola said. "The police, FBI, they're all after you. You should go away somewhere, hide."

"But my name wasn't in the paper."

"They didn't want to frighten you, make you run. But that's what you should do. You should run. Take whatever money you have left and hide out, maybe Mexico."

Butler chuckled. "Did you take him in your mouth back then, Lola? I bet that's it. His wife Irene wouldn't take him in her mouth, but you would. Is that what happened? Is that what you did in here?"

"We talked," Lola said. "That's all we did."

He jabbed his sparking hand toward her, came a half step closer. Lola standing straight, holding his eye.

"You're lying. You didn't talk. You fucked him. You lay with him on the floor like a dog. They were snickering outside. They knew what you were doing. You were using your body, you were using your mouth and your ass and your hands and your fingers. You were doing things to him."

Sampson shook his head. "You should've let that shrink drown him."

Butler took two sudden steps his way and caught him as he was trying to dodge to his left. He swiped the voltage across Sampson's throat, just enough to knock him backward onto the couch. Sampson slumped there, breathing hard, head wavering. Butler stepped forward and pressed his fingers against the soft flesh on either side of Sampson's head. His temples.

He cradled his father's skull in his hands. This man who had dishonored his mother, defiled her, seduced her away from all that was good and virtuous. Used his money to buy her affection, cor-rupt her. He tipped up Sampson's chin, and looked down into his father's eyes, and watched them open slowly. Clouded and dull. But still awake, still able to see Butler, see what was about to happen. Butler closing his fists. Staring down into his father's eyes to watch it happen, watch the seizure, watch the thin wire of mortality snap, watch the cool lights inside his eyeballs dim and sputter and wink out.

Very quietly behind him, Sugarman told him to stop.

Butler grinned to himself, let go of Morton, and turned around with a leisurely grin.

Sugarman was holding an ice turkey against his chest like a basketball he meant to shoot. It was half melted and had lost its defining details. Just an oblong lump of ice filled with a half-dozen silver and copper coins. Water dripped onto the straw mat at Sugar's feet.

Lola slid away to the door.

"Where you going, Lola? Out to see Wally Bergson now? Maybe Wally wants to have sex with you. Wally has more money than Morton does. Lots more. Is he your next target? Huh, Mom? Lining up the next one already, are you?"

Sugarman lunged forward and hurled the ice turkey at Butler Jack and came on behind it. And Butler made a mistake, a little one, but serious. He should have batted it away. He should have dodged, or even let that flightless bird, that block of ice, thump him in the chest or shoulder. Almost anything else would have been better than grabbing it.

The zappers activated, the sparks shooting through the ball of frozen water. Butler staring at it, the sizzle in his hands, the silver coins glittering with blue light. He knew the voltage wouldn't kill him, but it hurt. It took him to a new place of pain. The current seemed to gather in his nuts and pulsate. He felt his legs give way.

Americans called it grounding. The British said earthing. The same thing. Electricity seeking safety in the dirt. Negative charge seeking positive. Positive seeking negative. Nature always wanted to be zero. To be quiet and still and dead and empty and neutral.

There was a word for what Butler was feeling. There was a word for looking up and seeing his mother and father and his brother floating in the air like angels. A word for the dark roar of voltage blistering his circuits. A single word that encompassed all of this. A word with a history, that carried every moment of its past into the ever-changing future. There was a word for the pain and for the cessation of pain. There was always a word. But at the moment, that crucial juncture, he had none of them. He had nothing but the pure sensations, the sound of crackling wildfire, the sharp sputter of bacon left too long in the pan, the smell of flesh turning hard and black, the tinkle of silver dollars falling to the concrete floor.

CHAPTER

39

In the week Thorn was away, Rover turned wild. He refused to come when called. He stood in the center of the yard and stared at Thorn, then slunk away into the deep woods when Thorn whistled for him. Thorn tried putting out his favorite dish of grits and fried grunt on a stump beside the sapodilla tree, but Rover simply sat on the edge of the woods and stared at the dish.

Rochelle had abandoned the dog, left him to fend for himself. It had only been seven days, but it was a week that might take months to fix. The dog had lost his faith in humans. Lost his fragile domestic connection and now he cowered in the thick bear-claw ferns, his muzzle wrinkled into a snarl, while Thorn whistled and cajoled.

Rochelle had hired a local company to paint the house yellow. There was a bill from the painters on the dining room table. The shutters were green, the interior was a salmon pink. It looked like someone's sappy honeymoon cottage.

Rochelle had moved out of her apartment. Her parents weren't sure, but thought she might be traveling back to Boston to pick up her studies again at Harvard. They smiled at Thorn nervously and cringed when he stood up to go as if they thought he might be about to thrash them both for their daughter's misbehavior.

Jeannie came home from California pregnant. She was going to have twins next August. Sugarman was elated and terrified. He handed out cigars for a week before Thorn told him he had it wrong. Cigars came later.

Monica found a job five miles away in Tavernier. Cutting and pasting advertisements for one of the local papers. It wasn't much, but it was better than making beds and cleaning toilets, and it was close to her apartment, and gave her considerable free time to pursue her drawing. Her father and Lola and Butler would be going on trial separately sometime in the spring. With any luck at all, their defense attorneys would guzzle every last nickel of the family fortune. The papers had fun with it for a while. Reporters had shown up, trying to speak to Thorn. But they didn't stay long. Sugarman and Thorn caught the evening news one night and there was Morton, speaking earnestly to Brandy Wong. Somehow he'd managed to resurrect his smile. Telling her this was a huge, unfortunate mistake. They'd sort it out. He was looking forward to his day in court.

Thorn went fishing. He left at dawn each morning and returned at sunset. He had some luck at first at a couple of his familiar haunts, but it fell off and a week went by without a strike. Then he found some shallows that had formed in the last month or two from a shifting in the tides through channel five, and he caught seven bonefish there one morning, two tarpon and a permit in the afternoon. He stayed out in the skiff till it grew dark, drinking beer and staring at the surface of the water.

Monica started dropping by in the early evenings, and she and Sugarman and Thorn worked together with steel brushes and sandpaper, scraping away the yellow paint, moving foot by foot around the house, restoring the weathered wood. It probably only took three or four days for the painting crew to do the house, but it was going to require a month or two to scratch it clean. That's the way it was with some things, Sugar said one night as they were standing out on the porch watching the moonlight coat the bay with iridescent silk. "Some things are just a hell of a lot easier to do than undo."

Rover sat out in the yard that night and peered up at them while they drank wine on the porch. Thorn called out his name but the dog wouldn't budge. Sugarman tried with the same result. Then Monica went over to the rail, gathered herself for a moment, and whispered Rover's name so quietly that Thorn, standing beside her, could barely hear her voice, but the dog stood up, hesitated for a few seconds, then came running up the stairs, his tail beating with all his old forgotten joy.